Jessica's house loomed and he hid in the shadows for a time before creeping over the wall and making his way slowly to the window. He became very still and looked behind and to either side, checking that he was the only one abroad in the night, that no one watched. He put down the bundle and tested the window; she hadn't locked it, despite his warning. Part of him wished she had.

Louise Pennington, Baroness Bentinck, worked in advertising for five years before writing full-time. She was born in Bristol and has lived in Vienna, the background to her novel *The Diplomat's Wife*. Her other previously published novels are *The Dreambreakers* and *Sins of Angels*. Louise now lives in Sussex, and has a young daughter.

JESSICA'S LOVER

Louise Pennington

CORONET BOOKS
Hodder and Stoughton

British Library Cataloguing in Publication Data
Pennington, Louise
Jessica's Lover
I. Title
823.914 [F]

ISBN 0 340 60632 0

Typeset by Phoenix Typesetting, Ilkley, West Yorkshire.

Printed and Bound in Great Britain by
Cox & Wyman Ltd, Reading, Berkshire.

Hodder and Stoughton
A division of Hodder Headline PLC
338 Euston Road
London NW1 3BH

'. . . Soon as she was gone from me
A traveller came by
Silently, invisibly –
O, was no deny.'

William Blake

I

Women had always wanted Zak, there was just something about him, something raw and ripe and a little merciless.

And sometimes he wanted them almost as much as they wanted him.

Saffron had followed him all the way from Glastonbury and finally he let her seduce him, underneath the pier – a strident, laughing girl with jiggling breasts and a gold hoop through her nose. Her name amused him; conjuring images of that pathetic lost band of flower children he had left behind at the festival, one of whom had been his mother.

The girl's questing footsteps had dogged him wherever he went, following him like a lost stray, an eager puppy, a groupie. Even at sixteen she was well used, worn around the edges, a little chewed. Soft and creamy and stupid.

A warm breeze meandered off the sea as evening became night and Saffron's soft seeking fingers explored, touched intimately, pouring waves of reluctant pleasure into him. When Zak opened his eyes hers were half-closed in a kind of rapture, glistening and heavy as she exposed him fully and held his erection in her baby-fat fingers like a prize.

Little Saffron had been so ready, so easy to use. She had ridden him with a kind of desperate relentless energy: grinding her meaty hips with incredible strength as she squirmed frantically to work the magic on him. And all the time the sea had coughed and rammed and boomed and heaved within the iron vault of the pier, so that when he spasmed and cried out the sound was swallowed up with her exultant screams.

He didn't want her near him after it was done, so he made her go and then took a walk across the pebble beach to clean himself. The water was lukewarm and for a long time he sat there and watched the great animal move in and out, creeping further and further up the beach until it began licking the grey stones about his feet, tasting the dust of his Doc Martens. In the moonlight the vast pebble beach seemed alien and remote, like a lunar landscape, but Zak only had to lift his head to see the jolly old sink of a pier clotted with slot machines, cheap souvenirs and yobs sporting shaven heads and cans of lager, and girls – lots of girls, just like Saffron. He stood up and retraced his steps, found a stairwell leading to the promenade and followed the siren sound of the music.

A seawind struck his beautiful face full force, wrenching his hair back from his forehead. Zak lifted his face into it, and turned his gaze back to the town and the people, hundreds of them, surging like cattle in and around the fairground and the rides. He could see them quite clearly, even from the pit-end of the pier – neon lights rippled and winked in garish painted waves straddling the night sky, whoring and hustling the crowd, but it drew Zak all the same and, besides, he had promises to keep. There was something about a large crowd, hundreds of ordinary little people, swarming together. Waiting for the big swat.

Zak saw Saffron waving to him from one of the seats of the ferris wheel; she was there, just as she said she would be: a grinning, irritating girl who had sucked his cock like a vacuum cleaner. She bored him, like most of the women he had known bored him, except for the sex; that was something else – a searing impossible pleasure, a rocket of ecstasy, like a taste of deliverance.

A hot sweet ball of excitement began forming in his belly as he stood there, as the giant ferris wheel, still moving, began to go faster and faster. There was a noise, gathering strength, an ominous haunted-house groaning. People's heads turned and looked up, caught by the sound as Zak watched the wheel come round again and again, his old-young eyes giving nothing away. Saffron wasn't grinning any more, in fact her face was very still suddenly and dead white as if she was about to puke.

One of the rinky-dinky seats was slipping out of sync, and its safety bar fell away, clipping the furiously revolving wheel and catapulting the occupant from the security of the fragile swing chair and out into the night sky.

Saffron hit the road, feet first, both legs broke instantaneously with a great wet snap.

She had used him, after all.

Zak blinked with distaste and then moved on, sliding through the gawping, gathering crowd and into the street.

He wanted a *good* woman, a sweet and anonymous image he had made for himself too long ago to remember: a warm, forgiving, tender lady who would share her flesh only with him.

There was one to be had somewhere, and she was close, he could feel it. He craved his own love story, just as he craved respectability and all the trappings he imagined went with it without really knowing what it was – longed for something he had never had.

Jessica closed her eyes wearily and opened them again to look back at her reflection in the mirror of the bathroom cabinet. She was pale and just above her right eyebrow a spot was trying to form which would disappear once her period had come. Tomorrow. Her little loyal friend never let her down, regular as clockwork. She cupped her breasts which were a little tender, even sore, but full and swollen like a fecund Earth Mother which was funny, really, considering everything.

When she was a student she had been careless, even stupid with regard to contraception and had found herself praying hard several times for the telltale signs that would herald her monthly cycle: the smear of blood, the onset of menstruation which would tell her that her womb, thank God, was empty.

How could she have known, way back then, that it would stay empty, that all those years of taking the pill had been a total waste of time? What a great joke. God had a great sense of humour.

And there was nothing obviously wrong, apparently, nothing to explain why her box did not work, why she was infertile, out of order, a pretty tree that bore no edible fruit – barren. And what an unbeautiful word that was, sour and malign, conjuring visions of a dark past when women were rejected and cast aside as if they were blighted and cursed because they could not produce the desired goods.

She looked at herself full in the eyes and then impatiently shrugged off her thoughts and that sense of hopelessness which went with them; always waiting there just out of sight. What good did it do? All the weeping and wailing in the world wouldn't alter simple facts. Besides, it was Tom's birthday and she had no intention of mentioning the damned subject; she would be someone else tonight, someone sexy and desirable and waiting to please because he deserved it and she wanted to show her appreciation.

And Tom had been sleeping badly and the sounds he made in his sleep were not the sounds of a person having happy dreams.

Jessica studied her face for a moment longer then made herself smile right up to her eyes, it wasn't really so hard. Hadn't she read somewhere that if you smile often enough, really smile, it triggers off some kind of chemical reaction in the brain which acts like an anti-depressant? Just looking at herself with a silly fixed grin on her face made her want to laugh out loud.

She turned to the open window and looked out of the back of the house and on to the communal garden; a surprisingly large, almost semi-circular piece of land, the size of a small park. The curve, or arc, of the semi-circle was made up of fine Regency houses and each had its own individual garden or patio which opened directly into the communal garden; so unlike the squares of London or the Regency crescents of Bath where a communal garden was often to the front of the buildings and set apart from the houses by a road or path.

The straight edge of the semi-circle was a high wall spiked with glass in the middle of which a pair of black wrought-iron gates still stood. Once these grand gates had opened to horse-drawn carriages conveying the patrons of Brighton's invigorating sea air and, no doubt, some of the slavish followers of the extravagant and decadent Prince Regent – the future king, George IV. The gates had led into a magnificent curved driveway, a driveway now faded to dust and grassed over.

By virtue of its design, the Crescent was a world unto itself, a fan-shaped piece of earth almost cut off from the rest of the town.

And Jessica liked that sense of isolation, that feeling of exclusivity.

A movement caught her eye and she saw someone walking through the trees; a man, but young, with long dark hair. He sat down on a bench where two gravel paths formed a dusty salmon-coloured cross and leaned back, lifting his face to the heavy afternoon sunshine.

She had never seen him before and wondered if he were part of the set who had just moved into one of the converted flats further round the Crescent. It was functioning as an office – a party business, apparently, a trendy upmarket service offering pleasure domes for hire. And the boy in the garden looked as if he traded in pleasure, like a toy-boy, a sultry DJ, or one of those wild things who played in a rock band: a night creature. There was arrogance, too, even in the way he moved and he seemed so very, very sure of himself.

He looked up, as if he had sensed her eyes and Jessica felt blood soar into her cheeks as if he had just read her mind. He stood up then and began to walk towards the house.

Startled, she hovered at the window not knowing whether to stay or go, but then he waved taking the decision out of her hands and she waited there, watching him, until he drew close.

He stopped at the entrance to her garden and put a sun-drenched hand on the wooden gate. She looked down at him and could see, despite the distance between them, how beautiful he was. Not good-looking, not very attractive, not handsome – but beautiful; it was the only word that sprang into her mind and the only one that could fit.

'I'm looking for a ginger tom,' he lied.

Jessica frowned, puzzled. 'I'm sorry?'

'A cat – a big ginger tom. I wondered if you'd seen it?'

'Oh,' she said, shook her head. 'No, I haven't . . . but I'll keep my eyes open.'

He looked cursorily about the garden before switching his gaze back to her face and then he smiled.

It was quite something, that smile, and Jessica felt herself blush again, before her own mouth began tilting at the edges and she found herself smiling back.

'Well,' he said, shrugging his shoulders, 'that's that, I suppose . . . just have to keep looking.'

She nodded uselessly as he moved away, wondered why she should suddenly feel so hot and flustered, so odd and ill at ease. It's the heat, you fool, she told herself or good old PMT, of course. Nothing more.

'When?'

'Not now, Fay.'

'You promised.'

Had he?

Tom leaned up on his elbows and looked at her, following the line of her naked body until it reached the sweeping upcurve of her firm, round backside. Fay's skin was much paler than Jessica's – white as milk.

Outside the sky was a pale eggshell blue and the afternoon sun a large yellow ball low in the sky. Almost directly opposite and across the communal garden he could just see the roofline of his own house, partly obscured by some trees. A lack-lustre wind played with the leaves and branches so that they moved against one another, the patterns changing, forming pictures.

He closed his eyes and flicked them open again to stare at one of Fay's paintings, a huge canvas as tall and wide as a man: a few twisted pieces of grey metal lay in the foreground, so real that he felt he could reach out and take them into his hands.

In a fog-bound area, at the back and to the right, the paint took on more body and was swirling, thick and succulent. Here stood the figure of a naked elderly man: folds of wrinkled flesh, wasted muscle tissue, flopping shrunken penis – Fay had left nothing out. The man's mouth was angled slightly, into a small smile, and the smile made Tom feel uncomfortable as if something extremely disagreeable might be about to happen.

'That painting, the big one . . .' he frowned, 'what exactly does it mean?'

'Don't change the subject.'

They lay on a four-poster bed enclosed by swathes of white gauze and the air within their little love-nest was still and over-used, filled with the heavy musky scent of her perfume and the raunchy smell of sex. Tom shifted his gaze to her again. Fay was still lying on her stomach, her face turned away from him so that he could not read her expression. Automatically he found himself trailing a finger down her perfect back, still moist with sweat from their love-making.

'I really do want to know.'

She was planning to work here, turning the drawing-room of the new apartment into a studio. 'It means whatever you want it to.'

'That's a cop-out.'

'Well, you'd know all about that.'

Tom reddened. 'I never make promises I can't keep.'

'You said you'd think about it.'

'No . . .' he sat up, '*you* said that. Not me.'

Her hands balled into fists and she squeezed her eyes tight in frustration.

'You can't love her.'

'I told you in the beginning that I wouldn't leave her.'

'Jessica will understand,' Fay said; 'she's always been very good at that.'

'Don't talk that way.'

She remained very still until she had gained her self-control, only then did she turn over and look into his face and was glad to see the guilt lying like gloss on his skin. Tom was vulnerable when he was being defensive, like a child, and it soothed her anger a little, shifting the balance so that she became strong again, lustful, teasing.

'Tom,' she said gently, then, 'Tom, Tom, Tom,' in fond mocking tones, 'you're such a bloody hypocrite.'

'She is your sister, for God's sake.'

'But *you* married her.'

'What a subtle observation.'

'You're not very good at sarcasm, Tom, it doesn't suit you. Besides, perhaps you've forgotten how good *I* am at really observing things, and particularly people. I enjoy learning what makes them tick.' With great deliberation she trailed a hand down his body, ran a finger across his penis, cupped and lifted his soft, warm balls; squeezed. 'That's how I found out about you.'

He closed his eyes, swallowed. 'But you wouldn't be good at marriage, Fay.'

'And Jessica is, I suppose.'

'We've been through all this before.'

'She's not much good at getting pregnant . . .'

'Shut up.'

'Just stating a fact.'

They fell silent. She withdrew her hand.

Tom switched his gaze to the window, not trusting himself to speak, reminded all at once and with a sudden stab of sentiment that Jessica was his wife, his very good wife.

'Anyway,' Fay continued quickly, 'she may be my sister, but frankly, it wouldn't have made any difference if she'd been my mother.'

He turned and regarded her steadily; waiting, hoping that she would smile or grin, so that he could laugh at her heresy. Instead she brought her hand up to touch his face: caressing his cheek, his jaw, his mouth; the scent of sex on her fingers.

'After all, can I help the chemistry that's between us? It's hardly my fault.' Her mouth corners turned up a little. 'I love you, Tom. I need you here, with me, I don't think you know how much.'

The words sounded unnatural, pinched and tight, like stage dialogue, but Fay's face was slightly flushed and she ran her tongue along her lips and parted them as if she were suddenly a little breathless.

'Don't make me laugh.'

'No joke, Tom. I mean it.'

For a split second their gazes locked and Tom felt himself weaken as he battled against a desire to look away from her. Did she love him? As long as he wanted her more than she wanted him, as long as he remained her sister's husband. That was the whole point – the thrill, the excitement, wasn't it? Part of him believed that Fay was only capable of loving herself.

'That's not supposed to be part of "this" – us,' he said slowly, carefully.

'Feelings, like relationships, never stand still, they grow or die . . .'

'How poetic.'

'I'm serious.'

'Don't . . .' he said tiredly, 'just leave it.'

Her pale eyes iced up momentarily, then she pushed back the bedclothes with an abrupt sweep of her arm, got up and walked slowly across the room to the window. Even the anger that was boiling up inside did not change the little smile on her lips. Fay knew Tom's eyes would be following the sway of her naked hips, the way her heavy red hair tumbled down her back. She paused deliberately, leaning against the window-frame, one leg resting on the broad window-seat, and yawned, arching her back and thrusting her breasts outwards.

'God, you're so gullible, Tom! You still don't know when I'm joking and when I'm serious, do you?'

He flushed a livid red.

'And do you really think that I'd want to make our little arrangement permanent . . . actually be *married* to you?' She shook her head and let off a peal of laughter. 'Why should I? I get what I want and I live exactly as I please, not many people can say that.' She gave him a smile of thorough sensuality. 'Besides, I could never be faithful.'

There was a look of unpleasant surprise on his face. 'But you're faithful to me, now, aren't you?'

She shrugged.

'Fay?'

'You really want it all, don't you, Tom? Everything. Sometimes I could almost feel sorry for Jessica.'

'You haven't answered my question.'

'Scared of big bad AIDS, are we, Tom – or perhaps a nice little helping of herpes . . . ?'

He looked back at her with distaste.

She laughed and clapped her hands. 'God, imagine if you gave Jessica a dose!'

'Not funny.' He glared at her. 'Well, are you going to tell me, or not?'

'That's something for me to know, and you to find out.' Couldn't he tell, the idiot, that she was chock-full of the human version of insecticide (not forgetting the highly unbeautiful Dutch cap which was also up there somewhere . . .) in preparation for their little trysts? Or did he think the inordinate amount of fluid emanating from her nether regions was the result of 'deep valley' orgasms? Probably. All that revolting gunge which trickled out for ages afterwards that women, as usual, had to endure in order that, hopefully, they – a) wouldn't get pregnant, and b) wouldn't catch something disgusting. The last time one of her lovers had deigned to use a condom it had split right down the middle . . . 'Besides,' she sneered, 'it's taken you long enough to ask. The faithless pleading with the faithless. Rather ironic, don't you think?'

A sense of weariness overtook him. 'Why do you have to be such a bitch?'

Her eyes shifted slowly and although she was looking directly at him there was a glazed look on her face, as if she were seeing something else, not Tom at all.

'It's just in me, I suppose,' she said lightly, 'or, conversely – perhaps there's a little piece of me missing. You know, Tom, like I'm not really all there, not a complete human being at all.'

His eyebrows came together in a frown. 'Why do you have to say such weird things – play these infantile games? What's the point, for God's sake? It doesn't impress anyone.'

'Because I want to. And why not? Besides, being different is one of the reasons why you find me so irresistible.' She grinned and stretched and, as if to prove the point, began to move her hips slowly, rotating them provocatively before taking up an empty wine bottle and rubbing it between her legs.

He looked fixedly at her, scarcely able not to. He fought an urge to lick his lips, but already his mind was returning to their love-making and Fay's skill, those profane things she whispered which could still shock, still conjure thoughts of weird dark sex.

'I couldn't stand living with the same man. . .' she closed her eyes tight, feigning pleasure, 'day after dreary day, having him breathing down my neck, guarding my luscious little fanny,' she quickened the thrust of her hips, giggled, 'I'd die of boredom.'

'Fay.'

She put the bottle down abruptly and turned to look at him.

'You get things wrong, Tom.'

'Come here.' His hands were clammy with sweat.

'Did I tell you that the people downstairs tried to buy me out?' she said, ignoring him. 'The guy – Jonathan, I think his name is – wants the whole house, but I told him that I would never sell; this flat is perfect for my work and these attic rooms will make a fabulous studio. You see, the light's just right, slants straight from the north . . . clear as crystal.' She pushed her hair back from her face and looked up at the skylight windows.

No sea-view, that was the only drawback, but in the end she had opted for the pure north light – and Tom – instead, and the investment had proved worthwhile so far. He was convenient, energetic and very willing, if a little dull.

'Fay.'

She continued to ignore him, the smile on her face wistful, dreamy. 'Some kind of business, he said – something to do with parties. I *love* parties.'

She buried her fingers in her hair, tugging sensuously at the roots, then slowly brought her hands down the sides of her body to the flatness of her belly.

'I said, come here.'

'Sometimes I think you don't know what you want, Tom.' She began sliding her hands upwards to caress her breasts, fingering the extra nipple which had always repelled but somehow fascinated him far more – a pink fleshy jewel: very pale, very delicate.

'Come here, damn you.'

She shook her head.

His expression was hard, almost accusing. 'Stop it.'

She laughed and the sound was low, throaty.

'I don't want to stop.'

'You're playing games.'

'I like playing games, you should know that by now.' She opened her mouth and pushed her tongue out, licking the torpid air slowly, greedily.

'Not with me.'

'You most of all.'

'No.'

Her eyes grew round and innocent.

'But you misunderstand me.' She smiled invitingly, one hand cupping a breast, the other slipping downwards to the sensitive core between her legs.

A light sweat had sprung all over his body and in the heavy silence he could hear his own breathing. The sound of some traffic, a lawnmower, was a far-off soporific drone. Another world.

'Come back to bed.'

She looked at him long, full in the eyes.

'No,' she said, 'you come to me. We can do it here.' She giggled softly. 'Wouldn't you like that?'

He stared at her face, a doll's face with two dimples placed in soft seductive features. Tom swallowed, caught between excitement and fear: the window overlooked the communal garden. If Jessica, or anyone, looked up he could be seen. He opened his mouth to speak, but closed it again.

'Tom . . .' she breathed, as if the waiting was an agony.

He swung his legs off the bed, but still he hesitated, sitting motionless and watching her.

'Look . . .' she said in a little girl's voice, 'the cat scratched me.'

His eyes followed the direction of her hand, saw a faint pink line etched across her thigh.

'Kiss it for me, Tom,' she said. 'Lick the nasty scratch . . . make it better.'

Effortlessly seductive.

And all the time he was looking back at her and she was looking back at him.

'Please, Tom.' She lifted the hand away from her body and stretched her arm out in a yearning kind of way.

As he walked towards her there was a gleam in her eyes, close to triumph and, like a reward, she took his hand and placed it over her own, the one which played so expertly between her thighs. At the same time he sought out the nipple he wanted, the special one, making it rise to his lips and roll across his tongue as Fay opened her mouth around an animal-like sound of pure pleasure.

'Down,' she said, '. . . here,' and made him kneel, brought his face, his mouth to the scratch, made him lick and lick his way to the place she wanted. There was something more than gratification in having his head, any man's head, between her legs, a sort of power which was usually only given to the male of the species as a right.

There was nothing so delicious as balancing the scales.

And dear Tom was particularly talented in this field, surprisingly uninhibited as he slurped urgently away.

When she had had enough she made him sit, pushing him into the window-seat with her slim white hands. She sank down and sat on her haunches and stretched her lips wide, so that he could see the slick wetness of her tongue, the back of her throat, before she took him into her mouth.

He groaned as she began to work on him, grasped her head in his hands, moving it to and fro, to and fro until Fay withdrew to look back at him. Her eyes were dancing with glee; this was the best moment, a slow, unhurried moment before she gave them what they wanted. Time and again she brought Tom to the brink, only to draw back.

She paused once more, muttering something inaudible and he thought her voice infinitely soft, like a caress, but then she shot a glance at him up through her eyelashes and began to use her teeth. Behind the little almond-shaped eyes she was laughing.

He shuddered and his eyes leapt at the strange mixture of pain and pleasure, felt the muscles of his abdomen closing in like tightening coils as rapier blades of exquisite pain increased and spiralled upwards and outwards.

Fay wanted to punish him, just a little, just enough to make him squirm. She raked the tender skin once more and he threw his head back whimpering. Cursed her.

When he leaned forward again he saw that Fay's eyes had narrowed and grown watchful, her mouth was still open and he could see her fine teeth, small and white and sharp. His heart was thudding nastily and for an instant he felt a spasm of intense dislike, and apprehension that was like a sick thought.

'Bitch.'

Still gazing at him she broke into high breathless laughter then proceeded to lick him lushly, like a cat lapping cream, and the moment was gone.

Zak crouched down against a tree as the moon grew brighter and lit up the night. He waited until a thin sliver of cloud passed across its blank white face and the grounds of the Crescent became very dark again. An owl called from somewhere close and he shifted his position, anxious to move as his eyes roamed over the building he had targeted and the others on either side. Over the last few days he had discovered that there was only one light that really mattered, in the house, at the top, where the red-haired girl lived. And she kept that light on all night, as if she were afraid of the dark.

After the man had gone, she had stood at the window for a long time, her face a small pale orb, like another moon, looking out until, at last, she had disappeared from view and Zak had breathed a sigh of relief because now she would not see him steal across the bleached grass and into the house.

He took a step forward and climbed swiftly over a wall and into the silent garden of the house, which was no longer a garden but a forsaken patch of land gone back to the wild. An ancient birdbath overgrown with ivy and encrusted with lichen rose above the tall grass, stems of bracken and battalions of bindweed; it smelled warm and close and earthy, but spiced with that vague sweet scent of something rotting underfoot, like windfall fruit left to moulder.

A sound broke behind him and he tensed, but it was only the cat; it had followed him. The animal snaked around his legs, thrust its head up under his hand, nudging for a caress.

17

Zak sucked in a breath, annoyed that he had allowed the animal to distract him, then switched his attention to the thing that mattered most and began following the line of the wall until he came to a narrow stairwell leading to the basement; it was crumbling and wet with water seeping from a cracked drainpipe and clotted with dank rich moss the texture of velvet. Treacherous, that moss, like ice; he had slipped and almost fallen the previous night. Now he pressed himself against the wall and slid down into the darkness and with confidence because he knew the way almost by touch.

A heavy wooden door, once painted brown, now chipped and peeling from years of neglect stood between Zak and the rooms within. He put his shoulder against it as he had done the night before and the night before that, smiled as it gave way and then became very still, listening to the silence now as a sweltering wave of stale air wafted into his face; it reeked of age and disintegration, as if no window or door had been opened in years.

Zak's broad, fine forehead creased into puzzled lines as he waited on the threshold, but then he shrugged, letting his eyes grow used to the blackness before stepping inside. He felt for his lighter and fished it out of a top pocket, flicking the wheel until a fragile flame filled the room with yellow light. A wide deep fireplace still clogged with ashes, stood in front of him on which he had left a candle in a bottle waiting to be lit. This done, he surveyed the empty room again, taking renewed pleasure in its size, the thick solid walls, the very fact that it was old and unloved. He walked across the patched linoleum floor into the smaller inner room which had once been a kitchen and where, a few days ago, he had begun to store his few belongings. Some pipes sloped raggedly up a flaking wall and in a corner stood a massive square sink with a single tap of brass coated green with verdigris and bandaged in rags.

He stood the candle on the sink in the shallow depression where soap had once sat and stared at the room for a long time before placing his fingertips up against one wall. He began edging his way around the perimeter of the room and every now and then he would pause, closing his eyes, as if he were listening to something distant and faraway.

Finally he picked up the candle again and moved to the window, running his hand along the deep stone sill and disturbing a large fly which buzzed irritably as it sought refuge from the light of the candle.

Zak looked through one of the broken slats nailed across the stained glass and stared up to where the overhanging branches of a tree laced the sky with shadows; moonlight poured through the gap to bathe his flawless face in rays of blue and amber.

Outside in the overgrown garden there was a brief flap of wings, followed by the squeal of some small animal and its death-cry made him twitch.

He could be happy here; it was almost the perfect squat.

Jonathan slammed the door of his car and stood still for several moments looking up at the house. It was almost everything he had been searching for. Of course, it would have been even better if he could have roped in the rooms above the office, 'lived above the shop' as the saying went, but maybe that would have been stretching things a bit, particularly as the basement was 'in need of some modernisation' as the estate agent had so sweetly put it, and that was an understatement in any language.

In his mind's eye he saw the two rooms again – riven with cracks and damp and ancient filth – and he shuddered a little. There was a bad-meat smell down there which seemed to defy logic (a dead rat in a wall cavity?). He pressed the thought down, revolted. A pit would describe the basement more accurately, a shit-hole with original nineteenth-century features (including the kitchen sink), but at least it had enabled him to knock down the price some more.

Despite everything it was a beautiful building, part of a Regency crescent which swung round in a huge arc embracing a very substantial communal garden, something Jonathan considered to be a big plus since, from the rear at least, it gave the happy illusion of living in the country. The front façade, facing the street, had been newly painted white, the railings and door black, the brass fixtures treated so that they gleamed white-gold in the burning sunshine.

He began crossing the narrow road, then stepped back in disgust to avoid putting his foot in a pile of fresh dog turds still steaming and crawling with flies. The warmth of the day seemed to cook the stench and it rose into the air like a tremulous heat haze. Jonathan closed his eyes for an instant and swallowed hard before making a comically large stride over it, cursing all dog-owners in the process.

He had never felt at ease with our four-legged friends, or anything, for that matter, possessing more than two legs, which covered pretty much everything non-human, but particularly creepy-crawly things, like spiders, flies and bugs in general; he found them extraordinarily distasteful, but it was something he preferred the rest of the world not to know. Deep down he felt his phobia (for he supposed that was what it must be) was unmanly – a weakness, and

something someone like cool-hand Keith would no doubt
find extremely funny.

He took another deep breath to regain his composure
and made himself pause before the wide heavy door which,
he realised all at once, was impressive by itself; perhaps he
would have a brass plaque fixed beside it with 'Party
Classics' inscribed and his name underneath. But he would
need the permission of the girl upstairs, the red-head who
had practically told him to piss off when he explained
that he would be interested if she ever thought of selling-up.
A hard cow, a real testicle-shriveller despite the face and the
nubile body.

He loosened his collar and shrugged, dismissing her from
his mind. Instead, he made a conscious effort to focus his
thoughts on Emma, his girlfriend, before pushing open the
door. She was leaning over her desk, her face hidden by a
curtain of hair.

'Sorry I'm late,' he said.

Emma looked up at him, felt the resentment she had
been hoarding fade instantly despite the little resolution
she had made to herself; Jonathan always had that effect,
always won without even trying. Even now there was that
eagerness inside, boiling-up, just at the sight of him.

'I was worried.'

'No need.'

'I thought you'd call.'

'There wasn't time.' He straightened the blotter on his
desk unnecessarily.

'It went well, then?'

'Everything went like clockwork, not a hitch – the
food, the fire-eater whom we will definitely use again,
the music . . .' Jonathan sat down. 'But it was so damn
hot in that marquee, dancing crazy, everyone was sweating

like pigs. And Keith was great – almost outdid himself.'

'Perhaps you should give him a rise.' He was short of cash, had actually told her as much. He had also hinted very strongly that maybe Jonathan didn't appreciate him enough.

'Oh, no,' Jonathan shook his head adamantly. 'That would only give him big ideas. Besides, he's hardly Radio One material,' he snorted with laughter, 'aping all that American speak . . . all that "hey man" crap. DJs like him are two a penny.'

'That's not fair, you know that. He's better than average, Jonathan, much better. Everyone loves him.' Keith had a way of making you laugh, even at yourself, and he could dance like no one she had ever seen, transforming that short, stocky body into something magically fluid, almost beautiful. But his mouth let him down because he could be crude and mocking and too smart; Jonathan hated that.

'Okay, okay,' Jonathan held up his hands in mock defence, 'point taken.' He grinned, flashing perfect white teeth.

'We don't want to lose him.'

'We won't lose him.' He sat down heavily. 'Besides, you've got a soft spot for our little Keithy, haven't you?'

'Not really.'

'Oh, come on.'

'Not in the way you mean.' How could she? Jonathan was the sun who loomed in her limited heaven, her very own Mr Universe. There was no comparison.

'Just a joke,' he laughed, 'besides, he's plug-ugly. That mouth of his should have an entry in the Guinness Book of Records. I can't understand what girls see in him.' He shook his head recalling the little clique that had hung round Keith all the evening with their tongues hanging out. 'I really can't.'

The smile she returned was a pallid thing and touched by shame as her thoughts somersaulted back to Keith's birthday; when his greedy wine-stained lips had found her neck and for an instant pleasure had come in a heated rush and she had wanted more. But that had been Jonathan's fault; late again, making her lonely and needful.

'You look tired,' she said. 'Can I get you something? A coffee?'

'Lovely. Thanks.'

Emma pushed her chair back and stood up. He watched her walk into the kitchenette, thought how pretty she was in a fresh, unspoilt sort of way. He was very lucky. He was a lucky man.

'Any calls?'

'I've listed them,' Emma popped her head around the door, 'and you'll be pleased to know that we've confirmation of that big Rottingdean party, the tennis club and the twenty-first in Sussex Square.'

His face lit up.

At that moment she was close to being happy because he was so obviously pleased, and that meant he would be in a good mood tonight when she had him all to herself. Inevitably Emma found her thoughts turning towards the future and the Harrods catalogue lying in a drawer of her desk, and if the corners were a bit dog-eared it was because she had gone over and over the choices, carefully circling all the gifts in red: sets of bed-linen, glassware, china, French casserole dishes. The list was endless, but wedding lists usually were. And Jonathan would mean it this time, no more waiting and wondering; he had promised as much after the abortion.

Emma stared unseeing into the mug of black coffee. It had all seemed so terrible then, but he had persuaded her that it was not the right time, that she should be sensible and do as he asked, and so she had. It was as simple as that. He had been very understanding about it all in a strong, silent sort of way, but there was that image tucked away in her mind of him sitting quietly beside her, squeezing her fingers so tightly that the bones had ached. Willing her to go through with it.

And sometimes when she went to bed she would lie in the dark room puzzled, anxious, hands on her belly, scrutinising one thing after another. Nearly eleven weeks. She had even had a scan, seen the tiny funny body moving, fledgling arms and legs stirring, fragile heart pump-pumping. Not much more than a blob, not even a sustainable blob. But hers. Grief would hit her like a padded fist and she would cry silently so that no one would know, and especially not Jonathan. He couldn't bear to see her cry; it was as if he couldn't cope, didn't know quite what to do, and his face would close against her and she hated that. Losing him when she needed him most.

Jonathan was drumming his fingertips on the desk as she emerged from the kitchen.

'Three quotes, three acceptances,' he shook his head almost in disbelief. 'You know, it really is beginning to take off . . .'

Emma paused in mid-stride, coffee in hand.

'You didn't have any doubts, did you?'

'I always have doubts.'

She frowned, not understanding.

'Why didn't you say something?'

'I worry enough for both of us.'

'But that's not right,' she put the coffee down, 'I mean, we're a partnership, aren't we? After all, when we get married we'll share everything, even doubts and worries; that's what it's all about.'

A fly settled on the sleeve of his jacket, crawled to his wrist and immediately it was flicked away with a violent sweep of his arm.

'Bloody flies, they're all over the damn place.'

'It's the heat I suppose,' Emma said vaguely, then darted a careful glance at him. 'By the way, the estate agent telephoned, there's a balcony flat coming up for sale in number seven.'

'That's the other end of the Crescent,' his voice had sharpened, 'right at the beginning.'

'It's probably as near as we're likely to get to the office, and it sounds wonderful.'

'I'm not sure we can afford it.'

'If the girl upstairs had been willing to sell, you would have found the money from somewhere.'

He tensed at the edge to her voice, but made no answer.

'I think we could rent . . . I'm sure that's an option,' she pressed, willing him to agree, 'and we have to find somewhere soon. I hate living apart like this – staying with my parents. It's not much fun.' Emma glanced down at her hands, 'I hardly see you.'

'All right,' he said, 'I'll think about it.' Jonathan lifted his gaze and surveyed her, surprised and a little disturbed by her persistence, 'And that's a promise.' Below the round adoring eyes and white silky neck Emma looked surprisingly bosomy and it made him feel uncomfortable.

'I'm wearing one of those "wonder-bras",' she laughed, but it was a small laugh, nervous and unsure.

His eyebrows drew together in a frown.

25

'Why?'

'I thought . . .' A hot flush crept up from her neck.

'I like you the way you are.'

There was a moment's strange little silence.

'Shall I take it off?' she asked quietly and with odd formality.

'For God's sake,' he said with exasperation, wishing he had never spoken, never noticed. He looked at the telephone, willing it to ring and save him.

'I did it for you.'

'There's no need to do things like that for me.' It took an effort not to let the irritation show.

'I thought you'd be pleased.'

'Emma . . .' He stood up and moved around his desk, put his hands on her shoulders, 'I told you, I like you the way you are. My little girl.'

She found herself pressing gratefully against him, burying her face in his shoulder, but feeling the offending bra graze his shirt and she wondered how, so often, she managed to misread him.

Jonathan looked at her partly bowed head, kissed it lightly then stiffened and shot a glance at the doorway because someone was standing there and watching them.

Zak grinned and held up a tin can dangling from a handle, like a miniature bucket.

'Could I scrounge some water?'

'Who the hell are you?' Jonathan moved Emma to one side, 'and how did you get in here?'

'I came in the back door. It was open.'

'Have you ever heard of knocking?'

'I did, but no one seemed to hear.'

Instantly Jonathan was playing back the last few minutes in his mind, felt his face redden.

'Why do you need our water? Don't you have a supply of your own?'

His eyes flicked over the boy: probably early twenties, average height, average build, except that there was nothing average about him.

'There's something wrong with the plumbing,' Zak continued. In his mind's eye a picture took shape of the basement and the lone brass tap sticking out of the flaking wall. 'I only need enough for some coffee.' He put his head on one side and held up the can again, disarming them both with a smile that was somehow innocent and inviting at the same time.

Jonathan regarded him suspiciously, but was caught by the angelic smile and the face that looked back. Zak's taut muscular frame was clearly outlined beneath a black tee-shirt and tight denim jeans, so tight his thighs strained at the material, crotch bulging. He felt himself flush again.

They stared at each other until Jonathan's eyes slid away.

'All right, go ahead,' he offered grudgingly, 'but don't go mad – there is a hose-pipe ban, you know.'

Zak gave a mocking bow which made Emma giggle.

'By way of thanks, perhaps I could make you both a coffee?'

'I already have one.'

Zak's gaze fastened on the solitary mug. 'Must be cold by now.'

'Thanks, but no thanks – that goes for my girlfriend too.'

Emma tensed in silent protest, but Zak ignored the rebuke. Sometimes he thought he had spent his whole life learning how to handle jerks like this one. A worm of sexual malice moved in him and he almost wanted to laugh because

27

this guy, this jerk, didn't even know what he was.

'I'm Zak, by the way.'

Jonathan sniffed in contempt and instantly Emma was turning to look at him in surprise.

'Hi,' she said quickly to make amends, 'I'm Emma – and this is Jonathan. The kitchen's to your left.'

Zak nodded and smiled, then moved out of view and into the tiny room, immediately dismissing them from his mind. His eyes began roaming over the white, white walls – shining stainless steel sink (pink rubber gloves dropped casually over gleaming tap), pink plastic dispenser containing matching sponge and cloth, the coffee percolator sitting on a surface of pristine Formica, a strip light blazing overhead. A 'No Smoking' sign. Very new, very hygienic; he doubted if anyone had so much as farted in here.

But it was almost sheer pleasure to turn a tap, watch the water pour in a torrent over and through his fingers, the silver drops plip-plopping from the tips of his chipped and blackened nails. He began washing his hands very carefully. There was a small brush, pink of course, used for scouring pans and he brought it to his nails, picking out the grime with meticulous care.

It made him think of his mother – no running water for her, no pretty prissy kitchen, no apron or waste-disposal unit. She couldn't stand 'all that materialistic crap'. He saw her in his mind, and the other travellers, and their shabby convoy of trucks, coaches and caravans weaving their way from the delirium of Glastonbury to Wales and an old safe spot, but far away from the sea which he loved. He had left them with mingled feelings of relief and regret, mostly relief, but they hadn't understood him; they never had, not even his mother – Astra (not her real name, naturally), child of the universe and everyone's Earth Mother, everyone's lay.

Way, way back Zak had been born by the sea, near a flat silent landscape of Norfolk coastline: scattered copses of gnarled, wind-broken trees and strange little ribbons of water carrying twigs, seeds, fragments of dead life and forgotten things down to the sea. That sound and that smell of the sea had stayed with him – always there, for ever and ever.

Zak switched off the water, wiped his hands on his jeans. But it was good here, not the same, yet it would do for a while. The Crescent swung off a main road which ran directly to the sea front and sometimes in the early morning there was a mist, like a bloom on the grass, which would get heavier as the year wore on and the days grew colder: thick grey mists ghosting up and rolling in from the sea.

Thick grey mists ghosting up and rolling in from the sea.

Zak stiffened as a memory churned up and stared unseeing at the white kitchen wall. His mother had cornered him at the leaving and thrust her face into his, pulling her handsome features taut so that her face seemed stretched as if the skin might break. She had said something obscure, something vaguely threatening, and for an instant his arms had goosefleshed, and sometimes his mind would stubbornly return to that no matter how hard he tried to avoid it. He began washing his hands again, very rapidly, over and over.

'Hi!'

Zak started.

'Keith's the name.'

Zak shook the outstretched hand, a big hand despite the squat stocky frame, and smiled back at the little man whose over-large mouth was widening into an enormous grin. Very red the lips, thick and fleshy like pieces of rubber. He wore a shell-suit the colour of blood with a silver flash down one side, his hair was tied back in a pony-tail over which, like antennae, sat the earphones of a Sony walkman waiting to blast his eardrums with sound. One of his feet moved constantly as he spoke, tapping by itself, as if music were playing in his toes.

'Zak.'

'Cool,' Keith said with approval. 'You're new here?'

'Just scrounging some water.'

Keith snapped his fingers. 'A DJ – right?'

'Not me.'

'A friend of Jonathan's?'

'Not exactly.'

'For your information, Keith . . .' Jonathan was suddenly hovering at his shoulder, 'we've only just met.'

'What are you so uptight about?'

'I'm not uptight.'

Zak met his eyes, saw the lie.

'It's about time I left.'

'Hey, man,' Keith said, 'not on my account.'

'Like I said, I only came for some water.' Zak slid the water-can beneath the spout in the sink and tried to turn the tap again, except that it would not move.

'It was okay just now . . .' He closed his fist around the gleaming chrome head and used more strength.

'Let me have a go,' Keith offered.

'It's all right, it's beginning to shift.'

Slowly, reluctantly the tap began to turn and water trickled, then spluttered forth, brown with rust and thick with sediment.

Grains of mud, sludge and dead insects poured into the shining stainless steel sink, a corrupted sick stench of rotting things rose up and into the air like a noxious gas.

'Jeeesus Christ . . .' Keith swore again. 'Shit – that is dis-gus-ting, that is *other-world*, man.' He put a hand over his nose. 'Like something died in the goddamn pipes . . .'

Behind him Jonathan clutched his stomach and retched.

Jessica was sitting on the patio waiting for Tom, wearing the slinky black number Tom liked and feeling slightly ridiculous. But the night was a dream, a silky seductive summer night full of languid promise except for the heat, the almost unbearable heat. And, incredibly, this was the end of September. Crazy.

There had been no rain in weeks and the distance from the patio to the wall which separated the house from the communal garden did nothing, even in the fading light, to soften the harsh edges of the drought. In some places the unremitting sun had stripped the skin from the land so that there was no grass, nothing, only brown scabrous patches of scorched earth.

Even with the assistance of daily washing-up water her own pear tree still thirsted, still looked skeletal – a temple of wiry stalks and branches covered with a fine film of dust.

Native trees and shrubs had withered. In the communal garden itself it seemed the time of the more exotic breeds planted by generations of hopeful gardeners, now gloating and flourishing unnaturally in the abnormal climate along with the insects which were literally having a field day. Not like England at all. But tonight the air was heavy, almost humid, and Jessica hoped thunder might be brewing somewhere just out of sight, and the rain would come, days of it perhaps, righting everything.

And she would conceive.

A wry smile tipped the edges of her mouth. Anything could seem possible if she had much more of the rich yellow wine, when that old friendly floating feeling would come, like a comforter: a heady, happy hoper.

She pushed the thought carefully away and focused her mind deliberately on her husband. Tom was late, but Tom was often late these days; perhaps he was working too hard. And this was his birthday after all, or had he forgotten? That would be like him, not wanting to be reminded that he was a year older – a year off forty – and it made her laugh, his vanity, that serious, nit-picking side he had which was both endearing and idiotic at the same time. She shifted her position in the hard metal seat, aware that her bottom was beginning to feel vaguely sore because she wore no panties beneath the little black dress. Suddenly she wondered if he might think it obvious and crude and was tempted to run upstairs like a schoolgirl and cover herself.

'Pull yourself together, Jess,' she said softly to the night air, 'this is your husband, for God's sake . . .'

She poured some more wine into the waiting glass and thought of the boy who had come by earlier in the day: a beautifully made boy, skin the colour of honey, thick black amazingly long hair, and the shadow of a beard on his jaw. A nineties' Jesus. A vision of his face formed in her mind and her fingers itched for charcoal so that she could sketch the perfect features and set them down on paper. It had been a long time since she had really wanted to do a portrait – years – and she didn't even know his name.

A door slammed and she jerked her head towards the door, heard the heavy familiar footsteps of her husband as he moved through the house.

'I'm out here . . .'

'I wondered where you were.' Tom was standing in the doorway.

'I was wondering the same thing about you.'

He swept an impatient hand through his hair. Tom had very straight hair the colour of toffee, which constantly fell across his face.

'Sorry . . .' he said, 'did I snap?'

'Almost.'

'Bad day.'

'Oh?'

'Can't we go inside? It's so bloody hot out here.'

Jessica glanced at the garden for a long moment, then stood up.

'Is that what made you late?'

'What?'

'The bad day.' He looked confused and boyish and Jessica found herself wanting to smile.

'Partly,' he said, 'I had a call for a valuation in Kemp Town.' He turned away, back into the house.

'Anything interesting?' She followed him, glass in hand, into their drawing-room.

'A chair,' he had the lie prepared, 'quite grotesque, actually. I was told on the telephone that it was Jacobean, but it turned out to be Victorian which was a bit of a let-down.'

'Why was it grotesque?'

The guilt came creeping, rising.

'Because it was covered in carved animal heads, mostly monkeys, grinning. To be frank – it was just plain ugly.'

'Poor you . . .'

'Quite.' And there *was* such a chair, except that he had seen it the week before in a sale-room.

'I thought,' she grinned, 'as it's your birthday – '

Tom groaned.

' – we might make an evening of it,' she said, 'I've cooked something a little more exotic than usual, a Thai dish – even chilled a couple of bottles of wine.'

Tom focused on her glass and smiled with an effort. 'So I see.' He loosened his tie.

'Try and sound a little enthusiastic.'

'Oh, take no notice – you know how I feel about birthdays.' He rubbed his forehead with the palm of his hand. 'I'm tired, that's all. Any calls?'

Jessica picked up a piece of paper from her desk. 'Dennis Santana.'

'Who?'

'Dennis San-ta-na.' she mouthed comically.

'Oh, God, yes . . .' Tom drew a sharp breath, 'I almost forgot. He wants a chat about some restoration work before he buggers off to the States.' *Fay would ruin him if she didn't kill him with exhaustion first.*

'And Fay.'

'Fay?' His heart began to thud.

'She said you promised to pop over – something to do with the windows.'

'Oh, that,' he sighed inwardly with relief, but anger bubbled at Fay's recklessness; it was probably her idea of a joke. 'Yes, I remember now, she called me at the office about it.'

'I hope to God she doesn't think that we'll be at her beck and call now that she happens to live right on our doorstep.'

Not we, Jessica – me.

Tom loosened his tie some more and undid his top shirt button. He took a deep breath, closing his eyes for a moment as he recalled their love-making and how Fay had switched effortlessly from beguiling vulnerability to chilling viciousness, but even as the thought took shape he was aware of a kind of sick excitement building up.

'She always said that she wanted a place with a view of the sea.' Jessica continued, 'something we definitely don't have here.'

'Obviously she changed her mind.'

'I wish she'd find a man – I mean someone permanent.'

'Perhaps she's too tied up in her work,' he offered, wishing his wife would drop the subject.

'Not Fay,' Jessica said with dry humour. 'She needs men, or rather their adoration, like most people need air to breathe.' Oh, her work was important to her, she had never doubted that. It was even becoming well known in the right art circles: strange surrealistic landscapes which prompted shock and unease.

Jessica thought of her own sketches with a sinking heart, black and white views of Brighton and Sussex, tame and parochial when compared with her sister's, but they sold well locally which had been important in the early days of their marriage when Tom had not yet established himself and money had been short. One of these days, she promised herself, she would try to recapture the originality she had once prized so highly and which she had sacrificed with hardly a second thought.

'That sounds a bit dramatic . . .' Tom's voice broke in, but it was true.

'Don't forget she's my sister, and I talk from a great deal of experience.' Her little sister: lovely, talented and spoilt. Fay who, too often, had caused Jessica anguish in the past; but they had buried all that, hadn't they? Made up, friends again – if rather distant ones.

'Okay. Okay.'

'Anyway,' she said, 'what's the matter with her windows?'

'Stuck. Jammed.'

'Maybe you should go across now and get it over with,' Jessica said, 'before supper.'

Tom shook his head. 'Tomorrow. It can wait until then.' Fay would only make it as difficult as hell for him to get away. He remembered her expression when he left: sulky, defiant, tantalising on purpose.

'Are you all right?'

'Yes. Why?' He darted a glance at her.

'You just seem a bit edgy, that's all.'

'It's this bloody heat, I expect,' he said quickly. 'Why don't we have a drink?'

'I'll make them,' Jessica offered, 'you sit down.'

He watched her as she moved across the room to the drinks cabinet. Jessica was wearing that dress, the black one which clung to every curve, her thick chestnut hair hung loose and big hooped copper earrings jangled against her neck.

'You look nice.'

She grinned with pleasure and did a little twirl. 'I wondered when you'd notice.' Her gaze met his and she felt sure the eagerness she felt would be in her eyes. How long had it been? A month? 'Gin and tonic?'

'Please.'

She poured two and brought them over to the chesterfield where he was now sitting.

'What the hell's that?' He spoke and pointed at the same time.

Jessica laughed.

'Your birthday surprise.'

'Oh, my God!' he exclaimed and then he was frowning. 'What's happened to the Venetian glass?'

'For heaven's sake, Tom. I needed the space for your

birthday present, so I've stored them carefully away. All right?'

'Sorry,' he responded sheepishly and then looked warily at his gift. 'What is it?'

'Go and see.'

'I'm not sure I want to.'

'Don't be such a spoil sport.'

He took a large mouthful of his drink, then stood up and walked across the room to a shining brass pedestal. A dove grey blanket completely covered what could only be a very large cage. Tom pinched a corner of the blanket between his fingers, hesitated, then pulled hard and the bird squawked and blinked as light shone down unmercifully, swamping its small world and dazzling tiny, beady black eyes.

'A cockatoo.'

'You said you wanted one.'

'To be precise, I said I thought that they probably made interesting pets.'

'Same thing, really.'

'Hardly, Jess.'

'Oh, don't be such a misery. What would you have preferred – a pair of socks?'

'It's a bit of a shock, that's all.'

'Not it – he.'

'He.'

'And 'he' can talk, you know.'

'Can he?' Tom said bleakly.

'He says "boring" very clearly,' Jessica responded ruefully.

'Oh.'

'For God's sake, Tom, it's a cockatoo, not an atom bomb. Cheer up.'

He regarded his wife, then the magnificent white bird

which was scrutinising him very carefully. 'All right, all right,' he said with apprehensive amusement. 'It – he – is beautiful.'

She watched him steadily. 'Happy birthday.'

Tom smiled, not a large smile, but toothy grins never had been his style.

'Thanks, Jess.'

'How about a kiss for your lonely wife?'

He looked embarrassed and couldn't disguise it. He thought she must smell her sister on his clothes, on his skin. Yet he had showered before leaving Fay and taken what he presumed would be normal precautions under such circumstances.

'Is it such a big deal,' her voice faltered, 'a kiss?'

'Oh, God, I'm sorry,' he said quickly, 'I've been a bit preoccupied lately, haven't I?' He flushed, thinking of Fay, what he had been doing with Fay.

'It doesn't matter.' But it did. In fact, it was beginning to matter a great deal.

He took Jessica's hands and pulled her close, kissing the soft red mouth, feeling the familiar outline of her body, and he thought he must be going quietly out of his mind to risk this. All that he had.

Tom stroked her hair and realised with something close to horror that it was the same texture as Fay's, yet clearly several shades away from that distinctive red colouring. He swallowed and cast his eyes around the room at all the familiar things he loved. And Fay was a world away, a shockingly lustful world away, and he wondered how he had allowed himself to be enticed and seduced so completely. When he thought back, there was no how or why, only sex – rich, black sex which made him dizzy with terrible possibilities.

38

And he had not been forced into her arms; there had been no compulsion. He could have said no and meant it simply because she was Fay, someone he had never liked and yet always wanted, and in the way men really wanted women: acting the whore. It was as if he were being driven too far down a road on which he had only intended travelling a certain distance and there was no way of turning back.

Maybe it was this pregnancy business, always hanging there, like a bloody cloud over his head.

Tom glanced down as he felt Jessica open his shirt and rub her hands across his chest, then her soft needful fingers were trailing down to the fine cotton of his trousers as she searched for his zip. In a few moments, he knew, she would release him before taking him into her mouth, but the thought disgusted him. He felt sleazy and repelled because only an hour ago it had been Fay's lips, Fay's hot open mouth sucking, licking . . .

But with Fay there was no pressure, no duty.

'Jessica . . .'

His wife wanted sex, she wanted love-making sex (baby-making sex?) and so she was trying to please him, just as she used to, and he was touched by shame. He sighed and the sigh became a moan, but then he was pushing her gently away, clutching her arms and forcing her to the floor. He pulled her dress up, almost angrily, trying to feed on his anger so that he would be able to do what she wanted.

Tom pushed her thighs apart and moved into a crouch above her, massaging her breasts, running his hands down her body, making himself hard and ready so that he could make it more easy to slide himself inside her, but all the time he was thinking of Fay.

Jessica's eyes were closed and he was glad of that because otherwise she might see all the feelings he was sure were written on his face, feelings he would rather she did not see. He took a gulp of air as she arched her pelvis to accept his thrust and brought her legs up, wrapping them around him as he began building-up the old familiar rhythm, taking her with him, but then her eyes opened and she was looking into his.

Tom could feel the pounding of his heart, followed by leaping, jostling panic. There was a strange feeling inside, a relentless seeping at his centre. His mind went back to Fay and all at once he could feel himself coming, and he was coming too fast, his cold control bursting through all his good intentions – he convulsed, jerked, and then slumped forward with a small cry before sliding slowly, helplessly to Jessica's side. He left his arm lying across her body, as if the need just to hold her might serve as some compensation for his failure.

For a long time he did not move or break the awful quiet which pulsed between them. Jessica lay quite still, staring unblinking at the ceiling, panting softly and unfulfilled.

I will end it with Fay, he vowed silently. Tomorrow.

Outside the moon stared down, bloated and cheesy-looking.

2

There was another world on the ceiling, a place full of craters and lumps and gullies and cracks where spiders lived and other, nameless things. Zak's eyes travelled over and across the room and came to rest on the uneven corner where the secret was, the wall with a hollow sound and the staircase he had seen through a gap in the plaster – each step splintered and sunken in the centre, pitching and yawning downwards into shadow. A hidden place.

'Out of that hideous place shall come a garden . . .'

He spoke as though recalling an ancient thing, words he had heard somewhere, some time and thought strangely apt. Zak liked poetry.

He was stretched out on the floor, naked, watching a pool of sunshine brighten and shame the shabby linoleum floor, listening to the creaks, the little whispering sounds of the building. That was one of the things he liked about old houses; they were never really quiet, almost as if they were living things and had souls of their own. And why not? Walls absorbed energy, like people absorbed memories. Walls, rooms, houses witnessed the whole gamut of human drama – all of the lives that had lived here, all of the crying, the laughing, the grief. And the other things, the black things like envy, greed, malice, hate. Most people didn't notice these things, of course; they went through life failing to compute or perceive those invisible signals tickling their subconscious. A fatal mistake, really, considering everything.

In each of his fists Zak held a large can of beans and using them as weights, raised them into the air. His arms were pistons, his already well-developed biceps began to sweat and swell in the heat ... pumping twenty, forty, sixty, eighty actions. Zak dropped the cans and let them roll across the floor, then he turned over on his stomach and began one hundred press-ups. He wasn't exhausted when he had finished, just horny. Exercise always did that to him.

With a languid sigh he turned on to his back. Out of the corner of his eye he could see that the patch of sunlight was about to touch his knee; if he waited long enough it would cover him, so silently, turning his skin to gold, gilding his prick, his prize, warming him up. He thought of the girl upstairs, the red-head, the hard case, and disregarded her with hardly a second thought and let his mind roll on, focusing on the woman he had met yesterday, the woman with the lovely mouth and big warm smile. Zak closed his eyes.

'Is there something wrong' Jessica asked quietly, 'something bothering you?'

'No.'

'What is it, then?'

'I'm tired, that's all.'

'You've been tired before, but it hasn't affected our sex life to this extent.' There, she had said it.

Tom stared into his coffee cup, watched steam rise into the air.

'Christ . . .' he sighed heavily, 'I don't know, Jess.'

'Is it me?'

'No,' he said, 'of course not.'

42

Jessica switched her gaze from Tom's partly bowed head to the window and the garden. The sun blazed down, it was another glorious bloody day.

'So much for happy birthdays.'

'Don't be like that,' he said quickly, 'it was just bad timing . . . I love the cockatoo.'

'No, you don't.'

'Jess – I do. I know I wasn't enthusiastic at first, but that was last night, now . . .'

'Now I'm upset.'

'And I'm trying to make things better.'

'Yes, you are,' but it wasn't working, which made her feel worse than if he hadn't tried.

'But you're making it as hard as hell for me.' And how hard would Jessica make it if she knew the truth? Until Fay he had never lied to her, until Fay he had never been unfaithful, but he had managed to change all that in an appallingly short space of time and in spectacular fashion. Screwing her own sister; he must be going out of his mind. In fact, of late, Tom had actually begun to wonder if he hadn't gone a little crazy. Once upon a time they would have said he'd been bewitched, and wouldn't Fay just love that; the word had that weird sort of ring to it that would appeal to her. 'Let's go out for a meal tonight.'

'And that will make things better?'

'I said I was sorry, and I am. Why are you making this such a big deal?' Tom deliberately kept his voice low and reasonable. 'I've been working too hard and I don't seem to be sleeping well either . . . you know that.'

Jessica turned and looked at her husband, suddenly feeling defeated, wondering why she was making such an unaccustomed fuss.

'You're going to be late.'

'Jess . . .'

'Forget it, it doesn't matter.'

'It does matter.'

She met his eyes, wanting to cry.

'Oh, Jess, I'm sorry – really.'

'It's PMT, that's all.'

'Oh, Christ . . .' He'd forgotten, something he should have learned not to do by now. After all, the pattern of Jess's monthly cycle was practically branded into his skull: counting the days to the middle of the month and then coupling with his wife in a desperate scramble to conceive during those precious three days which turned out to be not precious at all. No precious cargo for them.

'Don't,' she said, 'I'm all right.'

'But you're not.'

Jessica said nothing, but there was a part of her that wanted to scream and put the pressing need for a child away somewhere and dissolve all the tension. Be free of it.

'Let me book a table – we'll go out, forget everything and simply have a good time.'

He thought abruptly of Fay; he had promised to call.

Jessica watched his face, focusing on the dark smudges beneath his eyes, found herself touched a little by shame at her churlishness. 'All right.'

'Good.' He kissed her. 'And wear your black dress again,' he smiled a smile full of promise, 'Please'.

She waved to him from the window and thought how handsome he looked despite the tiredness. Tom was a very attractive man; how often had her friends told her? She wondered what he thought of her when he looked at her good and hard. Jessica suspected that he found her a little wanting; after all, they had been married almost nine years and there was probably no novelty or excitement in sleeping with her any longer, but there had been no complaints or lack of enthusiasm on his part until recently. Perhaps it was a phase and something she would look back on and laugh about in a year's time.

The funny thing was, she still wanted and loved him in a physical way, always: the familiar feel of his skin, his hair, his smell, that lovely yearning pleasure when he made love to her. And she welcomed him in that way, always had done, there had never been any reluctance on her part; for Jessica, sex was an integral and delicious part of married life, a pleasure that was never merely endured, but savoured.

Except that lately, for whatever reason, there hadn't been much of that and she couldn't fool herself or pretend, because all she knew was that she missed it, wanted it back, wanted Tom back the way he was.

She leaned her forehead gently against the glass and for a long moment stared into the narrow sunlit street and the heat vibrating up from the tarmac; melting the roadway, the light dazzling, dusty and brittle. Her eyes came back to her fingertips which still touched the glass and almost at once she drew back; several flies buzzed fitfully on the sill, stupified by the crushing heat, and these were repulsively fine specimens: big, plump, blue-black. Jessica grimaced and made a mental note to purchase more fly-spray.

Her eyes strayed to the cockatoo; he was watching her from the corner of the room where the cage had been left the night before. Beside it stood a spray full of water, his mobile shower, and something she had discovered he adored. His pleasure had been amusingly obvious and it seemed to her now that his beady black eyes asked her once more, so that she found herself crossing the room to the cage to begin the spraying ritual all over again whilst the bird preened and squirmed beneath a cloud of cool misty droplets. He had to have a name, she realised, but that should come from Tom because the bird was his, except that he wasn't really interested. After all, she had wished the bird on him, so perhaps it was her fault, perhaps everything was her fault.

She put the spray down and with an effort switched her attention to the other thing, the impulse which had been gathering momentum over the last few days. She turned round and went to a large walk-in cupboard under the stairs.

Behind the wellington boots, tennis racquets and boxes of Christmas decorations were her paints, charcoal, an easel and fold-away stool, paper. She had put it all away a few months previously because she had hated what she was producing: tame and parochial views of the sea and surrounding countryside. Oh, they sold well in the souvenir and tourist shops, even on the good old pier but, God, she despised them for their mediocrity. Of course, it didn't help that Fay was so close, Fay with that extraordinary talent which was at last beginning to attract real attention. But her paintings disturbed Jessica, they always had, yet their power and surreal beauty, their difference, was obvious.

With something close to determination, she clamped an old straw hat on her head and then proceeded to drag the easel and its trappings out of their hiding place and onto the patio. Before sitting down, she walked back into the house to the kitchen and took a bottle of chilled white wine from the fridge. It was hot and she was thirsty – besides she wanted to cheer herself up and at the moment drinking plonk seemed the only way she knew how.

The cork made a happy popping sound as she extracted it and poured a generous dollop into her favourite glass.

As she brought it to her mouth she saw the trees over the rim of the glass, the two that had been struck by lightning the year before during one of those brief and infrequent hell-raising storms they had had. It had been beautiful, that storm, frightening and uplifting at the same time, and she had stood out in it with arms open wide and let the million bright rods of rain soak through her clothes to her skin. It was moments like that that made her understand how people had once worshipped the old gods of sun and rain with fear, fervour, even joy. Tom had thought she was mad.

The lightning had struck the sycamore with a blinding flash and a crack that sounded like a small explosion; the tree had split and burned at the same time, transferring fire to an old elder and unifying them both in one flaming torch which even the torrential rain had been unable to quench. And in that instant of burning she had shivered and withdrawn into the house.

Now the trees stood alone, two gnarled blackened stumps standing in a ring of dust because grass wouldn't grow there any more.

She wanted to sketch them and maybe the sketch would evolve into a painting, but even as the thought took shape she was thinking of the boy, the nineties' Jesus, who had stopped by yesterday. His face came before her eyes, as clear as some mystic's vision.

Jessica put her glass down, sat on her little stool and picked up a piece of charcoal and as she lifted her head to confront the paper he was standing there looking back at her, just beyond the wall which separated the patio from the communal garden. For a moment she froze, caught off guard, as if her own thoughts had somehow conjured him out of thin air.

47

And the look he gave was grave, but then he broke into a smile, like yesterday, and the immediate warmth of that smile quietly astonished her.

'Hi.'

'Hello,' Jessica flushed, 'did you find your cat?'

'Oh, yes,' but the cat wasn't his, it simply stuck to his heels like a piece of gum. He had needed a lie, a little entré into this lady's life. 'I thought I'd just come over and say thanks.'

'Well, I didn't really do anything.'

'You were civil and polite,' he was suddenly formal, 'not something that's exactly common these days.'

She raised her eyebrows a little with curiosity, watched him as he moved into the gateway.

'What are you painting?'

'I haven't even started.' She nodded towards the blackened stumps, 'Maybe the remains of those trees.' Her mind strayed back to her thoughts of a moment ago and her desire to paint him, wondered why she lacked the courage to tell.

'Lightning?'

'Yes.'

'What sort of trees were they?'

'The larger was a sycamore and the other an old elder.'

'Elder is supposed to protect against lightning.'

'Is it? How?'

'Legend has it that the Cross of Calvary was made from elder and was exempted from being struck by lightning.'

'Oddly enough, it was the sycamore that attracted the lightning; the elder caught fire because it was too close.'

'There you are – but burnt elder means bad luck,' he said this with a touch of humour, 'and I quote: "make a fire of elder-tree Death within your house you'll see". . . .'

'Ugh. Do old wives' tales happen to be a speciality of yours?' She was intrigued.

'I was brought up with them.'

'But you don't actually believe in that sort of thing?'

He shrugged. 'Much of it *is* nonsense.'

'Not all?'

'There are some tales which do have more than just a ring of truth.'

'You're kidding?'

'No.' He shrugged, 'But you're closing your mind and most people do that these days. Besides, I would never kid you.'

She met his stare and was vaguely startled, but then he was speaking again, breaking the moment:

'And after you paint the trees, what will you do?'

'When I was at college, I loved to do people, faces, portraits . . .' she paused, feeling awkward and finished lamely, 'but I let it go.'

'You shouldn't have,' he said earnestly, 'get it back. Do what you really want.'

As if he knew. An instantaneous and curious look of embarrassment came over her.

'At least try, everyone should,' he continued easily, 'otherwise what's the point?'

His voice was surprisingly deep, mellow, almost soothing.

'You have an interesting face,' she said all at once, surprising herself. But interesting was not the word.

'Me?' His expression became thoughtful and childlike.

Jessica smiled. He knew, he must, because he was quite beautiful: skin pale to dusky, neat finely carved features, a long lavish mouth, eyes very blue and framed by unbelievably long eyelashes as coal-black as the thick savage hair hanging down his back. A disconcertingly

49

beautiful face. And beneath the tee-shirt and jeans she knew there would be more beauty.

'Well,' she said, hesitant now, 'it was just a thought – silly, really.'

'I wouldn't mind.'

She didn't answer, but looked back at the paper, as if she had said too much.

'No one's ever wanted to paint me before . . .' he coaxed.

Something inside her could not believe that, someone somewhere must have been caught by that face. She could see him amidst the frescoes and gilded carvings in some shadowy Renaissance church or in an illustration in a book, drawn in black and white.

'Except my mother,' he added, 'but that doesn't really count, does it?'

'Why not?'

'She's dead,' he lied, 'apart from anything else.'

His face was closed; there was no dampness, no manifestation of feeling in the candid eyes.

'I'm sorry.'

'It seems a long time ago,' he said and for the first time he glanced away from her. 'And it was not a good likeness. My mother was better with words, that was her thing.' And astrology and folklore and cures and charms and omens and ritual. Astra comprehended the world and its perils through the old ways – superstition, divination, druidism. A true pagan, that was his mother.

'Did she write?'

'Many things.' Things he would rather forget. His face became thoughtful and gentle as he twisted the conversation back on itself. 'But could you do a good likeness? I think you could, you have that look.'

'I do?'

'Oh, yes.'

His eyes spoke to her, too clear not to be recognised, and a small still voice whispered to her in some dark cell of matter.

'Perhaps it's not such a good idea . . .'

'Why not?'

'Well . . .' she faltered, searching feebly for an excuse, 'it would mean sitting for long periods.'

He shrugged and the çorners of his mouth began to tilt upwards and there was that smile again: a clever, trusting smile that made you think the gesture could be just for you, that he had never done it quite that way with anyone else.

'When you've finished your trees, then?' he said, deceptively mild.

Jessica looked back at him, hesitation still preventing her from making an immediate response, but then, 'Why not?' She met his eyes again, heard the sudden raucous squawk of the cockatoo, like a protest, but the noise seemed distant, as if it came from somewhere far away. 'All right.'

'Good. I'd like that,' Zak said.

Fay sat in front of the mirror and began to brush her hair, heavy careful strokes which went on and on and on. It was something she did each evening, a ritual, and something which could soothe like almost nothing else. But she was angry; Tom wasn't coming, Tom had chickened out. The message on her answerphone had only said that 'something had cropped up,' but also 'they needed to talk'. Clearly he wanted to finish it or, at least, felt that he *should*. How very gallant of him, how very sensitive finally to consider good old Jessica after he had screwed her baby sister to hell and back several times over. Of course, Jessica could have her puerile husband back, but when Fay said so and not before, that was only fair, under the circumstances.

Fay continued brushing her hair, a luxurious red mass so different from her sister's. Jessica, admittedly, had a certain charm, a certain warmth, something which had been evident even when they were children, a warmth Fay never had and never missed. Curious.

Besides, she and Jessica had lived separate lives really, certainly once their parents divorced: Jessica with Mummy, Fay with jolly old Daddy whom she could twist around her little finger. Sometimes Jessica seemed remote, not like her sister at all. But Fay was inherently selfish and knew it, and there was no changing in her, even if she had wanted to, which she didn't. That had been tried once when she had been 'a bit of a problem' in her teens and what a waste of time – not to mention money – that had been. For an instant Fay's eyes darkened resentfully. As if they had really believed there was something actually *wrong* with her.

The telephone rang jarring her out of her thoughts and she stiffened, waiting for the four rings to sound before the answerphone took over. It was Tom. Fay stared at the phone in contempt, but then walked slowly across the room and picked up the receiver.

'Hello, Tom.'

He stopped abruptly in mid-sentence, made a funny hiccuppy noise and she thought the little sound he made almost comical. She could imagine his face – pale, with that pretty greedy mouth of his hanging open like a great wet fish.

'Fay, about tomorrow . . .'

'I thought you seemed more concerned about tonight.'

'That was never really on, you know that.'

'No. Actually, I didn't.'

He sighed. 'It's getting impossible.'

'What is?'

'This. Us.'

'We've managed very well up to now.'

He sighed again. 'It's Jessica.'

'Has she found out?'

'No. God, no . . .'

'What then?'

'It's affecting our relationship.' Immediately Tom wished he could gather the words back, choke on them. Christ, how infantile he must sound, how incredibly crass. 'I shouldn't have said that.'

'God, you're pathetic.'

'I didn't mean . . .'

'Yes, you did,' she snapped, 'and you're not going to do anything about "us" because I don't want you to.'

'That's ridiculous.'

'I mean it, Tom. You should know better than this. You should know better than to call and give me this shit.'

'For God's sake. We've had a good run, a good time, or whatever you want to call it, what more do you want? Fay,' he said carefully, 'all good things come to an end sooner or later.' But they had not been good. 'Good' evoked things of value, of worth; pleasant things.

'How clichéd. And this little call is merely laying the groundwork for this grand decision of yours – breaking it to me gently, so to speak. Very thoughtful.'

'Stop it.'

'Stop it,' she mimicked. 'I will stop our little fling when I feel like it, Tom. Not before. Otherwise, I could very well find myself doing things that you would not like in the least. Certainly things that Jessica might find just a teeny-weeny bit repugnant.'

'And you would, wouldn't you?' He said this with

53

resignation and dislike because he knew what she was capable of; Fay had never lived her life by rules and regulations, other people's boundaries, and reluctantly he admitted to himself that that was probably half her attraction for him.

'I kid you not, Tom.'

'But it can't go on, I mean not indefinitely . . .' he said with a touch of despair.

'Now you're being melodramatic and childish. Besides—' she yawned, 'we can talk about this when you come over.' Her tone was soft and silky now, Fay's bedroom voice. 'We can do that thing you wanted . . .'

His mind was suddenly filled with that 'thing', that fantasy, that dark sexual trick she had tantalised him with the last time they were together. The memory inflamed his mind and body, but unexpectedly and for the first time there was a trace of revulsion in him, a flicker of nausea.

'I have to go.'

'When can I expect you?'

'I'll call you.'

'You'd better, Tom.'

He quietly replaced the receiver and remained there, standing very still, letting his head fall back and staring helplessly at the ceiling. For an instant he wondered whether there had ever been a moment of sanity when it had seemed possible to stop before something irrevocable happened, but if there had been he could not remember and perhaps somewhere inside him he must have wanted it to happen.

'Who was that, Tom?'

He jumped. Jessica was standing there and watching him.

'I thought you were asleep.'

'I think I drank too much coffee at dinner.' She was

watching him steadily. 'Who was it?'

'Linda.'

'Your secretary? Why on earth do you need to speak with her at this time of night?'

'I had to check some details about that Eastbourne auction tomorrow,' he said rapidly. 'She'd forgotten. Seems to have been a bit preoccupied lately.'

'That's not like her.'

'Well, she certainly seems to have had a lot on her mind,' he shrugged. 'Maybe she has problems at home.'

'It seemed a long phone call.'

'No.' Panic washed over him. 'Not that long.' What had she heard? How long had she been there?

Jessica scrutinised him carefully, his face seemed inflexible, set and very, very careful.

'Jess – it was Linda. It was a work call.'

'Was it?'

'Who else would it be, for heaven's sake?'

'I don't know.'

He moved towards her, placed his hands on her arms and held her tightly.

'Jess, you're being silly.'

There was a moment's odd little silence.

'Nothing is right,' she said softly. And now she realised that, but then there were things one did not admit, not even to oneself, except perhaps when it was too late.

'It's a bad patch, that's all,' he said with more lightness than he felt. 'Everyone has them.'

She looked at him long, full in the eyes until he wanted to drop his gaze, except that he didn't dare, and the confused expression he saw on her face was at once doubting, sad and bewildered.

* * *

'Christ, he's living downstairs . . .'

Jonathan's voice was strident and appalled.

'Who?' Emma responded. 'What do you mean?'

'That bloody boy.'

She frowned.

'You know,' he hissed, barely able to contain his irritation, 'that Zak.' Even the name seemed to grate, fashioning visions of Zowie Bowies, Twinkles and Trixie-Bells. Pretentious sixties' crap.

'Oh, him.'

'Yes, *him*,' Jonathan said. 'He's a bloody squatter.'

'You mean he's living downstairs?'

It had dawned, finally.

'Watch my mouth move, Emma – yes, that boy is squatting in *my* basement.' He shook his head with disbelief. 'What a nerve, what a bloody nerve. Coming up here with that load of bull about needing my water because there was something wrong with his plumbing – he hasn't got any bloody plumbing, he hasn't got any bloody running water, come to that.'

'Calm down.'

'Don't tell me to calm down. He's got no right, he didn't even ask, for God's sake.'

'Well, he wouldn't, would he?'

'What the hell's that supposed to mean?'

Emma sighed wearily, wishing she had not allowed herself to be drawn.

'Squatters don't ask, do they? They just move in. They *squat*.'

'Thank you for your pearls of wisdom, for your enlightening explanation, my sweet. I shall call them to mind when I kick his arse out of there.'

'Do you have to? He's not doing any harm.'

'That is hardly the point,' he snapped, 'and don't tell me you feel sorry for him?'

'Well, you're hardly likely to be using the basement for the foreseeable future.' In fact, he avoided it like the plague.

'We're talking principles here, Emma, not practicalities. Bloody hell – what is it with these sort of people that they think they can just walk in and take over decent people's property? They make me sick.' He took a deep angry breath. 'Parasites – all of them.'

She looked at him and said nothing, then shifted her gaze to her desk and the invoices, his ledger, a list of notes, his calls.

'The plumber's coming tomorrow morning.'

He shot her a quizzical glance.

'To find the blockage.'

'Oh yes the blockage . . .' Jonathan closed his eyes as a distasteful picture of the effluent-filled kitchen sink slid into his mind. And that God-awful smell! He pressed down the shudder so close to the surface.

'And is there a connection between the plumber and our uninvited guest, or am I being particularly thick?'

'He'll be working mostly in the basement,' she said. 'I thought you should know – and Zak.'

'You mean, our squatter.'

'Well, he might decide to leave once the plumber begins to explore the pipes and take things apart. It won't be very pleasant.'

'You must be joking!' He snorted with contempt. 'People like that choose to live in squalor – they don't mind a bit of unpleasantness, or some liquid filth leaking from a few old pipes. Probably adds to the attraction.'

She opened her mouth to speak and then closed it again,

knowing that it was useless to argue with him when he was in this sort of mood. He wore a sullen expression that, despite his handsome features, made him unpleasant to look at.

'Anyway, I'm going down there – now.' He strode towards the door and called over his shoulder, 'And if Keith phones, just tell him to hold on, I need to speak to him after last night.' He slammed the door behind him so that she could not hear anything more, not the fury barely withheld, not the exasperated mutterings, 'What the hell did Keith think he was up to . . . asking for a rise,' then, 'And over the *mike*, for God's sake. If he thinks he'll get away with a cheap trick like that he must be more of a fool than I thought – the little creep.' As he approached the garden embarrassment enveloped him all over again, followed by outrage which gave way to a spurt of hatred.

Emma watched Jonathan move through the door until he disappeared from sight, felt the beginnings of anger again and that little surge of resentment. He was so used to controlling their conversation, telling her what to do and how they would do it, that her opinion had grown to mean nothing.

She looked about the office, *his* office, *his* design: the chrome and glass furniture, the leather chairs, the spotlights, trendy pictures of the promenade, even the potted plants; everything had been chosen by him to suit his taste and she had gone along with all of it.

She couldn't even remember if it had been like this at the beginning of their relationship because it seemed so long ago now. At the time she had been flattered (and still was) that he had even looked in her direction, but she had only been twenty and a rather virginal twenty at that – something Jonathan had cherished like a prize – and just recently she had found herself wondering why, since his interest in her sexually could hardly be called passionate.

And she had never climaxed in all their time together, but she knew what it was – what it felt like – because she had found out all by herself, during all those times when she had wanted Jonathan and he hadn't been there. Emma liked to think of it as improvising, but she found it odd that the same feeling, the same physical pleasure, could not be conjured when Jonathan made love to her, but then he didn't really touch her, not down *there*. In fact she knew her body, at least its potential for delight, far better than he did.

Perhaps she should talk to him about it, that was what the problem pages in the women's magazines suggested and those grinning reassuring agony aunts who seemed to have all the answers.

Communication, apparently, was the key, but Jonathan was not very good at communication and just lately he had become more distant and tense and so hard to get near to, wriggling away from her affectionate approach, his face closed and set, his voice dry with sarcasm, and she had no idea how to deal with this side of his nature. But she had gone along with it, just as she had the abortion and the postponement of their marriage plans, like something blindly accepted yet only half understood.

She had been weaving intricate dreams of her life with him: building a future together, seeing him every day, every night, and now she felt puzzled suddenly and confused, as if she had missed something. But Jonathan was faithful (he never really looked at other girls), reliable and successful: he was a *good* person, and this mood of his would pass, just like all the other times, and everything would be all right again.

* * *

Jonathan stood on the dilapidated porch and surveyed the overgrown garden with something close to misery; he must do something about it otherwise it would really depress him on top of everything else. He didn't even need to see it; it was enough just knowing the unwholesome jungle was there and only a few yards away from where he sat in the office. He lifted his eyes to the communal garden beyond which was well tended at least, if rather wizened.

He took a deep breath and pushed angrily through the long grass to the ancient birdbath. A thick crust of bird droppings was being eaten away by a colony of red ants scurrying in and out of deep cracks and crevices. There was a strong scent of mould, of rotting things, and his nose wrinkled in disgust. An apple tree, gone to seed, had lifted some of the fence with its bulging root, twisted limbs clawing at the iron palings.

He would need a bulldozer to clear it, a bloody army to make it vaguely decent, and it would cost a fortune.

He hesitated at the top of the stone steps and looked down into shadow where the door to the basement stood shut and silent. Was he there?

Gingerly he made his way down the steps and stood outside a window, but the glass was silted with dirt and he could barely see inside. His gaze turned to the door which he remembered too well from his one and only visit when he had looked around the property: solid and heavy, chipped and warped, yet with a horrible permanence about it somehow, but it opened easily enough when he placed his shoulder against the wood and shoved.

And it wasn't cool down here as he had so mistakenly anticipated, it was baking and the heat from the basement rooms rolled towards him as if the door of an oven had just been opened: the smell was clinging, thick and sweet and he held his breath until the ghastly moment had passed.

There was no one there. He stepped inside and was confronted again by its dreary squalor, uniformly dingy, littered with an accumulation of various kinds of ancient filth, filth that had never been disturbed, never even moved from one place to another – yellowing newspaper, clots of fluff, dead insects, lumps of mud, dust and soot and God know what else. He was revolted. How could anyone live in this awful place?

He moved tentatively forward and saw the bed roll, a stump of a candle in a saucer full of wax beside it, an empty beer can, a small leather-bound book. Jonathan stooped down and picked it up, bringing the front cover close to his face so that he could read the title: 'William Blake'. A book of poetry.

'What are you doing?'

Jonathan wheeled around and for an instant could only stare with alarm at the black silhouette standing framed in the open doorway.

'As it happens . . .' the words gushed awkwardly, 'I own this basement.'

'Really.'

'Yes.'

'And so you want me to move out?'

'Squatting is illegal.'

'Not really, not once you're in.'

'I can have that checked, you know.'

'I'm sure you will.'

They regarded each other for a long moment.

Zak wanted to smile, instead he began removing his tee-shirt, pulling it over his head and throwing it to the floor. 'Hot, isn't it?'

Jonathan nodded dumbly. In the half-light Zak's upper torso was picked out in black and white, each muscle clearly defined and glistening with exquisite little clusters of perspiration.

'I won't be any trouble,' Zak said.

For a moment Jonathan could not speak because his lips felt unnaturally dry.

'You should have asked.'

'I thought it was derelict. I thought no one loved it.'

Love? This place? Jonathan's face was both puzzled and wary. He cleared his throat.

'Well, anyway . . .' he said in a funny squeezed voice, 'just don't damage anything.'

Zak suppressed a smile. What more could he do to this filthy hole, this rancid sink, that time and neglect had not done before him?

'I wouldn't do that.'

'No,' Jonathan replied stiffly. 'Well . . .'

'Anyway, it's only temporary until I find something else.'

'Something else?'

'Of course.'

'I suppose . . .' he said, 'in that case . . .'

'Like I said,' Zak added easily, 'I won't be any trouble.' There was a remote smile on his face as he stared at the other and Jonathan was forced to drop his eyes. His gaze fell on the poetry book which was still clutched in his hand.

'Yours,' he looked up. 'I wasn't prying . . .'

Oh, but you were.

'That's okay.'

'You don't look the type.'

'For poetry?'

Jonathan shook his head.

'Never seek to tell thy love, Love that never told can be; For the gentle wind does move, Silently, invisibly . . .'

Jonathan was momentarily startled, he looked back at Zak without speaking, unable to speak, crawling with discomfort and unease. He felt the boy's eyes on his face and wondered what it was in him that made him want to say such weird things.

'Don't be embarrassed.'

'I'm not.'

Zak smiled.

'I have to go.' Jonathan's voice had a slight unsteadiness to it.

'Of course.'

Jonathan swallowed and moved past, avoiding touch, but caught by a dreadful, distracted nervousness as if something huge and unknown was clamouring to get inside him. He stepped out into the glare of the sun and almost swooned, but the sense of nervousness was still spreading through him, like a stain.

Tom's desk was a mess. Jessica stood over it, trailed her fingers across the mass of papers and a pad with some of his incomprehensible doodles scrawled in black ink.

Her hand strayed deliberately to the middle drawer where his cheque stubs were, his Amex receipts, his diary. Just browsing, a little voice insisted, that's all. She shook her head in hopeless protest; God, what a fool she was.

The cheque stubs and receipts told her nothing and the diary, like his doodles, was incomprehensible. She sat down in his chair and went slowly through everything, each tiny slip of paper, each page and, in the end, they told her nothing, nothing at all.

If she could have felt relief, that might have been

something, but she did not. Well, what was it then, what was this tiny doubt that made her afraid? That he was having an affair?

Even their so-called 'night out' had turned into an anticlimax; there had been none of the old banter or real closeness and he had seemed distant somehow, preoccupied, almost nervous.

Jessica put the papers, receipts and diary back in exactly the way she had found them and closed the drawer. She moved across to the window which overlooked the garden and wondered where he was, what he was doing. Tom. He was her whole world and that was a mistake. No one should build their very existence around another human being; the responsibility, the burden, on both sides was too great. Except that these things happen insidiously, advancing imperceptibly over the years, building a false sense of security so that when something goes wrong there is no fail safe, no emergency exit, no safety net.

But she did not know, not for certain, that there was anything really wrong. Perhaps she was only jumping at shadows and, in truth, she could not imagine him with another woman, not Tom. They were happy, weren't they? Everyone had little blips in their relationships at one time or another – big blips, even, – but they got over them.

She should call Roz and confess her suspicions because Roz would offer sensible advice and make her laugh, but most of all she knew her friend had been down this road herself and probably would know all the signs to look for. Except that Jessica didn't really want to know what to look for, or to tell *anyone* what she was so afraid of. Besides, she was probably overreacting, PMT and all that.

Yet in the deepest part of her heart she doubted, everything. Jessica had been stirred by the first faint inkling that there was something out of sync in her life, that Tom was somehow *different*. She made a soft despairing sound and focused again on the garden, the familiar, the safety of everyday things.

The sun was shining down through the branches of her pear tree in thick mote-filled shafts and the shadows beneath were black and perfect as if someone had taken a knife and carved them there. Each branch, each tired leaf and wiry stalk stood out separately with its own life against the white paving stones of the patio. Where her easel stood.

Everything was as she had left it the day before, nothing had moved, not even the paper she had propped up against the frame.

She stood in front of the beginnings of her sketch and thought it a poor thing: hopeless, soulless, irretrievable. She tore it up, rolled it into a ball and threw it into the open doorway.

'Shit,' she said. 'Shit, shit, shit.'

She should have taken the boy's advice and done what she wanted, painted him whilst she had the opportunity; even now she was not sure why she had prevaricated. It seemed to her then that lately she had been full of little fears without foundation, that she bruised too easily – plagued by cowardice and for reasons she only half understood, if they were reasons at all.

'I need a focus,' she said softly, 'something to give me space from thoughts of babies, from this sameness – even from you, Tom.' Her eyebrows drew together in surprise because she had spoken aloud.

She sat in silence then, immobile, brooding staring at the blank piece of paper. She would ask the boy to sit for her when she saw him next. And it would be all her own this project, this curious determination to complete his portrait and capture that barbarous beauty on canvas. And there *was* something barbarous about him, Jessica realised that now, something savage and perhaps a little cruel. She frowned, rubbed her forehead with the palm of her hand and wondered why she should think such a strange thing.

Zak was lying on the grass, leaning on his elbows, letting the sun beat down on his back, and watching a clot of flying ants climb in and out of the cracked earth as they scoured the soil for their supper. Beyond him and beneath the dappled shade of a tree lay a dead pigeon on which the ginger tom cat was feasting – battle-scarred ears flattened back against its head, eyes furtive and shrunken to greedy black points. It was the same cat that had greeted him and followed him when he arrived in the Crescent: a monster that could purr.

He knew that if Jessica happened upon the grisly little scene she would shoo the cat away in disgust and give the pigeon a decent burial.

He could see her through the lace-work of trees: bare arms a golden brown, hair carelessly piled on top of her head. No straw hat today. Her shoulders were stooped over the easel, but she was doing very little, he could see that, even from this distance. She was unhappy, of course, and he was touched by a feeling that was both tenderness and pity.

He was sure that she did not know that her oh-so-respectable nerd of a husband was having an affair with the red-head; Jessica was probably only aware that something was not quite right any longer, that her safe docile little world was about to turn on its head and do a few somersaults.

And he would be there to catch her.

She was vulnerable, after all, and would need someone once she found out the bad news. Zak could offer solace and love and sex in any order she might please, except that she was not the sort of woman to be rushed, but he was prepared to wait because patience had always been his strong point and did, he believed, have its own reward. In fact he would be very disappointed if Jessica reacted in any other way, despite the fact that she wanted him, something he sensed she was hardly aware of herself.

He had also sensed her desire for a child, a bouncing little bundle of joy; he had felt the need coming off her in mild but unmistakable waves. Just like he had known her name – lovely biblical name, full of promise.

Zak's eyes grew dark and dreaming. 'Jessica,' he whispered.

She lifted her head as if, in some impossible way, she had heard him say her name, as if she perceived by low-grade telepathy that someone watched, and he knew those big trusting brown eyes were searching the garden, that the lines on her forehead had deepened sharply in puzzlement.

There was a gleam in his eye as he regarded her, a studied calculation and an overwhelming desire for possession.

Jessica was the sort of woman who would never suspect the depths of her own sexuality, an innocent in a way. And she would ask no price. She would not spread her legs and take him as a prize like so many of the other girls he had known, and as a reward he would make sure that his seduction of her would be something scalding, something that could never be thought away.

Zak smiled, a broad smile of thorough sensuality.

Something special for Jessica.

3

God, she was bored.

Fay watched the cat from the window. He had ceased feeding on the dead pigeon and was looking cautiously around for a place to hide his kill, but eventually he would bring it home to her, and when he did she would allow him, Max, a little display of triumph before taking the disgusting prize from him and dropping the bird into the waste disposal unit. There would be a short, predictable battle and Max would sulk, then sit or lie, and after a while he would carefully wash himself over and over until the stink of the juicy scent was gone and then he would purr throatily.

Max was a renegade, just as she was. He had simply appeared one day and stayed and, apart from the times when he insisted on following that revolting practice of marking out his territory by peeing in the odd corner, they had tolerated each other rather well. He would be her only permanent live-in lover. Men were bearable in short sexual bursts, other than that Fay found them childish, selfish, intrusive and tedious.

Yet she couldn't do without them. Even the very large and almost beautiful vibrator she sometimes employed was ultimately a source of frustration, second best, because it could not do the business in the way she wanted or come close to real coupling, real sex – all that heat, that friction, the smells, the sweat and the tension. Oh, no. She wouldn't try to kid herself about that.

To the left of Max and behind some bushes a boy lay stretched out on his stomach, staring into the distance. He was wearing black jeans and Fay noted that they were very tight, rounding his backside to sculptured muscled orbs. Above the waist he wore a vest, black and frayed, almost the colour of his hair which reached in a shaggy mane well below his shoulders.

She thought of Tom and his careful suits, his blazer and cavalry twills, and wanted to laugh. It was hard for her to imagine that he had been a real honest-to-God hippy once, that his hair had been as long as that of the boy lying in the garden, that he had gone to rock festivals and smoked hash cross-legged amongst all the other dick-heads.

And Tom was late. Angrily she folded her arms and unfolded them before walking over to the stereo and switching on the radio, but immediately grimaced at the sound of a love song pouring into the room – a popular favourite, a slush number, a real tear-jerker. Fay turned the music off, preferring silence to the sentimental dirge which flowed uneasily to that watertight compartment where her soul was.

She switched her attention to her flat and its starkness, its clear pure lines, and wondered what it was about the past that fascinated Tom so, his beloved antiques, because it depressed her – that sort of attachment; all those lives that had withered and gone, reflected somehow in a piece of furniture or a cracked oil painting: reminders of age and death and disintegration.

A shudder twisted her narrow shoulders and instinctively she turned her gaze to her own work which would begin to take real shape once she had scraped off the thick, still-wet paint with a palette knife and developed the roughened texture she required.

Another picture Tom would fail to understand.

It would be a garden: an angry, neglected botanical garden, not unlike the one she could see from her window except for the anger, of course, because the garden outside was too withered, too exhausted for fight or fire; and there would be a further difference. She planned that the leaves, but particularly the fruit of the trees, would be in the process of turning into something weird – animal heads perhaps, or insects at war with each other. Tom knew, surely, that certain female insects devour their partners after the sex act? Fay smiled and then frowned softly. Perhaps uniting and devouring were the same thing. But Tom wouldn't see that either. Tom would probably be disgusted.

She glanced at the clock and clenched her dainty fists with annoyance. The doorbell rang and she stalked across the room.

'Where the bloody hell have you been?'

Instantly Tom was looking over his shoulder.

'For God's sake, keep your voice down.'

'Why should I?' She swung round and walked away, leaving him to close the door.

'I've just driven like a maniac all the way back from Eastbourne.' His eyes flicked to the unfinished canvas and the lumpy, formless oil paint which looked as if she'd been plastering it on and gouging out shapes with her bare hands. He felt a twinge of distaste.

'You never drive like a maniac.' There was a sneer in her voice and Tom was vaguely shocked by an itch to slap her.

He watched her move to the window. She was wearing a diaphanous see-through thing which billowed and flowed behind her like a bridal train. Underneath she only wore her customary G-string: a tiny nylon triangle in a leopard-skin print from behind which a few red pubic hairs peeked. He found himself wondering if it was the same one, or if she had scores of the same garment waiting to titillate and provoke.

He didn't feel like being titillated and provoked. He had come because she expected, no *demanded*, that he come and if he did as she asked now, there would be no question of him returning later when he should be at home, with Jessica.

His wife's face took shape in his mind and that painful expression of doubt and confusion he had seen there, something he had achieved all by himself and in record time. What a shit he had become, a hollow-eyed lying shit.

'Stop thinking, for God's sake, it's getting on my nerves.'

'I only wish I could.'

'You're hopeless, Tom, do you know that?'

'Don't remind me.'

She turned and looked at him. 'Christ,' she fumed, 'I can't stand it when you're like this, feeling sorry for yourself, as if somehow all this were a kind of tragic accident into which you had so helplessly stumbled – or have you conveniently forgotten that our torrid little affair was very much half of your making . . .'

'All right, Fay—' He swept a hand back through his hair, 'I'm here, aren't I?'

Her scornful eyes were on him, daring him to look away. 'Yes, you're here.'

'But I meant what I said.'

'And what, pray . . .' she said drily, 'are we talking about now?' She glanced down and surveyed her nails as if she were bored; they were clipped quite short, but beautifully manicured – pink and glossy like her little mouth.

'About finishing this,' he said. 'Us.'

She stiffened just perceptibly and then looked at him with one eyebrow cocked.

'Oh, yes, our little conversation of last night. How could I forget? I expect you took all your somewhat dubious courage in your hands before picking up the telephone and giving me the glad tidings. Didn't you, Tom?'

'It's gone on too long.'

'Last week you wouldn't have said that,' she said slowly. 'Last week you were still willing to beg on your knees.'

'Don't talk such rot.'

'True, Tom.'

He hated her then, hated the way she made him feel so incrediby juvenile.

'I don't know,' he said flatly, suddenly weary of it, 'things are out of hand.' He had the feeling that she was deliberately driving him further and deeper than he'd ever meant or wanted to go.

'It's guilt, Tom, that's all.' Fay's voice was condescendingly kind, as if she were conversing with someone mentally retarded.

'I hope you're right,' and how he wanted to believe her, more than anything, 'but whatever the reason, I'm telling you now that this situation cannot continue. It just can't. I have to get things back . . .'

'. . . the way they were?' She laughed. 'Don't be so naïve.'

'I can try,' he said with more conviction than he felt. 'So we've had an affair, lots of people do, the world doesn't have to cave in when it's over. We both have full, even rich, lives to fall back on.' He swept his hand again through his hair, but in a despairing kind of way. 'We can still be friends.'

Fay guffawed, brought her milk-white hands together and began to applaud.

'Bravo, Tom, bravo.'

'Stop it.'

'Well, what do you expect? A bloody medal for your sickly little speech?' She planted her hands on her hips and glared at him. 'And *friends*? We've never been friends, as you so sweetly put it. I don't think you even like me.'

'That's not true.' Oh, but it was.

Her face was filled with contempt. 'You're a terrible liar, Tom.'

'Christ,' he burst out, 'why do you have to twist everything – make it all so damn ugly?'

'Maybe that's the way it is.'

He looked taken aback, but then his voice came to her softly, wondering, almost a whisper, 'You're so different from Jess.'

'Yes, thank God.' A long time ago that had been a phrase her mother had used about her, and Fay's face darkened.

They stared at each other, full in the eyes, until he wanted to drop his gaze.

'This is getting us nowhere.'

She remained silent.

'Look—' he groped hopelessly for the right words, 'what more can I say? What do I have to do to convince you that I mean it?'

'I think you've said quite enough.'

'Fay,' he said, 'please?'

'You're beginning to make me feel sick.'

'Don't *be* like that . . .'

'For God's sake, do *shut up*, Tom. We both know you're

here for one reason and one reason only, just like all the other times.' She sighed and her voice was light suddenly, almost sweet, 'So let's get on with it, shall we?'

She gave her shoulders a delicate shrug and the diaphanous see-through thing slid down her arms and on to the rug, then she smiled and began to walk slowly towards him.

Tom bowed his head for a moment, but it was a half-hearted gesture because already his eyes were lifting to her approach and fixing on the alabaster breasts, the rose-pink nipples and then dropping to her navel and further – down to the plump vee pressing against and filling the leopard print G-string. Fay.

A reluctant warmth burned in his loins, coursing through him, causing his face to redden and give everything away, even the dislike of himself.

'There's an antiques exhibition coming up,' he said abruptly, as if his words might stave off her advance. 'I won't be around for a few days.'

'Really?' she was twirling a lock of hair around one finger like a little girl. Her hair drove him mad; so long she could almost sit on it, so long she could tantalise and blanket him with it from crotch to mouth.

'It might be for as long as a week.'

She was close enough now to place her hands on his shoulders.

'Don't,' he said.

'Why not?' she teased. 'Don't be silly, Tom.'

'I'm trying . . .' his voice trailed off, 'really trying . . .'

'I know, Tom. But not now, you're wasting time. Fuck me first and then we'll talk about your little anxieties.' Later or tomorrow or next year.

He sighed dreadfully then, but she only pulled him closer,

her lips tracing the curve of his neck, pressing against his ear.

'But tell me,' she murmured, 'when and where is this exhibition?'

He swallowed. 'The week after next.'

She kissed him, filling his mouth with her tongue. Withdrew.

'Where?' she persisted.

'Edinburgh.'

'Let me come.'

He shook his head. 'I can't.'

'I suppose Jessica's going with you . . .' She felt a hot, interior dig of jealousy. 'You could have made some excuse.'

'She always comes on these trips.'

'Because she has nothing else to do.'

'Because she wants to.'

There was something in the way she was looking at him that he didn't quite like and he tried to disentangle himself from her, but Fay was already slipping her arms around his neck and tightening her grip.

'You don't get away that easy. You should know that by now.' She was amused and he was caught by the sly knowing smile as she began to move against him, wriggling up and down, sideways, rubbing and rotating her pelvis until she felt his hardness chafe her through the thin material of his trousers.

Her hands were on his crotch and he felt his trousers slowly ripple down to his ankles, felt the buttery softness of her fingers take him. 'Oh, yes . . .' she breathed and glanced up at him, 'oh, yes, Tom.'

Their eyes held each other, like a challenge, and he was only conscious of a tight wad of excitement building in his chest and stomach. Her hands slid round to his backside and her greedy fingers began to stroke, caress, explore.

'I always have liked your bum, Tom.'

He squeezed his eyes tight shut, caught between contempt for himself and the pleasure she could offer.

'We'll do that thing you wanted . . .' she whispered, 'I promised. Remember?'

Tom had difficulty in speaking because he had no defence against her greater knowledge, her dark delights sucking him in like quicksand. And he was still willing deep down, and somewhere inside he wondered how much it would cost him in the end.

'Take me with you, Tom,' she whispered, 'to Edinburgh.' She lifted up her hand to show him the black silk cord coiled around her wrist. She untied it and began lacing it between her fingers so that it pulled tight and slick. Interesting, that fine line between pain and pleasure.

'No.'

'Jessica won't mind,' she coaxed, 'not just this once.'

'No . . .'

'Yes, Tom.'

'I've put on *seven* bloody pounds,' Roz exclaimed, 'can you believe it? That's giving up smoking for you . . . not forgetting the holiday, of course – all that moussaka and red wine and lazing around on the beach. Must have played havoc with my cellulite.' She sighed resignedly. 'At least Gordon, God bless him, says he hasn't noticed that I've grown, as it were . . . but that's nothing to go by since he's got a thing about child-bearing hips.' Roz clamped her mouth shut, instantly regretting her words, but Jessica hadn't even heard; Jessica was staring unseeing out of the window.

Roz frowned. 'Are you okay? I don't think you've been listening to a thing I've been saying.'

'I have. Really.' Jessica looked back at her friend and tilted her lips into a bad imitation of a smile.

'You could have fooled me.' Roz searched her face.

'I have . . .' Jessica protested.

'And have you thought any more about France?'

'There's plenty of time.'

'We have to register for a place on the wine-tasting course by the end of this month.'

'I'm not sure . . .'

'It will do you good,' Roz said heartily, 'get you away from here for a bit, and Tom can spare you for a few days. It's only for a week, after all.' She sighed heavily. 'Jess, you need a break.'

'Do I?'

'Yes.'

'I promise I'll let you know – soon. Okay?'

'What's the matter?'

'What do you mean?'

'You should never answer a question with a question.'

Jessica looked at her friend carefully.

Roz looked back. 'Are you going to tell me what's wrong?'

'Everything's fine.'

'How's Tom?'

'Fine,' Jessica said, but her eyes gave everything away.

Bull's-eye, Roz.

'Had a row?'

'Does it show that much?'

Roz nodded and regarded her with curiosity; Tom and Jessica didn't have rows.

'Actually, we didn't exactly row . . .' Jessica picked up

her glass of wine and shifted her gaze back to the restaurant window and the busy street beyond. She pushed a leaf frond out of her line of vision and thought abstractedly that there were too many palm plants lined up against the glass and hanging from the ceiling; they shut out the light. 'Things just seem *different* somehow and I don't know why.'

'Have you tried talking to him?'

'Oh, yes,' she said, 'but he says there's nothing wrong, that maybe we're just having a bad patch – whatever that's supposed to mean.'

Roz tapped the stem of her glass, glanced warily at Jessica's profile.

'But things are generally okay between you?'

How do you mean?'

'Well – you know – sex?'

Jessica didn't answer immediately and by the time she did her silence had spoken for her.

'No,' she said quietly. 'They're not.' And it had come down to sex in the end, she thought sadly, or the lack of it, and that had been the beginning of her knowing that there was something wrong after all.

'Perhaps he's been working too hard? You know, he's tired. Men are very feeble in that way.' She thought of Gordon and his little willy-wonka and the effort it sometimes took to tease it into action, but you couldn't have it all, she mused, and he was sweet and kind and funny and comfortable to be with, rather like a well-worn and dearly loved pair of slippers.

'Yes, he has been working hard, or at least late . . .' the words seemed to hang in the air for a long moment. She met Roz's eyes across the table and felt her face redden.

'It probably doesn't mean anything,' Roz said quickly,

as if she had read her mind, 'and anyway, Tom's always been a bit of a workaholic, hasn't he?'

'I might have agreed with you once, but not now. Anyway, like I said, everything seems different,' she said softly and almost to herself. 'As if he's changed in some way and I haven't.' Moved on, she thought bleakly. With someone else? 'Sometimes I have this feeling that I'm standing still while other people's lives are busily growing away from me.'

'Jess . . .'

'There's no need to be concerned,' she said wearily, 'I'm okay. Fed up maybe, but okay.'

A woman paused outside the window to look at the menu fixed against the glass, on her arm was a basket filled with shopping and laying across the top was a magazine, its front cover plastered with enticing headlines (mostly sexually related) – 'You Too Can Have Multiple Orgasms!'; 'Married to a Transvestite'; and 'Is Your Husband Having an Affair?!' Jessica winced inwardly. Christ, for a little peace.

'Try talking to Tom again, for heaven's sake – tell him how you feel.'

'No. I'm going to leave it for a while. I don't want to become "the nagging wife" after being good old predictable Jessica for so long. I've even decided not to mention the dreaded subject of babies. What's the point?'

'Nothing doing, then?' Roz asked gently, pointlessly.

Jessica shook her head. 'I have my usual appointment at the end of next month and I'm back on the IVF list.'

'That's good, isn't it?' In truth, Roz found the thought of a test-tube baby distinctly unappetising – all that poking and prodding and rummaging about, all that *waiting*, all that money – but she supposed if she'd ever wanted a child as much as Jessica did she would probably try anything. Well, perhaps once.

'After the first few failures I made up my mind not to do it again . . . but you should know by now that I'm a glutton for punishment.' And she had already cautioned herself not to make too much of it – to do so would only risk another and greater disappointment.

'Oh, Jess.'

'Let's talk about something else, shall we? What's the use in going over all that old ground again.' Opening up all the old wounds.

Roz followed Jessica's gaze into the street outside. 'You said you'd started painting again?'

'Yes.' Jessica thought of the boy, the nineties' Jesus. How she had called to him from the upstairs window that morning, examined him as he stood in the parched garden looking back at her. He had worn a stud in one ear, a tiny pin-prick of gold which the sun had picked out through the black mass of his hair. He had seemed to her then like something out of time, a dream made flesh for her to paint.

'But that's great! I only said to Gordon the other night that you were wasting yourself.'

Jessica stared at her friend for a moment, the ghost of a smile on her lips. 'I don't think I'd put it quite like that. I'm not my sister, Roz.'

Thank God, Roz thought. 'And Fay's stuff takes some getting used to – to put it mildly.'

'She's beginning to attract a lot of notice.'

'I'm not surprised.' Roz raised her eyebrows.

'She's very talented.'

'If you like that sort of thing.'

'Roz . . . please.'

'All right, all right.' She had met Jessica's sister twice and the second time had been no better than the first. There was something instantly dislikable about Fay, a sort of barely veiled contempt for the world at large, and the contempt went hand in hand with the pretty careful smile which seemed to say that she didn't really care if you liked her or not. 'She's such bloody hard work, Jess. You must admit.'

'She's not interested in small talk and she's not interested in people generally,' Jessica said. 'Put it down to artistic temperament.'

'I don't know why you always defend her. She's been such a little bitch.'

'I'm being realistic.'

Roz raised her eyes heavenward. 'How is she, anyway?'

'Don't see her very much, which is probably just as well.'

'Even though she only lives a few houses away now?' Roz exclaimed. 'Seems crazy.'

'Even more crazy if you knew how much she always wanted a view of the sea.'

'Why did she buy it, then?'

'I have no idea,' Jessica said, 'except that the light is very good – all those converted skylights face exactly in the right direction apparently – which is important for her work. And she does seem to be working terribly hard, lives practically like a recluse. When she first moved in we asked her over for dinner a few times, but she never came, so we don't bother to ask any more.'

'How does she get along with Tom?'

Jessica shrugged. 'Okay. Uses him like an odd-job man, actually.' She smiled drily.

'What?'

'Oh, it's nothing really. Only that a couple of times her

windows have jammed and poor Tom has been called in to do the honours. She's even had him unclogging her U-bend, would you believe? Well something along those lines.' Her voice trailed off as if she were no longer interested.

'Really?' Roz snorted with laughter, but then her eyes narrowed just perceptibly as a curious, yet strong picture of Tom and Fay alone together formed in her mind.

And Jessica failed to see, her attention caught by a man pushing a pram across the street.

Roz caught a wary breath. She wouldn't trust that little bitch Fay with her tabby cat, let alone someone's husband. Even Gordon. But she was jumping at shadows, surely, and Jessica was her own *sister*, for God's sake, and apparently Tom didn't even *like* Fay. Roz darted a careful glance at her friend and tried to think of something else, something less disturbing, something nice, but at that moment nice thoughts seemed just a little beyond her.

And Jessica's eyes were on the man across the street, the one with the baby, and if she closed her eyes a little and left the leaf frond where it was she could imagine that it was Tom out there – same height, same colouring, except it couldn't be, of course. Tom was in Eastbourne, and there was no baby; only a pretty cosy picture she had painted in her head.

A gull screamed down to the sea and scooped up some delicious debris. Zak watched it soar skywards again then resumed his walk along the shingle, dry seaweed cracking under his boots; a few flies momentarily disturbed resettled on rotting mussels thrown up too high by the tide.

He was making for the far end of the beach which was almost empty except for a few naked men strutting about or lolling in the afternoon sunshine. They were 'naturists' apparently and Zak found himself wanting to laugh at the pretty word which at that moment could only offer the seedy examples ahead of him: flabby old men with wrinkled buttocks, a middle-aged businessman with a great white behind and belly, pappy breasts like a woman. Beyond the fat businessman a youth lay playing with himself as a woman walked by with her dog.

Zak paused some distance away and looked out to sea, to the white horizon of the English channel which was flat and waveless, and then with great deliberation he began to peel off his clothes. He felt the eyes of the fat man crawl over him as he picked his way through the stones to the water's edge.

He found sand and his feet luxuriated in the wet creamy coldness squirming up between his toes, gloried in the water which sucked and slid and lapped at his ankles. A fine, almost perfect afternoon except for the fat man's eyes. And the eyes, alight with excitement, spoke of an absorption with loathsome, violent things, a sickening fascination with degradation which emanated from him like a bad smell.

A momentary shadow crossed Zak's face as he turned to stare fixedly at him, and the fat man, misunderstanding, smiled and passed his tongue along his lips.

Zak's face betrayed nothing as he switched his gaze back to the sea and then moved languidly into the water, letting it slide up his legs and thighs, through the arch of his pelvis, trickling like a caress up and into his navel. He left the beach behind him and struck out for the nearest buoy, feeling utterly free for the first time since he could remember.

When he reached the buoy's anchor chain he stopped and let the sun beat down on his wet upturned face. He began pulling himself forward, at the same time exploring the chain with his feet and found a long jagged piece of driftwood trapped against one of the metal links by seaweed and flotsam. The buoy bobbed and swayed drunkenly as Zak trailed a hand across its plump yellow girth, stroking it almost tenderly then circling it with his arms. He imagined Jessica there with him, taking his hands from the other side, head thrown back, laughing – imagined touching her beneath the water, feeling her skin; her touching him.

He pictured her at the window as he had seen her that morning. She had called to him, face flushed, to ask if he was still prepared to sit for her. Oh, she had been nervous, he had sensed that, but she had clearly overcome any apprehension because there was a look of determination about her, something girlish and childlike. Sweet and soft.

It was quite remarkable how the future was beginning to take shape in just the way he wanted and the implications almost dazzled him. In the drowsy beauty of that summer afternoon he thought that everything seemed possible. He closed his eyes and felt a sleepy desire, a kind of mild lust which he could save and hoard for later when he was alone.

His reverie was abruptly disturbed by someone moving towards him through the blue wash of the sea. He watched closely as the swimmer drew near and an extraordinary indignation jerked in Zak's brain when he realised it was the fat man, who had stopped only a few yards away and was now treading water.

'Lovely day' he said.

Zak made no answer.

The fat man was almost completely bald and his skin seemed unnaturally white like something which has lived underground and come up for a time to bask in the sun. Rivulets of water coursed down his domed forehead and dripped from overgrown eyebrows.

Zak matched his greedy stare, pressing down furious distaste.

'Not a day to enjoy alone . . .' the man persisted and his mouth made a bad replica of mirth. And it was a strangely feminine mouth: small, heart-shaped, pink and pouting. Once the man had been pleasing to the eye, almost beautiful, but he had allowed himself to rot from within like an exquisite piece of fruit with a maggot for a heart.

'I like being alone,' Zak answered with a slow darkening of his face.

'Not always, surely?' the man said. 'Not a boy like you.'

'A boy like me?' And he knew what the fat man saw: a born voluptuary, a juicy-lucy lay, a sexy boy hung like a horse.

Zak stretched his foot beneath the water, found the jagged piece of driftwood, felt it graze his instep.

'Pretty,' the fat man said thickly. His calculating gaze had fallen to Zak's lips and now rested there. 'Very pretty.' He remained still for a moment before moving closer to the buoy, reaching out to it with one hand and looking at Zak from the other side.

Jessica's side.

The fat man was staring at him with a feverish hypnotic intensity. Beneath the water he touched himself. If Zak had been an attractive woman it would have made little difference, or a pretty child – boy or girl – no difference really as long as the focus of the fat man's attention could play a convincing role in the pornographic fantasy he had conjured in his head.

The look of scorn in Zak's eyes sharpened ominously, but he did nothing as the man began to edge round the buoy, and because he did nothing the man took his silence for consent. And when he placed his big hand on Zak's thigh, pressing suction-tight against the boy's perfect skin, Zak still did nothing.

The fleshy contact seemed to possess the sting of a mild electric shock and Zak felt something in his mind, a wave of revulsion as he picked up the dirty secrets stored the the man's memory, like black poison leaking into his veins. He remained quite still as the fat man's hands closed around his sex, but his eyes were dark and glassy and unseeing. A terrible voice, flat and hard said – 'Take your filthy fucking hands off me.'

The man jerked his head up, eyes wide and startled with a look very much like fear, his breath warm and thick on the boy's cheek.

'Grotesque, that's what you are, fat man,' Zak hissed, 'a monster with a sewer for a brain.'

The man opened his mouth to speak, but only a faint mewling sound squeezed from the dry-as-dust throat. His face had grown whiter, if that were possible, eyes huge and almost comically terrified.

Zak smiled, a weird chilly sort of smile, and the fat man withdrew abruptly, white body flopping, splashing clumsily and as he retreated he came up against the anchor chain of the buoy. One foot and leg scraped painfully against the jagged piece of driftwood which seemed to jump, suddenly, of its own volition and embed itself in the fat man's groin.

He shrieked in agony and blood began staining the water in an inky-red cloud, but Zak felt no pity at all.

Some gulls dropped from the sky, white and purposeful, like pretty vultures, and their screams were almost as loud as the fat man's, but as Zak moved away and swam back to shore the screaming became faint and unimportant.

*　　*　　*

The street was empty except for a stray dog and a tramp sifting through a rubbish bin and the sight pricked Zak with nausea and unease as if he were returning to the slovenly chaos of his growing-up. Only once had his mother made him scavenge: raking through black plastic bags full of other people's gunk, other people's filth, and he had never forgiven her and when she realised how she had wounded him she had tried to make it up to him. Oh, how she had tried.

Even now, he was still astonished that she had taken so long to understand that there was nothing she could do to make up for the life she had made him lead: the rootlessness, the humiliation, the men slipping in and out of the joss-stick stench of her bed after sampling her big strong body which was always so willing to receive and enjoy. So easy to use. Free love didn't die with the sixties, not whilst his mother was around. She still held a diehard hippie torch, still clung to all that cosmic, far-out, neanderthal cliché stuff which made him want to puke his guts up.

Yet worst of all was the sham she had created and actually believed – that the pointlessness of their lives held some meaning because they were *outside*. As if that were enough – everything – an end in itself: like the Tarot cards and the crystals and the nerve-numbing madness of the festivals and all the other New-Age crap she had force-fed him.

Her son, the Travelling Man.

But that life was *her* choice, not his, and because of it she had denied him everything.

His hands were balled into fists and when he stretched and splayed them open they trembled. And his were extraordinarily sensitive hands which could tell more through the cards and the crap than his mother's ever had. He had come across hundreds of so-called clairvoyants, faith healers, psychics, pier-end palmists, weirdos who wrote new music for dead composers, but most were con men – or women – quacks and liars, or naïve idiots in whom only people more naïve or more idiotic than they were themselves could believe. And the quacks and liars flourished because the world had never been short on people wanting to be relieved of their money – wanting spice added to their boring unloved lives.

His mother had called Zak 'a sensitive' and claimed that he had a real gift (emphasis on *real*), and he had seen a glimpse of envy in her eyes, and something else. He frowned and then blinked before looking up and realising he had arrived outside the house.

A large terracotta urn stood on the step beside the door crammed with flowers, but they were fast-fading: geraniums, fuchsias, trailing ivy falling to pieces in the searing heat. A fly buzzed against his ear, settled on his sweat-dampened skin and he brushed it impatiently away.

Jessica had gone out earlier, but that was three hours ago. He stared at the heavy wooden door, the knocker was a monster in brass, an impressive lion's head which he slammed down hard and then listened to the unmistakable echo that told him the house was empty, except for the bird; the cockatoo was squawking and whooping hopefully now as if it expected an answer.

Zak turned round and began to walk back down the street when he saw her coming towards him. She was looking at the paving stones, shoulders a little hunched, tendrils of rich brown hair straying from the loose top-knot at the back of her head. She wore a calf-length cotton skirt in tan, a white open neck blouse and soft leather sandals which exposed toenails painted golden-orange. She held a bulging carrier bag in one hand and across her chest was slung a small brown purse on a long strap. Cradled in her other arm was a bunch of flowers wrapped in green paper – irises and big white daisies.

He walked towards her, studying her with fascination, scrutinising one thing after another until all had been absorbed, and as she looked up he saw the lines puckering her brow, felt her sadness and was struck by an intense desire to defend and protect.

'Can I help?'

She looked at him in surprise as he reached out to take the carrier bag.

'I can manage – really.'

He took the bag all the same, despite her mild protest, then came beside her and they walked in silence the rest of the way until she stopped in front of the house. Zak glanced at the door and the lion's head, sunlight had turned it to gold.

'And tomorrow,' he said carefully, 'what time would you like to start?'

She looked blank and he knew she had forgotten.

'Maybe you'd like to make it another day?'

Jessica's face cleared and she shook her head. 'No, no. Tomorrow's fine, and we'd better make it early before it gets too hot. Would nine be okay?'

He nodded and they fell silent again.

'Would you like to come in for coffee?' she said abruptly and looked at the bag he was still holding. 'You've been very kind.'

'The name's Zak, by the way, and chivalry is one of my virtues,' he said gently, 'but no thanks, I have to keep an appointment with my landlord.' It wasn't so much of a lie and, besides, he sensed her need to be alone. The offer was only an example of her good, respectable middle-class manners, and he didn't mind that, in fact he found it endearing; as far as Zak was concerned it was only further proof of her suitability as a mate and in a curious way it made him desire her all the more.

'And I'm Jessica,' she said, dark limpid eyes squinting in the glaring sun. 'Tomorrow, then.'

'Tomorrow,' he said.

It seemed overly dark in the house, and cold. Jessica lumped the carrier bag on the kitchen table and began to unpack the shopping. In the corner and fixed against the wall was a telephone and she glanced at it as she passed back and forth, as a picture of Tom formed inevitably in her mind. She stopped once and actually placed her hand on the receiver, but then took it away again and walked across the room to switch on the kettle and make a coffee she didn't want. She leaned against the dresser, arms folded, and waited for the kettle to boil, but her gaze crept back to the telephone. She squeezed her eyes tight shut as if she would shut out the vision, except that it was too late; it had been too late all along.

Of course she knew the number of his office by heart, what she needed was the Eastbourne number which she didn't have. He should still be there now and she only wanted to speak with him for a minute, that was all, just a few inane words to reassure herself.

'Linda?'

'Hello, Jessica. How was lunch?'

'Fine . . .' Jessica replied hesitantly, 'but how did you . . .' Something leapt up inside her, some deadly intuition.

'Must have been a lovely surprise,' Linda's voice ran on, 'Tom driving all the way back from that Eastbourne auction . . .'

Jessica opened her mouth to speak and then closed it again.

'I can't see Derek doing that for me, not an ounce of romance in his soul. Worse luck.'

'Is he there, Linda?'

'Tom? Oh, no, not now. Sorry. He dropped some keys in and drove straight back again. It's one of those old sea-side hotels – a lot of Art Deco involved, apparently, and auctioning won't finish until late afternoon, or early evening.

'I see.'

'Can I give him a message?'

Jessica was staring at the window, a bluebottle buzzed fitfully against the glass.

'Hello – Jessica? Still there?'

'Yes.'

'Can I give him a message?'

'No. It doesn't matter.'

'Are you sure?'

'No, really. It was nothing.'

'Shall I tell him you called, then?'

'No,' Jessica said. 'There's no need.'

She felt a brief sensation of her stomach turning inside out and yet was surprised how calm her voice sounded as she said goodbye to Linda and replaced the receiver.

As simple as that, this knowing. Like something out of a silly plot in an afternoon soap. Her thoughts swept backwards, quickly, over the recent past and all those moments of anguish and uncertainty which she had carefully pressed down. She took a deep shuddery breath, but the air seemed clinging and over-used and she felt a little sick.

On the table lay the irises and daisies still wrapped in their green tissue paper. Automatically she found a vase and began to unravel the flowers before cutting the stems and placing them into the water one by one.

'I'm supposed to wait until he gets back,' Keith said and watched Emma closely as she bustled across the room.

'That probably won't be for another hour, at least.'

'Can I hang around?'

'No.'

'Why not?' He sounded aggrieved, but was only goading her.

'I'm busy, in case you hadn't noticed. Besides, Jonathan wouldn't like it.'

He repeated her words behind her back, mouthing them silently, insolently and then spoke aloud, 'This is about money – as always.'

'Is it?' But she did know. Jonathan had been raging about Keith's humiliation of him since the weekend and rightly, so she supposed, except that there was something funny, even clever, about Keith's little stunt, although she would never dare say so.

'But I'm worth it, babe.' He spread out his arms, clicked his fingers, spun round and back again. 'See what I mean?'

'Not exactly,' Emma said airily. 'You're supposed to be a disc-jockey, not Fred Astaire.'

'Not bad, kiddo, not bad. Got a sense of humour after all.'

'What's that supposed to mean?'

'Well, King Dick of Turd Mountain isn't what is termed "a barrel of laughs", is he? I thought you were two of a kind.' Except that he knew that they were not. Emma might be Jonathan's little galley slave, but on several occasions (inebriated ones, it must be said) she had given him reason to hope that there might be more to her than he thought.

'Have you quite finished?'

He grinned. Emma was boring and straight and a bit dim, but pretty and curvy and he fancied her. He had long nourished a fantasy of reforming her in a night of passion, but God – in the form of Jonathan – always got in the way.

'I'm not sure I've even started.' He began to laugh and was rewarded by a softening in her expression.

And he had to admit King Dick was good-looking, there was no doubting that, but cold and humourless and tight-arsed. And he would be useless in bed, good-looking guys usually were; practically every girl he had ever slept with (and there had been many) had told him that – it was the: 'lie down and worship my body, my dear' school of thought. Being ugly, on the other hand, could have merit; it had made Keith try harder and had, in fact, made him very good, even very, very good, between the old sheets. But loving women helped, he knew that too, and he loved them all.

'You should come out with me one night,' he added. 'I'd show you what it's all about.'

And it wasn't just the sex thing that attracted him to Emma, all that undiscovered territory; there was something in him that wanted to make her *laugh* – crease-up, crack-up, fall apart for just the hell of it. Keith had decided long ago that life without laughter and a little risk was no life at all.

'I don't think so, Keith.'

'Why not? You only live once. What have you got to lose?'

'No, Keith.'

'Come on,' he insisted, 'be *real*.'

'No.'

'Babe,' he shook his head sadly, opened his arms wide, 'you don't know what you're missing.'

'I'm not your babe.'

'Oh, man,' he sighed dramatically. 'What – is – your – prob-le-mo?'

For a fleeting moment she had an overwhelming compulsion to giggle. He was sitting side-saddle on the edge of her desk staring meaningfully, eyelids half-mast, his large mouth open just enough so that she could see the tip of his very pink tongue. He began to lean across towards her and as he drew closer she caught the pungent and overpowering smell of his cheap aftershave and she wrinkled her nose.

'Christ Almighty. What's the matter now?'

'Your aftershave.'

He blushed and she felt a little ashamed.

'Is your lord and master in?'

Emma's head jerked up; Zak was standing in the doorway.

'If you mean Jonathan – no, he's not.' She stood up and moved away from her desk.

'The plumber's left this . . .' Zak held up a drill. 'Amazing the things people leave lying around.'

'I'll call them,' she said.

'He didn't find anything.'

'Nothing?' She looked back at him for confirmation or an explanation.

'Nothing,' he said. 'Didn't you see the note?'

'No.' Her eyes travelled to Jonathan's desk and the pink flimsy paper which she had missed lying on his blotter. 'Jonathan won't be pleased. After all, that stuff in the sink must have come from somewhere and the basement seems the obvious place.'

Zak shrugged.

'Probably a dead body down there somewhere . . . boarded up in the walls,' Keith said peevishly.

Emma flicked a glance at him and sighed. 'Take no notice of Keith,' she said. 'Anyway, there *is* a smell.'

'The basement's neglected; it's bound to smell a little ripe . . .' Zak smiled crookedly.

'Ripe!' Keith guffawed. 'Man – that shit in the pipes was out of this world. Jonathan nearly passed out.'

'Probably been blocked for a long time,' Zak continued. 'Maybe now it's cleared, the problem's been solved.'

'Yeah,' Keith said doubtfully. 'Maybe.'

The door slammed behind him and he jumped.

'What idiot is using my parking space?' Fay stood in the doorway, seething with rage.

No one said anything.

'Well?'

Emma gaped at her for a moment. 'What parking space?' She asked. 'There are no parking spaces – not that I know of, anyway.' The girl was wearing a white halter, almost transparent so that her breasts were clearly visible.

'Wrong. I have one. And at the moment there's a bloody great black van sitting in it.'

'What makes you think it has anything to do with us?' Keith asked deceptively mild, eyes dancing across her breasts.

'Because it has Keith Valli, DJ, plastered across it in obscene gold letters a mile high.' And the letters were badly painted and raked backwards to indicate a speed that the antiquated vehicle could never hope to attain. 'Perhaps if you took your eyes off my tits for a moment you might be able to remember your own name. And it is Keith, isn't it?'

He nodded.

'Well, move it.'

He shook his head.

'You'd better.'

'That parking place belongs to no one and I got there first.'

'No way.'

'I won't need it for much longer.'

'I couldn't give a shit how long you need it for. I need it now.'

He stepped over to the window and looked out.

'There are a couple of spaces further up the street.'

'I want *my* space.'

'You'll have to wait.'

'Like fuck.'

Keith raised his eyebrows.

'Do you hear me?'

'I hear you.'

'Well?'

He shrugged. 'Sorry, lady . . .' Some lady. 'The van stays where it is.'

'You bastard.'

'Like I said – sorry.' And he opened his arms in a gesture that said there was nothing he could do.

Fay's eyes widened in disbelief.

'My brother-in-law happens to know a lot of very important people around here.'

'Oh, really,' Keith said with a trace of a sneer.

'Like the Police Commissioner, for instance.'

'Bully for him,' he said with less conviction than he felt. 'Who is your brother-in-law, anyway?'

'Tom Innes.'

'Never heard of him.'

There were two hectic bolts of colour in her cheeks as she glared at him, then she turned to Emma and finally Zak, but Zak only stared back because he was still trying to take in the new-found knowledge that this was Jessica's sister; this prize bitch, this little shrewish whore with the Pre-Raphaelite hair. In his mind's eye he saw her with her man, her lover, Jessica's shit of a husband, using that hair to tantalise; winding the red-hot tresses around him and his weakness like coils of rope.

Yet she was not so unlike Jessica, except that any likeness, for Zak, was a blasphemy. And inside she was ugly.

But even as Fay's gaze came to rest on him, her wide-set eyes had grown watchful and there was a change in her, an unfurling, a delicate papery thrill and a slow tingling deep in the pit of her stomach.

'Who are you?'

'I live here,' he said and glanced at Emma, 'in a way.'

Beyond Emma was the window and through it Zak saw Jonathan climb out of his car and walk towards the house.

'I think I'll make a move.'

'Why?' Fay said.

'Because I want to.'

'I let my temper get the better of me sometimes.' Her face had softened and her voice was silky now and close to being husky.

Zak ignored her remark and turned his attention to the others in the room.

'See you.'

'See you, man.' Keith winked and cocked an eyebrow towards Fay which Zak disregarded immediately.

'Yes – see you,' Emma said, 'and thanks for bringing back the drill.'

'No problem.'

Fay opened her mouth to speak, but snapped it shut as Zak walked away.

'What's going on?' Jonathan stood in the doorway, his gaze fixed on Fay, but he switched his glance quickly to Emma and her round startled eyes before turning back to Fay with obvious curiosity, dismissing Keith altogether.

'Someone has parked their bloody great van in my parking space,' Fay repeated sullenly, her eyes still following Zak's retreating back.

With great deliberation Jonathan placed his hands on his hips and stared at Keith, his expression at once irritated and smug.

'What have you been up to now?'

'Nothin', nothin' . . .' Keith said with exasperation. 'Christ Almighty! Unless parking the van in front of the house has suddenly become illegal. It's free parking around here, in case you hadn't noticed – I haven't broken any laws.'

'You're talking about *my* parking space.' Fay glared at him.

'That road doesn't belong to *any*one.' Keith waved an arm impatiently in the air.

Jonathan's gaze was drawn, magnet-like, to Keith's awful yellow shirt and the spreading patches of perspiration stain under his arms. He closed his eyes for a moment and then put up his hands to ward off any contradictions.

'All right, all right. Just shift the van, Keith.'

'Why the hell should I?'

'Because I say so.' He jerked his thumb in the direction of the street.

There was a look of thinly veiled disgust in Keith's expression and he knew it was useless to argue. This just wasn't his fucking day.

He said nothing as he moved towards the door, pulling it wide open before walking through. Jonathan waited for the sound of the slam as he closed it behind him, but it didn't happen.

Keith moved the van just as he had been told, right out of sight. Emma watched it draw away and was still able to hear the distant drone of the engine and the muted thunder of the ageing exhaust pipe long after it had disappeared from view.

It was early and the sun was low in the cloudless but still hazy sky, so that the heat seemed deceptively bearable and the day pleasant; a day full of possibilities. Zak had been waiting for over an hour, but he didn't mind; she would appear soon with her faithful easel and the other attendant little things that had come to represent Jessica.

He was sitting and leaning against a tree whilst the garden slumbered, except that it wasn't so much slumbering as dying, a sacrifice to the sun and this monotonous summer which seemed to have no intention of ending, but at that moment it seemed beautiful; even the drooping trees and dusty shafts of sunlight seemed beautiful. Zak lifted his head up and looked at the pale blue sky, felt the pleasing and familiar sensation of words forming on his lips – 'Can Wisdom be put in a silver rod? Or Love in a golden bowl?' He smiled, his memory never let him down; he could bring up whole poems or stories in his mind, and faces and scenes and conversations. Sometimes his head seemed full of words, other people's thoughts and dreams. He had often thought that if his life had been different he could have studied literature or history or the classics and been one of those shit-hot academics everyone made so much of, but then he had never cared very much for 'everyone', or their opinion – everyone meant society, meant authority, meant arseholes, and yet now, wonder of wonders, he wanted a piece of it for himself.

His mind returned to the lines he had spoken and he mouthed the words again, silently, over and over to himself. Maybe be could have been a writer.

He saw her then. Jessica was moving awkwardly through the door because she carried a birdcage in her arms and he could hear her talking to it, a white bird, and she was cooing through the bars so that it would not be afraid. She set the cage down on the patio and walked back through the door, hips swinging ever so slightly, innocently lustful, to return with a small table on which she placed the bird. She stood back and adjusted the position of the cage, wiped her hands on her jeans and disappeared inside once more.

Zak got up and began making his way towards the house and as he drew near he thought he could smell her scent on the warm air, her own scent, not something out of a bottle but subtle and sweet and smoky. It made him think of sex and the hot wet place between her legs. He felt a warmth building, that old raw lust which could make his head spin. To have Jessica, in all her secret parts.

He pushed open the gate and walked up the three steps to the paved patio. She was looking away from him when she reappeared but he could see the haunted expression on her face, the slight redness around her nose which told him she had been crying. Had she discovered that perfect hubby's halo had slipped, that it was hanging loose somewhere near his roving prick?

'Anything I can do?'

She jumped and sent a nervous hand to her throat.

'God – I didn't realise you were there.'

'If I'd had a trumpet I would have given myself a fanfare.'

She shook her head and smiled, but tremulously, as though it cost her an effort. 'No trumpets, please, my nerves couldn't stand it.'

'Is everything okay?'

She stiffened a little and turned away, reaching for a bottle of wine.

'Nothing a drop of plonk won't cure. I know it's a bit early, but would you like a glass?'

'I think I'll wait.'

'Very sensible,' she said, 'but I'll fetch another glass all the same.'

He watched her go, then moved over to the birdcage and stooped down to peer through the bars at the cockatoo. It seemed to peer back at him, in fact its black fish-eyes seemed to narrow as boy and bird stared at each other, but then it shrank away, shuffling quickly backwards along the perch, feathers ruffling, the plume on its head standing on end like the hairs on the back of someone's neck.

'Sorry to keep you waiting.'

He straightened. 'that's okay,' he said. 'Is the bird yours?'

'My husband's,' she said in a queer flat tone. She was looking at the garden. 'I wish it would rain – for days and days. I'm so tired of this bloody weather.'

'Everyone is.'

'Are they?' she said vaguely, then, 'I suppose so.' She stood there a moment longer before turning to him. 'Perhaps we should start?'

'Okay.'

'I thought you could sit here.' And she indicated a small folding chair. 'It's quite comfortable, at least for a while, and I've put the bird in your direct line of vision, to give you something to focus on when you get bored.'

'I won't get bored.'

'I think you will,' she said too brightly. 'It's one of the few certainties there are in life.'

He looked back at her and said gently, 'And life can be full of surprises.'

'Oh, yes . . .' there was a trace of bitterness now and she reached for her glass. 'You're right there.'

He sat down and she moved to her seat so that she was sitting at an angle to him.

'I'm only going to do a few sketches today. I won't start the full-blown picture until I'm sure what I want to do . . .' she paused, suddenly feeling horribly unsure of herself, 'or at least how I want it to develop.'

'You're the boss,' he said, 'and there's no rush.'

She picked up a piece of charcoal, rolled it between her fingers and looked at the glaring whiteness of the sheet of paper for a long moment before looking back at Zak and returning her gaze inexorably to the paper. A friendless Antarctica.

She couldn't do this. Her mind froze up, tight and helpless. She wondered how she had thought she could start in the first place, but she had steeled herself to begin working this morning despite Tom and his lies, his deceit. And she had tried so hard to push it all away, but the knowledge was clamouring to get in and once it did, she thought she might actually scream.

'I will have that drink.'

And she had said nothing to Tom because she was terrified. He had come home, had his bath, had supper and gone to his desk where he had remained. So engrossed in his own thoughts, he had failed to notice her silence and distress behind the excuse of a headache, but he could have seen it all in her eyes if he had bothered to look.

She reached for her half-empty glass like a blind woman and brought it to her lips. But she would say something to him, wouldn't she? She had to, because she couldn't go on like this. Yet what good would the truth do? What point in knowing?

'Jessica?'

She swallowed hard, her mouth tasted sour. Perhaps she was wrong, perhaps she was jumping to unbearable conclusions because right now she felt so ludicrously vulnerable. And in her heart she could not really believe it. Not Tom?

'Jessica?'

She blinked and shifted her eyes to Zak's face.

'Sorry?'

'That drink – I've changed my mind.'

'Oh, yes,' she said quickly and made a soft despairing sound, 'of course.'

He watched her lean down to the bottle of wine, wondered what she would say if he told her that her desolate thoughts were written in big grey letters across her face.

She moved towards him, stretching her bare arm out to give him the glass of wine which she had filled too well, and he steadied her hand because it was shaking and drops of liquid were falling to the ground and spreading across the patio like a stain.

With one hand he took the glass and with the other he took her hand, and he was smiling, a careful sad sort of smile. He knew instinctively that this was a moment to show restraint and not press or push, but to appear concerned, tender, almost affectionate. Gentle as a lamb.

Jessica's eyes were drawn to his beautiful face, his mouth,

the smile, and she found herself trusting him implicitly and wanting to tell him everything, spill out all that was in her mind.

His grip was firm and difficult to break and their hands fitted so well. He tightened his hold just slightly, until he felt his own delicious heat pour out of him and into her, through his palm, the tips of his fingers, and saw blood soar into her face and confusion and helplessness.

Oh, Jessica.

Sometimes, he thought, words don't say what we want them to. Sometimes it is better to say nothing at all.

4

Zak loosened his hold very slowly, then gently turned over her hand. Jessica's palm was white and softly shaking and for a moment he was tempted to bring it up to his lips, caress the tender salty skin with his waiting tongue; instead he smoothed it out flat so that he could look at all the lines.

'What are you doing?' Her voice was unsteady and some of the colour had gone from her face. She took a deep breath and felt the tension, the panic go and in its place the gradual calm of habitual control

'Attempting to read your palm.'

'Can you do that?'

'Sometimes.'

And she didn't want to know any more than that, afraid to look into his face and see truth, or that other quality which she could not identify, the one that looked out of his eyes sometimes but was never there when she looked back.

'I wish you wouldn't.'

'I won't tell you anything you don't want to hear.'

'Doesn't that make it a little pointless?'

'Palmistry originated in one of the earliest civilisations,' he said, ignoring her protest, '. . . the left hand discloses the attributes and inclinations we have inherited, and the right what we have made of them.'

He looked up then and caught her anxious glance.

'Why are you so afraid?'

She blushed and clenched her palm into a fist.

'I don't want to know, Zak.'

He was torn between telling her what he had seen and his own will, but it had only been a glimpse, and he could not be sure; did not want to be sure. His gift, that knowing from inside himself, jolting his senses. For an instant he was shaken by a feeling of loneliness and felt a sense of weariness overtake him.

'Sorry,' she said.

'Don't be,' he said. 'I should have asked first.'

'It's me,' Jessica added clumsily. 'I seem to have a lot on my mind.'

'I know.'

He stared at the closed fist which was resting on her knee, there was a small mole at the base of her thumb, a smaller one where her hand joined the wrist.

'What do you do, Zak?'

'Do?'

'For a living.'

'Guess.'

She smiled. 'Is it something to do with music?'

'Could be.'

'And it must be a nocturnal occupation . . .'

'Must it?'

'That would explain why you're here so much during the day.'

'Go on . . .'

She shook her head, the smile broadening. 'I think I guessed from the first time I saw you.'

'What did you guess?' he asked softly.

'That you're a DJ.'

Playing night music to prats and dead-heads. Now that would be interesting.

'Ah.'

'Why "ah"?'

'Are you always this good at guessing?' Not exactly a lie and that was important to him just then.

'No.' she said, 'no good at all.' And there was that look again, that shadow behind her eyes because she was thinking about her precious husband.

'Someone told me once that all things must pass.'

'Did they, Zak?' Her voice had dropped but her face was still and empty of expression.

'Nothing stays the same, Jessica, everything changes; that's the nature of things. And change can be good.' He knew she missed the implied message in his words, but something would sink in, something that would ease his way later, when real change had finally come.

'I don't think I'm very good at change.'

Her voice was so low that he strained towards her. He wondered if she knew that her sad mouth was almost perfect, the bottom lip a little more full than the top. His gaze followed the curve of her face to the neck and the opening of her white gypsy blouse. Sweet, the blouse, with its pretty braid and tiny embroidered flowers, pink like her mouth. He wanted to touch her. He imagined himself doing things to her, things she had never dreamed. Imagined that lovely mouth open and craving: made for love, for sex; tormenting him.

'Perhaps . . .' she said, as if she knew, 'we should start again tomorrow.'

Jesus. God.

'If you like.'

*   *   *

Emma irritated him, and just lately the irritation had got much worse. Jonathan wondered why it had taken him so long to realise it, yet the knowledge bothered him, nagged at him as if, even now, that were only half the story and there was something else which evaded him, hiding furtively beneath the surface of his daily existence.

Emma had been, was, his only real girlfriend; none of the others in the early days had lasted and now he could hardly remember their names, let alone their pretty vacuous faces. They had all been pretty, he was sure of that much because that had always been and remained his only criterion when it came to the opposite sex – well, that and a certain passiveness, a certain willingness to go along with everything he wanted.

He had lost his virginity with Emma, although she had never guessed, and at twenty-two he supposed it was a little late for a man, but women had never been one of his major priorities, never driving him into fits of passion and erotic adventure: distracting him.

And Emma had been a virgin, too. He liked that; it meant she was untouched, *clean*. There would be something disgusting in knowing that another man had been there before him, perhaps many men; something indescribably offensive in the knowledge that she might have been invaded and therefore tainted by someone else's flesh, someone else's hot grimy cock.

In many ways Emma was a perfect partner, and he did want, no, *need* a partner; being alone was not something Jonathan found particularly appealing. And, to be fair, he had known Emma a long time, so was it surprising that she should begin to grate on his nerves a little? It was her talk of marriage, of course; Emma's constant itch which she could never scratch. He felt sure that everything would be all right between them if only she would drop the blessed subject and leave him in peace.

Women still wanted weddings, preferably big and white and hugely expensive, even in these so-called enlightened times of the career-woman, but Emma was not a career-woman and had neither the desire nor ability to be one. What she wanted was a different number altogether: a husband, a house and a couple of kids.

And he didn't. But it was more than that; the prospect terrified and repelled him and he couldn't conceive of the cause or come close to understanding; that was the worst part.

His eyebrows drew together in a frown and he rubbed the back of his neck, felt himself sweating into his suit.

Jonathan was standing on the cracked concrete path looking at the garden. There were tufts of grass and clumps of dandelions sprouting between the paving stones and a distinct aroma of mould. He grimaced and reached into his pocket and drew out a pack of cigarettes and lit one up. He had only recently started the habit again, secretly relishing the scent of tobacco, the smoke; just the feel of a cigarette between his fingers was strangely comforting – a sort of relief.

He pumped the cigarette slowly, blew out a smoke ring from his mouth and through the haze saw Zak coming towards him.

Jonathan's eyes jumped like flies to the squatter's every movement. The boy was sauntering across the communal garden, thumbs jammed into his pockets, swaggering almost. As he approached Jonathan began to feel nervous and oddly clumsy, even out of place in his yuppie linen suit. Yet it was Zak who was out of place, who did not belong – the worm in the proverbial apple.

He flicked a self-conscious glance at the steel-blue sky, stuck a finger inside his collar and loosened his tie.

'Enjoying the view?'

'Not exactly,' Jonathan said tersely.

'Master of all you survey . . .'

'Ha, bloody, ha. Very funny.' Jonathan threw down his cigarette and ground it out too hard, too long. 'I'm taking a break from work, actually.'

'And having a clandestine puff while you're at it.'

'That's none of your business.'

'Sorry I spoke.'

Zak had paused outside the gate, one hand resting on the latch as if he had not yet decided he was going in.

'And you're rushed off your feet, of course?' Jonathan said sarcastically. 'I can see the sweat pouring off your brow.'

Zak smiled.

'Don't you ever get bored?'

'Not often. I read a lot.'

'Why don't you get a job?'

'There are approximately three million people ahead of me in the queue, in case you hadn't noticed.' Besides no one would employ someone like him – a drifter, a loner, an ex-New-Age Travelling Man. Christ, he didn't even have a National Insurance number.

Jonathan snorted with contempt and jerked his head towards the overgrown garden.

'You could help clear this lot, since you're living rent-free.'

Zak said nothing.

'I could make it a condition on your staying, you know.'

'Could you? I don't think so.'

'If I wanted to make your life difficult.'

'Go ahead.' Zak shrugged. He pushed the gate open and began pushing his way through the long grass towards the basement steps.

'For God's sake,' Jonathan said rapidly, with the strangest feeling of panic, 'it was only a suggestion . . .'

Zak stopped and swung round.

'What was?' he asked. 'Clearing the garden, or making my life difficult?'

Jonathan flushed.

'I could pay you something,' he said awkwardly, 'not much, mind you.' What was he saying, was he mad?

'You mean for the gardening?'

'What else would I pay you for?'

Zak looked back at him for a long time and Jonathan felt the flush come back, but deeper this time, more intense, spreading upwards from his chest. He swallowed repeatedly, his Adam's apple bobbing unbeautifully above the collar of his ridiculous suit.

'You tell me . . .'

'I don't know what you mean.' A tic twitched in Jonathan's cheek.

'Yes you do.'

For a brief moment Zak's mouth slid into that disturbing all-knowing smile which made Jonathan so uneasy, but then he was turning round and walking away. The squatter spoke once more, carelessly, over his shoulder, 'I'll think about the gardening, by the way . . . let you know tomorrow, or the day after.'

Cheeky bastard. Jonathan seethed impotently as he watched him go, but his inner anger was a poor thing compared to the blood which was now shooting through his veins.

* * *

There was a sheen of perspiration covering Tom's face and too much colour, as if he had been running – or something.

'Busy day?' Jessica asked.

'Mmmm.' He began sifting through the mail on his desk.

'Like yesterday.'

He looked up. 'Yesterday?'

She cleared her throat, her heart was an annoyingly hard pressure in her chest.

'You drove all the way back from Eastbourne – must have been something urgent.'

He gaped at her. 'How do you know?'

'I rang Linda.'

'What did she say?'

Dread was gathering in a corner of his mind and his eyes had grown round and dark, admitting his guilt like nothing else.

'You tell me, Tom.'

For a split second their gazes locked.

'I had a lunch.'

'With me, apparently.'

'Did she say that?' He tried to look astonished and failed miserably.

'Yes.'

'That's crazy . . . must have got her wires crossed.'

'No, I don't think so.'

'What are you getting at?'

'Who *did* you have lunch with?'

'A client.'

'Which one?'

'Jess,' he pleaded, 'what is this?'

'I want to know who you had lunch with.'

'For heaven's sake.'

'Who, Tom?'

'Dennis Santana,' he gushed.

'I thought he was in the States?'

'Apparently not.' Christ, if only he had thought of a convincing lie quickly enough, but just lately his brain felt addled, full of holes. Stupid.

'I'll check, Tom.'

'What in God's name,' he blustered, 'is this all about?'

'Shall I check?'

'Don't be ridiculous.'

'I will.'

Tom's face had turned a livid red.

'Is that a threat?'

'Call it what you like.'

'Why are you doing this?'

'I want to know what's going on.'

'Nothing,' he said. 'Nothing's going on. You're putting two and two together and making twenty-five.'

'Am I?'

'Yes.'

'I don't think so, Tom.' Her voice was hushed, too gentle and low. 'You never have been a very good liar.'

And Fay had said the same thing. He cringed inwardly, aware of that sick, scared feeling he had experienced as a child when turning the pages of a forbidden book.

'Jess, you're jumping to conclusions.'

She didn't want to look at him so she turned her face to the wall, the garden, her hands clenching and unclenching in an unconscious spasm.

'You don't make love to me any more,' she said abruptly in a soft, grieving voice, 'not really.'

'Jess . . .'

'Who is it?' She wheeled round.

'What are you talking about?'

115

'Stop treating me like a fool. Stop playing games.'

'This is crazy.' He shook his head, passed an agitated hand through his hair.

'Just tell me.'

'There's nothing to tell.' His eyes slid away from hers.

'I could call Dennis Santana now.'

'For God's sake.'

'Shall I?'

'What's the point if you're so sure he's in the States?'

'His wife will be there,' she said quietly, 'a nice woman – waiting at home for her husband like a good little wife.' There was a pause, 'Like me.'

'Stop it.'

'Or there's still Linda, of course. I could double-check with her – *again*. I think she'd be rather surprised to hear your version of events.'

'I do not want Linda embroiled in our marital affairs.'

'Haven't you already "embroiled" her, as you so quaintly put it? You've lied to her and to me.'

'You're jumping the gun, Jess. Believe me.'

'And you still haven't answered my question.'

'I don't intend to.'

She stared at him with disbelief, fought the fatal trembling of her mouth.

'Jess . . .' he pleaded. and was reminded of his time with Fay and another useless plea he had made.

The cockatoo which had been a silent witness to all that had passed suddenly burst into voice and Tom jumped.

'Christ,' he hissed, through gritted teeth.

The bird whooped again, cocked his head on one side and began a series of short staccato shrieks. 'Stop that godawful racket, can't you?' Tom reached over and banged the cage with the flat of his hand.

'Don't do that.'

'I can't stand his bloody noise.'

Jessica walked across the room, pulled the grey blanket back over the cage and the cockatoo fell silent almost at once.

'You've been found out. Don't take your bad luck out on him.'

'I haven't. And I wasn't.' But I was.

Her hand was still resting on the cage when she spoke again. 'That was a terrible waste of money,' she said quietly, and in a strange way that hurt almost more than anything else.

'I didn't mean to sound quite the way I did . . .' Tom said lamely.

'Oh, I think you did.' She looked back at him. 'He was a birthday present you didn't want. My mistake. And you don't like birthdays because you're vain and they remind you that you're growing older.' And he was only thirty-nine – laughable if it wasn't so pathetic.

Vain? Was he?

'I think . . .' he began.

'Let me finish,' she broke in, 'and you don't like the bird partly by association and partly because you think he's a damn nuisance. You look at him in the same way you have begun to look at me when I mention the word sex.' Or when I dress up to please you or lie awake waiting for you to make your move, one of the old familiar moves that told me you wanted to make love. And you have successfully reduced the ease and pleasure with which I used to approach *you* because I am so afraid of rejection and that wary look I see in your eyes. 'You don't want me. Not in that way.'

Tom was staring at Jessica as if he had never seen her

before. Her eyes were brilliant with anger, and there was that edge to her voice which signalled that this might be one of those rare occasions when she lost her temper.

'Rubbish.'

'No, it isn't.'

'This is getting out of hand, Jess.'

'I suppose it is.' And there was a part of her that didn't seem to care very much because she was so weary of the uncertainty, the not knowing.

'You're depressed.'

He was thinking of babies, of course, or rather the lack of them; her personal and very private hell-hole and something which seemed to wound her far more than it did him.

'Am I?'

'I think so.'

'And my "depression" could not possibly have anything to do with you?'

He glanced desperately around the room, found with relief the empty glass, the weapon, he was looking for.

'And you've been drinking.'

'What?'

'Every time I come home there's at least one empty glass hanging about . . .'

'That's a cheap shot, Tom,' she said quietly. 'The best form of defence is attack, isn't that right?'

'I'm just making a point.'

'That was one glass of white wine – not methylated spirits.' The fact that he was even partly right made her blood boil. 'What would you prefer? Valium or booze? A nervous-bloody-breakdown?!'

'Jess . . .'

'Don't keep saying that.'

'What? It's your name, for God's sake.'

'It's the way you say it.'

'You're being ridiculous.'

'You said that before.'

She searched his face, painfully aware that he was far away from her in spirit, fading. A deep, infinite sense of disappointment gripped her and an emptiness which was a little eerie; not like her at all. 'All right, then,' she said, 'swear to me that you are not having an affair . . .'

He was gawping at her again. Caught.

'Swear, Tom.'

'God, this is bloody childish.' The truth was in his eyes, too clear not to be recognised.

'You won't, will you?' she said carefully. 'Because you can't.'

Tom was swamped by nausea and fright. It was all coming home now, falling on him like a bloody great ton of bricks.

'The door was open . . . but I did knock.'

Jessica's eyes shot to the doorway. Fay was standing there swathed in a weird concoction of deep green resembling a toga, except this version was short and started halfway up her thigh on one side. There was a gold star nestling in her tousled mass of hair, more pinned to the material draped across her breast. Her feet were bare and she was eating a bunch of purple grapes, a wine-coloured stain decorated the corner of her mouth.

Like a child of Bacchus.

'I'm intruding, aren't I?' she asked, feigning innocence.

Tom glared at her, but her gaze was fixed on her sister.

'No,' Jessica said tiredly. 'It's all right.'

'Is it?' Her tone implied that she knew it was not, her tone was all concern.

'Yes,' Jessica said. 'Was there something you wanted?'

'A little late, I know,' she began, 'but I thought you two might like to come over for drinks . . . tonight, if it's not inconvenient, or maybe some other time?'

'I don't think so,' Tom said too quickly.

'Why not?' Jessica returned sharply.

'My reasons are two-fold, actually,' Fay continued. 'A London gallery would like to mount an exhibition of my work and I thought a small celebration was in order . . .'

'That's wonderful, Fay.' Jessica felt a wretched pang of envy.

'And I would also like to show my appreciation,' Fay added sweetly, 'for all you've done to help me settle in, particularly you, Tom, for unjamming my windows and doing all those other little things that I could not possibly have done all by myself . . .' She was looking directly into his embarrassment.

Blood soared into Tom's face. You bitch. You unprecedented little cow.

'There's no need, but thanks, and we'd like to . . .'

Tom's mind zoomed in on the word 'we', wondered if Jessica might possibly be coming round to believe him, wondered if the worst might be over. Sometimes consistent denial and lying worked, he had read that somewhere, like brainwashing. Please, God.

'. . . but not tonight, Fay,' Jessica said. 'I'll call you tomorrow and we'll talk about it.'

'Maybe you'd prefer to come alone, Jess. I'm sure Tom won't mind,' Fay persisted and flicked a glance at her lover. 'We haven't talked in ages. My fault I know, but I've been rather preoccupied, caught up in my own little world as usual.'

Jessica's eyes were puzzled, wary; a memory had churned up, an old window into the past silted with dirt from behind which Fay peered with that same sweet look on her face.

'I'll call you tomorrow,' she said again.

A shadow fell between them and for an instant Fay's eyes were flat and cold as if she sensed her sister's caution, her thoughts, but the moment passed and she was smiling once more, her pretty mouth turning upwards at the edges in that irresistible childlike way which, to a greater or lesser degree, had always got her what she wanted.

Jessica returned the smile with an effort, wondering wearily what it was Fay was after, what little game she was trying to play. She didn't need this now, not on top of everything else.

Her thoughts switched to Roz and their lunch, what Roz had said about her sister and her undisguised dislike of Fay. Naturally Fay wouldn't give a damn; as far as she was concerned Roz lived on another, uninhabitable, planet. And if her friend had been standing in the room at that moment she would have found it difficult not to laugh, in that infectious neighing way she had, at Fay's theatrical garb, her silly pose.

She would call Roz and give her a decision on France. It was almost like a reprieve. Jessica darted a glance at Tom and knew now that she would go. Let him stew for a week, let him rot in hell . . . except that she didn't really want that: but let him *miss* her some how, some way. Even now there was still a part of her that believed that he would.

'So you'll definitely come?'

'Yes.'

'And not just to spite Tom?'

Jessica looked at Roz across the kitchen table, she was tap-tapping her coffee cup with a perfectly manicured fingernail. 'No, Roz,' she said, 'not *just* to spite Tom. You were right; I need a break.'

'I was thinking,' Roz said too brightly, 'we could go to a health farm instead – you know, really treat ourselves. Book in to Champneys or Shrubland Hall, maybe even that place Joan Collins visits,' she frowned, 'now what's it called? . . . Stobo Castle, that's it, in Scotland.'

'Wherever you like.'

Roz's face fell; she was wasting her time and she had known that from the beginning, but it just wasn't in her to give up, even if her friend wanted her to. Jessica needed to get away from here, if only for a few days, just to have a change of scene and get out of the same four walls for a while.

And, for Roz, they were not particularly appetising walls. Sometimes it seemed to her that the Crescent and its environs were stuck in a suffocating time warp, that the black sockets of the windows of the old Regency houses looked out on the world with a fixed and resentful stare, as if they still yearned bitterly for the grandiose past they had lost. She had never been able to understand why Jessica and Tom liked it here so much and now, with the garden looking so sick, it practically gave her the creeps.

'What does Tom say?'

'I haven't told him yet.'

'Oh, Jess . . .'

'Why should I?'

'Okay, okay.' Roz held up her hands in mock defence. 'Have you talked any more?'

'No.'

'*Are* you talking?'

'Barely. He's trying desperately to behave as if there's nothing wrong.'

'Maybe there isn't.'

'I know there is. He lied.'

'People lie all the time.'

'You sound as if you're defending him.'

Roz shook her head. 'I just want you to be sure, that's all.'

'I checked and I'm sure.'

'You didn't?'

'I said I would.' She had even spoken to Linda in a round-about way, not about the lunch, but about the call Tom had made to Linda that night when she had caught him in the hall, telephone in hand, and he had reeled off one of his feeble explanations. Another lie, and not even a clever one. Tom had not thought to cover his tracks, probably because he never dreamed she would ever suspect him and now she wondered how many other little give-away signs there had been and which she had failed to see.

'Did you tell Tom?'

'No.'

'Why on earth not?'

'I don't know.'

'What are you going to do?'

'I want to know who it is,' she said quietly.

'Does it matter?'

'Maybe. I don't know.'

'Oh, Jess . . .'

'It's all right,' she said, 'really.'

But it wasn't. Nothing was right in her life, in fact everything was horribly wrong, and it would get worse before it got better, that's how the saying went, apparently. She wondered, bleakly, what poor fool thought that one up.

'You said he's going to that exhibition in Edinburgh.'

'Next week. Friday or Saturday.'

'And you're not going this time, of course?'

'No. I want him to go alone, I want some space.'

'What did he say?'

'He tried to persuade me to change my mind.' There had been a sort of look of anticipation about him as if he thought that would be his chance to make everything up. 'As if a dirty weekend over the border and a good bonking might paper over the cracks.'

'Put a dollop of brandy in my coffee, for God's sake . . .' Roz pushed her cup forwards, 'it's for my nerves.'

'Sorry.'

'Don't apologise, *please*, Jess.' Roz shook her head. 'I must say you seem very calm – too calm.'

Jessica reached into a cupboard for the spare brandy bottle. It was half-empty.

'Yes. Curious, isn't it?' she said remotely. 'I feel numb, actually.' But inside there was a sick sort of feeling compounded by grief and loneliness. 'I found myself crying last week – ' over the breakfast things, big fat tears rolling down her cheeks and dripping into the washing-up water, ' – and put it down to PMT, but I knew then, I suppose.' She pulled the cork from the bottle, stared unseeing out of the window. 'There was a smell once, a scent on him, and for an instant I had this feeling that there was something wrong about it, for just a fleeting second, but I let it go . . .' A woman's scent.

She realised that there were some things you suspect, those things you don't wish to acknowledge, but you lock them away behind the door you have closed in your memory because you don't want the pain of knowing. Except the pain comes anyway; sooner or later.

Roz examined her friend with careful scrutiny as she poured brandy into lukewarm coffee.

'Tom loves you, Jess, I'm sure of that. Despite all this.' The bastard better.

'He has a strange way of showing it.' She shrugged. 'Sexual betrayal, that's the official term. Did you know, Roz, that unfaithfulness comes second only to the death of a spouse on the stress league table? Maybe I'm in shock.'

'Men get the hots sometimes and it goes too far. It doesn't have to mean anything and usually doesn't.' And yet if Gordon messed around she would kill him. She couldn't stand all that again, not after Mark, her first husband, who had been neurotically unfaithful, amongst other things: baby-faced Mark, the proverbial wolf in sheep's clothing.

Before she had finally found the courage to extricate herself from his cashmere-clad embrace, she had begun to wonder if she wasn't one of those pathetic fools addicted to a terrible marriage. And she still had the ulcers to prove it.

'You mean they get bored.'

'Something like that.'

'What happens when I get bored – when my libido needs some attention, some bloody pampering?' And, God, just lately she had needed Tom in that way. But he had slipped away and given himself to someone else.

'I'm not being very helpful.'

'It doesn't matter.'

'You can get through this, you know.'

'Can I?'

'Both of you.'

'I don't know, Roz.'

There was something in Jessica's rigid, carefully arranged face which seemed to say that she could not.

*　　*　　*

He had started knocking back the sherry when he discovered that Emma had arranged the coming evening for him, down to the finest detail. It had begun with just one little glass to toast a new job, but Jonathan had let it go on, easing into the bottle with unaccustomed vigour, and the drink seemed to turn a screw in him so that he could feel the tension draw tight and spread, constricting his guts.

The strange thing was that Emma had no idea, no inkling that her coy plans for a night of passion were having quite the opposite effect. His aversion to her careful preparations should be emanating from him like a bad case of body odour, or a band of negative radio waves sending a clear and unmistakable message to that part of her brain where she was busy arranging his future like a dinner menu. But no, life just wasn't that simple.

And she wouldn't let it go; nag nag nag and the nagging and implied sex was tied up with pink lacy ribbons: lovey-dovey words about living together and marriage and kids. Wasn't it good – no, brutal – old Mother Nature up to her tricks again: making the sexy sap rise, giving the hormones an almighty kick up the arse in readiness for nest-building and a life sentence.

He was having one of his moods, Jonathan knew that, and when he was like this everything seemed distorted and twisted and inevitable, like he was being influenced and shoved along by forces beyond his control. Like a straw in the wind. But maybe it was, maybe it was *just* like that.

'I'm going out for some fresh air,' he said abruptly, pushing back the chair of his desk and standing up.

'Oh.' Emma lifted her head, batting her eyelashes at him, a tentative smile on her face. 'I thought . . .' but then she was frowning with confusion and hurt as he turned his back on her. 'When will you be . . .?'

'I don't know.'

He had to have some time to himself, just to let all the pressure out of his head.

There was someone coming down the steps. Zak stood back in the shadows of the basement room and waited for the person to reveal themselves. The sky was still a cloudless blue, despite the fact that it was dusk, but the shadows lengthened very quickly in the basement, situated as it was beneath the building and abutting the foundation wall of the garden, so that night came more quickly here than in the rest of the house.

Jonathan pushed open the door and Zak moved into his line of vision and folded his arms.

'What do you want?'

Jonathan only stared for a moment and in that instant Zak knew he had been drinking, he could smell it, something sweet, like the sickly stink of sherry.

'I came to see you.'

'What for?'

'I want you out.'

'Why?'

'Don't argue, just get out.'

Zak shook his head. 'I'm not going anywhere.'

'I don't like you,' Jonathan blurted out, 'I want you out.'

Zak smiled crookedly.

'That's not very friendly.' He paused, licked his lips. 'Anyway, why don't you like me?'

Even in the candlelight he could see Jonathan's face burning, his cheeks two hectic blotches of crimson.

'I want you out.' His voice was cold and furious and frightened all at the same time.

'You've already said that.' Zak held up a hand and counted on his fingers, 'Three times.'

'Just go.'

'I'm not going anywhere.'

'Please.'

Pitiful, that 'please'.

'But you don't want me to go.'

The heat flooded Jonathan again, passing through his whole body, weakening him.

'I can't . . .' he began, 'you see . . .'

Zak took a step towards him. 'No, I don't see.'

He was wearing skin-tight blue jeans caught at the waist by a wide leather belt with a large star-shaped buckle: it was silver and old and weird and for an instant Jonathan's gaze was fixed on its strange symbols, its fugitive gleam, but then he lifted his eyes to the squatter's upper torso, barely covered by a black leather waistcoat, and the skin that Jonathan ate with his eyes had turned deep brown, covered here and there by a down of dark hair where it ran across his chest and lower arms; tufts of silky black fur taunted him from behind the squatter's swollen biceps and underarms.

His gaze shifted to Zak's face, his lips, ached to trace them with his finger.

'Do it,' Zak said.

Jonathan jerked his head up as though he had been struck.

'Do it,' Zak said again.

The words hung in the air, hot and humid with meaning.

His eyes were on him, making his head spin. Jonathan opened his mouth, then closed it again, a feeling of dread was stealing over him, sick nervous excitement, gathering momentum.

'You want to ... and I don't mind,' Zak pressed, his voice deliberately softening.

Jonathan made a little anguished sound, felt himself harden, knew the proof would soon show through the thin material of his trousers, his precious linen suit.

'No,' he whispered.

Zak slipped off the waistcoat and for a long deliberate moment dangled it in the air with one curled finger.

Jonathan watched with a kind of horror and curiosity. He shook his head.

Zak dropped the waistcoat, brought his fingers to the big buckle of his belt and slowly began to unstrap it. He had been down this path before, understood every step of the game and he didn't care so very much, except to wonder how far he would have to go with this prince, this great nerd who was only just beginning to discover what made his prick really sit up and beg. He could even smell his sour desperate sweat, his eager sticky thoughts.

Nothing in Jonathan seemed to be functioning, not arms or legs or mind, but the expression on his face said everything, a mingling of dawning realisation and panic, as if he were about to babble an appalling confession.

And do that one thing, that secret thing he had buried so well and shared with no one. He had not, in fact, dared give it a name or even allowed the word to take shape in his frightened brain because that would mean no turning back and he just couldn't do that. Oh, no.

A strip of muted sunlight stole through the slatted window, playing on the squatter's chest; another danced across the fingers on his belt, his jeans, his zip. Outside, in the safety of that other place, Jonathan could hear a car drawing away, a child shrieking in play, the slam of a door, but here there was nothing but shadow and the thick heady sound of his own breathing, the nasty thud of his heart.

The tiny buzz-saw of a zipper sliding down.

Jonathan trembled and Jonathan ran.

Tom closed his office door, picked up the telephone and dialled the number he knew off by heart. When he heard her voice it was hard, no trace of the sultry, silky tones that Fay conjured when she felt the moment called for it.

'It's over.'

'Who is this?' she said serenely.

'Don't be bloody stupid.'

'Perhaps you'd like to give me your name, I've always found that such a useful tool when one is trying to communicate . . .'

'Fay,' he warned, 'don't push it.'

'Oh,' she said, 'is that *you*, Tom?'

'No more bullshit, Fay. No more pranks.'

'Now whatever have I done to deserve this?' She was mocking, laughing.

'I said that it's over,' he drew a breath, 'and I mean it this time.'

'I see.'

'What sort of trick was that to pull?' He ran on. 'What exactly did you hope to achieve by coming round last night and asking Jess to "pop over", for God's sake?'

He was close to panic; she could imagine the sweat lying like a string of beads along his pretty brow.

'I included you in the invitation, too, Tom, or have you forgotten?' she said sweetly. 'I was only trying to be sociable.'

'Like hell.'

'And it seemed as if I arrived at precisely the wrong time. Weren't you having a row?'

'That's none of your bloody business.'

'Oh, Tom,' she sighed dramatically, 'has Jessica finally guessed that you are no longer quite the paragon of virtue she married – that you are actually capable of extra-marital sex?' She chuckled in her throat. 'Or a quick fuck behind the bicycle sheds, to put it more colloquially.'

'Shut up.'

'You know, Tom, you shouldn't take it so hard; you're no different from all the other slimeballs walking around with a time-bomb waiting to go off in their Y-fronts.'

'Don't you ever know when to stop?'

'No,' she said lightly, 'I don't think I do.'

'You're sick. Do you know that?'

'Actually, I feel quite well.'

'You haven't answered my question.'

'Oh, yes, your question,' she mused. 'Perhaps you're losing your hearing, as well as your reason – I told you, I was trying to be sociable. All my life I have been accused of being quite the opposite: I simply thought it might be interesting to turn over a new leaf, so to speak – you know, see what sort of reaction I get.'

Using you, Tom.

'Just like that,' he said with contempt. 'What the fuck are you up to?'

'Tut, tut – language.' She paused, sighed again. 'I suppose, in a nutshell, I'm just a teensie-weensie bit bored.'

He closed his eyes.

'I mean, you've been such an old sour-puss lately, such a spoil-sport, I've literally been left to play with myself for most of the time . . .'

'Don't start that.'

'Why not?' she said dreamily. 'It's so therapeutic . . . right now in fact I'm . . .'

Except that she wasn't. In fact her hands were caked with paint and as she held the telephone between shoulder and ear she was picking at the lumpy scabs of colour until they fell away to reveal clean Fay-coloured skin.

But Tom saw her in his mind's eye: her hand, that finger pressing, squirming, driving deep into her tantalising thatch.

She quickened her breath deliberately, feigned a stifled moan of pleasure.

Tom swallowed hard, pressed his lips together. 'For Christ's sake, Fay. I'll put this damn phone down on you in a moment.'

'Oh.' There was a long moment of silence before she spoke again. 'You're no fun any more,' this was followed by another sigh. 'I'll tell you what, then, I'll agree to your pathetic demand if you grant me one little wish.'

'No.'

'Don't be difficult,' she sighed, 'and there's really no point in being unreasonable, Tom; after all, I do hold all the cards. What if Jessica does come round for a nice little chat? I might feel constrained to tell her exactly what's been going on between us.'

'I don't think you would.'

'I have nothing whatsoever to lose.'

That much was true.

'And you would tell,' he said sullenly, 'wouldn't you?'

'I might.'

'Bitch,' he said under his breath.

'Stop calling me that, Tom,' she said tiredly. 'You know how I hate repetition.'

'All right,' he snapped. 'What is it, then? What do you want?'

'That nice trip to Edinburgh.'

'No.'

'Well, Jessica won't be coming with you.'

'How do you know that?'

'I guessed.'

'Last night. You were outside listening.'

'Your voices were raised.'

'Really.'

'Yes.'

Tom sat back in his chair, rubbed the bridge of his nose between his fingers, felt exhausted. Maybe he would have a heart attack. He could see Linda, his loyal little secretary, sealing an envelope through the glass panel of his door and wondered what she would say and how loyal she would feel if she knew what a disaster her saintly boss was making of his private life. How had it all come to this? How could he have let things run so out of control, get so crazy?

'Well?' Fay's voice demanded.

'Do you mean it?'

'What – that I'll leave you in peace after Edinburgh?'

'Yes.'

'Of course.'

'And why on earth should I believe you?'

She shrugged. 'What other choice do you have?'

He said nothing for a long time.

'And this will really be the last time?'

She rolled her eyes to heaven. 'Yes, yes, yes, yes, yes. God, would you like me to have a document drawn up, you know, make it legal?!'

If only that were possible. Be free of it, *her*, then he could build bridges with Jessica, make everything all right again. Sleep at night.

And if only he had known that Fay was already making

plans to dismiss him from her life, her thoughts turning to the future and the delectable boy she had seen only a few days ago. He had literally taken her breath away, and it took a lot to do that; in fact, she couldn't remember it ever happening – not that need, not that overwhelming desire to reach out and touch and touch.

And she knew with the assurance of an artist who has studied and drawn scores of human kind that here was not merely perfection and beauty, but something else: an amalgam of sex, animal magnetism and sensual power. Even as his face, his body took shape in her mind she could feel herself shudder.

'I'm leaving on Sunday evening . . .' Tom said abruptly.

Zak, that was his name.

'. . . but we can't travel up on the same train, Fay, that's out of the question. I'll drive.'

He would be big, that lovely bulge in his jeans had told her that much. She clamped her eyes shut, felt a delicious chill run up her back, the tingle of anticipated pleasure between her legs.

'Are you listening to me?'

'What hotel have you booked?'

'The Caledonian.'

'Nothing but the best. You're really quite spoilt, Tom,' she said brightly, 'I'll see you there.'

'When?'

'Does it really matter?'

'Please yourself.'

'I always do.'

She heard the click of the phone as he replaced the receiver and with a snort of contempt stuck one white vengeful finger into the air.

*　　*　　*

'What's the matter?' Emma asked softly.

Jonathan was standing at the window smoking a cigarette. Outside it was dark, pitch, the night sky pitted by bright brittle stars, but in the distance man-made dots of light winked and glistened, mocking him. Surf boomed somewhere far below; it would be relatively cool down there, he thought, but up here the closeness of the night air was oppressive. A moth wounded itself against the bulb of the single lamp, insects buzzed on the sill and tried to settle on his nakedness. Peacehaven. Even the name made him want to puke.

'Come to bed,' she said coyly. 'It seems like ages.'

And it had been 'ages', and now he knew why. Well, at least he had a bloody good idea, thanks to Zak; as if the squatter had peeled back his skin and looked underneath, as if he had *known*, and before *he* did, which was more to the point. The memory made his throat grow tight and he broke into a sweat, but now there was anger, too, boiling inside and shame and confusion. God, God, God. He squeezed his eyes tight shut and swore.

'What did you say?'

He gritted his teeth. 'Fuck.'

Emma made a valiant effort at a giggle. 'Isn't that why we're here?'

He shook his head in despair, wondered why he didn't take his clothes and run, but even as the thought took shape and fled he heard her turn back the bedclothes and come towards him, and he stiffened at her inevitable approach, and then her fingers were on him, resting possessively on his shoulders and she was pressing her warm naked body against his: asking, wanting, needing. With a sinking heart he supposed it was the need most of all.

'I know you have a lot on your mind,' she said.

He almost laughed then.

'But how often,' Emma coaxed, 'do we have an opportunity like this? My parents won't be back until next week and we have the whole house to ourselves.'

Granted it wasn't much of a house, something she had realised long ago, just one of a hundred little grey bungalows perched on a hill, but it had spectacular views of the sea and coastline and on a good day you could see all the way to Brighton; and it was theirs for a *week*! Why couldn't he be gracious just this once? Why did he always have to make everything seem so complicated? And tonight she had gone to so much trouble to make it nice for him – the wine, the candles, the Chinese meal; everything he liked, for heaven's sake.

Don't spoil it.

'I can't . . .' he said.

She had lain her head against his back, he could feel her warm whispering breath, skin on his skin, wanted to draw away.

'Just come to bed.'

As if that would solve everything.

Her arms inched cautiously around his waist until she was able to link her hands, marking out her possession, and he leaned his head back in silent agony.

'Jonathan,' she said, 'please.'

Please.

A thought came into his mind: unbidden, un-nice, and there was a scream beginning to uncoil in the back of his brain, the sly spectre of panic which would soon alchemise into frustration and fury. He stubbed out his cigarette and turned round, still in the circle of her arms, and there she was looking up at him bright-eyed, bushy-tailed, hopeful.

For an absurd instant he thought he could tell her, pour out all the doubt that was in his mind, but he lacked the courage and courage, anyway, was a pale thing compared to the grinning blackness which was welling up inside waiting to claim him.

And now she was touching him, *there*. Brave girl. Clumsy fingers tugging, rubbing.

A hot dazzling blur fell over his eyes and there was Zak and Jonathan's heart began to pound, wanting him in this picture his mind had drawn as much as he had wanted him in those dizzying insane moments in the basement.

He placed his hands on the top of Emma's head, pushed her down and forced himself into her mouth. Jonathan found himself staring at her hair, the open busy mouth – vaguely fascinated, as if he were observing something remote and strange, far away.

He threw his head back and thrust deep into her throat, quivering with excitement as the rhythm began to build and build, the fantasy being played out in his head becoming more clear, searing, a heady erotic vision which was taking his body beyond his control. He became frantic and pushed her away, turning her round in one swift movement before bending her over in a kind of gutter ecstasy and driving himself into her trembling, unsuspecting backside.

He came quickly and with stunning force – all those old suspicions and dark desires unspoken, shooting out of him like poison.

But in the thickness of the heavy silence that followed there was only shame and confusion and dread because it would all, surely, be out in the open now. Rather like Emma's weeping.

Somehow she had kept herself from crying out, but when the first tears had dried and she was able to look at him again, Emma wondered if he knew or cared what a selfish, cold, rotten lover he was – even before this odd, hideous evening.

And he had hurt her. A lot. Her bottom was bleeding.

Jonathan was slumped in a chair when he turned and saw her looking at him. He shook his head miserably, not trusting himself to speak.

'You could at least say sorry,' she said.

'I'm sorry – okay? You know I am.'

They fell silent again: she was curled up, foetal-like, in the bed; he in the chair wrapped in a blanket.

'You ruin everything,' she said.

He sighed wearily. 'Would you like a cup of tea?'

'No.'

'Can I get you anything at all?'

'No.'

He had a headache, his temples thumped and throbbed.

'Why did you . . .' she began, faltered, started again. 'I mean, you've never said, never tried to . . .?'

He didn't answer, looked down at his feet.

'Say something, Jonathan,' her voice sharpened, 'anything.'

There was another thick, horrible silence.

'I don't know,' he said at last, 'it just happened.' He lifted his head up and made himself look at her. 'I'm sorry – really. Very, very sorry.'

'There are names for people like you,' she said spitefully, resentfully.

'Don't, Emma.'

'What do you expect?'

'You kept on and on . . .'

She sat bolt upright. 'And why wouldn't I, for God's sake? Everything I do to please you you sneer at. You hardly touch me – and when I try and touch you, you freeze up . . .'

'That's not true.'

'Oh, yes, *it is*!' she said shrilly. 'You're a mean, selfish, arrogant, thoughtless pig!'

He pulled a face, wincing at her outburst.

She started to cry and he couldn't stand that either.

It was another perfect balmy night, one of those perfect skies which was both brilliantly clear and curiously low, so low that it seemed possible to reach up and touch. Earlier the sunset had bathed the horizon in streaks of blood-red and orange as if the world were heated at the rim, burning up, molten gold. And Jessica had thought it unbelievably beautiful, as if it were a reminder that there were still some things worth living for.

She leaned her head back and scanned the sky again, drank in the velvety blackness and the stars which seemed more sharply defined than she had ever seen them before. Perhaps it was the moon, she thought: a full luminous disc suspended above the world like a Chinese lantern.

A pity to enjoy it alone.

A pity to be sitting here all on her tod with only a bottle of plonk for company. As if to emphasise the fact, another light was switched off further round the Crescent, and a cat yowled through the dark calling for a mate.

And where was *her* mate? Good old unfaithful Tom was in Edinburgh, probably screwing his bit of stuff. The thought made Jessica's eyes prick and burn and she reached quickly for the wine bottle to top up her glass.

'God . . . sometimes I wish I smoked.'

She sat at the little metal garden table, in a shaft of yellow light from the house. A star was falling just out of her field of vision and she wished on it until she realised that it was a plane on its way to Gatwick airport.

She shook her head with exasperation. 'Sod you.' Her hair was loose and impatiently she pushed it back from her face and the gesture caused her cotton robe to fall open and reveal part of a tanned thigh. Not bad. Mildly wobbly, but not bad all the same. She wondered sadly if Tom's woman had mildly wobbly thighs, or whether they were firm and strong and young (all the better to grip you with, my dear . . .).

He had gone without saying goodbye because she had deliberately made herself absent as he packed and made to go. There had been a note, though, a little sweet thing in his familiar gothic scrawl and she had torn it up piece by piece and flushed it down the loo. Perhaps she should have wiped her bottom with it – she had read that somewhere and it had made her laugh at the time (not now, though; 'now' was very different), but it wasn't her style and she was a little beyond pretending.

Instead she sat in the moonlight like an exile, feeling desolate, strange, weary and on the way to getting plastered. What else was there to do? What else, please, God?

'Jessica?'

She sat up with a jerk.

'God – you made me jump.'

Zak.

'Sorry. I seem to make a habit of doing that.' He came up the steps, hands in pockets. 'I saw the light, then you, thought there might be something wrong.'

'Just feeling a trifle melancholic.'

'How's the painting going?'

'It's not,' she said and thought of Tom and how he had not let his emotions come between himself and his precious

140

antiques. She, on the other hand, had practically fallen apart and let her 'fresh start' fall at the first hurdle. 'But I will get back to it – it's just a hiccup, that's all.' If only.

'Where's your husband?'

'In Edinburgh.'

But he knew that already; he had seen the ageing whizz kid throw a case into his car and zoom off in his flash BMW.

'Why Edinburgh?'

'He's in antiques and there's an exhibition.'

'Nice place, Edinburgh,' he said. 'You should have gone.'

'We've had a row.'

He said nothing.

She sipped her wine. 'He's having an affair.'

'I see.'

'Do you, Zak?' she said and there was an edge to her voice before she added, 'Because I don't.'

He looked back at her, thought how desirable she was now that her composure had slipped and a little wildness was seeping out around the edges.

Her eyes were on him and he could read her expression, knew what she would say next. 'I'm sorry, Zak, it's not your fault.'

Wondered what she would say if he told her he saw a baby suckling at her breast, a little dark-haired thing conjured out of the night-milk of his dreams.

'It's okay.' He smiled. 'You can say anything to me, Jessica, and I won't be offended.'

She shook her head. 'You're sweet,' she said, 'and too good to be true.'

He savoured the word for a moment before he spoke again. 'I've been called many things, but not "sweet".'

He leaned forward, placed his elbows on the table, his

brown sculptured arms glistening in the lamplight, and she found herself thinking again how beautiful he was, wondered how she could have forgotten.

'You must have a girlfriend?'

'Not at the moment.'

'I would have thought they'd be queueing up.'

'Perhaps I'm too choosey,' he said slowly.

'What are you looking for?'

He paused, looked at her beneath half-closed lids and brought his hands together so that the fingertips touched.

'A woman, not a girl.'

He caught her glance, stared into her eyes with a gaze that seemed to see beyond and into her brain, and she felt her heart begin to thud.

And he thought: I am tired of waiting, I am tired of letting you keep your guard up, I am tired of wanting you and not having.

On Jessica's face there was a look of faint astonishment, then disbelief, and inside the dizzying response which can come from sudden realisation. She put down her glass, miscalculated and knocked it over. As she moved to right it Zak took her wrist and the moment seemed almost an exact replay of the last time, as if, in some strange way, they had not moved on from that point at all.

There was that delicious heat again, that power surge simply from his touch; all the stuff she had pressed down and put away because she was terrified, but now she felt relieved, and the relief was a little like swooning.

'I'm so bloody lonely.' The weight of unshed tears hung in her voice.

'I know,' he said.

'I want . . .'

'I know,' he said.

She was not surprised that he knew, at that moment she would not have been surprised at anything Zak said or did. Even the force of his personality which was being brought to bear through his powerful fingers did not surprise, neither the desire which was burning its way through every nerve and vein and fibre of her being. Like a drug, like she was being shot through with something electric, mind-blowing, paralysing: all those things.

When he placed his warm seeking palm on her uncovered thigh that was no surprise either. In fact, that was the beginning of her knowing that she really did want him – it – after all.

And she didn't care, not just then; it was as though she had come upon one of those rare moments in a life that, long after they are passed, stand out in one's memory as a turning point, or, perhaps, the ending of something.

On a balcony in Edinburgh Tom was also a little drunk and, in a way, for much the same reasons as his wife. From the magnificent aspect of his hotel room he could see the famous castle, floodlit and defiant, and it made him think bitterly of his lover, his sister-in-law, lovely little Fay. He placed a hand against his face and felt the weals scored down his cheek, examined the evidence from his reflection in the ruptured mirror: there was blood on the tips of his fingers.

He thought wearily that Scotland was not an unfitting place to have blood on his hands, not near the seat of so many kings, so much bloody violence and intrigue which had literally torn this brooding country apart, but what it lacked in wisdom, it more than made up with in guts; and he had neither.

He had come back from a brief tour of the city to find

Fay waiting outside his room and his heart had sunk, but even seeing the dismay on his face had not deterred her. If anything it had provided her with a handy sensual spur as she proceeded to bully him into sex, but her ploys had failed to work and he had been unable to perform, at least in the way she wanted.

So she had stalked off in a rage only to return with a magnum of champagne as if that might help or act as a stimulant, which was crazy. Alcohol was the last thing he needed now – alcohol had safely killed-off his tremulous erection; it had withered and died despite Fay's skilful coaxing fingers and there had been 'insult' written all over her face, as if he had planned it that way, as if his impotence *must* bow to her irresistible ministrations and God help him if it did not.

He had discovered on one previous, unfortunate occasion that Fay was allergic to booze, or something like that; anything over two glasses and her chemistry mis-handled the toxins – put quite simply, she changed and the change was not an improvement.

So there had been another hysterical rage, a repeat performance of the first one except for the violence: the fists and the nails and the teeth. He had held her off as long as he could until his self-control had snapped and he had slapped her and the slapping had been like the lancing of some great perpetuating boil. There had been overwhelming relief followed quickly by doubt, because in the deepest part of his heart he knew that it had both scared and excited him more.

And she had come back for second helpings, flinging herself at him in a sort of glorious obscene rage, her voice breaking into high breathless laughter as if he had finally done that one thing she had been trying to goad him into all along, and he had fallen into it just as he had done every other thing she had steered him towards, as if he had no will of his own.

She had begged him to do it again, biting into his ear-lobe with her sharp little teeth to goad him into another meaty little scene. Except, curiously, it had had the opposite effect because bile had risen upwards into his aching throat and there had only been a tremendous feeling of revulsion.

Thank you, God.

And Fay had not liked that at all. So she had flipped completely and given him the performance of a lifetime, something which would really bring the house down. Oh, and she had done that all right.

The mirror in which he scrutinised his face was fatally fractured, a network of cracks spread out from a deep hole at the centre like a bullet wound. Two light fittings were smashed and the shower curtain torn from its rail, the television had survived by falling over on its face – something, perhaps, he should have done himself. At least the telephone still worked, despite the fact that she had yanked it out by the roots.

Of course, it wasn't simply the fact that he hadn't been able to 'get it up', that he had ultimately rejected her kinky sado-masochistic plans. It had been his desire to call Jessica which had finally blown Fay's inebriated fuse; she had emerged too soon from the bathroom and caught him with the telephone in his hand and her lips had literally curled back in a snarl. For a comic second he was reminded of one of those horror films, the silly sort when someone opens their mouth and reveals a ludicrous set of vampire-like teeth. He had smiled, even then, and the smile had been fatal.

Tom patted a cold compress against his cheek and

thought of Jessica. There would be no escape for him now, no feeble excuses; she would only have to look at him to see the livid love-marks of his affair clawed into his once flawless face.

And he *was* vain, she had been right about that.

So perhaps Fay's grand finale was, as they say, only what he deserved.

5

A moth fluttered against the window, a great red and grey thing hovering and bobbing up and down, up and down, so patiently, as if it were prepared to wait outside in the wilting night air until Jessica decided to get up from the bed and allow it entry.

And if Jessica watched, she watched without seeing, suspended in space as if time had slowed or stopped altogether; her body and mind taken up with other, more immediate things, and as she lay there she thought: everything has changed for me; I have changed.

Zak's hands were on her, making an intimate and protracted exploration which she was powerless and, in truth, unwilling to prevent. He had begun by holding her head between his extraordinary hands and kissing her cheeks, her brow, her closed eyes, the little neglected places at her hairline and ears, the places no one had ever thought to kiss.

And there was no choice in this seduction, he had made sure of that. Even as he laid her across the bed – *her* bed, *Tom's* bed – Jessica was only aware of a helpless desire to respond to all that he did; all that he proposed to do, as if all her senses had been primed, fine-tuned, heightened in some incredible way.

Oh, God, and she wanted and she wanted and she wanted.

She heard herself whimper like a puppy because his mouth seemed to be working some magic on her body: licking, raking, probing her stomach, thighs, knees ... God, under her arms. He turned her over and for an instant she felt out of her depth, afraid and utterly vulnerable – and imperfect – that he should see the small cluster of spider veins, like a bruise, at the back of her thigh, the blue shadow of her one and only varicose vein lying beneath the skin; her white, soft bottom which no other man had seen in years. Years. God, she was so afraid, yet so excited, as if she were about to lose her virginity all over again.

He trailed his fingers across her, put his lips to the places she hated, traced the blood lines with his tongue as if he had just picked out her anxious thoughts and laid them bare.

And then he paused and she could feel his eyes drilling into her body before he lay beside her and began again, dragging a fingertip down each side of her body, gliding his hands over and drawing languid spirals on her lower back, her buttocks and haunches, pressing and kneading with the palm of his hand until his own need compelled him to sit up and massage her in earnest, revelling in her sighs and moans and little animal squirms as he rubbed and gathered her warm forbidden flesh in his hands, between his fingers.

Oh, Jessica.

She felt damp all over, everywhere, and her skin tingled and seemed shot through with something more than sexual expectation, as if for the first time in her life she was really *alive*.

Slowly, and with great deliberation Zak lay on her, full length, the front of him against the back of her, hands and arms sliding beneath to cup her breasts so that he could press himself into her, so that she would feel every contour, every hollow and roundness, his hardness lying wedged against her lovely ass.

Oh, Jessica.

And she thought 'now, please, now', but instead he became quite still, not moving, containing himself so that she could only feel the movement of his mouth nuzzling against her neck, his breath weaving into her hair.

'Not yet,' he murmured. 'Not yet.'

His voice was low and secret and full of soft passion. He felt her shiver, watched the profile of her face as it lay against the pale bed cover, saw her eyelids quiver and her helpless lips part. He smiled and rolled to her side, buried one hand in her hair and brought her head close so that he could invade her needy mouth with his tongue. And all the time she could feel him – it – lying against her thigh. She wanted to hold and touch and take it in her hands, explore him. Have it. Fill herself and cure that woman ache, that heat pounding out of control between her legs.

Zak raised himself up on his knees and stared into her eyes and she shuddered at his beauty, at the enormous pole of muscle which shocked and yet made her desperate to submit, avid to yield – to get down on her knees and worship. Insane thoughts. But then he was running one lazy finger from her chin down and down and her body jerked with stunned delight as the searching finger found her clitoris, worked on it, teased and touched and tortured.

Oh, God. She flashed a pleading glance at him. And in that instant she thought: he looks like an ordinary man, eats and drinks like one, sleeps, laughs – just like me. And yet. And yet.

'Face to face they gaze,' he murmured, 'Their eyes shining, grave with a perfect pleasure . . .'

She reached up and grasped a great swathe of his hair in her hand and pressed it against her cheek.

I want his hot open mouth closing over mine, I want his strength and his flesh *inside* me. The words turned over and over in her head like some ancient shibboleth.

And my spunk, Jessica, don't forget the best part. All yours, my love lady, my sweet cunt. And there was triumph blended with his lust, an exquisite feeling of exaltation sweeping through his mind and body as he forced her back against the bed, hands above her head to plunge inside her and deliver them both.

Filling her with silent wonder.

Something pulsed and coursed through her, an almost unbearable intensification of all her senses, and more, a strange primitive mingling of power and life and creation which made her head swim for this new flesh, this body she did not know.

And the pumping was steady, relentless, controlled, until Zak let himself go, turning loose like a wild thing.

Unbelievable pleasure. Paralysing. She cried out, weeping, with grateful ecstasy as his savage thrusts went on and on and on and on.

Don't stop. Don't ever stop.

And he loved that abandoned cry which broke from her lips, the scream skewering upwards from her guts, so much so that he closed his mouth over hers and ate her voice, her words, her pleasure, the sex and the sweetness.

Oh, Jessica.

The taste of you, the scent of you, the feel of your skin. Everywhere I breathe.

*   *   *

'When will he be back?'

'Tuesday evening.'

She lay in the crook of his arm, his eyes were on her mouth, watching it move, savouring the moment.

'Will you let me see you again?' he asked, but knew the answer before she did.

'I don't think I have much choice.'

'Everyone has a choice,' he said. 'You can tell me to go and not come back. And I wouldn't.'

'You must know I don't want that.' She thought inevitably of Tom. 'Nothing is the same any more, Zak; it's as if my life has turned on its head. And I don't know what to feel about Tom, or even if we still have much of a marriage left . . .'

'Maybe you should try taking things, days, one step at a time. Stop planning ahead and trying to predict the future, because you can't. Anyway, at the moment your feelings must be pretty mixed up, maybe shut down in a funny sort of way. Who knows?'

'Some people would say I shouldn't have done this.'

Zak made a noise of mild disgust. 'Most people are hypocritical shits who shouldn't be the judge of anything.'

'Perhaps I'm no better than he is now.'

'Tom?' He wanted to spit. 'You want me to reassure you in some way, don't you? But I can't, so stop torturing yourself.'

'I suppose I almost can't believe that I've actually . . .'

'Committed adultery? Been unfaithful?' he sighed. 'Say it, Jessica, and you'll feel better.'

'You must think me a fool.'

Yet I needed this, *deserved* it, *earned* it. For a moment she closed her eyes.

'Oh, no, never that,' he said. 'Gullible, maybe naïve, but

these are traits I find difficult to resist, as you may have noticed.'

And she could still feel the aftermath of their sex, the undercurrents and shock waves of that amazing debilitating pleasure, even now. It was as if the earth *had* actually moved with their passion and that frightened her.

'He drove you to it in the end,' Zak added gently, 'and I was here.' Waiting.

'Yes, you were.'

'Don't regret it.'

'I can't.'

'We can have time together, you know that. I can even help you through all this . . .' And out the other side, my sweet, 'so enjoy it, don't waste it.'

'I don't want to waste it, Zak. I'm just pathetically confused.'

He smiled, beautifully, lushly. 'So be confused. I'm here. I don't mind.'

And by the time Tuesday comes around, you won't ever want that great nerd of a husband back, that quisling, that spoilt prick.

He brought her hand to his mouth, kissed the tips of her fingers and his eyes came to rest on a small bloody bruise just above her wrist.

'How did you do that?'

'The cockatoo,' she said. 'He's not used to me yet.'

Zak's eyebrows came together in a frown. 'Your husband's cockatoo.'

'I suppose it is,' she said slowly, sadly, not caring, but was deeply touched when he lifted her wrist and kissed the wound reverently, felt serenity turn to desire as his hand fell to her damp yielding breast, cupped it, squeezed it, then lay with his head in her lap. She heard him sigh softly, happily, and found her own hand reaching again to his incredible hair, the fingers slipping through the thick blackness with something close to gratitude and wonder.

She lifted her gaze to the window and stared out at the night stars gleaming above the trees and the rooftops and the cities and this bitter-sweet little scene which was all her own. So frightening how quickly the future could change, and in her mind she went over all that had happened, re-examining the past in order to try to put it into some sort of viable perspective, but gave up in bewilderment.

'Can I ask you something personal?' he said at last.

'All right.'

'Has your husband done this before – been unfaithful, I mean?'

She shook her head. 'No.'

But had he? How would she ever know? The image she had always held of Tom no longer existed, the person she thought she had always loved was someone else. Wasn't he?

'Do you know who the other woman is?'

'No.' Her voice was almost a whisper.

A sharp image of Fay formed in his mind.

'Perhaps it's better if I don't know.'

'Perhaps.' There was no need to tell her yet, all in good time. Instead he lifted his head and began teasing her nipple with his tongue, making her forget. Oh, the taste and the texture, the feel of her flesh in his mouth. And it was *his*, now, his mind said.

She shuddered and moved up against him so that their bodies touched in one long silken line and let him play with her: with his tongue, his lips, his fingers; indulging both their need and their loneliness.

'Where were you born, Zak?' she murmured.

He wound a lock of her lovely hair around his fingers before answering, and if she had looked into his face at that moment she would have seen remoteness and a sort of distancing coming down between himself and the world.

'I was conceived at Glastonbury, born on the coast of Norfolk,' he said flatly.

'I didn't mean to pry.'

Zak blinked, swallowed deep in his throat. 'You're not. I just don't like my past very much, that's all.' Those shitty, uneasy memories stealing over him like a chilling wind. He forced a smile. 'Ask away if you want.'

Jessica hesitated, caught by curiosity. 'Is it so important where you were conceived?'

'My mother met my father at Glastonbury.' She never let him forget it. 'In the sixties and seventies the Glastonbury-Avalon experience was a rite of passage – you hadn't *lived* unless you'd done the hippy-primitive thing and danced naked round the stone circle. All that sacred stuff about Druids and King Arthur and Joseph of Arimathea . . . that really got to my mother. She'd been trying for a kid for ages and then someone told her that standing stones have a phallic significance, that ancient earth currents flow through them as sacred semen, able to fertilise the land, crops, animals, and people . . .'

Zak felt Jessica stiffen ever so slightly.

'Did it work?' she asked.

'She thought so.'

'But you don't?'

'It was all down to the guy who was my father.' His mother had been drunk and high at the same time when she had told him about that long-ago night. About the man coming out of the rain: beautiful and big and wild and caked with mud, who had called to her in a language she had been unable to understand, but it was old, she had sensed that much, apparently – old and timeless and majestic.

Uther had raped her. And the rape had been played out with such fury and strength that each of his frantic thrusts had literally lifted her from the saturated earth, as if he would give her every last drop of his seed, draining himself. The assault had gone on and on, lasting for so long that finally she had passed out.

Uther had fucked her under the stars, she had told Zak proudly; 'but it was raining' he had replied and she had retorted, 'it didn't seem like it'. Then – 'but he raped you', he had reminded her, and she had said so simply, so smugly – 'to find true joy one must first accept true pain.'

'Zak?'

He was staring into space and Jessica brought her hand to his cheek, turning his face towards her. 'Are you okay?'

'Miles, years away. That's all,' he said. 'You see, Jessica, there was a certain chemistry between my mother and father, had to be – something special that worked the magic of conception.' Something meant. Something out of time.

'Nothing to do with the standing stones?'

He heard the barely concealed disappointment, the desperation in her question, knew what she wanted to hear.

'I don't know,' he said softly. 'All I can tell you is that Glastonbury, Avalon, the standing stones are *different*. I don't know how, or why, but the area was called "sacred" early, long before Christian times. People performed magic in the streets a thousand years ago. This hasn't changed at all, not really; they still believe in it.' And sometimes in the early morning when a silky mist steamed from the warm ground and settled around the Tor in a ghostly band, it was easy to imagine that it was, indeed, all true.

'I'd like to go.'

'You should,' he grinned. 'I'll take you.'

She said nothing, only smiling in response.

'It can still offer seclusion and peace,' he continued easily, 'and even a taste of mysticism if you're lucky. Maybe you'll meet Arthur and Merlin . . . they're supposed to come back, you know, when the world needs them,' he paused, his face half-serious, 'but the wonder wizard and our once and future king are a little late, don't you think?' He shrugged and sighed heavily. 'Anyway, I've had enough.'

'Why?'

'I don't want to go back to all that. I've had it up to here with those wankers and their search for celestial bliss,' he brought his hand up to his neck and made a sharp chopping gesture.

'What about Norfolk?'

'The coast,' he corrected her. 'That's different, and it means a lot to me, for some reason.' That flat silent landscape, the gnarled wind-broken trees and the sea that stretched for ever away from him. Home. The last place his mother had seen his father, but that was a lie, wasn't it? After Glastonbury she had never seen him again, he was sure. Yet she said he had come to them again, taking Zak into his arms, flinging him into the air and catching him like a real doting papa – on the beach, she had said, in the very early morning, with the salt wind stinging their faces. Was that the stuff of memory, or dreams?

His eyes flinched, touched by doubt and a little fear; the image he had of his father had the power to do that to him. Yet sometimes he wondered if Uther wasn't just bullshit – an exciting story his mother had made for herself conjured out of Arthurian myth; that would be just like

Astra. She had probably been doped up to the eyeballs on Lebanese Gold at the time.

'You've had an odd sort of life . . .'

'Oh, yeah,' he said tiredly, and you don't know the half of it, Jessica. 'And sometimes I wish . . .' it had been so different, that I had lived a life like other people and tasted the humdrum, the ordinary, *fitted in*. 'Forget it.' He shook his head, as if aware that he had already said more than he had intended.

He suddenly looked terribly young and vulnerable, his heart filled with obscure hurt for all that his strange rootless life had taken from him. Jessica studied the pained, almost adolescent, face and was struck by an unsettling desire to mother and love and touch him all at the same time.

She swallowed hard, tried to lose her thoughts. 'Will you stay – I mean, around here?'

'That depends.' Relieved, he turned to her and pushed her hair away from her face with a sweep of his hand, kissed the exposed neck as tenderly as a lullaby and then released her. There was a gleam in his eye, a sort of mischief. 'Merlin was supposed to have been supernaturally conceived. Did you know that?'

She shook her head.

'Sired by a devil on a maiden.' Zak looked into Jessica's eyes. 'That must have been quite something, don't you think?' He placed a hand on her thigh, slid his fingers between her legs up and into that warm wet place he loved.

Oh, Jessica.

' "I have been in many shapes, Before achieving this convenient form. I have been a drop in the air, I have been a shining star, I have been a word in a book . . ." '

All the time he was looking back at her and she was looking back at him.

'Shall I sire *you*, Jessica?' he whispered and then lowered his voice still further until she could barely hear because the blood was pounding in her head.

'Shall we fuck and spawn and beget . . .?'

And she felt limp, anchorless, intoxicated.

' "I have the knowledge of the stars",' he began, ' "Of stars which pre-exist the earth. I know where I have come from, And the number of the worlds . . ." '

'No more, Zak,' she breathed. 'Don't tease, don't do that to me.'

He placed his first finger across her lips to silence her, but all the time he was looking at her and she was looking back at him.

' "I have slept in a hundred islands, I have lived in a hundred cities. Learned Druids, do you prophesy of Arthur? Or is it of something older: Is it of me you sing?" '

She caught his finger, his hand and brought it feverishly to her mouth.

Zak grinned as she squirmed beneath his words, his touch, his fingers. Tormenting her.

'Want me, Jessica?'

'Oh, yes. Yes.' And the words were spoken like a groan, a plea.

'Want all of me?'

She began sucking his lips, his cheeks, his neck, his shoulders, digging her nails into his perfect skin.

They came together so fast, straining against each other almost violently and even as he took her and their juices ran and mingled he was seeing that image again, feeling it, the fearful one of his father raping his mother in the mud and the rain and in the shadowy mists of the standing-stones.

But this is Jessica, his mind screamed, and I am not my father.

It was revoltingly hot and the vinyl upholstery of the taxicab stuck to Fay's short-clad thighs as she shifted uncomfortably in the back of the car. She placed the earphones of her Sony walkman over her head and turned up the volume. What utter crud, but she did not switch off the music because it beat on her resistance and once again she found herself drawn by the sound, the rhythm, the soul, even if the lyrics, as usual, filled her with contempt.

The song was all about loving someone (not exactly original) and the someone, the man, was not like all the rest, apparently; he was sickeningly perfect, magical – a hero. Oh, *please*. And to which flawed, pathetic macho *persona non grata* did the deluded words of the song refer? She recalled another song equally as good, if not better in its way, but the lyrics must have been written by someone with a bad case of clinical depression because it was all about this girl wanting to top herself if her man left her . . . they were 'one' . . . and she would 'never be free' . . . . didn't *want* to be free, in fact. Bizarre. Imagine, for instance, not wanting to be free from someone like poor old Tom? Fay chuckled in her throat. And he would be poor old Tom, at least for a while.

For a moment she experienced a brief sensation of shame, then looked down at her nails; two of them were broken and she cursed softly. If he had just cooperated in the way she had wanted instead of being so stuffy, so tediously correct all of a sudden. Of course, she shouldn't have had anything to drink, then things might have stayed somewhere near normal, but was it really her fault if drink had a bad effect on her? He should have stopped her when he saw the way things were going; he knew what it did to her. It was *his* fault, really, because she could not be held responsible for her actions when booze was shooting through her veins and making her a trifle unreasonable.

The pier flashed by in a blur of people and balloons and hot-dog stands and wearily she leaned her head on the back of the seat. A little controlled, skilfully applied pain was very fashionable in these sado-masochistic times. It managed to stave off the boredom quite nicely, but Tom didn't seem to see it that way. So she had left him to stew amongst the debris of their affair in Edinburgh, to lick his wounds so to speak. Ha ha.

She glanced out of the window and watched the Pavilion float by, saw the tourists with their cameras snapping, snapping. Hadn't Jessica done rather a good painting of the Prince Regent's folly once? And sold it for something close to two hundred pounds, if she remembered correctly. Not bad, but boring. Perhaps if Jessica had been less boring Tom might not have felt compelled to stray; perhaps if she hadn't been so obsessed with *producing* and getting a bun in the oven Tom might . . . as it was, well. Fay shrugged inwardly.

Anyway, she was tired of Tom and his angst, his pathetic pleas and excuses, so Jessica could have him back with pleasure. There was that boy, after all, the delicious one with that fantastic hair, that face, that body, that enticing bulge – the thought of which had driven her to feverish bouts of masturbation during the long hours of the night when sleep refused to come. No one could do it better than she could, except perhaps the boy. That Zak. Fay's breathing was coming fast and heavy as her imagination took flight, but instead she closed her eyes and let her brain go to work, to plan and plot and sift through everything, all of the possibilities that lay ahead which would eventually get her what she wanted.

When the cab drew up outside the house it was forced to double-park and Fay struggled out of the back-seat with an array of carrier bags and a small overnight case before squeezing through a narrow gap made by the vehicles sitting at the kerb.

'Hello, Fay.'

Fay's eyes narrowed as she stared at the woman who had paused on the path: middle-aged, middle-class, dull; they had met at Jessica's a couple of times.

'I know your face . . .' she began, 'but . . .'

'Roz.'

'Ah, yes,'

'Been away?' Roz's gaze fell to the carrier bags printed in a garish tartan, the overnight bag.

'Yes.'

'Anywhere nice?' Edinburgh perhaps?

'Yes, actually.' And that's about all you're going to get out of me.

Roz looked and the look said everything.

'You should be wearing a hat, Fay.'

'Oh?'

'This sort of heat is very ageing . . .' Roz turned and began to walk away, '. . . particularly for someone with your sort of skin.'

A sharp retort hovered on Fay's lips, but she stayed it because there had been something curious in the woman's expression which had unsettled her, that overt dislike for a start. What had she ever done to her, for God's sake?

'Cow,' Fay murmured, too late, and stuck out her tongue at the retreating figure. Off to see saintly Jessica, no doubt, two little pals together, and there was that interior dig of jealousy again and she hated herself for it. She looked down at her hand, the plastic handles of the carriers were cutting into her fingers: she was dusty, tired and too hot and her feet felt incredibly heavy as she trudged the last few yards to the house and up the marble steps to the imposing door. It opened almost by magic.

'Fay . . .' Jonathan said jovially, 'I can call you Fay, can't I? Here, let me help you.'

He must have been watching her from the street; Fay looked back at him warily.

'Is there something you want?'

'Not exactly.'

'Look – I've travelled a long way and I'm extremely tired.'

'I'll be brief.'

Please.

'Emma and I are getting engaged.'

'Congratulations,' she said. 'Can I go now?'

'We're throwing a party.'

'Great,' she responded flatly.

'We'd really like you to come.'

Fay glanced over his shoulder, through the open door, watched Emma drop her eyes. She doesn't like me either, but what did she care for the opinion of someone as squeaky-clean as the nauseous Emma?

'I'm not a party person.'

For an instant he looked insulted.

'This won't be your average party, not by a long way,' he said. 'Believe me.'

'Really?' Her eyes were blank with boredom and she shook her head, felt any patience she had begin to fray around the edges. 'I don't think so.'

'Come on. Spoil yourself.'

God, what a line.

'No.'

Suddenly he seemed at a loss for words, hovering over her like some gigantic agitated fly. Buzz buzz buzz.

She moved past him and began climbing the stairs, then realised he was coming up behind her with her damned carrier bags. He followed her like a sniffy dog before dropping the bags outside her door, took an envelope out of his jacket pocket.

She looked up at him, too tired to protest any longer. Wasn't he disgustingly hot in that suit? The shoulder-pads alone would surely weigh several kilos, but he was an image man and the image was all important, even if it killed him in the process.

There was a fixed grin on Jonathan's lightly tanned face as he leaned down and planted the invitation in one of the tartan carrier bags.

'In case you change your mind.'

'I won't.' And this little performance was all in aid of him wanting her flat. Well, he was wasting his time. She was tempted to throw the blessed invitation after him as he sprinted athletically down the stairs, but decided against it because it was probably still throbbing hotly from his insipid body heat. Fay wrinkled her nose; there was something curiously unappetising about Jonathan-Mr Universe-Keeley, something hygienic and sexless and ultimately depressing.

'It's wonderful,' Roz said and then added, 'well, at least, it *will* be.'

The unfinished black and white sketch of Zak was propped up against the easel which still sat on the patio. Jessica was sitting beside it, charcoal in hand.

'Thanks,' she said softly, 'I thought I wouldn't be able to do it. I started then stopped, then began again and somehow it took off. It's been years since I've done a portrait.'

'Who is he?'

Jessica learned forward and adjusted the drawing unnecessarily, went over a line on the paper and waited for the telltale blush to fade before she looked back at Roz.

'A local,' she said, 'moved in a couple of weeks ago.'

'What a face,' Roz said. 'He's gorgeous.'

'Yes, he is, isn't he.'

'How did you meet?'

'He was looking for his cat and then came by again the next day,' Jessica paused, pulled her straw hat down a little harder, looked out into the garden. 'I was trying to draw those tree stumps over there, the blackened ones . . .' Roz followed her gaze as Jessica's voice ran on, 'but it was hopeless, nothing would come.' She paused. 'He was helpful – and interested, I suppose.'

'Lucky you.' Roz raised her eyebrows.

'He's a nice boy,' Jessica said defensively.

'If your portrait is at all accurate, I think the word "nice" is probably the understatement of the year.' She chuckled. 'Are you going to stop at the face and shoulders, or do you intend to do a life-size study?'

'I hadn't thought . . .'

'You know,' Roz added 'have him naked – as it were.'

'For God's sake, Roz.'

'Just a joke,' she said. 'Might cheer you up, you never know.'

'Ha ha.' Part of her wanted to turn around and look Roz straight in the eye, tell her everything, all that she had done, as if she were wringing out some irrevocable confession.

'Heard from Tom?'

'No,' Jessica said. 'I told him not to call.'

'When is he due back?'

'Tomorrow night.'

'What will you do?'

'I don't know.' She looked at the sketch for a long moment. 'I want to know who it is, how long it's been going on. *Why*, for God's sake . . . I've got a right to at least that much.'

Roz thought of Fay and those garish tartan bags. A coincidence? Things like that didn't happen in real life; real life was a bitch, as the saying went – someone with flowing red hair and delicate white skin who dished it up in your face.

'I know you do, but maybe it's better not to. If Tom has had a fling in a weak moment, then let it be, Jess,' she said earnestly. 'Let him crawl and beg and get on his knees – all those things if you want, but don't go into it too deep.'

'Why not?'

'Because you'll end up hurting yourself even more.'

Jessica looked down at her hands; her nails and fingertips were black with charcoal.

'Sometimes I think it was this baby thing,' she said miserably, 'you know, that he was fed up with it – all that temperature taking and bonking at certain dreaded times, all my angst. Years of it.'

'You don't know that.'

'No, but . . .'

'Let's have a drink.'

'You have one. I'm sticking to mineral water.'

'Why?'

'Don't say you hadn't noticed that I'd been drinking too much?' Friday evening began playing itself back in her mind. If she hadn't been drunk maybe it wouldn't have happened, complicating everything, churning her up, except there was a little voice telling her that she had wanted Zak, wanted the sex and the loving: needed it. Him. Even as she sat there, she experienced a spasm of remembered pleasure, felt her whole body shiver with desire. Oh, God.

'You're not cold, are you?'

'No,' Jessica responded quickly. 'Thinking too much, that's all.'

'Someone walking over your grave . . .'

'That's a cheerful thought.'

'Believe me, I have plenty of those, Jess,' Roz replied wryly.

'Gordon's okay, isn't he?'

'Oh, yes. Fine, actually. He's fishing somewhere along the Lavant right at this moment,' she said. 'No – I think it's this business of yours, bringing my own personal disaster back to me in all its lurid detail. This damn memory of mine doesn't help, of course . . .'

'What do you mean?'

'It's too good, too perfect. I have this awful habit of remembering everything in glorious stinging technicolour . . . you know, as if it were yesterday.'

'I know.'

'It doesn't go away, that's the trouble, at least not completely. You think it has and then something comes along – and wallop.'

'Do you ever hear from him?'

'The monster from the black lagoon?' Roz smiled drily, 'No. I never hear from sweet little Mark. Thank God. And I don't want to. Why would I want to hear from, let alone see, someone who almost crucified me? That would be rather foolish, not to say, insane, my dear.' Roz shook her head. 'Tom is a little innocent compared to my ex-husband.' And yet if her suspicions were right about Tom and Fay, how far would her grand assumptions get her then?

'I wish I could see it that way.'

'I know and I'm sorry; it was a silly thing to say. Besides, it's too soon to talk of comparisons.' Roz lifted her face to the sun and sighed heavily. 'You know, I never have understood how anyone can have an amicable divorce – sounds so bloody absurd.'

'You had a particularly bad time.'

'It's all relative, I suppose.'

'No.' Jessica said firmly, 'it's all hell.' She stood up abruptly. 'I'll fetch the plonk and give you that drink.'

'Maybe it's this dry as dust summer, Jess, the damn heat, driving everyone a little mad.' But Jessica had already disappeared into the house. For a long moment Roz stared into the deserted communal garden which slumped sullenly beneath the relentless afternoon sun (not dozed, that was too nice a word – no, it definitely slumped), and was empty save for the thrum of insects and a few birds too listless to fly. 'I know this much,' she said aloud, 'it would drive me mad if I had to look at this bloody garden every day.'

'You can't blame the garden,' Jessica said from the doorway.

'I wish you wouldn't creep up on me like that,' Roz said. 'And I really don't know what it is about this place. Even before this drought got underway I always thought there was something, well, *wrong* about it somehow . . .'

'But it's a beautiful garden,' Jessica protested.

'Maybe it's the close proximity of the houses as well,' Roz responded awkwardly, 'all those shadowy windows staring back at you from that great sweeping arm of a crescent.' Like an enormous, but not very welcome, embrace. 'It's enough to make anyone claustrophobic.'

'I think you've been reading too many horror stories.'

'Well, wasn't someone murdered around here?'

'For God's sake, Roz, that was years ago. The twenties, I think.'

'But they never found the person who did it . . .'

'How do you know? Besides, you weren't even born then.'

'Gordon told me. You know what he is for local history.'

'Even so, Roz . . .' Jessica protested in exasperation.

'All right, all right,' she said with a sheepish grin, 'so I have a vivid imagination.' Her gaze crept to the blackened tree stumps, travelled to the dusty depression in the earth where there had once been a pond, across a scabrous patch of lawn to a neglected summer-house where a small cherub statue, once a fountain-head, stood forsaken, the round plump bottom spotted with lichen and bird droppings, its sad little penis silhouetted plainly, but redundant now that the water had been cut off. Behind it nameless creepers crawled over and up the walls where two pseudo-Grecian torsos peered sightlessly through snares of briar, smothered by the eternal bindweed which still flowered despite the endless heat, its white trumpet-like blooms spreading unchecked across the colourless landscape like a contagious disease.

A place full of shadows and suffocating warmth and seething with insects. Roz stared at the summer-house with something close to dislike and as she withdrew her gaze saw out of the corner of her eye a figure emerging from the convolutions of foliage and her heart jumped.

'What on earth . . .?'

But it was only a boy, no, a young man and she pressed down a small sigh of relief.

And she had thought . . . what? She felt foolish suddenly, like a child who makes a monster out of a piece of furniture in a darkened room.

Jessica watched Zak come to her from the shadows of the summer-house, the trees, felt something inside her rise up in eagerness and placed a hand on her chest to try to quell the crazy beating of her heart.

Roz shifted uneasily in her seat as he drew closer and she turned to Jessica, but Jessica was very still, staring straight ahead, looking fixedly back at him. Puzzled, Roz switched her gaze back to the boy who was moving towards them with an air of impenetrable calm, and immediately recognised his face from the portrait, an enigmatic but, oh my, a face promising so very much.

And he did not see her, not at all. Roz might well have been sitting on the other side of the moon.

Keith was lying on his back staring up into the belly of his van; the clamps had fallen off his exhaust, which would explain the horrendous noise that accompanied him whenever he drove. He caught a weary breath, then cursed before letting his head fall gently back on to the road to watch Emma's legs as she walked towards him from the house. Her skirt was shorter than usual and she wore no tights, so he let his eyes drift up and down and back again as she drew closer; and she had painted pink nail-varnish on her toes. Pretty feet. She stopped beside the van and he felt her eyes looking down.

'Does he like your feet?'

She sighed then, one of those big, heavy girly sighs, and he grinned widely to himself.

'Who?'

'Mr Wonderful.'

'Jonathan has far more important things to do than worry about my feet.'

'Thought so.'

'What is that supposed to mean?'

Keith moved his head so that it was only inches away from her lovely bare legs, not a hair in sight, not a pimple or a scratch. Salivatingly smooth. He thought that if he stretched out his tongue he could lick that warm salty silky skin.

'It doesn't matter.'

Emma tapped her foot and Keith's eyes followed the exquisite movement of tanned muscle: ankle to calf, calf to thigh, up and up. Everything was working perfectly. He tried to ignore the tickling sensation which was beginning in his groin.

'He just telephoned,' she said briskly. 'You have to be in Lewes an hour earlier.'

Keith's germinating erection withered and died.

'What?'

He poked his head out and screwed up his eyes against the sun, through the blur saw Emma looking down at him; hand on hip.

'They couldn't get the extension they wanted,' she continued, 'so the disco has to start an hour earlier.'

'Great,' he seethed, crawling out from under the van. 'Brilliant.'

'What's wrong with that?'

'Only that the exhaust is falling off.'

Emma looked alarmed.

'What are you going to do?'

'Get it bloody well fixed somehow.' He placed the flat of his hand on the roof of the van and withdrew it immediately, hissing with pain where the sun-heated metal had burned his skin. He glared at the clapped-out vehicle. 'Until the next time.'

'Well, Jonathan's going to get you a new van.'

'Jonathan had better.'

'He always keeps his promises,' she said defensively.

'Oh, yes, I forgot. Finally, you're getting married.'

She blushed furiously.

'What did you do?' he said with a sneer. 'Threaten to break both his legs?'

'Don't be stupid.'

He laughed, but it was not a kind laugh and he brushed passed her, unable to resist the touching, then strode back to the office feeling that he had just scored a few brownie points in this, their latest encounter. His step faltered as he reached the bottom of the steps, wiped sweat from his brow with the back of his hand. But for what?

Emma scrutinised him sharply as he moved away from her. He was wearing a white tee-shirt with a gaudy message emblazoned across the back – 'Get Lost Dog Breath' – ghastly wide black shorts which reached to his knees and a huge pair of Reebok trainers with the tongues hanging out.

Her stomach was churning ever so slightly and she wondered why it was that Keith always seemed able to dig up something to sting her with, some uncomfortable 'home truth' to spoil her happiness. And Jonathan loved her, why else would he suddenly and so earnestly talk of marriage? There was no need for coercion on her part, not now, not after what had happened between them. She had forgiven him his strange behaviour that night and he, in turn, had been so grateful that the balance had shifted in their relationship and in a curious way she now held all the cards, except that Emma wasn't sure she understood quite why.

But she mostly liked the little piece of power she had gleaned from the results of that unfortunate evening, the feeling of being in control, the unspoken authority that she now seemed to possess which was close to a cautious and yet not entirely pleasing victory – as if, somehow, she had won a game unfairly by bending the rules.

A confusion of feelings played across her face as she stared up the street, as a BMW carefully weaved its way through the pathway left by cars parked bumper to bumper on either side of the narrow road and slowed to a stop further around the Crescent. Absently she followed the car with her eyes and the tall man who got out; it was Mr Innes, the brother-in-law of that bitchy red-head who lived above the office. Emma noted the bandage plastered across his cheek, brushed a fly off her skirt and walked back into the office.

'Hello, Jess.'

She had heard the closing of the front door and the familiar footfalls as he made his way through the house, so his voice from the doorway came as no surprise. It was almost easy, then, to contain herself and continue with the portrait, feel his eyes on her back, the sun beating down on her head.

'Hello, Tom,' she replied without expression, then, 'you're early, I didn't expect you until this evening.'

He didn't, couldn't, reply immediately because his throat was so tight he was finding it difficult to breathe. 'I wanted to come home.'

She stiffened, caught by the misery in his voice, then slowly turned to look at him.

'Good God.' she exclaimed. 'What have you done to your face?'

His hands were shaking and he put them aside.

'It looks worse than it is.'

Jessica gaped at him. The left side of Tom's face was horribly swollen and covered by a large piece of white gauze kept in place by numerous sticking plasters which reached across his nose and into his hairline like tram-lines. There were dark circles of exhaustion lying beneath his eyes.

'What happened?'

'You might call it a collision of sorts.'

She stood up and began to move towards him.

'An accident with the car?'

He couldn't lie, though he had meant to, but not now, it just wasn't in him any more.

'No.'

'What then?'

He made no answer.

'Were you mugged?'

He shook his head, sickened by the reality of the moment, felt acid seeping into his stomach.

Jessica stared at him with a kind of horror and curiosity as realisation dawned.

'Let me see.'

'Not now, Jess.'

'Let me see.'

It was useless to argue and he only hesitated for a moment, then began picking at the plasters one by one, pulling them away, ignoring the pain.

Fay's claw-marks had festered. The three weals she had scored down his cheek were pulled open by taut distended skin and oozing thick yellow pus.

'You need antibiotics for this.'

His eyes shifted wretchedly from her unblinking gaze. 'I know,' he whispered, 'I haven't had time . . .'

'She must have been very angry.'

Tom looked back at his wife carefully.

'That's not quite the word I would use.'

'No.' she agreed quietly, 'I don't suppose it is.'

'Jess,' he said her name so softly she barely caught the sound. 'It's over.'

She stepped back and regarded him steadily.

'Our marriage – or your affair?'

'Don't,' he said wearily, pathetically. 'Please, Jess . . .'

She waited for a second, then swung round and walked away from him.

'Jess?'

She was standing very still now, arms folded, in front of the portrait.

'Jess?' He followed and came behind her, hovering, wanting to touch her, but afraid to. Instead his eyes travelled to her drawing, focused on the striking face, the eyes which seemed to look back at him.

'You're working again.'

She said nothing.

'It's very good,' he said, then added after a pause. 'Who is he?'

'Just a boy.' Who slept in your bed and made love to your wife. The best sex she had ever had. 'Don't you think you'd better get round to the doctor's surgery?'

'I can go in the morning.'

'I don't think you should wait.'

'I want to talk.'

'When I wanted to talk, you weren't interested. My feelings, my needs, seemed to come very far down the scale of your all-consuming priorities.'

'I know,' he said, 'and I'm sorry – truly sorry.'

She closed her eyes and thought of Zak and what she had done with Zak, and when she looked back at her husband she found herself wondering bleakly what had happened to their carefully ordered lives.

'I wanted to,' Tom continued hopelessly, 'I didn't know how; everything was out of control.' And he had handled the whole thing so badly, he realised that now, misjudging and miscalculating all along the line.

'What was out of control exactly?' She looked at his damaged face, the hunched hopeless shoulders.

'I didn't mean it to happen,' he said lamely.

'It was "just one of those things" – was it, Tom?' she responded harshly.

'I can't explain.'

'No,' she said, 'I didn't think you could.'

'I was a bloody fool.'

'Oh, no, Tom, much more than that.'

'I never meant to hurt you,' he began, 'I thought it would be over and done with before you . . .' his voice trailed off.

'Before I found out,' she said tiredly. A part of her wished for that, wished that they could rewind their lives, change things, so that she would never know what he had done. But now there was Zak, too, and what would Tom say if he found out that his behaviour had unwittingly driven her into the arms of someone she hardly knew and where she had discovered things about herself she never knew existed.

'It wasn't something *planned*, Jess,' he said desperately. 'I didn't go looking for it.'

'You didn't think of me, either.'

'You can't believe that.'

She shook her head with disbelief. 'Do you know, Tom, you're full of platitudes – meaningless words which you try to make sound sincere.'

'No, Jess.'

'Was she so difficult to resist, then?' Her voice was full of scorn and her eyes examined him sharply, saw the livid glow of blood suffuse his battle-scarred face.

'Don't.'

'Well?'

'It doesn't matter now.'

'It does to me,' she said angrily. 'It matters very much *to me!*'

'All right, all right.'

'Who was she?'

He stared at her hard, wiped his forehead with the palm of his hand.

'Someone I met at an auction.'

'Who?'

'You don't know her,' he said quickly and felt guilt constricting his throat – searing, shuddering, appalling guilt; felt the crushing, awful heat weigh him down, his knees turn to jelly as he realised how close Fay was and would always be.

'I think you'd better go inside, Tom, the heat's getting to you.'

He didn't move and she stared back at him hard before taking his arm and walking him into the house.

In the drawing-room she made him sit down and pressed a large brandy into his hands.

'Drink it,' she said, 'you look as though you need to.'

'I'm all right.'

'You should see yourself.'

'I don't want to.'

'Well,' she said quietly, 'I shouldn't worry, I doubt if your friend's claw-marks will leave a lasting scar.'

'That's not what I meant.' He flashed a glance at her. 'And she's not my friend.'

'Not now. No. I don't suppose she is.'

'Jess,' he said, 'please.'

'Please, what, Tom?' she retorted, suddenly aware of rising gorge and yearned to say something harsh and fatal so that she might hurt him. 'Am I upsetting you in some way? For heaven's sake – and why on earth would I want to do that? You've only destroyed our marriage for some torrid little affair.'

'Not destroyed, Jess?' he broke in, pleaded.

'Or perhaps it wasn't so torrid, or so little? And how am I supposed to know because you've told me absolutely nothing? For all I know this fling of yours may have been one of many throughout our precious married life.' She paused and looked at him full in the eyes. 'It was precious to me, anyway.'

'I've never been unfaithful before,' he stammered, then stood up, 'never . . . believe me,' knocked the brandy glass over which in turn pushed a delicate Tiffany vase to the floor. 'Christ,' he exclaimed.

'It's all right, Tom, it's not broken,' she said with thinly veiled sarcasm.

'I don't care about the bloody vase.'

'I thought it was one of your favourites.'

'Does it matter?'

'Not to me.'

He just looked at her.

'I want to make all this up to you,' he said at last, but an expression of uncertainty appeared and then disappeared on his face, 'but I don't know how.'

'Neither do I.'

His eyes continued to regard her apprehensively, even with fear. 'You do want me to try, though, don't you?'

'I don't know what I want, Tom.' She thought of Zak

suddenly, felt a little panic stir in her stomach. 'Perhaps it would be better if we separated, at least for a while.' The words seemed to spill out almost of their own accord.

'No, Jess', he protested.

'What do you *expect*?'

'I told you, it's over and there'll be no going back. I give you my word.'

'Your word,' she repeated, 'and what good has that been to me?'

'I mean it. I promise you,' his voice was beginning to rise, 'I don't know why it happened in the first place . . . it meant nothing to me,' he went on, 'not in the real sense. I didn't *love* her. I don't think I even liked her.'

He passed an agitated hand through his hair in that old familiar way and she thought she could almost feel sorry for him, thought that if she weakened enough she could let him through the careful barrier she had built. It was the face, of course, so wounded, not like Tom's face at all, and that childlike look of disbelief.

'I love *you*, Jess. There never has been anyone else.'

'Except her, apparently.' In her mind Jessica went over all the deadly retorts she could think of, but gave them up because there was still a part of her that was reluctant to hurt him and reduce herself to his level.

'Oh, no. Not her,' he shook his head, 'never *her*.'

She looked back at him with curiosity, wondering at the vehemence in his tone.

'Who was she, Tom?'

'I told you,' he said, 'you don't know her.' And she didn't, he told himself, not really.

'Why, Tom?' she said softly, abruptly. 'What did I do wrong?' She looked bruised, regretful, cut off from him.

'Nothing,' he gushed, 'it was me.' He sat down, his

forehead was streaming with perspiration and he could feel the dull thunder of a headache beginning somewhere in his weary brain, 'Oh, God knows . . . it was everything.' He looked at the floor, brought his hands together, pushing and kneading them in an agony of anguish. 'You wanting a baby so much, perhaps . . .' he began.

Her eyes flew open. 'So it was my fault?'

'Of course not,' he blustered, 'I didn't mean that exactly.'

'Don't you want a child?'

'Of course,' he said rapidly, 'but it's become . . .'

'What?' she cried, 'what has it become?'

'I don't know,' he said helplessly. 'Sometimes I've felt swamped by it, sort of overwhelmed . . . and when we made love it wasn't for us . . .' he darted a glance at her, 'was it? Not for the pleasure, or the fun, or even a bit of plain old-fashioned lust. It became so bloody mechanical . . .'

Jessica stared at him for a long moment, stunned into silence because he was voicing what she had suspected, but not wanted to believe.

'Am I to blame for that?'

'No,' he spoke in a whisper.

'You could have told me how you felt . . .'

She turned round and walked over to the window. Dusk was creeping in like a thief, lengthening the shadows as the day lost its colour.

'What are we to do, Tom?' she said at last.

'I have to make this up to you,' he said again. 'I want things back the way they were . . .' he paused helplessly, 'although I know that won't be possible – but we can try, Jess, can't we?'

She said nothing.

'Jess?' He got up and came towards her. 'I've never let you down before, have I? Don't condemn me for a weak moment – something stupid, crazy. It won't happen again. I don't want anyone else, I never really did. Jess?'

She shook her head, not trusting herself to speak.

'We've been married too long and gone through too much together to let it all go. Haven't we?'

'That sounds like a carefully prepared speech,' she said. 'Why didn't you think of that when you were arranging your love trysts, when you were with *her* . . . doing all the things that lovers do . . .' Her voice was low, hurting, a whisper.

'We weren't *lovers*, not in the way you mean,' he said. 'It was just – sex.'

Her eyes were on him, full of reproach, utterly desolate.

'What have you done, Tom?' she said helplessly. 'Do you have any idea?' She caught a breath as if she were drowning, as a vision of Zak's beautiful face soared into her mind.

'Jess, please,' there was that note of urgency in his voice again, that fright. 'If you'll just give me a chance.'

'I don't know – I don't know what to say to you. I need some time. Space to breathe and think things through.'

His face was desperately set; he looked weak, shaken, and as if to twist a knife in the wound his mind switched to Fay and what would happen if Jessica knew the real truth. A sort of darkness crept over him.

'Okay, okay,' he began haltingly, 'I'll leave if you want,' but his heart jumped in quick and sudden panic unable to imagine what he was saying. Where would he go? 'I will,' he repeated unconvincingly. 'If that's what you really want.'

'Perhaps that would be best,' she said at last and without looking at him.

He gasped, speechless with incredulity, his mind buckling under the pressure of her apparent decision, his guilt and the whole hideous mess which he had fallen into with such lustful ease, right up to his neck. Which was, oh yes, exactly what he deserved.

When Jessica finally turned round to look at her husband he was standing there white-faced, mutely crying, and even the fateful claw-marks seemed smaller somehow and drained of colour.

Zak watched from the shadows of the garden, saw Jessica as she placed her hands on her puling husband's shoulders, gathering him against her. She was not to blame, of course; she had little choice, really, as things had turned out and could not go against her nature, which was part of the reason why he loved her – that warmth, that understanding, that forgiveness.

Yet he turned his face away, not able to bear to see the man who was her husband touch her, or see the liquid silver of his pathetic tears mingle with hers as Jessica sought to comfort them both.

And puling husband had not told her of Fay, of course, would not dare reveal that his whore was Jessica's own sister.

Zak moved into the protection of the shadows and slipped back into the communal garden. When he glanced over his shoulder he could no longer see them and then the drawing-room light was switched off and there was only the black empty window staring at him with the fixed unwelcoming eye of a dead man.

He stood there for a moment, immobile, brooding, then swung round and began to walk away. No good to look and wish and hope, or imagine what she might do next. Let him in her bed after what he had done? Would she?

Zak squeezed his eyes tight shut as something inside him rose up in protest, felt sick with jealousy and pain as crippling loneliness washed over him. From the heavy stillness, he heard the sharp bark of a vixen followed by the strange little sob which always came after, as if there were a child out there alone in the dark, not a fox at all. He was reminded of the travellers and his old life, and all those times he had slept, literally, under the stars. He stopped, waiting for the lean, low body to creep out from some undergrowth, but nothing happened and the silence came on him again like a burden.

He continued to walk and the walking became a trot and then a run through the thickening darkness, across the baked earth and bleached undergrowth; his footfalls thudding against the turf and churning up echoes as if something else were abroad in the gathering night.

He had left the door to the basement open and the ginger tom cat was lying on his sleeping-bag cleaning itself, but it stopped preening, one leg cocked at an angle, to look back at him as he came into the room. Zak ignored the animal and walked over to the fireplace and the stump of a candle, still lit, which was beginning to drown in its own wax. His heart was pumping too fast and he placed both hands on the mantelshelf and slumped against it, pressing his forehead against the wall as if he might blot out the wretchedness and frustration and desire, and that weird sensation of panic which seemed to be twisting his guts.

Wanting her.

He swung round angrily and stalked into the place which had been a kitchen; looking for something, but not knowing precisely what. He picked up a paper cup, threw it; an empty beer can went the same way, clanging and banging along the patched linoleum floor, bouncing against the skirting-board and rolling, finally, to the part of the wall where the secret was, the steps he had seen through a gap in the plaster, sliding downwards into shadow.

He stood stock-still for a moment, then crossed the room and pressed his palms up against the peeling wallpaper. Something. He ran his fingernail down an indentation he found through the material and began tearing away at the covering until he discovered the door which he had known all along must be there. And it was a very mediocre door: peeling cream paint and a hole where the handle had once been. Zak slipped his finger into the hole and pulled, the door wavered but refused to budge, he stepped back and gave it an almighty kick and the door swung outwards, away from him and so gently and silently that the silence was almost eerie.

He lit a candle and held it over the mouth of the abyss, because that is what it seemed to him, for whatever flooring had been there had long since rotted away. Only the ancient steps leading down from the open door still hung precariously over nothing but blackness, and the blackness was heavy with the stink of decay.

He stared down for a long time, as if drawn, closed his eyes and then looked up, saw a mass of fungi growing out of the low ceiling, great fruiting bodies like giant toadstool caps and dripping rusty-red spores which had probably drifted from cellar to attic, through wood, plaster, brick and even stone – germinating and infecting the whole house. The building was living on borrowed time.

As he stood there he experienced an odd, uneasy feeling, a feeling of being watched. Something. He reached inwards and across the blackness, gingerly catching hold of the door to draw it back. It shut with a sigh, a brief expellation of warm cloying air caressing his skin and he recoiled in distaste, but then wheeled round, caught by a sound behind him.

'It's me,' a voice said uncertainly from the outer room

and a figure came cautiously through the threshold of the kitchen towards him, 'Jonathan.'

For an instant Zak had prayed for Jessica, but Jessica was nowhere near, he had sensed that much. She was busy now, wasn't she, with puling husband? His face contorted as the image of her with him took over and then worse, a feeling of the thwarting of all his hopes and dreams.

'Zak?'

He sighed. It was the precious prince from upstairs, the one who was just beginning to learn about his sexuality and yet was still not brave enough to savour it.

'What do you want?'

Me. A taste of my flesh.

'I wanted to apologise,' he began, 'for what happened before.'

'I knew you'd come back.'

'I don't understand.'

'You knew you'd come back.'

There was almost a smile creeping over Zak's features as he watched Jonathan shake his head slowly, repeatedly.

'No.'

'Yes,' Zak said softly. 'Stop wasting my time – and your own.'

He walked towards him then, stopped a step away and smelt the pungent aroma of something like whisky; perhaps he had run out of sherry. 'It's called Dutch courage, isn't it?'

'What is?' Jonathan said unsteadily.

'Drinking doesn't just dilate the blood vessels you know, it dilates the brain, loosens all the cogs, sets you free,' he paused, 'for better or worse.'

'I don't know what you're getting at.'

'Maybe you haven't drunk enough this time.'

Jonathan swallowed. 'For what?'

'Me.'

Jonathan made no answer, not trusting himself to speak.

'That *is* what you want, isn't it? A taste to see if you like it?' Zak pressed, his voice low and secret.

For a split second their gazes locked. Jonathan's eyes were wide and terrified, but his tongue ran along his lips as if of its own volition, as if it knew something he did not.

Zak smiled thinly. 'But I think you know that already.'

He put the candle down, lifted his tee-shirt and pulled it over his head, slung it to the floor, unbuckled his belt and let his jeans fall. It was hot and clammy in that room and his perfect skin gleamed with moisture, shone like yellow gold in the candlelight.

'I didn't think . . .' Jonathan's voice faltered.

'Don't think,' Zak said softly, impatiently, 'just do.'

And in a curious way he wanted him also, wanted that sensation of human skin against human skin: the touching, the needing, the staving off of the pain that was Jessica – a little shallow pleasure to help him get through the night.

Jonathan was trembling perceptibly and Zak put his hands on his shoulders as if he would steady him, but then he pushed him down so that Jonathan was kneeling before him, his face flickering with fear and guilt and then closed with furtive excitement.

Zak threw his head back, let remoteness come down again, imagined it was Jessica's lips and cheek pressing against his belly; Jessica's hands, Jessica's mouth taking him with relief and gratitude.

He had learned the imagining trick a long time ago when he was a small boy, when one of his mother's lovers had preferred him to her and Zak had not known any better – all those mind-blowing caresses that knew nothing of love, only lust and starvation, but in the process he had learned all about taking and giving, withholding and submission. Pain. That, and what he had gleaned at his dear sweet mother's knee (what an education . . .). By the time he reached the grand old age of fifteen he had known *everything* and the sexual power he wielded was consummate, overpowering, irresistible.

Now it was Jonathan's turn, and Jonathan would pay for the privilege. And he would work hard, too, for this treat, this initiation, because bitterness was busy stealing through Zak, and envy and malice as his thoughts returned to Jessica, and Jessica's husband.

But there was always tomorrow, a voice told him, and the knowledge of Fay. He smiled to himself and gave in a little to the pleasure, let it quicken and then held Jonathan's head in his hands, moving it to and fro, to and fro, guiding him expertly in just the way he liked.

Zak turned his face to the window, the one of stained glass, and watched a shaft of moonlight shine through the colour of molten gold, almost orange, and thought of Fay's hair, that rippling mass of copper-red which fell around her pale face and way down to the swell of her tight little arse. There would be more copper-red, of course, growing on her plump fanny, between her legs – Fay's own little forest fire. And husband Tom knew all about that; he had burned his fingers there often enough.

Zak's eyes grew dark and far away as a spiteful thought, a child's thought, seeped into his mind, but abruptly this was swept away by his climax which was beginning to beat feverishly on his resistance. Even as his penis went through its convulsions his eyes were still on the window, but the light had changed and he thought he saw a face take shape in the glass and a voice from the deeper ranges of his mind told him it was a face he should know. A little dread crawled up his spine. Fear, bewilderment and shame moved within him followed by a terrible aching sadness far too deep for tears; but the face was gone.

And now he wanted Jessica like a child might want its mother. His eyes shifted miserably to the head and the lips that were eagerly feeding on him. He flinched inwardly. Oh, more than anything he had ever wanted in his aimless beshitted life he wanted Jessica. Zak shuddered, sighed dreadfully and jammed himself into the avid greedy mouth. To end it.

6

It felt almost cool at this time of the morning and the world seemed a serene silent place, the garden less care-worn, but later the sun would climb right up and fall on everything, and the hot light would bounce back in shimmering waves of the never-ending heat; as if the south of England had become the strange annex of some East African savannah. Jessica scoured the sky and thought that it would not seem out of place to see a spiral of soaring vultures circling far above her.

'It must rain soon,' she pleaded impatiently. 'This is crazy.' She stood at an open window savouring the quiet and not wanting, somehow, to go downstairs and face Tom who was making breakfast. Tom never made breakfast.

She looked across to the other side of the Crescent, following its elegant curve to the spot she wanted, where Zak would still be sleeping. Those enigmatic eyes would be closed and his beautiful eyelashes, long and thick and black, would be lying against his skin as he slept, accentuating every silky hair, every curve. If she knew exactly where he lived she would find him and tell him not to come and sit for the portrait this morning, not with Tom around.

She could hear her husband crashing about in the kitchen, and he was whistling. Tom didn't whistle, either. They were playing their designated roles, but it was all a painful sham, and even after the 'reconciliation' of last night they had

189

slept in separate beds; Tom, dutifully contrite and shamed, in the guest room and she in their own bed, with the still un-changed sheets which had draped her and Zak in their love-making only a day before.

'More tea?' Tom asked and so cordially she felt herself wince.

'No, thanks.'

'I thought I might not go into the office today.'

'Not at all?' she exclaimed. 'I thought that you might not go in this morning, but perhaps later . . .'

He shook his head and pointed at his face. 'With this monstrosity? Linda will think I walked into an unexploded bomb.'

Jessica met his eyes. 'Perhaps you did.'

'Oh, come on, Jess,' he ventured. 'Truce.'

'For God's sake, Tom,' she said with exasperation, 'it's hardly that simple.'

He flushed. Then, 'It's as simple as you want to make it.'

'And if you go on talking like that, you'll make me very angry.'

'I didn't mean to sound glib.'

'It seems you haven't meant a lot of things – being faithful,' she paused, 'and being unfaithful.'

'Smart, Jess,' he countered, 'but not clever.'

'Don't you think I have the right, Tom?' She felt furious. 'Or am I making a silly fuss over some trifling misdemeanour?' Her eyes blazed. 'Let's forget it, shall we? Let's brush it all under the carpet and pretend it never happened and we can go on just like before. Isn't that what you want?'

'You know that's not what I meant.'

'I don't know what the hell you mean any more, Tom.'

'We went through all this last night.'

'So we don't have to talk about it any longer?'

'Of course not.' He raised his eyes heavenward. 'One affair, Jess, just one,' he swept an agitated hand back through his hair, 'Christ, you'd think I did this sort of thing on a regular basis.'

'And how do I know that you don't?

'For God's sake.'

'I trusted you, Tom,' she said quietly, 'I really did.' And it was all gone. She found herself looking back at him through a blur of hot, hateful tears.

'Jess . . .'

He got up and came round the breakfast table, put his hand on her shoulder, but she flinched away and he was shocked by the expression of disgust he saw on her face.

'Okay,' he offered desperately, 'okay. Sorry, sorry. I didn't mean . . .' He backed off, plunged his hands into his pockets. 'We'll take things one step at a time. Just tell me what I have to do.'

She closed her eyes, took a deep breath and then opened them again.

'How on earth can I tell you what to do? What magical spell am I supposed to weave to make it all all right for you?' She looked back at him full in the eyes. 'Or for me?'

He gazed at her bleakly, in an agony of futile remorse and his heart began to thud nastily as a picture of Fay crawled into his mind.

'God, I'm sorry, Jess. So sorry.'

He sat down again and they fell silent.

'I just thought that . . .' he began again, 'well, that today we might let things sink in a little.'

'I had plenty of time to let things sink in before you

finally admitted what you'd been up to and, believe me, it wasn't very pleasant.'

'I know,' he said, his voice heavy with trepidation, 'and I've hurt you very much . . . And I'm sorry, more sorry than you can know.'

'Don't keep saying that.'

Words. She turned her head and stared at the sky outside the window so she would not have to look at him.

'But it really was the one and only time I've ever betrayed you.' God, he hated that word and, as if in muted agreement, his face began to throb horribly and he closed his eyes for an instant. 'You do believe that now, don't you?'

'I don't know what to believe,' she felt an immense lassitude descend on her, 'and I'm too tired to talk about it any more; I didn't sleep much last night.' She glanced at the kitchen clock. 'The surgery opened over twenty minutes ago; don't you think you'd better see Dr Landey about some antibiotics before your . . .' she paused, feeling faintly disgusted, '. . . your injury gets any worse?'

Jessica was right, of course, but he didn't want to leave her like this, not with so much said and unsaid, and this huge gulf lying between them, like the bloody Grand Canyon. So he hovered uncertainly on the other side of the breakfast table, wanting to leave, yet wanting to stay at the same time.

'Just go, Tom.'

He stared at her, trying to calm himself, felt the throbbing in his face go up five hundred notches.

'I'll be as quick as I can.'

'Don't rush on my account.'

'Jess,' he said despairingly, 'for God's sake.'

She wanted to scream at him or say something harsh and fatal and her mind was busy going over every cruel response she knew, but finally she gave them all up in helplessness.

'Just go, Tom.'

When she was sure that he had gone, Jessica stood up and went to the window, saw the empty space where his car had been and felt like weeping. Instead she flung a wet dishcloth half-heartedly against a wall where it clung feebly for a moment before sliding harmlessly down the blue and white Victorian tiles Tom had acquired at a knock-down price somewhere. A long time ago.

'You stupid bastard, Tom.' She picked up the cloth and threw it into the sink as tears cascaded down her cheeks. 'You stupid weak, thoughtless bastard.'

She sniffed and swung round, her eyes dully flitting over the breakfast things, and walked out of the kitchen, drawn to the only thing she wanted to do which might save her from herself.

Zak's picture was still leaning against the wall, just inside the patio door where she had left it, and it *was* good she realised as she surveyed it again, better than anything she had done in years. She stepped outside and wished Zak there without really thinking about what she was doing. Wanted him suddenly and with frightening intensity. She snapped her mind on the thought because it was hopeless, had to be, after all – what was he, twenty-three? Twenty-four? Which made her almost eleven years older. Ridiculous. And she was married.

Not something, perhaps, other people would allow to stand in their way, but she had always believed in all that old-fashioned stuff about the sanctity of marriage, 'for better, for worse': those heavy meaningful vows – otherwise what the hell was the point?

But where had Tom's vows been when he was busy with his nymphet? She squeezed her eyes tight shut as she imagined him making love to someone else – this other woman, his mistress, or 'tart' as no doubt Roz would have it. She swallowed hard and tried to switch her attention to the portrait, placing it back on the easel and stepping back to scrutinise it carefully, but at the same time desperately trying to overcome the desire to know the identity of *her*, the woman who had claimed her husband and perhaps wrecked their marriage.

And Tom would never tell; from his point of view that would be like sticking his head in a gas oven. Emotional suicide. Jessica sighed, looked back at Zak's black and white eyes. He would come soon, and she could have a little peace for a while because he could do that for her, make her see straight, calm her down; but what then?

In the cold light of day she knew she did not want Tom to leave and if that were so, she would have to try to make a go of it – give him the benefit of the doubt that his fling had, indeed, begun 'in a weak moment' (as her own had done?), but she wouldn't tell him that, not yet. In her heart she still wondered if there were not some truth in what Tom had said about how her need for a baby had somehow set the scene for his infidelity. How very convenient. And was that her bloody fault?

She felt outrage and anger begin to grow again and she bit her lip, slamming her sketching chair down beside the easel and then stopping abruptly, swept by a swift and appalling wave of desire as she saw Zak's familiar shape moving towards her across the garden. She wheeled round and went back into the house and then jumped with a small squeal as the cockatoo squawked and shrieked in protest because she had not yet fed him, or even given him his shower. There was a small mirror hanging in the downstairs cloakroom and she darted a glance at herself.

'God . . . I look awful.'

Jessica took a deep gulp of air and made her way to the kitchen where she splashed her face with cold water, drank a glass and then filled up the plastic squeezy bottle which she had adapted for the bird's needs before picking up the cage and carrying it out into the garden. She could shower him there; he liked being outside and it would give her a few moments to pull herself together. On the way out she grabbed at the straw hat hanging on a coat peg and clamped it on her head in the hope that it would throw a shadow over her face, hiding the red splodges left by her crying, the red nose, the tired eyes.

'Your nameless bird should have a sun-hat as well . . .'

Zak was already seated, watching her, and her stomach leapt despite all the sensible things she had told herself, that prissy little lecture on the sanctity of marriage. God, she was going mad.

'I'll put him under my pear tree,' she said quickly, 'what's left of it.'

They both glanced at the mass of wiry stalks and the few leaves which still remained unwithered.

'It hardly flowered,' she said, 'and no fruit, of course.' She shot a wrathful look at the sky. 'Damn this weather.'

'It will rain soon.'

'You sound so sure.'

'I am.'

'How?'

Zak tapped the side of his nose and looked at her from beneath half-closed lids. 'My secret.'

Jessica smiled despite herself, caught by his good humour, felt something inside her relax and some of the tension drain away. He will understand when I tell him, she told herself; he won't make it difficult. She began spraying the cockatoo, aware that Zak's eyes were on her as she turned her back, as her nerves began to fray all over again.

'How's your husband?' He saw how she stiffened at his question, clenched his knuckles as he remembered their embrace – not a lovers' embrace, he protested silently, more, surely, a thing of comfort?

'He's at the doctor's getting some antibiotics,' she said quietly. 'He had a little accident while he was away.' Her hand was squeezing the bottle too hard; a jet of water passed right through the cage to the other side.

'Are *you* all right?'

'I suppose so,' she said, then shook her head a little wildly. 'I don't know, Zak.'

He stood up and came towards her, took the spray from her and placed his hands on her upper arms. They were bare and warm and soft, he could feel the blood pulsing through her.

'Don't,' she began haltingly, 'please.'

'But you want me to touch you.'

'Oh, Zak.'

'Look at me.'

She turned and looked into his face, felt her knees grow weak. 'I'm trying to sort things out,' she said lamely, 'between Tom and me.' The words came out in a rush and were followed by a thick difficult silence.

'You want me to go?' His hands were still on her arms. Jessica's face was a study in misery.

'Tell me,' he said.

She shook her head and he could only look at her; the sun beating down on his back like a stick.

'I can't.'

His hands still rested on her arms, his fingertips tracing lightly across her skin, and he could feel the drive and the fear, the advance and retreat; the longing.

'Well,' he said, 'we'll work then.'

Zak let her go, moved away and sat down again.

Jessica stood very still, her eyes following him as he walked back to his seat. She tried to sort out her feelings into words, but clamped her mouth shut because she was not sure she could trust herself to say the right things in the right way. She was not even sure that she wanted to say them. There was a part of her which knew that if he touched her again she could not turn away.

She came across to the easel and slumped into her chair and just looked at him.

'I can't tell you what to do, Jessica.'

'I know that.'

'He wants you back.'

'I don't think he feels that he ever really lost me.' That irritated, too.

'And you?' But he knew that already, knew what was in her mind.

She looked down at her hands, then forced herself to match his stare. 'I have to try, Zak,' but her voice sounded oddly uncertain.

The phrase grated on his mind, nauseated him.

'He's told you everything, I suppose,' he said. 'Confessed.'

Jessica blushed. 'Not exactly.'

Of course not. There would be no going back for puling husband if Jessica knew about him and her sweet little sister. That would be termination time for Tom: curtains, finito, *the end*, old chap . . .

A door slammed somewhere inside the house and Jessica jumped, her eyes widening in alarm.

'It's Tom,' she said, 'he's back already.'

Zak shrugged. 'It's okay, Jessica,' he said calmly, 'we're working, aren't we?' He could hear the footfalls falter, once, twice, then come towards them, sensed the panic in Tom's racing steps when he realised his wife was not in the house, heard the barely concealed sigh of relief as he stood in the doorway surveying them.

Close up, Tom was taller than Zak had expected, broad-shouldered, well-preserved. He carried a jacket, flung casually over one shoulder like one of those slick sick-making dudes he had seen in the magazines. A handsome prat, a real poseur.

'Hi,' Tom said awkwardly. 'Hard at it, I see.'

'Did you get your antibiotics?' Jessica asked, then wished she hadn't because she wondered whether she sounded like some fussing mother-hen of a wife, pampering him too much – the old Jessica.

'Oh, yes,' he held up a small brown bottle and rattled it with forced jollity.

Tom crossed the patio and stood behind his wife, placed his jacket possessively over the back of Jessica's chair and glanced at the portrait, then at Zak, smiling back at him uneasily. He tapped Jessica on the shoulder, made her look up at him.

'When will you finish?'

'I'll finish the sketch in a few days,' she said carefully. 'Then I'll start the painting.' She shot a look at Zak.

'Probably won't need your . . . um . . . male model, then, I suppose.'

'Actually, I will,' she said, 'and I think you mean Zak.'

'Sorry,' he gushed, 'yes, of course, Zak.' His eyes swept, whiplash quick, over the boy.

Zak's eyes narrowed and grew watchful. Sorry, he says, in his gratingly 'proper' accent. He thinks I'm garbage. He thinks I'm the dog turd he steps over in the street. He thinks he knows, unlike his wife, what I am because his pretty blue eyes have told him everything – assessing and costing up my worth as if I were one of his precious fucking antiques.

Tom's eyes darted away from the boy who was making him feel so oddly uncomfortable and settled on the cage and the cockatoo.

'Bird's looking well,' he said.

Jessica sighed, willing him to go and take this strained awful atmosphere with him.

Tom meandered over to the cage.

'It's still nameless, I take it?'

'Yes.'

He scratched his chin, aping thought. 'How about Cleo – or Mildred?'

'It's a he, Tom.'

'Oh, God,' he stammered, 'yes, of course.' Could he say nothing right? And in front of this boy; he cringed inwardly. 'Well, let me think . . .'

'You don't have to do this now, Tom.'

He stared meaningfully at her. 'Yes, I do, because I should have done it before.'

She opened her mouth to speak, then closed it again. Let him do it now and get it over with if he thinks it might make any difference.

'George,' he said triumphantly, 'after the Prince Regent.' He bent down and peered between the bars.

Zak was gazing hard at Jessica's husband, indignation burning in his breast, but the corners of his mouth began to turn slightly upwards in a sardonic smile as a spiteful thought came into his mind.

The cockatoo was sitting, unmoving, on its perch and staring at Tom; its flat beady eyes had melted down to fine black points which looked almost as sharp as the bird's exquisitely curved beak.

Tom's face was perhaps half an inch away from the bars of the cage, he could smell the close musty aroma of seed and feather and bird excrement.

Zak took a deep breath and felt the hot ripe air of that sun-filled day hit the back of his throat.

Tom found his vision swimming slightly, felt a little sick as the bird inched closer, looking at him sideways through one eye.

Zak clenched his fists, there was a glazed look on his face, but inside there was soundless laughter, a sort of dark hilarity.

The bird had stopped moving and now its beady black eyes seemed to lock gazes with the human watching it, sent a tremor through the man called Tom as if he were impaled there, as if he were caught, by something outside himself.

The bird flashed forward in a blur of feathers, beak and claws. Jessica gave a little scream and her arm shot out towards her husband, as if she had sensed a moment before it happened what the bird intended.

The cockatoo's finely honed beak slashed through the flimsy white gauze on Tom's cheek like a sharpened blade; it even slashed through Tom's damaged flesh with relative ease, tearing a piece away and leaving an almost perfect triangle of pink mutilated flesh dangling from his face.

Automatically Tom's hands flew upwards to shield himself as pain ripped through his cheek, his face and seemed to shoot through to his brain and explode there. So excruciating was his agony that he did not even cry out, instead he sank to his knees gasping and retching.

'Tom . . . oh, God . . .' Jessica knelt beside him, put her arm around his shoulders as a small river of blood began to ooze through Tom's fingers. She looked up at the cockatoo with something close to horror and then clamped her eyes shut on the bird with a wild guilt. She hadn't fed him, she had forgotten; maybe if she had, maybe if she had . . .

Zak was standing up, watching them both.

'Shall I call a doctor?' he asked.

Jonathan was different, Emma realised – happier. True, business couldn't be better and their relationship had improved, but even so . . . She looked at him sitting across from her, the sun was shining through the back window and a beam of mote-filled light was falling down on his blond head as he scanned a column of figures relating to their engagement party (no expense spared now, she could hardly believe it). At this point her mouth tilted upwards into a dreamy smile. And on Saturday, he had promised, they would buy a ring, *the* ring, which would replace the cheap dress ring she always wore on that finger, as if she were ashamed in some way that it was still officially unadorned.

She glanced from the offending finger back to her almost-fiancé. The shaft of light had got brighter, she thought, and made him look boyish, almost angelic, but what her eyes would not see was the weakness in his mouth and the fineness of his facial bones which were, it must be said, rather too fine.

It only struck her that perhaps he seemed happier because he had finally come to a real decision about making a future together. Even their sex life seemed better, or at least was happening more frequently, although she had resigned herself to accepting Jonathan's limitations; he had never been exactly highly-sexed, in fact (she sighed inwardly) his libido would probably score a poor five on a ratio of one to ten. But you couldn't have everything and he had finally come round to her way of thinking. Granted it had taken a little pushing on her part, her dreamy smile faded a little here, but he had seen sense in the end.

Jonathan stood up, caught her smiling at him and gave her a broad grin. He had beautiful teeth. He walked over to the window and looked out into the garden, something which had become a habit just lately.

'I think I'll take a breath of fresh air,' he called over his shoulder.

'Fine,' she responded, 'I'll put the kettle on and we'll have a coffee when you get back.'

He nodded and then made his way outside to the still neglected garden where he stood for a long moment.

Emma watched him stretch, watched his shoulders rise and fall and for no apparent reason was reminded of that odd night at her parents' house when he had behaved so strangely. There had been no doubting his libido then; Jonathan had seemed like a different person – a different lover. But she wouldn't think about that. The dreamy smile faltered and died and she frowned, unable to comprehend this mystery, and walked into the kitchen.

Jonathan had seen Zak from the safe environs of his office. The squatter was walking back towards the house from the other side of the communal garden, from the same direction they had met that first time, and he wondered where he had been. What did he do with himself day after day? How on earth did he spend all that time alone? He watched the boy draw closer and lit up a cigarette; his hands were trembling.

Zak pushed open the gate and began wading through the long grass and the weeds of his precious landlord's property; he could feel Jonathan's eyes upon him and he did not look up.

'Hi,' Jonathan said.

One simple word, a word that, for Jonathan, said so much, so many things.

'I said "hi".'

'Hi.'

Zak was almost at the top of the mouldering steps now. He wanted his room, he wanted peace, he wanted to think. What he didn't want was Precious Prince.

'Is that it?'

Zak stopped abruptly and looked at him from the corner of his eye.

'Yeah,' he said, 'that's it.'

'I thought . . .' Jonathan's heart was knocking frantically. 'I thought . . .'

'What?' Zak snapped.

Jonathan looked quickly back, over his shoulder.

'Well,' he said uncertainly, 'the other night . . .'

Zak rolled his eyes heavenward. 'That was then. This is now.'

'What's that supposed to mean?'

'Whatever you like.'

'That's no answer.'

'I don't have to give you any answers.'

Jonathan's eyes widened in disbelief.

'Yes, you bloody do.'

Zak cocked his head back and looked at the sky. 'Not now. Okay?'

'Not now . . .' Jonathan repeated numbly.

Zak shook his head. 'Exactly. Just leave it.'

Jonathan took a step towards him. 'Who the hell do you think you are?'

Zak turned to look at him. 'Me?' He pressed a finger against his chest, the leather of his waistcoat was burning and sweat was pouring down his back in a steady trickle. 'I'm nothing, man,' but it was not he who was nothing, it was not he who had got down on his knees and begged.

Jonathan stopped and stared at him, his face a mixture of sullenness and stupidity.

'I thought . . .' he began again.

'I know what you thought,' Zak said, 'but I'm tired. Okay?' He set his foot on the top step, to move away. Christ, it was hot. Hot. If he could only find a shower, let the water run down and over and over and over . . . He thought of the sea, only a walk away, and promised himself a visit: to float and swim and submerge himself in the great blue animal.

'When?' Jonathan couldn't help himself. He was desperate. His gaze came to rest on Zak's hair for a moment; it was tied back in a thick black pony-tail and trailed halfway down his back. His fingers itched to reach out and set it free, feel it, crush it, wallow in it. He was hardening now, just by looking at him.

Zak felt a sense of weariness overtake him.

'When?' Jonathan pleaded.

'I don't know.'

'But you . . .'

'I didn't *do* anything,' Zak said tiredly, 'it just happened.'

'No.'

Zak's eyes shifted slowly until he was looking directly at the tall blond young man.

'Yes,' he answered coldly, precisely, 'that's just the way it was.'

Jonathan clenched his fists and stared up at the sky.

'You could have told me to go,' he said at last, but was

no longer able to meet Zak's unflinching stare. Instead he allowed his eyes to be drawn to a small garden spider which had spun its intricate web in the branches of the tree above their heads. He swallowed deep in his throat, loosened his collar. An insect buzzed through the torpid air, hovered by Jonathan's neck, and he brushed it away with a violent sweep of his arm.

'You were drunk,' Zak said flatly.

'And you weren't.'

'You're my landlord.'

Jonathan balked as if he had been slapped.

'Is that why,' he hissed, 'is that why you let me . . .?'

Zak shrugged.

'You cheap bastard.'

Zak looked back at him, full in the eyes, and said with chilling simplicity. 'You – came – to – me.'

'No.'

'For Christ's sake – stop giving your soul so much hassle, stop lying to yourself for once.' Zak jerked his thumb in the direction of the office, 'Stop lying to her.' Not that he really cared about Emma, but she had been good to him and he never forgot a kindness. Or a slight.

'Mind your own bloody business.'

'She suspects.'

'No.'

'She'll find out anyway, sooner or later,' Zak said softly. 'Particularly if you actually do go through with all this sweet crap about marriage.'

Jonathan's mouth was hanging open and his lips felt curiously cold.

'I said, mind your own business.'

'A little advice never does any harm, but usually people never take it; in fact, they usually go their own suicidal way and sod anyone else who happens to get in the way.' Zak glanced at the office.

'You wouldn't dare.'

'I told you, I don't need to.' Suck on that, he thought with an interior grin, and strolled down the steps without looking back.

Jonathan watched him walk away with a dull, half-questioning look on his face as the boy was swallowed by the shadows and the slam of the ancient brown door. A sick sheen of sweat broke out on his forehead and he felt his stomach begin to shrivel and fold in on itself as silent tears formed in the corners of his eyes.

Wanting his squatter as he had never wanted his Emma.

'What's he doing out there?' Keith asked. 'Seems to spend half his time admiring the view these days.'

'He wanted some fresh air.'

'Zak's there again.'

'Well, he does live downstairs.'

'They're arguing,' he said. 'Well, it looks like it from here.'

'I think Jonathan wants him to do something about the garden – you know, cut the grass, that sort of thing.'

'Fat chance.'

'Zak might.'

'Zak won't.'

'How do you know?'

'Not the type,' Keith said assuredly, 'he's sort of arrogant, don't you think?'

'I thought you liked him.'

'I do, as far as you can like someone you hardly know.'

Keith sauntered over to the window and peered through the glass. Jonathan was standing with his back to him, but

Keith could see the nervous movement of his arm as he pumped away at his cigarette.

'Must be smoking twenty a day, at least,' he murmured.

'What did you say?' Emma asked from the other side of the office.

'Nothing,' Keith replied, 'nothing important, anyway.'

He watched Zak turn away and disappear down the steps, saw how Jonathan stood there staring at the space where the squatter had stood and then he swung round and Keith was shocked by the contorted expression he saw on his face, an unenviable blend of misery and desolation.

'Keith,' Emma said, and when he did not respond she moved around her desk to come to the window. 'Keith?'

He jumped and twisted round as he heard her draw closer and she started at the sudden movement, at his look of astonishment, his large mouth hanging half-open.

'What is it?'

He forced a laugh and without really knowing why, quickly took her arm and steered her away from the window.

'What are you doing?'

'I want to look at the schedule for next week.'

'You already have a copy,' she said, her eyebrows drawing together in a frown. 'I gave you one yesterday.'

'Oh, yeah,' he said, feigning puzzlement, 'so you did.' Keith scratched his head. 'Must have been something else I wanted,' and he gave her a look of thorough sensuality and the large mouth, which moments before had been agape, now stretched into a wide cheesey grin.

'Don't be disgusting.'

'You love it, really.'

'Stop it, Keith.'

'Never.'

He began to move closer, inching towards her with great deliberation and then crouching down, arms dangling, in a bad imitation of a mating gorilla. He began thumping his chest and making whooping noises as he closed in.

'Don't be ridiculous,' her back was now against the filing cabinet, 'I'll scream.'

'Whoop . . . whoo . . . whoo . . .'

'I mean it.'

Keith stopped abruptly, tired of his little act and wondered why he was bothering.

'Christ, you're a waste of space, Emma. Do you know that?'

'And you're incredibly juvenile,' she said primly.

He sighed, suddenly bored. 'As Rhett Butler would say – "Frankly, my dear, I don't give a damn".'

He heard the door open and then close behind him and he wheeled round to see Jonathan walk back into the room.

'What's going on?' Jonathan snapped.

Keith examined his face sharply and saw no sign of the emotion that had so ravaged his features only minutes before.

'What the hell are you looking at?'

'I wish I knew.'

Maybe he had imagined it.

Fay had bought herself a pair of binoculars and she lay stretched out on the roof of her apartment looking through them. She had watched Zak walk from Jessica and Tom's across the communal garden and back to the house, and once he came inside the gate she could only hear his, and one other, muted voice because of the angle of the roof, and then silence. And she listened to the silence for a long time, staring unseeing into the empty garden until a small movement caught her eye and she saw Max run out from beneath a bush, tail erect, big square head pointed in the direction Zak had gone. The cat jumped on to the garden wall, coasted cautiously round the edges of the long grass and disappeared from view.

'Paying a call on the mouth-watering Zak, are we, Max?' Fay murmured. 'Lucky old you.' She sighed, turned over on to her back and closed her eyes. And Zak had been wearing that black leather waistcoat again, something which seemed to possess the ability of accentuating every muscle and contour of his beautiful and utterly desirable body.

Her eyes snapped open; but what had he been doing at Jessica and Tom's? He didn't know them – him, her – did he? For an instant her face held an ugly jealous expression, but then she was squinting in the sun as the searing light bore down on her unprotected eyes and flesh, and she recalled that unsettling remark Roz (what was her other name?) had made about her skin. Bitch.

Fay pulled on her robe with angry little movements of shoulders and arms, climbed down the skylight ladder and back into the apartment.

She stalked through to the part of her home which was the nucleus, the heartbeat, everything: bedroom, living-room and studio all in one – a massive high-vaulted room full of light and space. She stopped to study her unfinished canvas and wondered what it was about it that made it so different from anything she had done before.

Because it seemed so real?

She peered into a garden gone mad, and between the twisted limbs of trees and black-stemmed irises, toads and beetles squirmed in the mud of a stagnant pool. Through a tangle of brilliant green leaves a red squirrel watched, its face that of an emaciated old man; above and behind two thrushes perched, their beaks full of razor-sharp teeth. In the background she had painted a clearing in which stood a circle of standing-stones choked by dog-rose and bindweed and flooded by moonlight. She frowned, puzzled, because the standing-stones had been an afterthought and she didn't have afterthoughts.

Directly through the centre of the circle and into the hazy distance beyond, were rock-ridges and spurs and shadowy gullies, their sides slick with moisture and grey lichen turned silver under the moon. Tall ancient trees grew alongside with thick and fissured bark where woodland toadstools hung in clumps of sulphur-yellow.

There was still much definition to be done but, even so, the imagery was oddly tactile. It seemed to her that she should be able to reach in and touch it with her hands. Walk there.

She shrugged, inwardly dismissing the painting from her mind, turned round and looked across the room to the four-poster bed with its swathes of snow-white gauze sitting in the centre of the room like a stranded iceberg, cold and uninhabited. A shadow fell behind her eyes because there was no Tom now to warm the sheets and entertain her when she got bored. But he was out of order anyway, so to speak, and besides she didn't want him now. And even if she did, he would probably have a nervous breakdown if she made any more of her famous libidinous demands.

Fay turned round on her heels and stood in front of a huge mirror which was leaning, temporarily, against a wall, the heavy frame overloaded with gilded foliage through which mythical figures peeped – satyrs, centaurs, chimaeras. A very old mirror, Tom had told her, and worth quite a bit despite some damage where the odd leaf or branch had been clipped off, or a face worn right away to a featureless smudge. It had brought her luck, she was sure. Ever since she had discovered it in that flea market in Kemp Town everything had gone her way: her work, the flat, Tom, and there was no reason why things should not go on in exactly the same sort of way (modified here and there, of course). It was something Fay had always taken for granted – life treating her well, the lucky breaks, men, things, getting what she wanted.

She smiled back at her reflection and shrugged the robe from her shoulders, letting it drop to the varnished floorboards to run her hands down her body, studying herself, pinching flesh here and there, lifting her pert breasts and inspecting the outline of her bottom to ensure that everything was still as firm as it had been the day before, and the day before that. She was, she thought, perfectly formed and her delicate skin was, well, milk-white and with hardly a blemish. Stuff the short-lived glow of a sun-tan; particularly if it meant ending up like a wrinkled prune, and she had no intention of letting that happen, or witnessing her precious flesh begin to wobble and sag and dimple and go the way of those ghastly menopausal ladies she had seen revealing all on the beach. Oh, no.

She stretched and buried her hands in the rich mass of her hair, her skin goosefleshing with sensuous pleasure as she tugged at the roots.

What a pity not to live for ever. She could understand so well all those people, down through time, who had tried to discover the secret of immortality. And why not? Was there something so wrong in eternity, for just a hand-picked chosen few?

Her mouth puckered into a small, pretty frown as she

looked lovingly back at herself, but a reluctant vision stole into her mind: in ten, twenty years, what would she see?

Part of her protested – not to age and wither and shrink and die. She would do anything.

Fay felt an odd, vague anguish and a little shudder shook her as she stood there – so still and pale, almost sweet, like a life-size porcelain doll. Abruptly she shook off her disquieting thoughts and glared back at her reflection.

'You're doing a Tom,' she told herself sternly, 'and turning soft.'

Gradually her mouth began to tilt into a slow smile as she switched to the subject that mattered to her most and a strong image of Zak formed in her mind, an image and a host of furtive erotic thoughts that had been there all the time, lying in wait like a minefield.

'Where is he now?'

'Asleep.' Jessica's hold on the telephone visibly tightened and she glanced at the ceiling as if she might see through it and see Tom lying on his side, just as she had left him – knees curled up, one hand, childlike, raised to his torn cheek, a narrow trickle of saliva escaping from his partly open mouth.

'What are you going to do with the bird?' Roz closed her eyes for a second as she imagined, too vividly, the cockatoo tearing into Tom's poor face. 'Do you still intend to keep it?'

Jessica sighed. 'No. I'm taking it back to the breeders, probably some time this week. I don't think there's any other choice under the circumstances. Funnily enough, Tom hasn't said anything about it; actually, he hasn't said much at all, which is hardly surprising.'

'Have you any idea why it attacked him like that?'

'I hadn't fed it – perhaps that made it bad tempered.' She paused, rubbed at her temples, 'I meant to, of course . . .' But she had had other things on her mind, other thoughts.

'Did it do much damage?'

'Yes,' she said softly and was touched by pity. 'It did.' The left side of her husband's face looked as if it had been involved in a small explosion. Most of the top layer of skin had been sheared off, revealing raw lacerated flesh, and there was a hole big enough to take the top half of someone's thumb . . .

'Poor Tom.'

'Yes.'

Through the open drawing-room door she could see the cockatoo sitting serenely on its perch.

There had been blood on its beak and tiny flecks of ragged skin and pink matter hanging from and sticking to the white perfect feathers.

God.

For a strange illogical moment, it seemed that everything had begun when she brought the bird home and presented it to Tom on his birthday night, when all her carefully laid plans had gone so disastrously wrong – the night she wore no knickers and he hadn't even noticed. Funny; she had forgotten that idiotic, pathetic piece of useless information, had hoarded it away somewhere in the back of her addled brain. She felt a surge of despair and her mouth was suddenly full of the need to cry.

'Jess?'

'I'm so tired, Roz.'

'I expect you are,' she said firmly. 'You've had a shock too, you know, and more than one just recently.'

'I'll go and put my feet up and read a magazine or something.' Except that she couldn't imagine doing that – *relaxing*, being herself, being normal again.

'For God's sake, make yourself a strong cup of sweet tea and put a great slug of brandy in it.'

'Your recipe for everything.'

'Not everything, my dear,' Roz said wryly, 'but it helps. By the way, how's that boy?'

'That boy?' Oh, but she knew.

'Zak,' Roz said, 'isn't that his name?'

'Yes,' Jessica said, felt her heart pound. 'He's fine.'

'He's stunning.'

'Roz,' she said, 'not now.'

'I have to say that it seemed very clear to me that he wants rather more than his portrait painting.'

'Roz . . .'

'I *saw*, Jess.' In fact, she had never seen anything quite like it and could have sworn volts of electricity passed between them. And him. He was loaded with . . . charisma? Animal magnetism? Both those things. She surprised herself by a twinge of envy.

'It's just a crush.'

'Pull the other leg . . .' Roz said, and so calmly. 'I saw *you*, too.'

Everything they had wanted to say – everything they wanted – on their faces.

'Don't be silly,' Jessica said quickly, but in her mind's eye she could see him and there was her heart again, hammering away like a schoolgirl's heart.

'Go and have that brandy.'

Jessica sighed a little with relief. 'I'm going to do just that.'

'I haven't booked Champneys yet,' Roz said, 'but don't think you're going to wriggle out of it like you did the wine-tasting. Consider giving yourself an early Christmas present, for heaven's sake.' She paused. 'I am. Besides, you've damn well earned it.'

'Give me a couple of weeks to sort things out and we'll talk about dates. I promise.'

'All right, all right,' Roz said reluctantly. 'But bear in mind that we're just into October now and I'm talking about *this* year and not next.'

'Okay.'

'And if you change your mind about dinner tomorrow night, just call.'

'Okay. Thanks.'

'Give my best to Tom.'

'I will.'

'And Zak.'

'Goodbye, Roz.'

Zak. Jessica put the phone down and stood very still. what was she doing with her life? She didn't have the faintest idea. Her gaze fell again on the cockatoo and she felt a flicker of nausea, a sort of dizziness, and little beads of perspiration formed on her brow, the back of her neck, between her breasts. There was something about this heat, a sort of dangerous languor that seeped into everything, pushing change into the ordinary, the everyday things so that nothing seemed the same any more.

She closed the drawing-room door and stepped out on to the sunlit patio and stared at the garden still baking in the late afternoon sunshine. And the view was beginning to weary and depress her; it brought no comfort and no relief from her confusion and apathy; it conspired, like the endless scorching sunlight, to make things worse. The weather, like her life, was at odds with the normal scheme of things; strange and out of control.

Jessica paused by her easel and looked at the portrait,

traced the outline of the face gently with a fingertip. Wondered where he was, what he was doing.

It was a small fire, built inside the hollow made by some old bricks, and as it burned it painted moving shadows on the walls, the ceiling and dusted the windows with yellow light. Zak sat cross-legged before it making a carving out of a piece of wood he had found in the garden, and as he worked away no expression moved his features, no thought altered the dark, far away look in his eyes; only the light of the flames flickered with life, casting shapes against his face and making him appear waxen and illumined from within.

He sat there a long time until he heard the first footfall and slowly lifted his gaze to the open door. It wasn't Jonathan, this time; it was a woman – and it wasn't Jessica.

Fay stood watching him, her pale doll's face still as stone.

'I'm looking for my cat.'

'Your cat?' he responded quietly.

'Yes, she said. 'The big ginger tom.'

'He's been and gone.'

Her eyes were on him, eating-up his partial nakedness, the bare chest, the deep black of his hair tied back in a careless pony-tail, the mouth. Her lips felt very dry, but she would not allow herself to lick them. Instead she fixed a frozen little smile on her face.

'What are you doing?'

'I'm whittling, or carving – call it what you like.'

'What will it be?'

'Not sure,' he said. 'Sometimes I see a shape in the wood, sometimes the wood seems to shape itself. I just follow the lines and notches and wait for it to show me direction.'

She sat down opposite him.

'You make it sound as if it were alive.'

He looked back at her beneath half-closed lids. 'It is.'

She raised her eyebrows, but said nothing for a moment, then, 'Why do you live here?'

'Because I want to.'

'Actually, in a strange sort of way, I like it, too.'

'No, you don't.'

A flush entered her cheeks.

'Why shouldn't I?'

'Because it's a hovel and hovels aren't quite your thing, are they?'

She looked down at her hands, examined her fingernails. 'Sometimes,' she said slowly, 'things that you are not used to can seem fascinating.' Her eyes shifted to his face and rested there. 'Sometimes an extreme, any extreme, can seem intoxicating. Don't you think?'

'You mean you're bored.'

'Not exactly.'

'So your little affair is over, then?'

Her eyes widened with curiosity. 'How do you know?'

'I saw *him* – *you*– often.'

Fay threw her head back and laughed with delight. 'Tom would curl up and die if he knew.'

And he thought that, just then, she *was* lovely: her skin, her hair, the pretty lips (if rather smaller than he liked). It was the firelight, of course, working its magic, until you looked into her eyes and saw what was mirrored there.

'He's married, isn't he?'

'Tom? Of course,' she said matter of factly. 'That's half the fun.'

'But I'm not married.'

She smiled at him and said drily, 'Aren't we perceptive?' then shrugged, 'But you're different, that's why, sort of dangerous-looking.'

He longed to laugh.

'Isn't she your sister?'

'Who?'

But she knew.

'His wife.'

'Oh, you mean Jessica. Yes.'

'Doesn't that bother you?'

'No,' she said, 'We've never been very close.'

'A nice woman,' he said and looked into the flames.

'You know her?' she asked sharply and remembered how she had seen him come from Tom and Jessica's.

'A little.'

Fay felt her face burn with irrational jealousy.

'And?' she demanded.

'And nothing.'

She regarded him for a long moment. 'She's crazy to have kids, so crazy that she drove Tom to me . . .' she said meanly. 'It's sad really.'

He stared at her hard for an instant and her empty pitying smile faltered a bit. There was something in the way he was looking at her that she didn't quite like. He fell silent and switched his attention back to the piece of wood held in his hands, began to work away at it again.

Fay scrutinised him, felt growing irritation.

'Don't you like me?'

'I've never really thought about it.'

Her patience, at least what little Fay possessed, was fading fast. She wanted him, had wanted him, she thought, for what seemed a long time, and so she stood up and began to remove her clothes: a cotton skirt and silk vest; she wore nothing underneath.

'Look at me, damn you.'

Zak looked. Rossetti's Mariana. Except that sweet Mariana had not had an extra nipple, as far as he knew; a dubious honour belonging to the likes of Anne Boleyn who had not, in the end, for all her connivings, pleased old King Henry at all. Latterly she had been called 'a common stewed whore', 'a harlot' and, of course, 'a witch' – wasn't that what her extra nipple (as well as her extra finger) was supposed to denote?

His gaze fixed on the odd pink piece of flesh which was situated just beneath and to the right of Fay's left breast. Tom's hot open mouth had closed upon this teat with avid greed, many many times – she was telling him with her eyes.

'Well?'

'What do you want me to say?'

'Isn't that rather a stupid question?'

He shook his head and smiled, and once more began whittling away at the wood.

She stalked around the fire and stood behind him; he could feel her wanting coming off her in waves, smelt her sex smell like a dog might pick up that of a bitch on heat. She was breathing very heavily.

'Fuck me,' she said.

He snorted softly with contempt. 'You don't want to fuck, not really, that's just the beginning for someone like you. You want to play at pain; you want the thrill of torment because fucking holds no wonder for you any more.'

She crouched down, placed her hands on his bare shoulders, ran her nails down his back and whispered against his ear, 'As if you had read my mind. Amazing. You even make it sound poetic.'

I can do a lot more than that.

Zak brushed her away as if she were a bothersome fly and she lost balance, falling back on her shapely bottom with a small squeezed cry.

'Why did you do that?' she asked petulantly.

'Because you were touching me.'

'Don't you like that?'

'No.'

'Liar.'

And a little of him was lying, a little of him was drawn by the dark chemistry of revulsion and desire, just as he ·had been drawn by Jonathan. All his life it had been like this for him – destined to be a sensual spur to all he met, male or female, and the trouble was, when it really came to the crunch, he couldn't resist the sex (or a tantalising taste) and sometimes he hated himself for it.

He heard her move behind him, went to turn his head when a flash of pain seared his naked back.

Zak steadied himself, then shifted from his sitting position to a standing one. For a long moment he only stared at her, at the rod she held in her hand, a bamboo rod he had found and planned on burning, along with all the other twigs and sticks and dead ends of trees.

'Give it to me.'

'Why should I?'

'Because I shall give it back to you.'

Fay's face was sharp and her eyes glinted, but she smiled sweetly.

'Once more.'

He sighed and turned around; felt more than heard her arm draw back and the whistle-hiss of the rod as it came down again, but Zak barely flinched.

'Give it to me,' he said. And she did. He picked up several long twigs and put them together until they formed a long narrow bundle. 'It should be birch: a rod made for punishment.'

He wondered about her vocabulary of pain, whether she knew about bruising and bleeding – how to make shallow little cuts that bled for a long time; and the pressure points: those sensitive spots which hid in the dark places on the body. Places to touch and press and twist and make scream.

She thought she knew it all, and she knew nothing.

Fay laughed softly. 'I knew it,' she said gleefully, 'I knew I wasn't wrong about you.' She came up close and pressed herself against him, tried to invade his mouth with her tongue, tried to kiss, but he turned his head away so that her lips only found the hollow of his neck.

'Bastard.'

He said nothing. Kissing was not part of the performance; it was too intimate, too close, and he had always understood why prostitutes, too, refused to include it in their repertoire. Something had to be saved and savoured, some mystery left untainted.

Not part of the deal, folks.

Not for this prize bitch.

She removed his jeans so quickly it almost made him smile and her hands and fingers rubbed and probed and grew very busy in making him hard and ready and big.

The bigger the better for the shrew.

And then she bent over so that he would take her from behind.

Zak took the bundle into his fist and as he penetrated her he began to trail it across her back, her buttocks and as he thrust harder, so he brought the bundle down harder.

Flailing twisted branches on a blighted terrain.

He didn't want to do this.

Poking an open sore with a stick.

But a part of him did. Oh, yes.

Fay was whining and tossing her head, so that a red waterfall of hair brushed and spread and brushed and spread the grains of dirt, the dust, the dead insects on the patched linoleum floor. He reached forward and jerked her head back with a lock of hair so that she moaned and squirmed as strands pulled out and came into his hand. He could feel her little convulsions, the shivers shaking her milk-white body even as he secretly coiled the uprooted hair around his fingers.

He stopped abruptly, waited and watched until her shrew's face turned to look at him, and then he threw the bundle to the floor and withdrew.

'What the hell do you think you're doing?'

'I've finished.'

'No, you haven't.'

He made no answer and moved away from her. She was still on all fours, her alabaster backside pointing ludicrously at him as if it were begging for more. Which, of course, it was. He walked into the inner room and over to the big square sink in which he poured some bottled water and began to wash himself, all over. He felt obscurely dirty.

'How dare you,' she hissed at him from the doorway, her knees were black, 'how bloody dare you!'

He soaped his arms and chest, under his arms, threw water over his face, began to soap his thighs, his penis, under the foreskin, between his legs.

'I'm talking to you.'

He picked up another bottle of water, unscrewed the cap and poured it over his head, so that it cascaded all down his body and he shivered despite the heat.

She glared at him, aware of the implied insult in his meticulous washing.

'I said, I'm talking to you.'

'I heard.'

'Well?'

'I told you – I finished.'

She shook her head. 'No, you didn't.'

'As far as I'm concerned, I did.'

'You didn't come.'

'I didn't want to.' Not inside you.

'What about me?'

He shrugged. 'You got what you came here for – a little bit of pain.'

'That wasn't all and you know it.'

'I can't help that.'

He was drying himself now, throwing his mane of black hair over his head, which formed a curtain across his face so that she couldn't read his expression. Instead her eyes travelled over his nakedness and, even now, after what he had done, her mouth still watered with wanting and the wanting was an agony.

'This is part of it, isn't it?' she said quietly.

He looked up then. 'What is?'

'Part of the pain.'

'If you like.' He didn't care what she wanted to think or what devious dream she was weaving in her pretty depraved little head; he felt that it had nothing to do with him. He brushed past her and into the other room, pulled on his jeans, and all the time her eyes followed him.

'Where are you going?'

'Out.'

He slipped on the black leather waistcoat, tied his wet hair back in a pony-tail again.

'I'll wait.'

He wheeled around. 'No.'

'Yes.'

'I said no.'

She folded her arms and stood in sullen silence as he slipped some espadrilles on his feet and then bent down and proceeded to nudge over the bricks surrounding the dying embers and damp out the fire.

'Why not?'

'Just close the door behind you when you leave.'

He wanted Jessica, that's all he could think of as he distanced himself from Fay and the still, over-used air of the neglected basement. He wanted peace, he wanted rid of this dull sense of shame which was beginning to grow big in him.

It was night now and overhead a three-quarter moon spread its fragile light over the gardens. He felt cushioned and protected by the dark and as he walked across the dusty grass he hummed a little and his steps began to grow lighter. Night, he thought, is a time when things unfold, when memories are most vivid but least reliable, when people's inhibitions loosen and they are at their most vulnerable. A profitable time.

Zak moved away from the carefully laid gravel paths and through the covering of trees and stunted shrubbery until he came close to the house where Jessica was.

There was a light on at the top (where Tom would be) and another on the ground floor and as he drew near he saw her, through the glass pane of the patio door, walk from one room to the other. She was alone. Her hair was loose and she was wearing that robe again, the white cotton one she had worn that first time. The only time, his mind said.

As he climbed silently over the low garden wall, his eyes spotted Tom's jacket still resting on the back of her folding chair and he sighed softly with satisfaction. A gift. And he had thought this would be the most difficult part. Zak felt for the little nest of hair he had coiled so carefully around his fingers and pushed way down into his jeans' pocket, lifted it out: several long, long wavy strands of Pre-Raphaelite hair.

He stood over the chair, stroked the beautifully tailored jacket once, twice. Cashmere? He didn't even know what it was.

Two strands of red hair were laid strategically across the shoulders, another he caught up in the lapel, three down the back (just to make sure); they snagged on the fibres perfectly and even glistened in the pale-pearl light of the moon.

He stepped back and took a deep breath of night air and then walked towards the closed door of the house. He couldn't see her now, but she was still alone; puling Tom nursing his wounds in a room upstairs. Did she run up and down those richly carpeted stairs with hot drinks and toddies, cooling his fevered spoilt brow?

He knocked on the glass. Called her in his mind.

She appeared silhouetted against the glare of the kitchen light, he could see her legs through the thin material of her robe, the place where her thighs met her crotch, and then she was moving towards him, unbolting the door.

'You shouldn't have come.'

'I wanted to make sure you were okay', he said gently, 'and your husband.'

She glanced apprehensively upwards and then stepped out on to the patio, pulling the door almost closed behind her.

'I'm fine,' she said. 'Fine. And Tom will be all right in time.' A little plastic surgery, the doctor had said, and he would be as good as new, but somehow she doubted that. 'I've given him a strong sedative which should make him sleep.'

'Let's walk,' he said.

'I can't.'

'Just for a few minutes.'

She plucked at her robe. 'Not in this.'

'You look beautiful,' he said simply, 'and no one will realise even if they do see.'

She made no answer.

'Please, Jessica.' He took her hand and a delicious chill ran up her body, weakening her completely.

She followed him across the patio, down the stone steps and into the garden and away from the light. They walked slowly for a while and the only other sign of life they saw was a man walking his dog.

'More people used to use the garden,' she said absently, 'but now they don't seem to bother. It seems to have lost its charm for them.' She felt hot suddenly, damp all over, heard her voice prattling on. 'It's this damned heat, I suppose.'

Zak said nothing, neither the heat nor the garden was of any interest to him; he was only aware of the pump pump of blood pulsing through his veins. He steered her across the grass, towards the summer-house, stopped beneath the shadow of its crumbling rear wall where he pushed her gently up against it and began to kiss her lightly, teasingly.

'I shouldn't be here,' she said feebly.

'Oh, yes, you should.'

'I'm such a bloody fool.'

'Don't say anything.' He began to undo her robe, but she stiffened and he faltered.

'No.'

'Ssssh,' he responded and placed a finger over her lips. 'Trust me. It would be perfect, Jessica. The way it should be – on the earth, under the stars.'

He couldn't wait.

She swallowed hard as his hands found her breasts.

'No,' she breathed.

He looked back at her, shaken by lust and longing and yet not wanting to push her too fast. Time enough tomorrow, or the day after when Tom had gone.

'Then I'll just touch you,' he pressed, and his voice was a caress in itself: silky, benign, intoxicating. 'Nothing more. I promise,' he said patiently, but wondering how he could bear it.

Zak brought his hands up into her hair, down to her neck, circled it very slowly and then trailed his fingers across the top of her shoulders. Using one finger on each hand he traced two parallel lines over the curves and valleys of her moist, soft flesh.

'A woman should be soft,' he murmured, 'soft and warm and lovely.' He gave a long shuddering sigh. 'Like Jessica.'

'Oh, God . . . Zak.'

'Ssssh,' he whispered.

There was a gentle delight in all that he did, driven as he was to make her alone feel pleasure. As he looked into her face he thought her appeal was the sum of the faults – a sensuous mouth a touch too wide, a nose a touch too long and a jaw that was strong for a woman; and Jessica was sexy and Jessica was good. She was also respectable, middle class and financially secure. All the things he had always wanted, but never had. And other things, things he could not easily put into words.

She was what he wanted. And he would have her, wouldn't he, if everything went according to plan?

He kissed her more deeply, stroked and pressed, his fingers playing expertly and carefully as if he might wordlessly reassure her.

She placed her hands either side of his head, felt the dampness still in his fabulous hair and dragged it free of the pony-tail so it fell forward over his shoulders, on to her breasts and she cried out a little at the sensation.

When Jessica met his gaze she thought his deep eyes seemed touched somehow by regret and dreaming, and she was reminded of his impossible youth, because sometimes he seemed older, so much older than her.

A shadow fell across his face as if he had read her thoughts, and Zak's expression changed and now there was a look of deep sensuality, a sort of arrogance because inside he knew he could make her forget her doubts, her uncertainties – make her do exactly what he wanted.

He began to kiss and lick and rake a pathway down her body and her mind seemed to close, shutting out anything but the dizzying, indescribable pleasure.

She felt her will drain away even as a weak protest died on her lips. He brought her legs up around his neck, a small smile on his beautiful mouth.

'He it has found shall find therein,' he began softly, 'What none other knows . . .'

And then the beautiful mouth found her wet turgid sex; began to kiss and probe and nibble and torment.

And she thought she would go slowly, exquisitely, out of her mind.

Her robe had slipped way down her arms and she let it fall: let the air and the darkness and the night scents steal over her body, deepening the feeling of nakedness, an earthy primitive sensation which made her giddy. For an instant she looked down and saw a face silver with moonshine and black with shadow, a magical face, terrible in its beauty.

Blood pounded in her head and she felt her belly and thighs twitch and quiver as scalding delight began to burn its way through every vein and nerve and fibre. Felt the wriggling, darting arrow of his tongue reach up and up and up and she thought, this is not possible, not possible, and she opened her mouth to scream.

Zak took her hand as they walked back, interlocked his fingers with hers until they came within sight of the house.

'You'd better go,' she said quietly.

'Do you want me to sit for you tomorrow?'

'Yes.'

Zak smiled. Yet inside he ached for the coupling his body craved from her, and the aching wouldn't go away; it would stay with him until she rid herself of puling Tom, then she would let him in. And it would be all the sweeter for that.

'Don't forget the jacket,' he said.

Jessica frowned in puzzlement and followed the direction of his gaze.

'It's been sitting there all day,' he added. 'You shouldn't take a chance and leave it out any longer – it might rain.'

She was smiling and he liked it when he was able to make her smile.

'If only, Zak,' she said quietly, and lifted her eyes to the canopy of bright brittle stars as if wishing and hoping alone might bring about change; all the changes.

He waited in the shadows of the trees until the lights in the building had all been turned out, then retraced his steps back to the patio of the silent house.

Zak stroked the vacant easel fondly as he brushed past it to reach the window, then pressed his face up against the glass. Inside the darkened room he could see the white shape of the cockatoo, asleep on its perch.

Zak stood there a long time.

7

Fay felt as she had done when she was a little girl, and bad weather, or some other misfortune, had prevented her from savouring a treat like a party or a picnic and she would stamp her feet and cry with a child's shrill range.

Once Zak had left and gradually slow realisation dawned that he was not returning, at least not immediately, she had prowled, still naked, around the basement rooms like a sniffing animal, desperate to wreak revenge on his clothes and belongings for his humiliation of her, but all the time something stayed her itching hand because she still wanted him and the wanting was beginning to eat away at her with the hunger of an obsession.

Instead she scrabbled around until she found his store of candles and gained mean pleasure by lighting every one of them and placing them very precisely along the mantelshelf, the windowsills, the thick rim of the kitchen sink until the basement was lit up like a Christmas tree. Then she knelt down amongst the dust and the debris and consoled herself by going through his back-pack, his pockets, even his rolled-up sleeping-bag, flicking open his books and shaking them for any secrets; pulling out his few clothes and examining them disdainfully before stuffing them roughly back in his pack.

'Just a bum' she said meanly. 'Just a dead-head with big ideas.'

Except that the 'bum' had rejected and humiliated her in spectacular fashion.

It was a game, of course, and she liked games, only provided that she won them, naturally, but there was plenty of time. She stood up and looked about the shabby interior and wrinkled her nose in disgust. In a corner she spied an empty can which Zak had filled with water and into which he had placed some nondescript flowers. Fay longed to kick it over, crush the flowers underfoot, but did not dare, and then she saw the door, the hidden one, still half-concealed by pieces of yellowing wallpaper which lolled away from the doorframe like flaps of dead skin.

She pulled at the door in exactly the same way Zak had done, inserting her finger in the rough hole where a handle had once been, but, unlike Zak, she not only pulled, but pushed as she battled impatiently with the door and so was totally unprepared for the sudden ease with which it opened. Outwards.

Fay screamed in terror as its momentum carried her forwards – a big slack-jawed grin, stretching in the dark, and the dark embraced her in its noisome cloying warmth as she scrambled frantically for purchase. She managed to take the leading edge of the door between her knees and quickly realised that she had no choice but to 'ride' it as it swung away from the room behind her and into space.

Rusty hinges creaking, groaning, shrieking.

And she thought: it will break away and fall and I will fall with it.

Fay shot a horrified glance downwards. Please, God. Please, God. Please, God.

With agonising slowness the door swung back and she half-jumped, half-sank to the patched linoleum floor where

she sat hunched and breathless, covered in various kinds
of ancient dirt, cobwebs and a dusting of fine red spores.
God, the smell – rank, like rotting vegetables. She shivered
with disgust and revulsion, began slapping at her white
skin, slaking off the filth with nervous, trembling hands
and as she did so she saw that her knees and knuckles
were bleeding and the inside of her thighs had almost
been rubbed raw. In fact, she ached from head to foot.
In fact, all in all, it had been a completely unsatisfactory
and hideous evening.

And it was Zak's fault.

Fay rose to her knees and rubbed at her temples. She had
the distinct feeling that a headache was brewing somewhere
not so far away, like distant thunder. Brilliant.

She stood up, still a little unsteady, and stared at the door
for a long moment before kicking it hard with the flat of her
foot.

'Bastard.'

He had promised himself a swim, a skinny-dip in the dark,
when all the world was sleeping.

A romantic notion, because even as Zak approached the
sea-front, he realised that most of the world seemed wide
awake and still swarming around the ebbing night-life of the
Palace Pier. Abruptly he turned left and began to walk east,
away from the crowds and on to the beach. A few lovers,
arms entwined, strolled near the surf, gingerly avoiding
getting their feet wet, yet the sea was amazingly calm and
black, like a great slick of oil.

He walked on, past them, gradually leaving the noise and
the hubbub behind him and for a time the only sound he was
conscious of was the crunching of his feet on the stones. He
looked up towards the first promenade, the second and then

to the lights from car headlamps still racing along Marine Parade.

Zak tried to visualise the landscape as it once must have been, when the largest and most destructive invader had simply been the encroaching sea and not mankind.

Sometimes he wanted to wipe them all out with a great sweep of his arm. Sometimes he felt he shouldn't be *here* at all; sometimes he felt there was something running loose inside him, telling him he didn't belong.

Up ahead he saw a fire and the silhouettes of people around it drinking – and speeding – from the look of them. Rap music blared from somewhere and a man toasted bread over the flames; some of it had charred and Zak could taste its gritty burning smell on his tongue.

He gave them a wide berth and didn't stop walking until he had left them way behind. It was a long beach and the pebbles made his legs ache, but he kept walking, following the line of the little railway track which ran holiday-makers from one end of the beach to the other. 'Peter Pan' someone had said it was called – the railway line that never grew up. He had ridden on it once, sat next to the driver and caught a few rays from the open carriage as it creaked and wobbled its quaint way along the rim of the beach. Two years ago? Zak couldn't quite remember and his brow wrinkled up in puzzlement. Usually he remembered everything. Everything.

He stopped and rubbed his knuckles in his eye sockets, then sat down and for a long moment just stared ahead before beginning to strip off his clothes.

The water was warm and silky and mind-blowing: an all-over body massage. In the distance he saw a ship and way down the beach the lights of the town and the pier, and it was picture-postcard beautiful. He let himself float, lying in the water looking at the moon and the stars, lying in the water and thinking of Jessica and tomorrow, and tomorrow, and tomorrow.

He closed his eyes and when he opened them again the world had changed.

Zak blinked and jerked himself upright in the water.

There were no lights and there was no sound, except for the scraping of the sea on the shingle. There was no promenade, no pier, no concrete slabs of buildings, no windows, no cars, no road. Nothing moved, nothing was familiar. Zak was looking at an empty and uninhabited coastline. Above the beach there was a slope and above the slope was a dense forest of trees which swept up in a great black swathe to cover the surrounding hills.

And the moon shone down, flooding everything with its pale-pearl light as Zak's eyes widened with shock and disbelief.

He had never felt so much vast emptiness, never felt so small and alone, never seen anything quite so nakedly and purely beautiful.

And somewhere within that thick featureless landscape a wolf howled its mournful cry like an omen.

He started as way up on one of the hills something burst into flames. Further along the coast more flames leapt into being, tiny nests of fervent gold scintillating in the folds of darkness, and more and more, as if a message were being passed through the lighting of massive beacons so that they might be seen from a great distance. In the old way.

But this was a dream, wasn't it? A vision, or maybe some sort of psychic experience? Except that it seemed frighteningly real. And this was the past, wasn't it, not the future?

Such things had happened to him before, he explained to himself; but another, mocking, voice said, not ever like this, man, not *ever* like this. He felt suspended in space as if time had somehow slowed or stopped altogether.

Panic swept over him as a sudden and frightening thought flashed through his mind. What if this were real in some way? What if he couldn't get back? What if he were stuck here in this dark world of old mysteries for ever?

And out of the darkness came the dull thud of a drum beating, a measured dead sound which went on and on. Bug-eyed he stared at the great beacon on the hill and cold sour dread lapped over him.

Someone had died.

The beacon seemed to grow larger, more restless, and sparks soared into the air to dissolve in the black, star-hung sky, and Zak's gaze flinched as if he were watching some horror. He fought to control his breath as fear began to grow big in him and the fear to blossom into stark terror.

Uther, father mine; come to claim your shameless son.

He knew all this.

His head went back in silent agony as Jessica's face poured into his mind and he longed to weep.

In the filmy light of dawn Zak awoke on the pebble beach, face down, feeling cold and shaken. The sound of a car horn burst raucously into his exhausted brain, followed by the steady drone of traffic, and he rolled over on to his back and stared at a pale blue sky.

A dream, he told himself with relief, a fantasy – his secret self playing old tricks because that part of him knew things, could contemplate anything, imagine anything with unbelievable clarity.

Other lives beating on his brain?

Crap.

Way out, across the water, a lone seagull wheeled, cried and circled slowly in the sky, performing the same motion, crying the same cry, just as thousand upon thousand of its kind had done before it. As if life had not progressed at all, but only turned over and over on itself in a timeless, aimless cycle.

Zak shivered and began putting on his clothes.

Her fingers were shaking so much that Jessica found it difficult to keep the strands of copper hair in her hand. They were very long and silky, beautiful. Fay's hair.

'For God's sake,' Tom protested, 'I don't know how they got there!' And he didn't. How ironic that this time, of all times, he was actually telling the truth. As far as he could remember he hadn't worn that particular jacket recently, except for yesterday's visit to the quack and, besides, he had been meticulous in checking sordid little details like that whenever he had seen Fay. Meticulous; almost paranoid, in fact. He couldn't understand it.

'I should have known,' she said stonily. 'I just should have known.'

'Don't be ridiculous.'

'And you can stop that,' she said, 'it's a little late for playing games now.' Her eyes blazed. *'I know! All right?'*

He stared at her hopelessly, knew that his face was probably a much whiter shade than pale, he had felt the blood drain right down to his boots as soon as he had seen what she held in her hand. It was rather pointless, he decided wordlessly, to lie any longer and in a horrible strange sort of way, it was a relief.

'All right,' he said.

Jessica's mouth fell a little open as if, even now, she found it hard to believe that he had done this thing.

'And you said I didn't know her.' Her voice was quiet, but laced with icy contempt. 'You disgusting coward.'

'I know how it must seem . . .'

'Don't.' She clenched her fists and squeezed her eyes tight shut as if she would blot him out. 'Of all the women in the world you had to choose . . .'

'I didn't *choose* her.'

'What did you do, then?' Her voice was shrill now. 'Pick her name out of a bloody hat?'

'Okay,' he responded shakily, 'okay.'

'Why?'

He shook his head.

'You don't know?'

He said nothing.

'Was it sex?'

She thought of Fay and him together, Fay laughing because Fay would laugh; all the little talks they must have had after the sex and the love-making. Poor Jessica, poor pathetic good old Jessica.

'I want you to go.'

He made himself match her stare. 'Yes,' he said, 'I thought you'd say that.'

'Funny, really, Tom,' she said in a small voice, 'but I'd almost come to accept an affair, almost blamed myself, in an odd sort of way.' She looked back at him, all bewilderment and hurt. 'But not this.'

She took a deep gulp of air. 'You can stay the night, but that's all.' She could hardly bear the sight of him. 'I'm going out.'

'Where?'

'Does it matter?' she asked.

'You won't do anything . . .'

'. . . foolish?' Her eyebrows arched sardonically. 'Because of you? I don't think so, Tom.'

'Then, where . . .?'

'We're separating, Tom. Where I go and who I go with, is none of your business.'

Separating. The word struck him like a silent earthquake.

'Can't we . . .?'

'No.' Her eyes were drawn to his face and the damage there which could be seen more clearly now that the heavy bandage had been replaced by thin white gauze. 'Was it worth it, Tom?'

He watched her in appalled silence as she left the room.

For a long time he sat in an armchair staring into space. This is what it feels like, he told himself, when someone dies, when the roof of your life is blown off. He looked at his soft pampered hands, the carefully manicured nails, then let his gaze travel around the elegant room. And it *was* elegant if, he realised all at once, a little studied, a little too much like the aping of a stately home, its interior designed by one of those ghastly women with gratingly plummy accents. His fault.

It was Jessica who had given it the warmth it so badly needed, who had stopped him from entirely turning their home into a museum for his beloved glass and silver collections.

He got up and looked back at himself in the Regency mirror which hung so serenely above the fireplace (original, of course). Around him, like exhibits, were the 1820 Aubusson carpet, the Italian chandelier, screens signed Jacob Frères, the French Empire clock (which Jessica hated), gilt-handled fire irons. He glanced above his head at exquisitely stencilled walls and cornicing, the dado in *faux marbre* – panelled with *trompe-l'oeil* mouldings. Naturally. For a long moment Tom's stomach flickered ominously with nausea.

He wandered out to the hallway and down the passage into the kitchen. Jessica's domain. All wood and odd pots and strings of garlic; a sort of decorative disorder, cluttered with back editions of *Private Eye*, cookery books and an assorted array of exotic spice jars.

He wandered out again and hung miserably in the hall in a kind of daze before pushing open the dining-room door where the cage was and the cockatoo. He didn't know why he did this; he had no desire to see the bird (God, no), or the room. In fact, he had avoided it like the plague since the 'accident'.

In fact, the cage was empty.

Tom froze for a second and stared disbelievingly at the cage door which stood open. He hovered uncertainly on the threshold of the room, suddenly conscious of his fractured nerves and terminal fatigue, a heady mixture, now spiced-up by a juicy pinch of fear.

He brushed a shaking hand back through his hair and stepped into the room, flicking his eyes back and forth, up and down. In the bloody chandelier? Under the table? The bird was not there, and at that point he didn't know whether that was a good or a bad thing. In any event, he closed the door behind him and leaned against it before taking a deep breath and placing a hand protectively over his injured cheek.

Above him a group of flies buzzed and in the bird's cage more buzzed and settled and grew quiet as they went about their distasteful business.

Where was the damn bird? Where could it be?

Anywhere, a voice said in his head; the bird could be hiding anywhere in the house. But birds didn't *hide*, not in real life. It was frightened, lost. Wasn't it?

'Shit,' he said aloud, his voice cold and furious and scared all at the same time. 'What the hell is going on here?'

Tom waited until his pulse had stopped racing before venturing out into the hallway again and trying to gather his wits. He stood in a shaft of fading sunlight shining through the glass panel of the back door, feeling dull and stupid. Somewhere a rusty hinge creaked and he jumped, like a child who hears a noise in the dark, and he cursed himself for being such a baby.

His eyes travelled up the stairs, but he decided to return to the drawing-room to check that out first. And he found nothing. The bird (he wanted to call it George, but found that he couldn't) was not downstairs, he was certain of it. Tom looked gingerly back up the staircase and began to climb.

It was so quiet in the house it was almost eerie; he could even hear the squeak of his shoes on the carpet and, God, the pounding of his heart in his ears. The stairs coiled round at one point before straightening again and he could see the upper landing, the familiar sight of his framed Victorian cartoons running right along the wall. He frowned; one of them was out of alignment and when he reached the top step he automatically reached forward to tip it back into place.

Except the bird got there first.

With a shrill yelp Tom jumped back, but claw and beak had already made their purchase in the flesh of his lower arm and when he frantically tried to remove them with his free hand the bird flew into his face and this time Tom really did scream, whipping his head to one side so that claw and beak fell on his ear, his neck, but he was able to bring up both his hands and drag it, shrieking, away. Even when he held it, vice-like, in his trembling fingers it still jabbed and stabbed like a thing gone mad.

There was a flat cracking sound and then silence.

The bird's head lolled and Tom knew it was dead. He made an odd choking sound and abruptly let it fall to the floor as if he had been scalded, where it lay looking up at him with black accusing eyes. He made a comically large stride over it in order to get to the bathroom where his legs betrayed him as he tried to vomit, and as he fell to his knees he only succeeded in dry-retching, tearing his throat in the process with the useless effort.

When he had finished he put the loo seat down and slumped there, staring through the door at the little heap of feathers. His mind was grey and dulled and numb and he wanted a drink, badly.

Tom waited for a long time before trying to stand and then leaned weakly against the basin and considered his reflection. The bird had got his ear; there was no mark, but the lobe was swelling like a tomato.

With a great sigh he picked up a towel and walked slowly towards it. The bird was dead, he knew it was, yet the child in him almost expected it to revive instantaneously and lunge again for his face like some unspeakable ghoul from a latter-day horror film.

He scrutinised it carefully from a safe distance, found himself wondering why it had disliked him (because it had, must have . . .) – his birthday present: the only homicidal cockatoo in existence. He dropped the towel over its body with something like relief and swallowed deep in his throat, trying to push his weird thoughts away because he just didn't want to think about them, it, any more.

And what the hell would Jessica say? The ghastly question

flashed through his mind like a thunderbolt and he squeezed
his eyes tight shut in despair. Could he really say that he
had throttled the cockatoo in self-defence? And how had
it got out of its damned cage, anyway? She would say he
had done it, and on purpose.

And he wanted Jessica back. More than anything in
the world, he wanted her back.

He stared at the wall for what seemed a long time and slow
realisation dawned that the Victorian cartoon print was still
out of alignment and that there was an unmistakable scratch
in the silk wallpaper where George had left his mark. He
tilted the print carefully upwards with one shaking finger
and once it was back in place the scratch couldn't be seen.
Perhaps Jessica wouldn't notice and even if she did, she
would hardly think the cockatoo had been the culprit.

Tom gave a long shuddery sigh as nausea swept over him
again, suddenly conscious of the contact between his skin
and the material of his trousers in the area of his groin – it
was damp and clinging because he had wet himself.

'He said nothing?' Roz asked as she set coffee cups on a
tray.

'Not really,' Jessica said. 'In a way we'd said all there
was to be said.'

'I can't help feeling that Fay played a very big part in
all of this.' She was sure of it, in fact, and recalled the
Edinburgh trip, that smug look on Fay's lily-white face.

'I don't care,' Jessica said quietly. 'I can't forgive him.
How could I?'

'She was probably just using him. That's the sort of thing
she does, isn't it?'

'Oh, yes, but what difference does it make? He knew
right from wrong, he knew exactly what he was getting

into, despite the fact that he must have known how much it would hurt me.'

'How's the coffee?' It was Gordon.

Jessica turned her face away, as though it were bad manners to show her pain publicly.

Roz and Gordon exchanged glances over her head.

'Sorry,' he said, 'didn't mean to barge in.'

'It's okay,' Roz said, 'we're coming in now.' She looked back at him meaningfully, making a shooing gesture with her hand and he promptly disappeared.

Roz stared at the space where her husband had stood for a long moment and knew how lucky she was. Gordon was not perfect, but he would never deliberately hurt her, never let her down if he could help it. A big warm kind man who put up with her biting sarcasm and menopausal angst with amazing calmness and diplomacy. She wondered if she had told him lately.

'I shouldn't have come.'

'Don't be silly,' Roz snapped out of her thoughts. 'Besides, you were invited. Remember?'

'I know, but not like this.'

'Rodney and Suzy don't mind; they're hardly unworldly, after all.' She picked up the coffee tray. 'Perhaps if you do decide to divorce Tom, and that's a *big* "if", Jess, Rodney might handle your case; he's hot stuff, you know.' Ruthless was actually the word. An image of her ex-husband formed in her mind: Mark had hated Rodney by the time the divorce came through.

'There's no "if" about it, Roz.'

'All right, all right,' Roz said defensively. 'Just don't burn all your bridges yet, that's all.'

'I haven't burned anything, Roz. Tom's the one whose been busy doing that.'

'I'm sorry, I shouldn't have said that.'

'It's all right. Really.'

'Are you sleeping?'

'I have some pills.'

'Do they work?'

'Oh, yes,' she answered bitterly, 'I go out like a light.'

Roz looked at her friend and was reminded, unhappily, of herself. 'With Mark, I was on anti-depressants and tranquillisers – it's like serving time.' And she had been afraid to come off them because she thought that Black Depression would come back and gather her in its appalling cloak all over again.

'It will only be for a while.'

'I hope so, Jess.'

'I'm not the neurotic type. Remember?'

Roz sighed heavily. 'I don't mean to sound like a clucking mother hen, you know . . .' she glanced warily at Jessica. 'I can't believe all this, either – you always seemed so right together and Tom, he . . .' she thought of Fay and wondered what she was saying, why she was saying it. 'Oh, I don't know. It's such a bloody waste, that's all.'

Jessica made no answer, lingered a little as Roz took the tray into the other room. She wanted to cry. The bitterness of what had happened was beginning to sink in and she felt sick as well as tired. And how much she had wanted to know who it was, what little bit of stuff had claimed her husband. God, what a joke! Through her gathering tears she could see her sister's eyes, her little pointed chin, that small sure smile on her lips and, inevitably, her mind somersaulted back to their childhood; all those moments of anguish and confusion and treachery which only began to pale when her parents had split and they had separated into two camps. Remembering her sister's guile, her jealousies, her anger, the tantrums, that small sure smile; remembering.

Like she had told Tom, she should have known.

But she could not forgive him because he had known too and in the end that knowing had made no difference at all. Her husband had gone willingly into the spider's parlour, embraced the spider, even had sex with the spider.

How many times?

Was it better with her?

The pain seemed to grow worse; in a colder, uglier way.

'You will help, won't you, Zak?'

He looked wearily into Emma's pretty face, thought there was something curiously hygienic about it and realised she rather reminded him of Doris Day.

'I don't know the first thing about being a DJ.'

'If Keith lined up the music for you, all you'd have to do is put it on to play.'

'Even I know it's not that simple, Emma.'

'Oh, *please*', she whined. 'It would only be for an hour at the most.'

She moved past him into the basement rooms and began looking around. He sighed with irritation.

'Why can't Keith do it himself?'

'There's a gig on the same night as our party. We didn't plan it that way, it just happened, and Jonathan doesn't think it would be good for business to turn it down.'

'That figures,' Zak said drily, but Emma missed his little dig totally.

'We're starting later now, as it is.' She was examining the first room with careful scrutiny, focused on the windows. 'I could run up some curtains for you, if you like. It might make this place seem a bit more homely.'

'No thanks,' he said quickly. 'What about the boss?'

Her forehead buckled into a frown.

'Jonathan,' he prompted.

'Oh,' she said limply, 'yes, of course. I see what you mean, but he'll be busy with other things – the guests and so on.'

'Lucky old Jonathan.'

'Anyway, he's hopeless on that side of things, gets sort of tongue-tied,' she mused. 'He's not a practical person in the least, you know. In fact, he's useless with his hands.'

You wouldn't say that if you knew what I know, my dear. Zak raised his eyes heavenward.

'Why me? There must be other DJs on your books besides Keith who could manage to squeeze an hour in.'

'Of course, there are,' she said importantly, 'but they're all out that night on jobs – even the free-lancers. Weekends are the worst and they're always booked well in advance.'

'Have it during the week, then.'

'It wouldn't be the same,' she protested. 'Besides, all the invitations have gone out.' She sounded like a child of six.

At that moment he thought that perhaps Emma and Jonathan were ideally suited. Two dim-wits together.

'Why, if you must get engaged, do you have to have all this performance and ritual?' He hated ritual. 'All this expense and show? Why don't you just *do* it?'

'It's more fun this way.' Her gaze fell to the sapphire and diamond ring on her finger.

'And what if it all goes wrong? What if nothing comes of it, or you decide too late that you hate each other?'

'Why should we do that?' she said, hurt. 'We love each other.'

Love. He wanted to spit.

'You hardly know him.'

'What do you mean?' Her eyes gave him an odd look.

'What I say.'

'We've been together nearly *seven* years. I should know him by now.'

'People can live together for a lifetime and still not know each other.'

'I don't understand what you're getting at.'

This was none of his business, nothing to do with him.

'Forget it,' he said abruptly. 'Just forget it.'

There was a sad look of reproach on her face, as if she were asking him why he should want to say such strange things.

'When is the party?' he said at last.

'The last Saturday in October.'

'All Hallows' Eve.'

'Pardon?'

'Hallowe'en to you.'

'Oh yes,' she said vaguely and her eyebrows drew together in a frown. 'That won't mean bad luck, will it?'

Zak rubbed his forehead with the palm of his hand and succeeded in shielding his mouth from her gaze, because his lips were twitching at the edges as if he might smile. He shook his head in mild exasperation. 'I shouldn't think so, Emma.' And even if it did, what more bad luck could she have than marrying Jonathan, someone who couldn't, and didn't, love her? In fact, he doubted if Jonathan actually liked women at all; he was still too involved with the sex side of things to realise they were people as well.

'Will you do it, then?'

He felt sorry for her.

'Yes,' he said and instantly regretted it.

'Do what?'

Zak turned round and wondered how long his landlord

had been standing there in the open doorway and what he had heard.

'What are you doing down here, Emma?'

'Maybe she should ask the same thing about you.'

Jonathan's eyes flashed at Zak, they said – 'You mean shit, you bastard' and behind the cursing Zak could feel Jonathan's wanting coming off him in suffocating waves.

Meanwhile Emma blushed. 'I've asked Zak to stand in at our party for that hour Keith can't do.'

'Oh, really,' Jonathan said. There was a sneer in his voice. 'And does he have the relevant experience?'

'No, I don't as it happens,' Zak snapped back, 'so why don't you find some other poor fucker?'

'Hey, hold on,' Jonathan said quickly, placatingly, 'not so fast. It was just a question.' He caught hold of Zak's arm as he brushed passed. 'Don't go.'

Zak glanced behind him. Emma was dim, but she wasn't that dim. Instantly Jonathan let go of his arm and looked at his girlfriend; there was a strained smile on his face.

'We'd both like you to do it,' he said, 'wouldn't we, Emma?'

He kept smiling, his face was very white and Emma wondered whether he might be sickening for something.

'Oh, yes,' she piped up.

Jonathan found himself transfixed by her cow-like expression, felt a strange sensation of general despair, as if events were beginning, somehow, to overtake him.

'I don't know,' Zak said and in a voice that discouraged any further discourse. He stepped out of the basement and into the sunlight.

'Think about it, then,' Jonathan called after him, 'there's no rush,' and, as an afterthought, 'the money will be good.'

He watched the squatter walk away, moved to the window

where he continued watching him until Zak disappeared from view.

'What was he saying to you?' He spun round.

Emma stared at him blankly.

'You were talking . . .' he went on impatiently, 'before I came in.'

'Oh, yes,' she felt herself redden, 'about the disco.'

'No,' he said, 'there was more to it than that.'

'I can't remember,' she faltered, 'something about marriage, I think.'

'Whose marriage?' he snapped.

'Ours,' she said and wished she hadn't, 'anybody's.'

'Go on.'

'I don't know. I don't think he believes in it.'

'Is that all?'

She looked bewildered.

'Oh, never mind.' Jonathan shifted his gaze back to the window and the cracked sill where two flies were busy copulating. He recoiled instantly. 'What the hell are we doing standing around in this godforsaken hole, anyway?' He cast his eyes around the basement and wrinkled his nose in disgust. 'It stinks.' There was always that smell here, a moist rotten smell the source of which had evaded everyone, even the murky delvings of the local pest-control agency. And they had told him he must have 'a very sensitive nose'. Unbelievable. If anything were found when he finally got round to renovation, he would sue the bloody surveyor for negligence, that's what he would do.

'Let's get out of here.'

There was revulsion on Jonathan's face, but he knew with a sinking heart that he would be back, because he just couldn't help himself.

*   *   *

Zak was glad to leave them and their smothering talk behind him, and he had no desire to be dragged into their pre-nuptial celebrations, their balloon-infested farce which would all end in tears, anyway. Did smart-ass really think he could live two lives at the same time? Hadn't anyone told him yet that these were the 1990s and you could screw whatever gender took your fancy, when you fancied, where you fancied without breaking the law or losing your rep-u-tay-shun? Spoilt for choice, really – but DON'T FORGET THE CONDOMS, FOLKS!

And don't tell the girlfriend.

What a beautiful world.

A shadow momentarily dimmed Zak's eyes as he walked beneath the trees; but he was worse than Jonathan because he didn't care, he didn't care at all. In fact, he had never cared about anything or anyone in his whole life until now.

He would do their precious hour for them, but mainly because he needed the money and he sighed heavily, weary and exasperated by that side of his life. More than anything, money meant freedom from being shat upon.

So he would play out Hallowe'en for them, if that's what they wanted, but even as the thought took shape his mother's face formed in his head because she would damn him for that if she knew, for defiling one of her sacred Old God feast days, one of the 'Grand Sabbaths'. And for money, too. Oh, she would love him for that, all right.

Zak was surprised and irritated by a sudden stab of nostalgia. His mother's little tribe would probably be 'settled' in Wales by now, for the winter, Astra and her 'brew-crew' tucked away under a leafy wood somewhere, aping the hunter-gatherers of millennia she so admired – 'our ancient ancestors who (apparently) understood the chemistry of life in a more – not spiritual way because that word has really been abused – but more cosmically . . .'

He could hear her now.

After the winter she and the others would be on the move again because as far as his mother was concerned there was always something better waiting around the corner, but they would end up at Glastonbury, eventually, in time for the festival.

Zak faltered as he broke through the trees, as the memory of his weird 'vision' on the beach began to unspool in his mind, and somehow it brought back the leaving of the travellers and his mother when she had mouthed her threats and warnings so close to his ear that spittle had congealed on his skin – Astra's ugly prophecies told like a promise.

Crap, of course, and Astra was full of it.

But for some little time he stood there, head partially bowed, letting the sun beat down on his shoulders, doubting everything. When he lifted his head he saw with relief Jessica's house through a break in the trees and he ached towards her with a longing that was passionate and hot.

Everything would be all right now, he told himself. He could move in once her husband had packed his bags and left, and that would be soon, he had made sure of that.

'You bastard, Tom.'

'I didn't do anything, Jess,' he wailed.

'So it opened the cage door all by itself?'

'I didn't say that.'

'I'm glad you didn't, because it would make me appear more of a gullible fool than you already think I am.'

'I have never thought you gullible or a fool.'

'No?'

'Of course not.'

Jessica took a deep breath. 'What happened to the cockatoo, then? Where is he?'

Tom felt his face going hot. 'Look,' he spread out his hands in helplessness. 'Just after you left yesterday, I discovered the cage door open and the bird gone. That's all there is to it.' God, if only.

'Oh, come on. Do you really expect me to believe that? I'd respect you more if you just came out with it.'

'Came out with what?'

'That *you* let him go.'

'But I didn't.'

'There was no one else here, Tom.'

'Maybe you hadn't closed the cage door properly after you fed him.'

'After recent events, I more than made sure the cage door was closed. It snaps shut, actually.'

'I didn't let him out, Jess.'

She gave him a strange uncertain suspicious look. 'I don't believe you, Tom, and I think you did it out of spite.'

He screamed inwardly and stared out into the garden as his eyes found and focused upon the spot where he had buried George (having first bound him securely in an old Union Jack tea-towel).

What a fiasco that had turned out to be: all that fumbling around in the bushes, crouching in the dark and digging into sun-baked, hard-as-bloody-rock soil because he had been terrified simply to bundle it into the waste bin in case Jessica found it, which was unlikely, but he hadn't been prepared to take any more chances on his abysmal luck.

For a few mad moments he had contemplated telling her the truth, but how could he have put into words the fact that he had actually strangled the damn thing – something a day, a week, a month ago he would not have dreamed possible?

'I'm leaving anyway,' he said with a sigh. 'What difference does it make?'

'I suppose I thought that, even you, wouldn't sink as low as this.'

He had a sudden desire to weep hot tears of frustration.

'I could go on saying "I didn't do it" and you still wouldn't believe me, but what's the point?' He shook his head. 'And, really – why *would* I do it, for heaven's sake, since you could only blame me?'

'In a fit of anger, maybe . . .' she said quietly, 'People do strange things when they're under pressure.'

'Thank you for giving me the benefit of the doubt,' he responded bitterly.

She ignored his remark and walked over to the window.

'He will die out there,' she said, 'of starvation or thirst or both, and if not that, the other birds will probably gang up on him. They do that, don't they?'

'Don't count on it,' he brought a hand up to his injured cheek. 'That bird wouldn't have looked out of place wearing an SS uniform.'

He thought his little witticism might raise a ghost of a smile in the old Jessica, but no, his wife only shook her head, and so gravely that the action nearly brought a lump to his throat.

'His flare up was my fault, Tom; I hadn't fed him, remember? and I shall always be sorry for that and what he did to you because of it.'

'For God's sake, you shouldn't blame yourself,' he said;

'maybe he was just plain mean.' Bloody psychopathic would be more of an apt description. 'Besides, you're forgetting that he simply made worse the damage that had already been done.'

Sweet little Fay.

'I hadn't forgotten.' A faint distaste arose in her. 'How could I?'

'I didn't mean to start . . .'

'It doesn't matter.'

'It was over then, Jess,' he pleaded suddenly, desperately. 'She wouldn't let me go.'

'I don't want to hear about it.'

'Sometimes it felt as if I were being dragged along . . . like I didn't have any free will . . . I don't know.'

'Fay is very talented, and the talent obviously extends to the bedroom . . .'

'That's not exactly what I meant.'

Oh, but it was.

'Or perhaps you simply needed a change of scene, Tom – a different body because the novelty of mine had worn off.' She looked back at him, full in the eyes. 'That happens to a lot of men, apparently.'

'*NO*, Jess.' But in a way it was true.

'Except that fucking my sister seems a trifle incestuous, don't you think?'

He blushed furiously, shocked, too, by his wife's use of such a crude expression.

'Of course,' she continued unsparingly, 'I've probably become rather predictable over the years, rather boring, what with my nagging angst about having a child. Our child. I mean, it must have been very irritating, come to think of it. I suppose some people would say I drove you to it.' Fay would, anyway.

'Jess, please.'

'Must have, Tom – to do what you've done.' Her face was blank with fatigue and misery. 'My own sister. Pretty staggering really . . .' she continued in a dead sort of voice. 'You and Fay. It feels rather like I've been slammed in the stomach by a truck.' And the truck wouldn't back off, it was hanging in there, sinking into her by slow degrees. She wanted to ask someone when the pain would go away.

He couldn't bear to see her like this and not be able to touch her, comfort her. 'God, I wish it had never happened,' he blundered on hopelessly. Wondered why, during all that meaningless physical pleasure, all that clandestine bonking, and afterwards, when he had been swamped by guilt, he had been unable to imagine the terrible reality of this pain which had been rolling towards them with the inevitability of a tidal wave.

'Can you go now, please?' she said.

Tom froze for an instant, then nodded dumbly, astonished that he didn't totter and sway and fall over; but instead his legs began to move, carrying him across the room and through the open door where a packed suitcase stood, looking back at him.

Fay scraped a little more paint off with a palette knife until the inner structure of the garden-forest began to appear. Then she reinforced the precise outlines of the trees and the standing-stones in thick paint with a brush. Her head ached and she was sweating profusely and kept bringing the back of her hand to her brow to mop up the perspiration gathered there, but the urge to finish the painting was much stronger than the urge to stop and rest. It was becoming, like Zak, a sort of obsession.

In fact, the canvas seemed to possess the curious ability of making her feel both elated and depressed. The reality and strange beauty of the garden and then the forest made her spirits soar and yet at the same time there was an oppressive sense of hostility in those weird and wonderful, yet startlingly real trees. She stepped back and surveyed the picture again and was struck by an odd thought that it posed a riddle, yet would never offer a solution, and she had no idea why she should think this.

She looked again into the clearing where the standing-stones stood and beyond into the mists of hazy distance for what seemed miles and from where a man would come.

Fay frowned. What man? There was no man, would be no man because she hadn't planned on one. She leaned forward and studied the picture with uneasy avid interest, then closed her eyes and rubbed at her temples. She needed a break and she would have one, now. The exhibition was a month away yet, enough time to make everything neat and tidy, or 'on top', as they say.

Her eyes moved to the bed and for the first time she wondered if she had not timed things badly and got rid of Tom too soon. She needed regular sex; she was used to it, wanted it.

And Zak was playing hard to get.

She sighed heavily with impatience and frustration. But he would come round to her way of thinking in the end; they always did. Even poor old Tom had tried to ignore her little flirtations in the beginning, but he had stood no chance at all. He had known that really, Fay chuckled, wanting her all the time he had kept saying no.

Still smiling, she lay down on the floor and decided to catch up on some pelvic floor exercises, fifty contractions to be exact, and when she had finished she relaxed her whole body and lay staring at the ceiling, feeling horribly horny. What was the point of performing her little fanny-tightening exercises every damned day if there was no one to appreciate it? She swore softly and thought of Zak.

She got up and walked over to the window, scanning the gardens for any sign of the boy. Her eyes strayed to Tom and Jessica's place which she could now see quite clearly through a gap in the almost leafless trees. Fay caught a sharp breath of disbelief. Zak was sitting on their patio, opposite Jessica, and wasn't that her easel he was facing? Good God, was her big boring sister actually attempting to paint him?

Several emotions stampeded through Fay – jealousy, hatred, confusion, humiliation, outrage. What was he doing with Jessica when he could be here, with me? And he had called her sister 'a nice woman' and there had been that look on his face – hadn't there? She searched out her binoculars and peered through them, picked up the image of her sister's profile which told her absolutely nothing. Impatiently she shifted the binoculars to the squatter's face which she was able to view full-on, noting his features with microscopic intensity. Fay felt something twist in her guts, an appalling stab of desire, but more than that, she saw something in his expression which profoundly disturbed her, made her mouth go dry, her pulse resound in her head. Zak's face was full of a telling softness.

'I don't believe it.' She threw the binoculars down, whirled round and stalked over to the telephone.

'I want to speak to Tom.'

'He's not taking any calls at the moment.'

'Tell him it's his sister-in-law.'

'Well, I . . .'

'For God's sake – ' Stupid bloody woman ' – just tell him.'

Fay glared into the receiver until she heard his voice, his little familiar cough. Rolled her eyes.

'What do you want?'

'Just wanted to know how you are,' she said with as much conviction as she could muster.

'I asked what you wanted.'

'Tom,' she said sweetly, 'please.'

'I'm going to count three and then I'll put the phone down.'

'Tom?'

'One . . .'

'For heaven's sake . . .'

'Two . . .'

'I've just seen Jessica,' she snapped, and it was, well, partly true.

'What?'

'With that boy.'

'What the hell are you talking about?'

'I thought you should know.'

'Perhaps *you* should know that Jess and I have separated.'

Fay gaped into the receiver.

'And,' Tom continued, 'that boy is sitting for her – she's doing his portrait.'

'Yes,' she said, 'I realise that.'

'What did you say to her?' He laughed, then stopped just as suddenly so that the laughter had the rough abruptness of a sob. 'Although, believe me, there is nothing you can say now that would make the slightest bit of difference to the massive balls-up better know as my marriage.' Or, rather, my life – the two, after all, were inextricably linked.

'She knows about us.'

259

'Full marks, Fay.'

'Oh.'

'Goodbye, Fay.'

'No, Tom. Don't hang up,' she said quickly. 'She'll have you back once she realises that the thing between us is really over.'

Thing. The word clanged and banged in his mind. He had seen a horror movie once called *The Thing*.

'You just don't get it, do you, Fay?'

'What?'

'Jess will never have me back.' He was trying to believe it – and something told him that he'd better get used to the idea. Yet he still found it hard to believe that their life together could be blotted out with such ease, that all those moments of love (because they had loved) and companionship and shared dreams and shared angst could be erased so abruptly. Tears were very close and he clamped his eyes shut on his weakness. And he *had* wanted a baby as much as she but, in the end, sex had somehow got in the way, which was rather absurd when he let himself think about it.

'Oh, don't be melodramatic.'

'Stay away, Fay,' he said ominously, 'from both of us.'

'Of course, she'll have you back,' she pressed on, 'all she needs is some time to get used to what's happened; she loves you, she always has. Always will.' She felt an unexpected twinge of – shame, envy?

'Now you're the one who's being melodramatic, or should I say totally unrealistic,' he said with bitter and unhappy relish, 'which is really rich, coming from you – of all people.'

'You're wrong, Tom.'

'Am I?' he replied. 'About you, or Jess?'

He put the phone down and Fay cursed, but all the time her eyes were on the window and her brain working on and around the subject that mattered to her most.

She would go over and talk to Jessica; explain everything. Of course, it wouldn't be easy, but given time she would see sense. Jessica had always been that sort of person – sensible, practical, predictable – and certainly not the type to take risks with her future. She was just teaching Tom a lesson, that's all, which was understandable. If their situations had been reversed, she would have personally strung Tom up, probably castrated him first, except that she would never waste that much energy on someone like her brother-in-law. The Toms of this world were meant for women like Jessica – homebodies, broody-mares, nest builders. Fay shrugged inwardly, but then she and Jessica had always been very different.

Chalk and cheese was how their mother had once so sweetly put it, which was why Fay had finally gone to live with their father once the divorce had gone through, because dear old Mum had never been able to understand or like her. Well, to put it bluntly, she couldn't stand the sight of her. She had tried, of course, but sometimes Fay had caught her mother eyeing her with a mixture of bewilderment and unease, as if she were trying to fathom some strange insect through a pane of dirty glass.

Jessica had always been the favourite.

She felt a sullen glow of resentment and a little moisture of self-pity made her eyes prick and burn.

But Jessica wasn't going to have Zak.

She moved away from the window and over to the gilded mirror which still leaned against a wall. She was wearing very tight denim shorts, and a pink vest full of carefully torn holes through which the areolae of her nipples sometimes peeped. Her hair was piled on top and she pulled it free so that it fell around her face and down her back in a magnificent swathe. Nothing on her feet, very Bohemian, and Zak would identify with that – with her – because he must see, surely, how much they had in common?

Zak saw her first, strolling towards them across the grass which was no longer green, but an unhealthy ashy grey. She was trying to appear nonchalant, but it wasn't working because tension had drawn tight the muscles beneath the white skin of her pretty sly face.

Jessica had not seen, Jessica was engrossed in the picture as she had been since he had come to her this morning; submerging her unhappiness in her work. She had told him Tom had gone, but apart from that had hardly spoken a word, and he had bathed in the silence because they were alone at last and he was confident that in time the unhappiness would dissipate and he could move in and replace her husband.

Tom was sorry, of course, monumentally so for all that he had done; but people usually were once they had been found out.

Zak scrutinised Fay with interest as she drew close, wondered how she would open her carefully prepared little speech, because she would have one ready and waiting for Jessica to swallow whole, like a great big putrid sweet.

She stopped just inside the open gate, smiled at him greedily, conspiratorially, before switching her attention to Jessica.

'You should have told me, Jess,' Fay began brightly.

Jessica froze for an instant and then very slowly lifted her head and looked back at her sister. She said nothing.

Fay shrugged and went on, 'I mean, that you'd gone back to portraits . . .'

Jessica's eyes moved beyond Fay to the communal garden baking in the heat, the dusty grass, the criss-cross of hot gravel paths and the crumbling summer-house where Zak had loved her.

Fay's eyebrows came together in a frown and she thrust her thumbs into the pockets (no more than slits) of her shorts.

'I hope you're not taking that . . .' Fay paused, '. . . that other business too seriously. It was a "flash in the pan", as they say.' Her voice was too casual, almost silly; the voice of someone ill at ease.

'Tom . . .' she began again, but stopped abruptly when Jessica flinched.

'Would you mind coming back later, please, Zak?' Jessica said quietly.

'Sure,' he nodded, got up.

Fay blushed, irritated and embarrassed at the same time; she had wanted him here as a witness to her big apology because she wanted to show him that she, too, could be nice, that she, too, could gain entry to the 'League of Good Women', just like her sister. Vomit. Puke.

Zak brushed past her and she shivered with delight, turned her head so that she could take one more mouth-watering look as he walked away. When she looked back Jessica was bent over the portrait again and Fay pressed down a snort of disgust. She was getting the silent treatment. Big-fucking-deal.

'Tom wants you back, Jess.' Warily she began walking up the steps, caught by a sudden desire to see the portrait.

When she stopped, Fay was perhaps four feet away and

could see her sister's work very clearly and what she saw filled her with dismay and envy.

'There's a black leather sports bag sitting in the hall,' Jessica said without expression. 'It contains some more of Tom's things. Perhaps you could give it to him, please.'

Fay bit back a sharp retort. I'm not your bloody slave.

'He's not staying with me, you know.'

Jessica got up and walked into the house, picked up the bag and returned to the patio.

'Just give it to him.'

'You're really taking all this too personally,' Fay continued petulantly. 'What happened between us was just one of those things, for God's sake. It meant nothing.'

'Perhaps someone will carve that on your headstone.'

Fay bit her lip, brow furrowing. 'What?'

'It meant nothing.'

Dull heat filled Fay's cheeks and an ugly silence fell between them before Jessica thrust Tom's bag into her sister's arms, and so hard that Fay almost stumbled backwards.

'Now leave me in peace.' Jessica began packing up her paint tubes, the easel, picking up the portrait.

'The trouble with you,' Fay started, 'and always has been, is that everything has to be so damn black and white in your tedious little world, so right or wrong.' She took a deep angry breath and her voice began to rise as her sister approached the open door. 'Real life – big sister mine – is not like that – some of us are human, you know; we make mistakes, take risks, *live*.'

Jessica closed the door and the wretched image of her sister behind her.

'Not all of us are angling for a bloody sainthood.' Fay's voice ran on and then trailed off when she realised she was wasting her breath and her time. 'You silly boring shit,' she muttered morosely and then threw Tom's bag over the wall and into the next garden.

Even as the bag disappeared from sight she was already wondering where Zak was, what he was doing, and she swung round and down the steps before running back across the communal garden.

The sun was at its highest and the heat in that walled garden seemed to emanate from below as much as above, thick floating pockets of tremulous air which wavered and danced as Fay ran through them: firm ripe haunches moving like an animal's in her tight shorts, slim white legs stretching and pumping, and the hair, oh the hair, fanning out behind her like some wayward nymph from a Greek myth. In another world, another time, Fay might have been Hecate, Medusa, Augustus' lovely lethal Livia, Morganna in Arthur's Camelot . . .

Because inside, Fay's heart would always be the same – ruthless, greedy – and now it gave a little start of glee; Zak was still there, standing inside the garden of the house, talking to that wanker, Keith – he of large mouth and little brain.

She sidled up to the gate and pushed it gently open. 'Hi.'

Both men turned and looked at her at the same time. Keith's eyes crawled over her with great, if wary, interest, but Zak barely glanced in her direction before resuming their conversation.

'Wednesday afternoon, then,' he said.

Keith blinked, pulled his eyes away from a peeping nipple, 'Oh, yeah, sure.' He swallowed. 'I can probably fit in another afternoon before the actual party – just for half an hour or so.' He shot another look at Fay who was staring at them fixedly, desperately trying to impress. 'There's nothing to it, really, and you won't have to do much patter.'

Fay's brain was rapidly ticking over.

'What's this, then?' she said. 'Becoming a DJ, are we?'

Zak made no answer, saw her move closer out of the corner of his eye.

'Oh, come on,' she persisted, 'won't you let me in on your little secret?'

'It's no big deal,' Keith said coolly. 'Zak's standing in for me at Emma and Jonathan's party – just for an hour until things begin to hot up and before I, literally, come in.'

'Sounds like a good arrangement.' She was looking at Zak all the time, tormented by the nearness of him, sweat trickling down her back, between her soft alabaster thighs. Wanting him.

'So long as it works,' Keith said importantly. 'Zak needs to familiarise himself with the lights and the equipment. It's got to be right.'

'Oh, sure,' Fay said condescendingly.

Keith sucked in a breath, suddenly aware that she wasn't really listening; he simply didn't exist for her. Arrogant preening bitch. She was the sort of girl he came across every once in a while; there was one in every office block, every tennis club, every disco. The sort of girl who would think it terribly funny to spill her drink down another's dress, or cut you dead in the street, or leave you waiting and waiting in some place when she had had no intention of turning up in the first place.

For a brief moment Fay switched her gaze to Keith's face, as if she had sensed his eyes drilling into her skull, saw her own dislike for him mirrored in his eyes. *Touché*.

Keith looked at Zak as a thought struck him. 'If you like,' he said, 'I can show you the equipment now.' He made a big show of looking at his watch. 'I've got some time. It's back at my place.'

Zak nodded, glad of the reprieve. 'Okay.'

'I suppose . . .' she began.

'No, sorry,' Keith said with obvious insincerity, 'you can't come. This is business.'

He watched with satisfaction as Fay pouted with disappointment, saw how she opened her mouth to speak only to close it again.

'Bye,' he said grinning, 'see you around.'

Fay seethed with humiliation as they walked away, leaving her standing alone on the path like an exile, and she wondered for an instant why she was allowing herself, so uncharacteristically, to be put in such a demeaning position. The answer was horribly simple: because she just couldn't help herself. In this somewhat unusual situation, her body was sending out the messages, the signals, and giving her these feverish highs which her mind had no power over. And all because of some man. Now that was scary, but it was also very, very exciting.

Fay continued up the path towards the office where jerko Jonathan and his future bride would be sitting behind their reproduction desks, mobile phones glued to their clueless ears. And wouldn't they get a surprise when she told them she had changed her mind about their precious party. She would wear her sweetest smile, of course, and tell them that she would be delighted to accept their invitation, after all.

The digital clock's illuminated dial told Jonathan it was three twenty-six in the morning (and forty seconds). He could hear Emma's even breathing, feel her left thigh lying against his own, and he moved ever so slightly so that a small space might separate them. He was still not used to her sleeping with him (would he ever be?) in his very smart, pristine studio flat and it had been her idea to have regular 'stop-overs' on Friday nights, and in all honesty, and particularly after what had happened on that other, unmentionable, occasion, he could not refuse her. He had no excuses left.

They made love – had sex – in a mechanical kind of way and then went to sleep; it was quite simple, really. Jonathan closed his eyes during their sex because that was the only way he could go through with it; imagining it was Zak beneath him, Zak's mouth, Zak's hands, but then he would brush against the plump little mounds of Emma's breasts, or get a good strong whiff of her cloying perfume, and the dream would end abruptly and usually with the sudden and irrevocable deflation of his erection.

He did love her, he told himself, well, at least he *cared* about her . . . in his own way. Why on earth would he marry her otherwise? Because you don't want people to know, a voice piped up – people like your parents: good old Annie and Derek. Christ, the bowling club would have a field day! And his brother, macho, rugby-playing Ian who would probably beat the hell out of him before getting pissed out of his brains and crying into his beer. Ian's friends were his friends, too – true they weren't all beer-swilling twerps like his brother, some of them were actually decent blokes, but they would laugh; they would all laugh and snigger behind his back.

And Keith. Jonathan squirmed inwardly. Keith would think it the height of hilarity.

I am not brave, he said to himself, and it isn't my bloody fault, his mind ran on, I didn't want this. Did I? Did I? Did I?

Before Zak, everything had been manageable. Before

Zak, life had seemed uncomplicated and almost easy. The squatter had walked into his life and somehow changed everything.

I love him.

The words seemed to jump up and down in his mind, in huge dazzling neon-lit letters.

It was a crush, his sensible self told him. Zak is beautiful, anyone can see that, anyone could convince themselves they loved someone as physically desirable as that, if they wanted. But it's not love, it's just lust and possession.

Jonathan thought it was hell and he caught a deep trembling breath even as his mind began to replay (yet again) that secret time with Zak. In the dark that tic in his cheek twitched and his pulse began to race very fast. His hands drifted to his chest; he dragged fingertips down his belly and beyond to his hardening penis and his soft tender balls.

He moaned in the darkness, in the closeness of the night air, and wondered hopelessly why his fantasies couldn't revolve around someone as luridly sexual as that quirky red-head, Fay. When she had come into the office that afternoon she might as well have been wearing nothing at all, for all the difference it made. Most men would have been foaming at the mouth.

Not me.

Jonathan sighed dreadfully and resumed the play on his sex. It was comforting this play, soothing; it reminded him of when he was a boy and he had found solace from school and home under the bedclothes. All that seemed a long, long time ago now because these days the play did not stay as 'play' any more, it became a heated game with himself, a frantic fantasy filled with erotic visions of Zak.

And then he would come. Oh, yes. Jonathan would shoot the moon.

Just as Jonathan took his pleasure, Zak was swimming up from sleep in the neglected basement.

When his eyelids flickered open and he realised where he was, his first thought was of Jessica and how she had not wanted him tonight, how she had (very gently) told him that she wanted to be alone. Part of him had wanted to pressurise her – and he could have done, and won – but his stupid pride wanted her to want him herself: no tricks, no cute messages, no Zakky magic. Now he wished he had simply been his old ruthless self and done what he wanted, which would have delivered them both.

He clenched his fists in an agony of frustration. Would that have been so wrong, helping things along a little? Something told him it *was* wrong, just like all the other things he had done with such merciless ease. Bad things; but he closed his mind to them.

The thrum of an insect batting against the window made him blink and he rolled over in his sleeping-bag and looked at the moon through the little stained-glass window. He was restless and the restlessness was telling him that he didn't want to stay here any more, not in this filthy sink of a hole.

Even the shadows seemed filthy, a dirty grey sort of colour, and because of this eternally hot windless summer, they never moved, never danced across the room, but only dawdled interminably as the moon shifted slowly around the sky.

Zak's eyes grew heavy again, began to droop and close. Behind him the hidden door swung silently open.

As he lay there, floating between sleep and wakefulness,

he was touched by a groggy feeling of unease which increased steadily even as he slid back into sleep.

A smell made his nostrils twitch, a singey smell, like ashes and damp smoke. The smell on the beach. It told of beacons and battles and betrayal and death; standing-stones in a clearing flooded by moonlight. The end of something.

It was the time between dog and wolf, the time of near-darkness when mists roll in from the sea and the wind makes the trees moan.

Zak's body twitched and trembled and his eyes began to dart back and forth beneath his closed lids. He muttered occasionally, his face distorting in a kind of blind helpless panic, legs pistoning as if something nameless and terrible chased him through the canyons of his mind. Then he screamed.

His eyes ripped open and he jerked upwards into a sitting position, looking into the dark as goosebumps rippled up his legs and arms, placed a shaking hand on his chest to quell the nasty thudding of his heart.

Something was not right.

He turned his head slowly, leaned on one elbow and looked behind him and was confronted by the black mouth of the secret door yawning open: black and old and deep, and the sight brought a helpless chill.

What the fuck was going on?

Zak got to his knees and clutched blindly for his jeans, but all the time his terrified eyes remained fixed on the open door.

On his face there was a frozen waiting expression, and a small still voice whispered that all his carefully laid plans would come to nothing, that it was a child's game he played, and the voice dried out the moisture in his mouth, made the flesh shrink against his bones.

But he fought the fear and the panic erupting in his mind.

This is an old house, an old house with memories, he told himself, and things seem different in the dark.

And there were things – nothing to do with him – old and hidden things in the world that some people could detect, things that left a mark down through all the years; palpable like damp and ancient dust and the musty smell of disintegration.

Nothing to do with him. Nothing to do with the beach thing or the lies of his mother. Nothing to do with the mystery man who was his father, an image which, frankly, scared the living daylights out of him.

Why? He didn't know. He didn't *want* to know.

Zak stumbled, got up again and ran out into the moon-drenched garden, and when he stopped running and his head had cleared he tried to gather strength inside himself, to feel the power of his thoughts giving him sustenance. Still looking back, he slipped on his jeans and felt anger begin to burn a little in his belly, eclipsing his fear. Looked with disgust on the sheen of nervous sweat saturating his skin.

A frigging nightmare. That's all, Zak, a frigging nightmare.

Yet the images, the face, stole back into his memory with horrible clarity.

I don't believe,' he whispered, 'any of it.'

With great deliberation he turned his face away and looked towards the place where his future lay innocently sleeping.

This was *his* time, and he would have what he wanted in this world and in the way he wanted it, and that included Jessica.

8

Zak leaned gratefully against a tree and slid down into a crouching position, all the time his eyes looking back. The overgrown garden above the basement was a mass of hunched shadows, the twisted branches of the tree embracing the fence a tangle of black skeletal fingers. Not exactly an inviting prospect. No, there would be no returning to the filthy hole tonight; he had allowed his mind to play one trick too many and that was more than enough.

The rest of the building was also in darkness, except where Fay was and sometimes the lights stayed on all night; amber rectangles falling on the chaos of the garden like bars of gold. Fay's dubious proclamation to the world that she was free.

Zak wrinkled his brow in irritation, because her sister, apparently, was not.

He cocked his head and looked at the moon, another few days and it would be full which would mean he had been here for just over a month, yet it seemed longer, much longer than that. And how far had he got? He shifted his gaze to Jessica's house and he thought of her face and an odd little pain arose in his chest.

If Jessica had let him stay he wouldn't have found himself in this pathetic (no, pitiful – let's get it right) situation.

He began kneading and pushing his hands together in an agony of frustration.

Why hadn't she let him stay? Why? Why?

She needed him, more than ever she needed him, and yet she chose to be alone tonight of all nights when puling Tom had just left her. Was he such a great loss? After what he had done, she must know that she was better off without him – trust was all, wasn't it, and respect? She could start again, begin a *new* life filled with possibilities.

With me.

As if drawn, Zak stood up and started to walk towards the house, imagined her sleeping in that big bed with the expensive white coverlet where they had made love with such sweet ardour. He paused on the patio beside the empty easel and looked up at the shadowy window where she was, then moved to the drawing-room window and peered into the darkness. In the far corner sat the cockatoo's cage, silent and empty, and he wondered how Tom had coped with the second assault the bird had made upon him and what exactly he had done when it had happened. The evidence (or lack of it), would point to dear old George literally flying the coop. And good luck.

Zak placed his fingers on the wooden frame of the window and more out of curiosity than anything else tried to lift it, and it gave easily, slipping upwards with barely a sound.

He smiled. Foolish Jessica – dangerous to leave the windows unlocked; you never know who might get in.

Zak climbed through with hardly a second thought and just missed hitting a lamp with his foot. He drew in a breath and then looked cautiously around the room; in the darkness he could just make out large pieces of furniture, brass or gilt glinting dully in the moonlight, a mirror above the enormous fireplace.

He padded noiselessly across the carpet and straight through the open door and up the stairs. He knew exactly where he was going and what he would do.

Her door, like the others, was open and he moved inside and stood looking at her. She was lying on her back covered with only a sheet and the material seemed almost luminous, touched as it was by moonlight. Her shoulders were bare and on one side a knee and thigh protruded. She was naked beneath the linen sheet.

Jessica's face was soft with sleep and her breathing came deep and steady. His eyes flitted to the bedside table and the small brown bottle which contained her sleeping-tablets.

Zak watched her for a long time before pulling back the coverlet, and she didn't stir. He waited and looked, following every line, every curve, the white bits where the sun had not been, moonlight icing her mouth; cataloguing every detail. Then he sat down and waited again before placing a hand lightly on her calf. Waited before reaching upwards to touch a thigh; waited, hand hovering, to cup a breast and squeeze it gently, lovingly. Jessica's mouth opened a fraction and then closed again.

Zak looked at her very hard, concentrating all his will on her sleeping mind.

He brought his hand to her pubic hair and trailed a finger softly through, dipped into her slit, drove sure and deep and held it there and was swept by a crushing and incredible wave of desire.

What he could do, and she would not be able to stop him. Anything.

His sex was a rock-hard bulge confined by his blue jeans and he released it with a shuddering sigh. He climaxed immediately and without preamble; just by looking at her, just by having his finger inside her. He felt shocked and shaken with disbelief because it had never been like this for him before.

He closed his eyes and when he opened them again nothing had changed and Jessica still slept, but something had altered within him; he felt a little dirty, a little ashamed, as if he had sullied something precious.

The word is violate, Zak, a voice told him.

There was a sour taste in his mouth and he flushed deeply. Then, as if in atonement, he leaned across, tenderly kissed each nipple, and then the soft moist place between her legs. Lastly, he brought his mouth to her belly and laid his cheek against it before lifting the linen sheet over her again, but leaving her shoulders bare, just as he had found her.

Moonshine flooded the room and when he straightened the pale-pearl light fell on the tears standing in his eyes.

Outside, Zak leaned into the shadows of the house; his hands were shaking and a feeling of wretched loneliness overwhelmed him. He folded his arms tightly across his chest and lifted his gaze to the night sky and wondered what the fuck he was doing with his life.

Trying to make a better one, wasn't that it? Trying to leave behind all that shit his mother had so sweetly bequeathed him; except his methods would be considered a little unorthodox for most people's tastes.

He took a deep breath, brought his gaze back to earth and stared out at the silent garden. He felt a little better, not great, but better. His eyes came to rest on an old tree-house which someone had thoughtfully built into the middle of a big horse chestnut; most of the lower steps leading to the top were missing, but that wouldn't be a problem for someone determined and agile like himself. It would be a breeze, in fact. It would also be a good place to stay for the night, because he was still in no mood to face the basement with that haunted house of horrors called his imagination.

A bad dream, he told himself again, but there was another part of him which wondered and doubted and made him cringe inside himself.

The birds began their dawn chorus way before the sun cleared the horizon and Zak groaned softly; his body ached all over, as if his muscles had frozen to the bones. Very slowly he uncurled himself from his foetal position on the floor of the tree-house and sat up.

He had a unique view and it would have been pleasant if his body had not complained so much. No one was awake, there was not even the distant sound of a milk float to be heard, and the thought made his mouth water for a good cup of coffee, 'a brew'. The night's events seemed blurred and indistinct now, almost unreal, but it was always like that in the cold light of day when dreams and nightmares and imaginings seemed like so much flotsam. He would go back to the basement (temporarily), eat and drink and then try and get some more sleep. But he would also close up the door, good and tight.

Zak yawned and pulled himself into a standing position.

He would also have to consider what he was going to do about Jessica. He blushed again at the memory of what had happened when she was sleeping, what he had done – an aberration, he protested silently, a small lapse on his part that should not happen again. If she would only let him in, let him stay, then it *couldn't* happen again. She needed to be shown that living on her own was not good for her, not healthy. He could convince her, of course; it would just take a little time.

He sucked in a gulp of air and took in the view again. It was really quite something, he could even see the smooth white rim of the sea in the near distance. He shifted his gaze back to the trees and down into the garden, and his eyes locked on some movement beneath the withered remains of a holly bush. It was the big ginger tom cat, Max, and he was busy, intent on unearthing something with his great fat greedy paws.

Zak watched him, saw how the cat's tail frantically snaked backwards and forwards as it strove to exhume the object of its desire, and it was getting there because something blue and red poked through the sandy soil. A cloth?

Curious, Zak climbed down the tree and made his way over to the spot where the cat was feverishly digging. He squatted down a little way off and waited.

It was a bundle and the bundle was wrapped in a coloured cloth, maybe a scarf or a tea-towel.

Zak picked up a heavy stick and used it to push the cat out of the way which proved just as difficult as he'd anticipated, but when he caught the animal's furious glance and stared back hard and black, Max began to retreat.

Don't mess with Zak, pussycat.

The bundle was half-in, half-out of its hole and Zak poked it gently with the stick, was uncoiling the cloth with its jagged point when he saw the snow-whiteness of feathers through a dusting of soil.

Poor old George.

Naughty, murdering Tom.

Zak flicked the cloth back and tightened the bundle into some semblance of order. He would take it with him, back to the basement; he wasn't quite sure why, or even what he might do with it, but he would think of something.

*   *   *

'We don't have time for this,' Jonathan said sharply, looking up at the block of purpose-built flats, 'and it's too far away.'

'We lost that lovely place with the balcony because you managed to find fault with it,' Emma complained. 'Don't you want us to find a place and live together?'

Jonathan stared at his shoes, the pavement, not wanting to answer.

'Let's just take a peep, anyway,' she persisted, not willing to be put off. 'There's no harm in looking and it sounds fantastic.'

He lit up a cigarette and took a long drag before speaking again. 'Where is this guy, anyway? He's late.'

'No. We're early,' Emma said and then gushed with relief, 'That's him – just drawing up.'

The estate agent emerged awkwardly from the environs of his Ford Escort, a tall gangly man, who waved and then proceeded to leaf self-importantly through a note-pad he had taken from his pocket.

'Lovely day,' he called loudly, stuffing the note-pad back into his jacket and walking towards them.

Jonathan raised his eyes to heaven.

'Barry Dymoke,' he said and stretched out his hand to be shaken. 'We spoke on the phone.'

'Yes,' Emma enthused, 'hello. This is my fiancé, Jonathan Keeley.'

'Hi,' Barry pumped Jonathan's reluctant hand, then added predictably, 'These are fabulous apartments.'

Jonathan said nothing, his attention momentarily taken by Barry's terrible skin. How would it feel, he wondered with horrible fascination, waking up to a face like that every morning?

'Shall we go in?' Barry's voice broke abruptly into his thoughts and Jonathan blushed.

And the foyer of the 'fabulous apartments' was just as Jonathan had expected, all glass and gleaming marble and potted plants. He heard Emma gasp with pleasure, and winced. All the way up in the lift (the size of a walk-in cupboard), Barry gave a running commentary on the advantages of living in Kebbel Lodge, so it was a relief when the lift stopped and he was able to step out into the corridor; except here, of course, was the flat awaiting his unwilling eye.

'All the apartments have access to the communal gym, a swimming pool . . .' Barry paused for a second, 'a crèche . . .'

Emma reddened prettily and Jonathan saw. God, kids. He stared at the back of her head with growing trepidation as they walked into the flat, then pressed the thought down and tried to concentrate on the matter at hand. The living areas were spacious, he had to admit, but totally without character: square boxes relieved by large plate-glass windows.

'Quite a view.' Barry was standing in the lounge/diner staring out of the window.

Emma followed and there was another little gasp. 'Come and look, Jonathan – you can see the Palace Pier and even the Marina from here.'

How very dramatic. Jonathan sighed, moved dutifully across the room and stood beside her.

'You can even see the office,' she piped up softly.

'It's too far,' he said.

Emma didn't respond to his remark and Jonathan wondered if she'd heard as she turned away from him, following Barry into the kitchen.

'Fitted.' The estate agent speak ran on, 'everything's here – including dishwasher and waste-disposal unit.'

Wow.

Jonathan trailed in the rear as they moved into the hall and on to the bathroom with bidet and jacuzzi; master-bedroom en suite, and finally the box-room, or nursery, where Emma hovered very pointedly.

'That's it, isn't it?' Jonathan said.

'That's it,' Barry repeated cheerily. 'and quite a bargain, if I may say so.'

'We'll think about it,' Jonathan responded abruptly, forcing a smile.

'Of course – and naturally we have other, very attractive properties available in your price range.'

'Fine.' Jonathan deliberately glanced at his watch. 'But right now, it's getting late and I have a business to run.' His words came out in an awkward rush, and were immediately followed by an uncomfortable silence.

'Right,' Barry nodded tactfully, 'I'll see you out.'

As they drove away, Emma sat stiffly, not speaking.

'It's too far,' Jonathan said.

Emma said nothing.

'Well, it is,' he went on defensively, 'you must see that at least.'

'I heard you the first time, actually.' Her voice was clipped, offended. 'And even if it had been next door to the office, you still wouldn't have wanted it. Would you?'

'You know I don't like modern buildings,' Jonathan said sulkily.

'Yes, I know, but it had all those other things to offer, like a gym, a swimming pool . . .' she hesitated, 'a crèche.'

'You're not pregnant, are you?' And as soon as he had

said the fateful words, he wished he could call them back.

Emma froze for an instant before slowly turning her head to look at him, but he kept his eyes glued to the road.

'How could I be?' she said quietly, ominously.

'Well, he said, 'you know . . .'

'You always wear a condom, Jonathan,' she said bluntly and he felt himself redden with surprise and embarrassment, 'and I'm on the pill.'

He forced a poor but jocular sort of grin. 'Couldn't be much safer than that, then, could we?'

She said nothing for what seemed a ghastly length of time.

'I didn't mean . . .' he began as unspeakable memories of *the abortion* rose up and slated him, 'about – you know . . .'

'I'd rather not talk about it, if you don't mind.'

He gulped and felt his heart sink, but there was irritation, too, and he wanted to scream, wanted to get back to the office, get out of here and the stifling confines of the car. He looked at her out of the corner of his eye; she was staring out of the window and he was suddenly touched by shame. 'Sorry,' he said, 'sorry. Really, Em.' He placed a conciliatory hand on her knee.

For a moment she didn't respond, but then she covered his hand with her own and he knew it would be all right. An odd thought struck him that Emma made things too easy, too comfortable for him. If she were harder, or perhaps more worldly, their relationship might have ended years ago. As it was, well . . .

'You do want us to live together?'

'Emma,' he said, 'we've been through all this.' He withdrew his hand, placed it back on the steering-wheel.

'It's just that, over the last few days, you've become all moody again . . . I thought that after – well, after that time

282

at my parents' house, I thought things had changed, you seemed . . .'

'All right, all right.' God, he didn't want to go into *that*.

'So you do?'

'What?'

'Want us to live together?'

'Yes,' he hoped he sounded more sincere than he felt, 'of course.' And was astonished that he was able to form the words without choking.

She sighed softly with relief. 'That's all right, then.'

Jonathan gazed bleakly heavenwards and thought of Zak and the thought hurt like a physical blow. He must be going mad. He darted a furtive glance at Emma's innocent profile and told himself that she need never know, people did what he was doing all the time – kept secrets – and no one ever found out. She looked back at him at that moment as if she had sensed his eyes and smiled in a way that he was coming to dread.

He swallowed hard, feeling distinctly uncomfortable and a little disgusted with himself. It was Zak's fault, he told himself again; everything had been all right until the squatter moved in and things had begun to unravel and fray around the edges.

'How long now?' Zak asked.

Jessica placed the canvas on to the easel and looked back at him.

'A week, maybe.'

'Sometimes it feels like I've been sitting here for ever.'

'I'm sorry.'

'Oh, no,' he grinned, 'don't misunderstand me. I don't mind in the least.'

She caught the eager look in his eyes and wondered how much longer she could keep him at arm's length. Not much. Besides, she didn't really want to, but now, right now, she only felt sick inside and numb and bitter. No good to anyone.

'Someone tried to force my door last night,' he lied.

Jessica's eyes widened. 'Really?'

'It was a guy, but I chased him off and he disappeared into those trees,' he gestured towards the far side of the communal garden, 'and then I lost him.' He looked pointedly at her. 'You didn't hear anything, did you?'

'No,' she looked concerned, 'nothing.'

He scrutinised her gravely. Seeing her in his mind's eye as he had seen her last night. You didn't even hear me, Jessica, or feel my touch, sense the longing pouring out of me. A tingle like a mild electric shock passed through him.

'Make sure you lock up properly,' he thought of the window, 'you can't be too careful these days.'

'I know,' she said, 'and thank you for the warning.'

'It gets around,' he added slowly, 'that a woman is living on her own.'

'Does it?'

He nodded.

'Jessica,' he began, 'maybe you shouldn't be alone, particularly not at the moment.'

'It's all right, Zak. I'm fine.' Liar.

'No, you're not.'

He got up and went over to her, crouched down on his haunches so that he was looking up into her face.

'If there's anything you want me to do for you,' he said, taking her hand, 'anything at all – just name it.'

She was exquisitely aware of his eyes on her, and his hand in her hand sending warm, wanting signals seeping

284

through her skin, up her arm, and beyond, weakening her completely, and she felt herself shiver despite the heat.

The doorbell rang and Jessica jumped, glancing nervously at her watch. 'She's early, but that must be Roz; she's staying with me for a couple of days.' She saw a shadow momentarily dim his beautiful eyes. 'It's just for a couple of days, Zak. That's all.'

'Sure,' he said, 'if that's what you want.'

She watched him carefully, willing him to understand.

'Roz is an old, old friend – she might help me clear my head a bit.'

He nodded and smiled with an effort as she walked away, into the house, to let Roz in. Then he cursed softly because just lately it seemed as if someone were deliberately putting obstacles in his path, which was a crazy thought, but that's just what it felt like.

Zak got up, not wanting to stay now that her 'old, old friend' was intruding on his space. He wanted Jessica alone, he wanted to be in her house and walk barefoot on those plush rugs, shower in her shower, sit and drink coffee with her in that big cosy kitchen, read poetry to her amongst the plump cushions of the sofa, lie with her in that great big bed. Oh, yes, and lie with her most of all. Every day, all day; have her when he wanted, where he wanted. Sudden heat burned in his loins and he felt himself harden with amazing rapidity. Two days, she had said, and he wondered how he was going to last that long.

'False alarm . . .' but Jessica's voice trailed off as she stared at his empty seat. 'Oh, Zak,' she murmured with regret and quickly scanned the communal garden, but there was no sign and even if he had still been in view she wondered whether she would have called out to him. She was relieved and disappointed at the same time. It was better, wasn't it, to play things down just now? The trouble was she wasn't really sure – about anything; everything was so bloody awful, so miserable, so confusing that she wasn't even certain she was capable of making a rational decision at the moment.

Tom phoned every night, but she didn't want to speak to him; she wanted to scream at him.

Her mind switched inevitably and reluctantly to her sister. What had she ever done to Fay to deserve this? But that wasn't the issue, she reminded herself with familiar and painful logic: Fay just didn't care. There had always been a strange sort of treachery in her sister, 'a lack of guilt' their mother had let slip once, and this latest stunt should hardly have come as a surprise. But it had. Understatement of the year, Jessica.

She slumped down on to her chair and tried to lose her punishing thoughts. She looked at the portrait, the best thing she had ever done. The sun was shining across Zak's eyes in a deep band and he seemed to be looking back at her in that way he had. It aroused her, made her knees turn to jelly like a lovesick teenager; a look that seemed to say so much, so many things.

Jessica took a deep breath and observed with something close to astonishment her shaking hand because she wanted him and very badly, there was no doubt about that, but when he came close the strength of her wanting frightened her a little. And he was so much younger, she reminded herself again, and so unnervingly attractive. It didn't seem possible that he should want *her* when there were other younger and more lovely women around.

A purely physical thing, she told herself, something chemical. Must be, but it was crazy.

So it had been easier to keep him at arm's length; cowardly, perhaps, but easier.

There had been none of this sort of longing with Tom; they had simply met at university, then something had clicked and it had grown into love, except that 'love' seemed a rather overused word these days.

They had *shared* things together with ease, all the things that should be shared, the silly things like Sunday papers in bed, long walks on Brighton beach (even in the rain), restoring wrecks of furniture that had been left to die. Friends. And all those other tiny, meaningless details shared down the years, which had bound them inextricably together. She felt a funny tightening in her throat. They had had a good marriage. At least, she had thought so.

And now she would never have a baby.

Jessica sat back, her eyes wandering aimlessly to the thirsting garden which was more than merely thirsting, but dying in all probability; just like everything else in her world.

She thought of the boy and the emotions he churned up in her and an urge to get drunk took hold: blearily and wretchedly – sodden with plonk and grief.

'Oh, Zak,' she whispered and the sun's heat seemed to scorch the words away, like withered stalks pulled up and cast aside for burning.

He watched her unseen from the tree-house, saw her consternation and was tempted to go back, but her friend was arriving so what was the point? He should have stayed instead of stalking off like a sulking child. Even if he wasn't able to touch her, he would be close, he could study her, and he liked to do that – to follow the way she moved, tilted her head, held the damned paint-brush in her hand. A real poet would know the words for how I feel, he thought, but I don't and anyway, perhaps she would laugh because I'm so much younger than she is. A nobody with nothing to offer a woman like her, a one-time New-Age traveller with a raggedy-arsed past that would make her heave.

He made a soft despairing sound, felt the sun seep through the leaves to beat on his tired eyelids and then his stomach rumbled. Reluctantly he thought of food and the last can of baked beans standing on the kitchen windowsill in the basement. He didn't feel like baked beans, in fact, he was sick of them, but they would fill the gaping hole in his belly for a while until the next time. He was almost stone broke and calculated that he had about ninety pence in his jeans' pocket and that was it: finito. What then, Zak? What the hell do you do then? Beg? He had too much pride for that. There were other ways.

He made his way back to the house and only paused for a second at the top of the basement steps, but it irritated him that he had paused at all. Wasn't he over that stupid shit? Hadn't he sorted all that creepy stuff out in his head? It had been a nightmare, Zakky boy, he told himself, but somewhere inside he wondered what it was he was trying to do: explain to, or fool himself. He slapped the thought aside and as he came up to the threshold swore and pushed the door open with his foot, suddenly angry with himself.

He walked into the first room and was immediately aware of how stuffy it was, how rank and unwholesome. It seemed to disgust him more and more.

He sighed heavily as he crossed the room and into the other, but stopped dead in the doorway, the hairs along the nape of his neck standing on end.

The hidden door, the door he had so determinedly closed when he had returned that morning, stood wide open.

He seemed to stand there a long time before making his feet move, before letting a small still voice remind him that this was daylight and the sun was shining through the dirty windows and that the door was just a door – was just a door that had fallen open. Wasn't it?

He walked slowly towards it, trying to calm his racing heart, and as he drew nearer he began testing the boards with his feet and they gave like sponge to the pressure. He squatted down about three feet away from the yawning opening and pushed the door closed again with one finger and when he placed pressure on the floorboards once more it popped open. Simple as that.

No spooks, no nothing. All in his mind.

Maybe someone had been down here sniffing around, maybe Jonathan, or Fay.

What about last night? he asked himself.

Perhaps he hadn't closed it properly, or maybe the weight and movement of his body had tripped the floorboards?

He pressed his foot down hard again and the wood began to split and crack and groan and turn to powder.

'Shi-ite . . .'

He stepped back gingerly and wondered how far the rot had spread; everywhere in all probability, and he had been sleeping on it and at any time the floor might have caved in, plummeting him into the unlovely murky depths beneath.

And it was highly likely that no one would find him for quite a while. Poor old Zak. What a way to go.

He picked up his things and threw them into the adjoining room and when he had finished he looked at the jumbled pathetic heap and it seemed to take on everything his life stood for, which basically came down to a big round zero.

Over in the corner lay a plastic bag and in the plastic bag rolled up in some brown paper was the body of George;

a little the worse for wear, of course, a little maggoty, but nevertheless it would serve the purpose Zak now had planned for it, and as he surveyed the raggedy bundle he clenched his fists and tried to suppress the odd, uneasy feeling trying to creep up on him.

An expression of pain weaved its way across his face and he shifted his eyes with relief to the window. He didn't want to do it, he really didn't, but Jessica had left him no choice.

Zak swung his legs backwards and forwards. He was sitting on the wall of Jonathan's precious patio thinking about Jessica and what he was going to do to change things. He was also waiting for Fay to notice him, which she would, sooner or later.

The basement was out as far as sleeping arrangements were concerned, would be out as far as *anything* was concerned and that was why he was sitting on the wall waiting for Fay.

He knew he wouldn't have to wait long; she had been watching him from the window of her apartment for quite a while and now she had finished biding her time and was making her move, and he didn't even bother to look round as she came sauntering down the path towards him.

'Hi,' she said silkily.

'Hi.'

'Catching a few rays?'

'Something like that.'

She sat down beside him and followed his gaze into the garden.

'They're going to start turning the water off soon,' she said, 'you know, rationing it, for an hour or so at a time.'

'Oh, yeah?'

'Driest year on record, apparently,' she turned and looked at his profile, licked her lips. 'Unbelievable this heat . . .' she was staring at him hard now, 'must be a little unpleasant not being able to have a good shower, or lie back and enjoy a deliciously long bath.'

'Sometimes.'

'You can always use mine, you know.' She paused. 'Any time.'

'Is there an entry fee?'

She smiled. 'Not exactly.'

He said nothing.

'Why don't you come up now?' she coaxed.

'I don't think so.'

'Why not?'

He shrugged.

'We could have a bath together.'

He leaned his head back, looked at the sky.

'Oh, come on, Zak,' she pleaded softly.

He shook his head.

'Why the hell not?' Her voice began to rise a little. 'What is it about me that's such a bloody turn off?'

'You're not really my type.'

Her eyes slitted with anger.

'You cheap bastard.'

He turned and looked at her full in the face.

'Which doesn't mean to say I won't come up.'

Fay's expression was now a mixture of fury and bafflement.

'What the hell is that supposed to mean?'

His mouth seemed on the verge of smiling. 'How much do you want me to come up?'

A strong picture formed in her mind of their previous encounter in his tacky squat; what he had done and how he had deliberately left her squirming with humiliation and an almost-orgasm, the lack of which had nearly driven her insane. Yet it excited her more than she cared to admit and the excitement incited arousal, made the flesh twitch between her legs.

'Is this a game?' she asked sharply. 'Do you want some kind of forfeit?'

'I think you misunderstand,' he replied, 'I said *how much*.'

She gaped at him in disbelief as the words struck into her understanding.

'You want me to *pay* you?'

'Why not? People pay for sex all the time, in different ways.' With their self-respect mostly.

'I've never paid for sex in my whole life.'

'Not many women do, or have to,' he mused, 'interesting that, don't you think? Paying has always been seen as a male obligation – paying money that is.'

'Are you serious?'

'Well, I think I'm worth more than a hot shower,' he said, 'don't you?' He held her gaze, then deliberately focused on her mouth and grinned in a mocking kind of way.

Fay thought he was the most erotic thing she had ever seen and even as she looked back at him, her face alight with excitement, her mind was already conjuring up visions of fantastic pornographic situations. Any price.

And if her vision had cleared for an instant Fay might have seen the scorn in Zak's eyes sharpen ominously. She might have seen ancient and desolate things reflected in the inner sanctum of those lustrous blue eyes.

It was one of those claw-footed baths – huge – standing isolated in the centre of a vast black and white bathroom.

There was chrome, too, lots of it, glistening and cold and severe, jutting out of the walls as geometric towel-rails or light-fittings or radiator grills, one twisting and zig-zagging up the paintwork like some weird and unravelling montage. Opposite the bath and attached to a stark white wall was a mirror framed in wrought-iron rusting at the edges, beneath it a polished chromium hatstand had been coiled into the shape of a black African slave. A stuffed fox with tattered, moth-eaten ears snarled impotently beside the original tank-sized flush toilet (the only foxes he had ever encountered were generally running away, fast, and in the opposite direction).

Way above his head a naked light bulb hung.

'You like it?'

'It's different.' Like a hospital waiting-room care of Salvador Dali.

'I love space and light,' she said with pride. 'I have a cleaning lady who does the marble floor for me. I like things *clean*. I hate dust and dirt in a house, and those little meaningless objects cluttering up a place . . .' Fay stopped suddenly, as if she had said too much. 'I'll run the bath. There's soap and oil and talc over there. Would you like a drink while you're waiting – some wine? Whisky?'

'Tea.'

She raised her eyebrows.

'Mint, camomile, Earl Grey?'

'Just plain tea.'

She left the room and he stared at the water pouring into the huge enamel bath, steaming up in great clouds, began stripping off his clothes.

She came back with a tray on which she had set a miniature silver tea set, completé with sugar tongs.

'Get in,' she said and placed the tray on the floor,

'I'll serve you your tea while the bath fills up and you soak.'

She watched him as he climbed into the tub, his hard perfect body not seeming out of place in what was essentially her territory. Her eyes fastened on his flaccid penis and she swallowed, deep in her throat. He was larger than Tom and yet she had been more than pleased with what her brother-in-law had had to offer, but Zak was of Errol Flynn proportions, in another league, and she shuddered just a little, containing herself, determined not to mess things up like last time.

'Sugar?' she asked sweetly, averting her eyes.

'Three,' he said.

She smiled. 'Lumps or teaspoons?'

He looked back at her without amusement. 'Teaspoons.'

The cup and saucer were delicate white and charcoal-grey things, he could see the tea through the wafer-thin porcelain as she brought it to his mouth.

They watched each other across the rim of the cup until he had finished, like a ritual, and then she started to remove her clothes.

'I want this bath alone,' he said.

She stopped dead, her eyes round, black, mutinous.

'When I've finished,' he said smoothly, 'then we can do what you want.'

Fay stared at him for a long moment before picking up her clothes and walking silently away.

When he was ready, Zak called her and she came to him naked. He lifted her then, into the bath water and began to soap her body everywhere, every crevice, every orifice and when he had done that he made her get out and dried her himself, and when he had done that, he oiled her, even her hair, pulling it hard and straight down her back, and he twisted it into coiled red ropes and then used it to tie her hands.

An insect buzzed through the hot air, then two more, three.

And Zak was cruel.

He was as cruel as Fay wanted on that marble floor; watching her anaemic hips squirm and lift and tremble as he pressed and pinched and nipped all those damp tender secret places, made her whimper and writhe and babble frantically like a gibbering doll as he brought his tongue, his teeth to her nipples, her groin until blood showed through and her neck muscles stood out, her lips strained over little white teeth. Until she was weak and limp and gutted.

Twisted her flesh into skewers, made it burn.

And she asked for more, so he gave her more and the asking went on and on and none of it mattered, he told himself.

He went on with the rut, battered into her like the barbarian, berserker that he was, all the way up – impaling: fists and fingers and cock smashing and driving and brutalising; unearthing all the caked and curse-laden treasures from the darkest ranges of his memory.

None of it mattered.

Not the poison seeping out of him, nor the beats of pain in time with the pumping of his heart.

He knew everything, could contemplate anything, things no one else could imagine, and the knowledge was killing him inside.

'Why on earth should he call you?' Jessica exclaimed. 'What good did he think it would do?'

'Gordon, not me,' Roz corrected, 'and I suppose he's looking for a sympathy vote.'

'And Gordon gave it to him . . .'

'Of course not,' her friend replied, 'but he wasn't hostile either.'

Jessica picked up the coffee pot, refilled their cups.

'What did he say?' she said quietly.

'What do you think?' Roz sighed. 'He's desperate to make things up . . .'

'For heavens sake.' Jessica pinched the top of her nose in disbelief.

'He's devastated, Jess.'

'Oh, don't Roz,' she said wearily, 'I've heard it all before. He was calling me every day,' every night, 'before I told him to stop.'

'And nothing more from Fay, other than that strange visit you told me about?'

Jessica shook her head, not trusting herself to speak, so they fell silent and she moved disconsolately to the window. Always to the damned window, always looking out like a blasted bird in a cage. An image of the missing cockatoo formed in her mind and her heart sank further. Another mistake, another catastrophe to help her along the way.

'Book Champneys, Roz, will you?' she said all at once. 'Maybe by the time Christmas comes round I might feel like going.'

'Are you sure?'

'No.'

'Oh, Jess.'

'I've thought of taking a holiday, going away.' She thought of Zak. What about Glastonbury? Could they? Was she brave enough to take that sort of risk? Why not? A little voice whispered – you want him, he wants you. Why not?

She glanced back at Roz, wanting to tell her, spill out her thoughts, but she said nothing and turned back to the window, felt her insides jump because there he was, walking towards the house, to her, as if he had sensed her wanting before she did, but she sucked in a breath as Fay came up behind him, running, red hair flowing out behind her, flinging her arms around his neck.

Hot blood crashed into Jessica's head and outrage and grief and disbelief.

Then he was disentangling her greedy arms, pushing her away, saying some furious thing and Jessica closed her eyes.

'What is it?' Roz's voice seemed to come from somewhere far away.

Jessica shook her head.

'Jess?'

Jessica turned round. 'It's nothing.'

'You've gone white – whatever's the matter? Do you feel ill, sick or something?'

She took a deep breath. 'As it happens, I do.' And it was true.

'Shall I get you some Andrews?'

'I told you, Roz, it's nothing.' Only her sister twisting a good sharp knife in the wound.

'I think I'm beginning to sound like your mother.'

'Oh, no, Roz,' Jessica protested, forcing a smile. 'I'm sorry.'

'Two days is a long enough stay under the circumstances.'

'I've loved having you here,' she said, speaking the formula, but her real self was outside, in the garden, and when she glanced back Fay was gone, but Zak was still coming and she felt a little dread.

'I know, and I've loved being here, but you can have too much of a good thing. Maybe you need time on your own now, although I shall worry about you rattling around in this bloody great place.'

'I'll be all right,' she said, 'I'm supposed to be a big girl now . . .' but she felt like a child, a very small and insecure child, 'and I've spent a great deal of time here alone. Tom was away a lot, remember?'

'I remember.'

Roz studied Jessica as she turned away from her again, saw that same stiffening in her body as she looked outside.

'How's that boy?' she asked, 'Zak, isn't it?'

Jessica didn't reply for a moment, then – 'He's about to arrive, why don't you find out for yourself?'

Roz looked at her friend sharply, wondered at the sudden edge to her voice.

He tapped on the glass panel of the garden door, watched Jessica come towards him and thought how tired she looked and then saw the anger held in her eyes and knew she had seen.

'Hi.'

'Hello, Zak.'

Over her shoulder he could see that friend of hers peering at him.

'Thought I'd come over and make sure you were all right.'

'I'm fine,' Jessica said tightly, 'just fine.'

'Anything I can do?'

He smiled and the smile was so warm, so genuine, she felt that heat flooding her again and she hated herself for it. She had been a fool ever to think that he really cared: a sop to her ragged, ever-decreasing ego, a knight of sorts arriving just at a critical and needful time in her life. The sort of thing that happened in those sickly 'True Romance' magazines.

But real life isn't like that, Jess. In real life people get hurt and love is gut-wrenching agony.

'No, thanks.'

'I could come back later.'

'No.'

He wanted to explain, but didn't know how without hurting her more.

'We could work on the picture.'

Please, Jessica.

'No. I'm very tired.'

'I won't tire you.'

Please.

'No, Zak.'

'I'll call in tomorrow.'

'Please don't.'

'You know I'll come.'

She looked back at him for several moments before closing the door softly and even when she was no longer in view he had difficulty drawing his eyes away from the place where she had stood.

Oh, Jessica. Don't leave me. Don't make me do this thing.

It was the dark end of the day again, night-time, when memories play tricks and people are at their most defence-less. A moonlit night, a still one, like all the others before it. As if the world had stopped turning for this interminable heat-filled summer. But it would end soon; Zak felt it, knew it, and the rain would come, smashing down on to the land in torrential sheets, flooding everything; there would be lightning and furious claps of thunder, like hammer blows from the gods. A fitting end to a summer that could never come again.

Not quite over yet, though.

He had walked down to the front and stood on the pier for a while, watching the sun sink below the horizon and blood-red light spread and haemorrhage across the fading skyline. The West Pier, the old one, had been silhouetted against the sunset; a pitiful hulk, crippled and broken and unloved, falling bit by bit into the sea, but it had lost none of its dignity down through the years. Zak thought it beautiful.

When he turned round and looked back to the eastern side, his eyes narrowed and grew watchful, it made him think of that other time when he had come here alone, the scary time when things had turned inside out, like a flap opening into eternity.

You're going nuts, Zak.

In fact, he made himself doubt that that night on the beach had happened at all and promoted it more and more into the realm of fantasy. But there *are* things, another voice whispered, uncharted things outside of human understanding. You, of all people, know that.

He thought he felt a gentle pull, a tug, a feeling of being drawn to the sea, but then blinked in puzzlement and fright and jerked his gaze back towards the bright lights of the town and reassuring reality. He was tired, that's all.

He walked away, all the way back to the park called The Level which bordered the Crescent, and then lay down on the grass for a long, long time and stared at the stars until he felt good and ready and sleep had claimed everyone else in the world.

The bundle felt vaguely warm, clutched as it was so tightly under his arm and Zak didn't like that, didn't like that warmth; it conjured images he would rather not think about.

The night had come down hard in the garden, there were few lights and the stunted trees and bushes soaked up the moonshine like water. He flicked a glance up at Fay's window and walked on, he would face her later and if she made things really bad he would simply leave and sleep in the tree-house, or maybe hold the tiredness off until tomorrow and sleep outside beneath a shady tree.

The funny thing was he didn't mind being awake now, didn't mind the aloneness in a way; in fact, he preferred it because it got him away from the dreams, dreams that were beginning to weave themselves inexorably into the pattern of his life. They were not *nice* dreams and not exactly bad either (nothing like the monster of the other night), but definitely not nice – disturbing was the right word and he had started to dread closing his eyes and falling into sleep because then he would have to suffer the dreams. And suffer was also the right word.

Jessica's house loomed and he hid in the shadows for a time before creeping over the wall and making his way slowly to the window. He became very still and looked behind and to either side, checking that he was the only one abroad in the night, that no one watched. He put down the bundle and tested the window; she hadn't locked it, despite his warning. Part of him wished she had.

He slipped inside in exactly the same way, followed the same path, only deviating once to study the flowers, yellow roses he had left her that morning, carefully arranged on the hall-stand. They had neat golden heads like thimbles on long green necks, all wrapped-up petal-tight like little gifts. The first flowers he had ever bought, and to say sorry, forgive; purchased with the Judas money Fay had given him.

When he reached the bedroom he stood again in the doorway and watched her sleeping face, the contour of her body beneath the sheet, but there would be no touching this time. He moved quickly, stealthily around the bed and placed the bundle on the empty white pillow beside her and as he withdrew his hands he stared down at them; they were shaking and he put them aside.

He could have frightened her into needing him in a less dramatic way, he supposed, but the cockatoo was a sort of trump card, a way of alienating puling Tom for good. Zak sighed, felt grey melancholy descend on him.

She should not have made him resort to this, she should have let him in.

'Where have you been?'

'None of your business.'

Fay's voice rose shrewishly. 'It *is* my business when I pay you to be here!'

'I needed a walk.'

'Not on my time.'

Zak fished in his pockets, pulled out some notes and dropped them to the floor and they fluttered down like little birds deprived of flight.

'Stuff your fucking money.'

She stared at the notes, lifted her gaze back to his face again and realised what she had done.

'Don't go, Zak.'

'I don't want to stay.'

'Take the money back.'

He shook his head.

'I didn't mean it, I promise you,' she pleaded. 'I lost my temper.'

'So I noticed.'

Above her a daddy-long-legs danced up to the fluorescent light, swooped jerkily to a lamp-stand, bobbed to the sky-light. Autumn. Change was coming at last.

'Stay,' she said, 'I've baked a lasagne and there's chilled white wine if you want it.' She wouldn't drink, of course, not after Edinburgh and Tom. Alcohol was poison in her veins, would turn her on her head so that she lost all control and Zak would definitely make an exit then.

He surveyed her with a feeling of inevitability, but said nothing.

'Afterwards,' she began, 'we could . . .'

'I'm tired.' He thought of Jessica.

She bent down to pick up the money so that he would not see the fury burning in her face.

'Whatever you like,' she said, calculating, fixing a smile on her mouth, but he wouldn't get away that easy.

She let him eat until his belly was full, gave him a big mug of black coffee and a dainty dish of mints and thick powdery turkish delight, then, without speaking, pulled him gently to the four-poster bed and undressed him and he gave in without a murmur or a protest which surprised her; but it didn't matter, all he had to do was lie back and she would do the rest. She *would* have what she wanted.

When they were both naked she straddled him, but held herself just above and trailed her breasts across his mouth, his chest, his belly, his sex, did this again and again. All the time her almond-shaped eyes watched him and then she moistened her lips and began to use her little pointed tongue; flicking it back and forth, over and over, coaxing and stroking the beginnings of his erection, lifting his scrotum and teasing his balls, rolling them between her fingers, slipping the hard point of a finger-nail up and inside, dragging it down in a silken burning streak towards the shaft of his now, very erect penis.

Zak was silent; Zak had not said a word and his eyes were closed.

Fay studied him with admiration, thought of Tom; he would have been frantic by now.

She moved her body, sealing herself across his thighs and looked down, saw that his face was lighted with the strangest of smiles. She lifted herself just enough to take him inside, brought her body weight down again and let him fill her, threw her head back, arching her back and grinning in delight and triumph.

Fingers dug into his neck.

Flesh grinding against flesh, slowly and deliberately, creating a delicious friction; Fay gazing at him, at that still, remote smile on the beautiful mouth.

An exotic sensual boy who belonged nowhere.

Fay's grin widened. Only with me.

Her grin did not waver, it stayed on her face as she built up the rhythm of her hips, wriggling, squirming back and forth, sideways, faster and faster, felt the first ecstatic mushrooming of a huge ring of pleasure.

'Oh, Zak,' she cried, 'oh, yes, yes, yes . . .'

His face was set and closed, the lamplight picking out his features, lips a little open now.

'Jessica,' he whispered.

Fay heard and Fay froze.

'Jessica.'

And then he opened his eyes and she saw the truth there, too clear not to be recognised.

There was an ugly silence which only lasted a matter of seconds, but seemed longer, much longer than that.

'You bastard,' her voice was unsteady, 'you lying shit.'

'I haven't lied to you,' he said quietly, feeling his hardness break and shrink to nothing.

She snorted with contempt, eyes glittering slits of fury.

'You and her?' she hissed, 'I don't believe it.'

He made no answer.

Fay squeezed her thighs, hard.

'Get off me,' he said.

'I asked you a question.'

Abruptly he pushed her back and slid upwards at the same time. Fay lost balance and fell sideways with a little scream.

Zak swung his legs out the other side, picked up his clothes and walked away, feet padding softly across the bare and varnished floorboards.

'You fucking bastard . . .' she crawled towards him on all fours, 'don't you dare walk out on me.'

She got up and ran after him, caught him in the hall and threw herself at him in a dark and all-consuming rage: hands and fists lashing out, knees flaying upwards. He brought his arms up to protect himself and in one unerring movement thrust her against the wall and slapped her so hard her head jerked back and thudded against the paintwork. She stopped then, as suddenly as a plug being pulled.

'Don't go,' she whispered.

'I want to.'

'I'll behave.'

'You don't know how.'

'Please.'

He shook his head.

'It's three in the morning – you can't.'

'Do you think I care about that?' His voice was full of scorn.

'Anything, Zak . . .'

'No.'

'Please.'

'No.'

'I promise I'll be good.'

'You?' he sneered, made a small sound of disgust.

Even as her eyes blazed with anger she was thinking that his mouth was divine, and so perfect that the sneer took nothing away. Nothing at all. Madness.

'And you – are you good, Zak? I doubt it somehow. I would guess that in the sort of place where you come from "good" sucks. I mean . . .' she spat, 'I don't know many guys – any, in fact – who would be prepared to rent themselves out for a hot shower.'

'Or many women who need to pay for the privilege.'

She scoffed and the corners of her mouth turned slightly up into a sardonic smile. 'I bet you've done things I'd never dream.'

He said nothing.

'Jessica doesn't know all there is to know about you, does she, Zak? And if I were to start delving into your murky past I expect I would find enough weird gunk to fill a sewer.' Her eyes shone with spite. 'You don't like me, but perhaps we have more in common than you think.'

'No.'

'You enjoyed what we did.'

He shook his head.

'You did, I could tell,' there was that smug smile again, 'I can always tell.'

He stared at her hard and darkness seemed to crawl up his back and beckon him in. Fay saw and for the first time felt a tickle of fear; her eyes darted to Zak's tightening grip on her wrists.

'You can let me go now.'

'I didn't enjoy you . . .' he said softly and there was a part of Fay that would have preferred a scream or a shriek, not this slithering softness in his voice that made her flesh creep. 'It was like having sex with something dead, or decaying . . .'

'Let go of me.'

Zak let go.

The fear left Fay as soon as she had closed the door after him and then she merely felt foolish and thwarted and manipulated in a peculiar kind of way.

'Creep, bastard, shit . . .' she stomped back into the studio-cum-bedroom and over to the window, tried to make out his form as he left the house, but lost him to the darkness. 'Louse, slimeball, parasite . . .' threw a tube of paint across the room, 'bloody prick-teaser . . .'

The paint landed a small way from her almost-finished canvas and she scowled, knowing that she wouldn't sleep now, knowing that she had every intention of continuing with the picture. What else was there to do now but work? Zak had put paid to the rest and with bells on.

She stood in front of the shrouded canvas, feet slightly apart, hands on naked hips, and with a petulant jerk pulled the sheet away from the unfinished painting and scrutinised it sharply for flaws and untruths. This canvas, of all those she had done, was uncannily short of such things and she had no idea why. There was something else, too; up until this point in her career she had quietly prided herself on producing work that made the average punter feel at the very least uneasy, or as the master, Max Ernst, would have it – 'make people scream'.

Her gruesome garden had started off that way, but now it was, quite simply, different and nothing like the picture she had originally visualised. Now she wondered if her earlier stuff hadn't been a little obvious because somehow this one's horror was not in the seeing, but in the sensing, as if somewhere, somehow, something unthinkable waited patiently within the trees and undergrowth, the forest and the standing-stones beyond. Curious.

She tilted her head on one side and frowned. And now there was a man in it.

Zak was glad to get out of Fay's place, eager: all that sterility and fluorescent lighting – all that black and white and chrome beating coldly on his brain. He faltered for an instant, feeling perplexed, uneasy. *Her* and her ugly little theories.

Fay was full of shit and she hated him now, he supposed, but it didn't matter, and it wouldn't matter to her either – not later, or tomorrow, or the day after – because she wanted him as much as he wanted Jessica, and that could bother him if he let himself think about it.

Instead he took a deep breath of air and walked softly through the garden towards the tree-house. The shrubs and earth and trees were moon-drenched and without colour, so white they seemed no longer real. His face was hot and he turned it up to the dark sky as if there might be some mouth-watering breeze weaving its way through the night air to cool his skin.

'All things must change,' he murmured, 'To something new, to something strange . . .'

Oh, yes, there was a change coming and coming soon.

9

A shaft of sunlight was falling on her half-sleeping face and Jessica turned over, willing her heavy eyelids to open, weighted as they were by the drugs she had taken the night before. Inside she chided herself; as if doping herself up might stave off those endless hopeless thoughts flitting in and out of her mind like blowflies.

She was curled up in bed, knees touching her belly and staring blearily at the radio, a sleek black thing which had been a gift from Tom's mother. She reached up and switched it on, heard the eager, ever-willing tones of a DJ tell her he was 'taking a trip back to the seventies'. Where had he been then? In play-school?

An old Bowie number filtered into the room, 'Young Americans'. She had been doing her A-levels way-back then and living in Bristol. She had had a boyfriend called Andy, her first *real* one, her first love, and he had driven an old Ford Anglia, rusting at the seams, and given her a pair of hooped earrings hidden in a box of After Eight Mints amongst all those slivers of paper-clad chocolate. He had taken her virginity and she had given it willingly and wanted more because she discovered she was made that way. In the end she had hurt him and she had never meant to do that.

Silent tears began working their way into Jessica's eyes.

He had had long dark hair, just like Zak. Odd that, she

thought vaguely, wearily. She shifted her gaze to the ceiling and moved on to her back, depressingly conscious that one side of the bed was empty and uninhabited.

A fly buzzed very close to her face.

Slowly Jessica turned her head and instead of emptiness her eyes found the bundle and the bundle was alive to the day, seething in fact, and the fly which had buzzed so close to her face had now settled on the brown paper and was busy disappearing inside, just as a wriggling clot of maggots was busy worming its way out.

Even at the moment of her screaming Jessica's mind was busy processing the sickeningly sweet smell of something rotting which had been permeating the hot humid air long before her eyes had opened.

Zak poured scalding coffee into Jessica's cup and started to top-up his own when the doorbell rang.

Jessica jumped.

'Shall I get it?' Zak asked.

'Please,' she replied. 'It's probably Roz.'

And it was. He wanted to smile at the look of surprise on the woman's face (a nice woman, but intrusive) when he opened the door, caught some of her confused thoughts as she blinked dazedly back at him.

'Where's Jessica?'

'In the kitchen.'

'Is she all right?'

'A bit shaken,' he said, 'naturally.'

'God,' she fumed, 'makes you wonder what the hell the world's coming to . . .' She moved past him into the kitchen where Jessica sat nursing a cup of coffee.

'Darling,' Roz gushed helplessly, 'I'm so sorry. How are you feeling?'

'I'm okay,' she said. 'Really.'

Roz looked at her doubtfully. 'How did they get in?'

'I left a downstairs window unlocked.'

'Oh, Jess.'

'I know, I know.' The police had looked at her as if she were a little mad, too. Maybe, just lately, she was.

'Did they take much?'

'No,' she said quietly, 'not that I can tell. That's what's so strange.'

She drew her coffee cup to her face, both hands clutched around it, the knuckles so white the bones shone through. Someone walking through her house, up her stairs, watching her as she slept. She shuddered, stared at the steam rising from her coffee with vacant eyes. 'It's the bird I don't understand. Why? What sort of mind would think up a trick like that?' An image of that bundle on her pillow slid into her head again. God, the smell ... the horror of it ... lying next to her, and for how long?

Zak looked away, to the window and the world outside. *Mea culpa, mea culpa, mea culpa.* I promise I will make this up to you, Jessica, I will. I will.

'Some burglars – or should I say certain very sick individuals – do unspeakable things these days ...' Roz began, 'you've probably read about them in the papers and know the sort of things I mean. No one can afford to take chances any longer,' she said pointedly. 'You must be more careful.'

Jessica knew exactly what she meant and Roz wasn't implying such old-fashioned niceties as merely gagging and tying someone up; she was thinking of a new age of wonders ... things like rape and sodomy and torture and human excrement plastered over walls and furniture, tainting all the things people had loved and grown with.

'I know, I know,' Jessica said. 'Anyway, the police have already decided that these – and I say 'these' not even knowing whether there was more than one involved – were not your common or garden burglars because nothing seems to be missing. They also seem to think it was only one person, and probably someone who held a grudge.' She sighed. 'They even asked me if I had any enemies and when I said my marriage had just broken up they hinted at Tom.'

'But Tom wouldn't do something like this.'

'Would you like a coffee?' Zak broke in.

Roz looked up, startled out of her thoughts. 'Yes, thank you.'

'I didn't think so either,' Jessica said.

'Didn't? You can't mean . . .'

'I don't know what I mean any more.'

'Tom wouldn't – you *know* he wouldn't.'

'He never did tell me exactly what happened to the cockatoo; apparently it disappeared into thin air.'

'Maybe it did . . .' Roz ran on, but faltered as Jessica opened her eyes wide at her, 'I mean, flew away that is; birds do, given the right opportunity.'

'He had every reason to let it go . . .'

'And who could blame him?'

'Milk and sugar?' Zak broke in again.

Roz looked up. 'Just milk, please.'

'But he didn't.'

Roz gave Jessica an odd look. 'What on earth do you mean?'

'The cockatoo was still wrapped in an old tea-towel of mine – one I never used, but I recognized it despite the fact that it was filthy with soil.'

'What are you saying?'

'That it was dead when Tom – and it must have been him, Roz – got rid of it, buried it, or whatever.'

'Are you trying to tell me that he *killed* it – deliberately?' She shook her head in astonishment. 'Don't be daft.'

'I'm not trying to tell you anything, I'm just telling you how it was found.' Jessica sighed heavily. 'Maybe Tom wanted to vent his spleen on something; he was in a bit of a state at the time, as you might expect. And the bird did seem not to like him, however much that may defy normal logic.' She played with her coffee spoon, watched Zak as he filled her cup. 'Oh, I don't know.'

'That's just not Tom, Jess,' Roz said with a trace of reproach.

'How do you know who Tom is?' Jessica said bitterly. 'Because I certainly don't.'

'Sorry,' Roz ventured, 'I wasn't thinking.'

'Oh, it's all right,' Jessica gave her a strained sort of smile, 'and take no notice of me, I'm touchy, that's all.'

'What about Fay?'

'Yes, naturally I thought of her.' My strange heartless unnatural sister. 'But hasn't she done her worst? She's got Tom, even if she doesn't want him any more. Why would she bother with this little performance? Besides . . .' she finished impatiently, 'I'm not sure she even knew we had a cockatoo.'

'Did anyone else know you'd lost the bird?'

'Only the neighbours.' Jessica closed her eyes in exasperation. 'And I put one of those ads in the newsagents, you know, the postcard variety – "white cockatoo lost, please call Mrs Innes, reward" – that sort of thing.'

'Jess, it could have been anyone.'

'That's what I said,' Zak said.

Roz darted a glance at him, suddenly aware of his eyes on her and she flushed.

'Zak saw a prowler in the gardens the other night,' Jessica said, 'he even gave chase, but lost them, I'm afraid. He bothered to call in and tell me and in the process reminded me to lock up securely which, as you already know, I didn't.' She regarded him steadily. 'He's been very kind.'

'I can see that,' Roz said. Every home should have one. 'How's the portrait going?'

'Fine.'

'What do you think of it, Zak?' Roz looked at him again, he was leaning against the kitchen sink, arms folded, hair tied and hanging down his back, a shadow of a beard on his jaw. Dark and sexy with a touch of the savage. She was struck by the odd thought that there was nothing of the twentieth century about him, somehow, despite his faded blue jeans and Doc Martens. There was something *different* about him, something *old*.

'Jessica seems to see a lot more in me than I do.'

Roz smiled. A clever answer; a little over-modest perhaps, but nevertheless clever.

'When do you think you'll finish?'

'Soon.'

'What will you do then, Zak?'

'I'm not with you?'

'I assume you're unemployed.'

'Oh, no,' Jessica interjected, 'Zak works nights, he's a DJ.'

'I see,' Roz exclaimed with interest, saw blood seep into his unreadable face.

'Busy?'

'Not bad.'

'What do you call yourself?'

He frowned. 'Just Zak.'

'I could hire you for my niece's wedding in March.'

He shrugged with indifference.

'Not up your street?'

'March is a long way off,' he replied cagily.

'I always thought that that was the idea – you know, booking in advance and all that, ensuring your future and keeping the shekels coming in.'

'I like to live on the edge.'

Roz raised her eyebrows.

'How provocative.'

'Makes life more interesting.'

'I don't doubt it,' she parried, 'but I'd always be a little afraid of falling right off that edge . . .'

'Oh,' he said, his voice deliberately softening, 'but I've never been afraid of heights.'

'No,' Roz said, 'I don't suppose you have.'

She was looking into his eyes, thought there was something almost hypnotic in the way he held her gaze, and then he was smiling, not at her, but at Jessica and there was nothing sweet in the smile, nothing ordinary.

It was a small slanting smile, the sort that went deep, like a dark stone thrown into a still pond.

From the fifth floor window of his rented studio flat Tom could see a large black wellington boot lying on the deserted beach and a little further away, underneath the pier, another gift from the sea had drawn a pack of gulls eager for rich pickings.

He had taken a walk down there and along the front that morning and actually managed it to Hove and back and without really being conscious of the effort.

315

Adultery and its grisly trappings concentrates the mind so wonderfully.

But the heat had got to him finally and at his journey's end he had sought refuge within the cool shadows of the Palace Pier, sitting on the stones like a day-tripper, and the stones had been blissfully cold which had surprised him until he realised that this patch of beach was never sun-warmed, had never been touched by the hot light of this strange summer, trapped as it was beneath the pier's great iron bulk.

Just after he'd got back, the police had arrived, two of them; a big one and a little one.

Now he was prime suspect in the murder of a cockatoo and the exhumation of its corpse. Notwithstanding the grotesque charge that he had defiled his wife's – correction – *their* home by pretending to break in and plant the revolting remains of that manic feathered fiend on her pillow (his, actually).

He had told them everything, of course, broken down, in fact, and he still wasn't sure whether they believed his actions had stopped short at the disposal of George's body. They had fallen silent at one point and in the strained stomach-churning atmosphere which followed he had seen how the little one had looked at him and in a way that made him want to crawl up and die – an unbeautiful blend of contempt and disgust; had felt both their burning gazes lock on the horror that was the left side of his face. Phantom of the Opera mark II.

Why would he do such a thing? For God's sake, he would have to be completely off his rocker to do something sick like that, but someone had, some brain-diseased pervert who enjoyed preying on women living alone.

And that someone had known where he had buried

George. Had he been seen grubbing around in the dark that God-awful night?

It was bizarre, all of it: completely, horribly and un-utterably bizarre.

Fay could have done it, but dead birds and certainly rotting ones, were definitely not her scene; she was paranoid about cleanliness, personal or otherwise. Besides, he could hardly imagine her wasting her precious time prancing around in the middle of the night to wage war on a sister on whom she had already delivered a crushing, if not mortal, blow. It didn't make sense.

Well, the police would no doubt make up their minds about that. Tom stared bleakly out to sea, but he didn't really think that they would come away from Fay's sterile abode with any more interesting leads; they would simply home in on him with more force, probably convinced that he was off his trolley and intent on wreaking revenge on his poor traumatised wife for kicking him out. Of course, they knew already that he had had an affair with her nubile younger sister.

What a twisted shit they must think him.

God, what a mess.

He switched his weary gaze to the telephone, picked up the receiver and dialled.

'Jess?'

There was a pause.

'Jess?'

'Hello, Tom.'

'Are you okay?'

'Yes.'

'I mean – really?'

'Yes.'

'You don't want me to come . . .'

'No.'

He cleared his throat.

'I didn't do it, you know.'

Another pause.

'I didn't, Jess.'

She sighed. 'I take it the police have been round.'

'You could say that.' In spades.

'What happened?'

'Well, I think you could safely say that I'm their number one suspect.'

'You didn't tell me the truth about the bird, did you?' she asked quietly, 'I thought you were lying, even then.'

'You wouldn't have believed me.'

'Tell me.'

'Part of what I told you was true,' his voice was shaky, 'the bit about finding the cage empty – I was flabbergasted, to put it mildly, when I walked into the dining-room and saw the cage door standing open.'

'It wasn't open when I left.'

'Well, I didn't open it, no matter what you think, and why would I, for heaven's sake? As far as I was concerned the less I had to do with the damned thing the better.'

'All right,' she said. Paused. 'And?'

'I went looking for it.' The memory stung him with appalling clarity. 'It was hiding somewhere at the top of the stairs.'

'Hiding?'

'It's the only word that fits,' he said haltingly, 'and then it went for me again,' like a bat out of hell, 'but I managed to get my hands up in front of my face before it could do any more damage.'

'Tom,' she said tiredly, 'this just doesn't add up. It all sounds so . . . crazy.'

'I can't help that,' he said. 'It happens to be the truth.'

'And then?'

In the solitude he blushed, wondered how on earth he was supposed to tell her what he had done next and how he had done it.

'Tom?'

'I stopped it.'

'How?'

'You won't understand.'

'Just tell me,' she responded in that quiet patient voice.

'I broke its neck.'

Jessica closed her eyes.

'I didn't mean it to happen,' he raised his eyes heavenward, 'I grabbed it . . .' his voice trailed off weakly; such a delicate little neck, '. . . and it just happened. I didn't have much choice.'

'Oh, Tom.'

'If you don't believe me,' he said quickly, panic creeping in, 'take a look behind one of the cartoon prints on the wall of the landing and you'll see a scratch. It did that when it came at me.'

'All right, all right.' There was a part of her that didn't want to hear any more.

'And then,' his voice was running now, the words spilling out in a horrible rush. He wanted to be sick. 'I went downstairs and was going to bundle it in the bin when I realised that you were likely to find it there – or at least there was a fairly strong possibility – so I decided to bury it.'

'Wrapping it in a tea-towel first.'

'Yes.'

'And that's it?'

'Yes.'

'I wish you'd told me all this before.'

'Do you think I don't? Do you think I wanted this?' He heard his voice begin to rise but couldn't help himself. 'And do you really think I'd creep into my own home and leave a disgusting object like that next to my own wife?' He gulped helplessly, plunged on, 'And whatever you may believe to the contrary – I happen to love you very much.'

'All right, Tom.'

'It's not all right,' he said, 'it's not bloody all right at all.'

She looked into the mouthpiece of the telephone and waited.

'I'd better go.'

'You do believe me, don't you, Jess?'

'I believe that you didn't leave the cockatoo on my pillow.'

That was something, wasn't it? he thought desperately, swamped by despair and homesickness.

'I suppose I can't really expect any more than that, can I, Jess?'

She was long in answering.

'No, Tom,' she said, 'you can't.'

Zak could feel Jonathan's eyes boring into his back, but he did not turn around, instead he continued getting his things together, just a few odds and ends to give Jessica the impression that he only intended a short stay.

'Are you leaving?'

Zak made no answer.

'I said – *are you leaving*?'

Zak put down the bag he was holding and swung round.

'What business is it of yours?'

Jonathan blushed. 'I just thought . . . well, I'd like to know.'

'Why?'

He looked at Zak full in the eyes. 'You know why.' He spoke softly, almost in a whisper.

'Your problem is not my problem.'

He picked up his bag again, began filling it.

'Stay,' Jonathan pleaded, 'I'll have this placed cleaned up – decorated.'

'It should be condemned.'

'No,' he said, 'it just looks that way.'

'It's rotten to the core.'

'It's old, that's all and, okay, some floorboards might need replacing, but it's got plenty of character.' He slapped the mantelshelf with the palm of his hand and somehow managed a grin. 'Only needs a bit of TLC – you know, Tender Loving Care.'

'Won't you face anything, man? Where are your brains – in your big ambidextrous prick?'

'Stop it.'

Zak shrugged and turned his back and Jonathan watched him in silence for a time.

'Where have you been these last few days?'

'London, Paris, New York . . .'

'Ha-bloody-ha.'

'Look,' Zak said, 'I don't have to answer to you, I don't have to answer to anyone.'

'Maybe that's your problem.'

Zak sighed heavily, patiently and stared hard at the man standing in the doorway; his shoulders were bent, hunched, as if the load were very heavy.

'And I'm not the answer to yours.'

Jonathan's face crumpled for a brief moment and Zak sucked in a weary breath, touched by pity for this confused, unbrave man who could not be honest with anyone and least of all himself.

'You are going to be miserable for the rest of your damned life if you don't get rid of the shit clogging up your head. Marrying Emma will make more shit – a bit like a rolling stone gathering no moss, but in reverse. And you'll be right up to your eyes in it.'

'Shut up.'

'Don't do it, man.' Zak suddenly had a compulsion to persist and persuade, perhaps because his own dream was so close to realisation he could afford to feel almost happy and with the happiness came generosity and even compassion, for too long strangers to him.

'You wanted me that night.'

'No,' Zak said. 'I wanted someone else.'

'Liar.'

'I'm not lying. I don't lie.' Not as a rule.

'You let me . . .'

'Only because you were here, because you wanted to and I wanted *it*.' Zak emphasised the last word with great deliberation. '*It* – not you. There's a difference.'

'You offered yourself.'

Zak closed his eyes in exasperation.

'I thought I'd do us both a favour,' he said patiently, 'all right?'

'I don't understand.' Jonathan looked bewildered, desolate.

'I thought you did.'

He shook his head, blushed deeply and Zak saw that his eyes were moist. I don't need this, not now.

'I've got to go.'

'Where?'

'A friend's.'

'The someone else you wanted?'

Zak nodded.

'You'll be back, though, won't you?' he pleaded.

'I'm helping out with the party, remember?' He would still do that for him; he didn't want to, but he'd do it. A little voice murmured: wasn't it called conscience money, Zak?

He moved to pass him, but Jonathan still stood in the doorway.

'Don't go.'

'I have to.'

'Please.'

'Get out of the way.'

Jonathan was shaking and perspiration seemed to be oozing from every pore. He felt close to panic.

'Zak . . .' The name sounded distorted, caught as it was between a sob and a moan.

Jonathan sank to his knees, put his arms around the squatter's legs, trembling cheek against his thigh.

'For Christ's sake . . .' Zak seethed.

'Bloody hell.'

Jonathan froze at the sound of the familiar voice just as Zak squinted up into the sunlit garden; Keith was standing there and watching them.

Instantly Jonathan was getting to his feet and smoothing back his hair with clumsy unsteady hands, dusting-off the knees of his trousers.

'What the hell do you want?' His voice still shook and all this Keith noted with avid interest.

'Sorry,' he replied and observed how two crimson blotches, like big rosy apples had formed in Jonathan's golden cheeks, 'am I interrupting something?'

'Nothing at all.' Zak stepped through the doorway and out into the day. 'In fact, your timing was impeccable – you couldn't have arrived at a better moment.'

Keith frowned in puzzlement and followed Zak with his

eyes as he came up the stairwell, switched his gaze back to Jonathan who was standing very still and watching the squatter walk away. His face was drained of all colour now, drawn and bleak.

'I asked you what you wanted,' Jonathan snapped.

His eyes were set on Keith, two glittering slits of resentment.

'And I asked if I was interrupting something.'

'Don't be stupid.'

'Looked like something to me,' Keith said nonchalantly. Everything was clear to him now, like glass.

'Such as?'

'Well, you weren't praying to Mecca, that's for sure.'

Jonathan was thinking fast and came up with the pathetic and most obvious. 'I'd dropped something . . .'

'Oh, yeah,' Keith said and nodded in a mocking sort of way, 'I should have thought of that. What did you drop?'

'Is that really any concern of yours? My lighter, as it happens.' He patted his pocket and made his legs move towards the steps; he didn't like Keith looking down at him, studying him, drawing uncomfortable conclusions from the ghastly little scene he'd just witnessed.

'Ah,' Keith mouthed, clearly not believing him. 'Got it safe now, have we?'

'Of course.' Jonathan began climbing the steps two at a time, but his legs felt like lead and he wanted a bath because he had this sensation of feeling grimy all over and wanting to scrub every crevice, every hollow, all those dark forbidden places which were at once so tantalising and yet so squalid, so ugly. The wanting was a fever, he thought miserably, and when the wanting was over . . . Oh, God.

'Is it the same as this one?' Keith asked and produced a familiar lighter from his pocket. 'Yours, I believe.'

Jonathan looked stupidly at his lighter and thought he might die.

'Where was it?'

'On your desk,' Keith purred, holding it up for inspection as if it were a prize, 'where you left it.'

Jonathan said nothing.

'Emma thought you might need it,' Keith continued easily, 'says you've been smoking more than usual just lately. I wonder why?'

'Drop dead, Keith.'

'I've locked up everything,' Zak said. 'Checked the windows, the front and back doors, even the cat-flap.'

'We don't have a cat-flap,' Jessica laughed.

'I know,' he said, 'I'm getting paranoid.'

'I think one of us is enough.'

'You're not paranoid,' he responded gently, 'just scared.'

She was standing at the window, watching her reflection in the glass. It was pitch outside and she could hear the muted thunder of rock music coming from somewhere; maybe someone was having a party.

'It's good of you to do this for me,' she said.

'I want to do it, you know that.' He eyed her with all the needful wonder of a lover, thought she looked beautiful in the long black kaftan she wore, wanted to reach out and pull her to him; touch and smell all that clean hair and skin. Drown in it.

'Yes, I know,' she said, 'but I don't know why.' She looked down at her hands. 'I assumed . . . when I saw you in the garden with Fay . . .'

'You shouldn't have assumed anything. That wasn't fair.'

'You don't know my sister.'

'I know *of* her,' he lied, but what good would the truth

do him, or her, now? Jessica could never understand. 'Very sure of herself, isn't she?'

'Oh, yes.'

'Forget it, Jessica,' he pleaded silently. 'She has nothing to do with me.'

'I suppose,' she began, 'after Tom . . .'

'I'm not Tom.'

'You lose something, don't you?' she said sadly. 'And more than trust when someone betrays you like that.'

He opened his mouth to speak, then closed it again as the telephone rang.

'That'll be Roz,' she said, 'or Tom – making sure I've locked the windows.'

Tom wasn't only puling, Zak had decided, but also mad to risk someone like Jessica for Fay. Mad *and* puling. She was picking up the phone now, he could hear her voice and bits of jig-saw conversation floating into the room. It was good old Tom trying to wriggle his way back in.

Zak turned to the window and looked out into the garden, thought his heart was as dark as the blackness waiting there.

'That's that,' she said behind him and he swung round. 'Just Tom, checking up. Probably afraid a real burglar might get in and steal his precious silver.' She forced a smile and Zak smiled back unconvinced.

'I'll sleep on the sofa,' he said.

'Oh.'

They looked back at each other full in the eyes until Jessica dropped her gaze.

'If I take the spare room,' he smiled, 'I might walk in my sleep.'

This was a game they were playing, a silly childish game because they were both afraid, and she more than him.

His Jessica, full of caution and fear and confusion; but he wouldn't push it, couldn't push it; this moment, this time was just too important to work the magic and steal what was not yet his.

'Shall I get you a blanket?'

'I've brought my sleeping-bag.'

'You needn't have done that.'

'I didn't want you to think . . .'

'What?'

'That I'd take anything for granted.'

She sighed deeply, and he was acutely aware of the rise and fall of her breasts.

'I know you wouldn't,' she said. 'I trust you, which is probably a strange thing to say after recent events – and perhaps more than anyone I've met in a long time. It's even more strange when you consider that I hardly know you.'

If she knew, if she really knew all the things I have done.

'You're kind,' she added, then paused, 'and seem to ask nothing in return.' Except her, and she thought she must sound incredibly naïve. They wanted each other, didn't they? And if she stayed in the room much longer she would end up staying, she would end up begging him to satisfy the need inside itching to get out. It was only sex, she cried silently, that's all, but when she was near him she could hardly think of anything else. The need was so great it made her back off and nervous, made a coward of her.

'I'm no saint, Jessica.'

He cringed inwardly. What had Fay said? That in his murky past she would find enough weird gunk to fill a sewer; except that the weird and the gunk did not necessarily go together, but she had been close.

It was his tragedy that he found the weird, the little

power in him, so irresistible, almost beautiful and yet it was inextricably linked to the ugliness which could so often spawn from it. All his life it had been this way. The first time, when he was three, a big black and white dog had snarled at him because he had pulled its fur. The dog had died: no mark, no nothing; the animal had simply stopped living.

'Are you all right?'

Jessica's voice was soft, melting, full of concern and he longed to do what Jonathan had done and throw himself at the feet of the one and only person who held him in thrall. In time there would be others for Jonathan, but not for him, never for him. Jessica was his only chance in this life to love and be loved in return.

'Tired, that's all,' he said.

'You won't be comfortable down here.'

'I'll be fine.'

He knew she would come to him later, even if, on the surface of her mind, she refused to recognise the fact, but she would come to realise it when she lay in the dark in that big empty desolate bed and was tempted to use her hand for comfort. She would come to him then.

'We'll finish the portrait tomorrow,' she said.

He nodded.

'Good night, then.'

'Good night, Jessica,' he said. 'And no pills, remember?'

She smiled finally and like a little girl who has been found eating some forbidden sweets. 'No pills, Zak.'

'You don't need them.'

Not now.

'I know.'

* * *

There was a wind. Zak opened his eyes from an almost-state of sleep and looked at the window, saw a tree-branch sway a little and tap-tap against the glass. He got up and padded over to peer outside into the darkness and the garden.

The wind dropped suddenly and the black outlines of trees no longer shifted and rolled, creaked or wailed, so that all was strangely still again and Zak felt a vague sort of anguish, a nagging feeling reaching down to blood and bone. Someone there? No. The dark playing tricks.

He waited and looked until he didn't want to look out there any more and began fumbling for the cord which would pull the curtains closed and when he had done this he leaned against the rich drapery and wondered at the mad beating of his heart. He lifted his eyes to the ceiling and wished himself with her and not alone, but then he was chiding himself for his weakness, as if he were some child waking up to the blackness of the night and seeing in his bedroom furniture the gibbering, bulbous shapes of ghouls and bogeymen.

When he lay down again it was with relief and sleep took him easily, as if it had been waiting there for him, for just such a moment.

And in the dream that followed he was standing at the window again and in exactly the same way. Outside the wind had picked up once more and shafts of moonlight spilled through the flailing branches of trees to dance wildly on the parched and broken earth. He could hear the wind's sad sough gather strength into a tortuous whine and then a scream, shrieking through the bushes and trees like an escaped lunatic.

It did not seem like the garden he knew; the dream had turned it inside out and from where he stood there was nothing but the tall shape of an enormous stone, a sinuous monolith standing isolated in the place where the summer-house should have been. The monolith was covered with thick curling moss and his eyes seemed to see it as though through the lens of a high-powered telescope –

It started to rain then, just as his nightmare began.

– and he saw that the moss was not moss at all, but a mass of living organisms: white worms crawling over the stone, eating it alive.

As he looked, as he saw, as he digested this horror, a face gradually took shape amongst the seething worms and the pallid light of the moon.

He knew who it was.

The face had a mouth and the mouth opened and grew wider and wider, a relentless angry mouth – a vast black hole boiling with ancient worms and filling with water finally let loose from the heavens.

And when the dripping mouth was full, the water spilled out in a torrential wave to claim everything.

Coming for you, Zak.

When Jessica put her arms on him, the scream which had been imprisoned by the dream broke free chilling her blood, and then he sat up with a tremendous jerk. Zak's face was clammy with sweat and white with fear: nostrils flared, neck muscles standing out like pieces of cord.

'Zak!' She shook him hard. 'Zak?'

He shuddered and gasped like someone who has just come close to drowning.

'Zak. It's me. Jessica.'

He turned his head slowly and looked at her with wide staring eyes.

'It was so real,' he whispered.

She drew him to her and her warmth against him dragged

up his loneliness and he began to cry and when the crying was over she took him to her bed where he slept in her arms, the deep exhausted sleep of a baby. Except that Zak talked and the talking went on and on through the night in relentless, helpless waves and Jessica listened for a long time until she was too weary to listen any more.

They slept late into the morning and when she awoke his arm was still flung across her body, still clinging to her like a life-raft. She touched his hair and he moved just perceptibly before lifting his face to look at her, eyes wide open.

'Have you been awake long?' she asked.

'A while.'

'You should have woken me.'

'After last night,' he said drily, 'I thought you might need your sleep.' He brought his hand to her cheek and trailed a finger across her lips.

'You talked about your father,' she said slowly, carefully, and he sighed and turned his face away, watched the sunlight fall into the room. 'Called his name,' she added, 'I think.' And other things, strange shocking words and demands that made her cold inside.

'What did I say?'

'That he's coming.' Over and over.

'Sometimes I think he is.'

'Is that such a bad thing?'

He didn't answer immediately and then his voice came low, quavering. 'I never knew him. I'm not even sure what, or who, he is.'

'I don't understand.'

He sighed softly, pressed his cheek harder against her belly. 'It's all weird stuff.'

'Tell me.'

Oh, God, and he wanted to – get it all out of his head, all

331

the garbage and the worry (not *worry*, man, fucking horror), rid himself of the burden once and for all.

'Have you ever experienced *déjà vu*?'

'Yes, I have, as a matter of fact, but that happens to a lot of people.'

'Or been somewhere, sometime, and thought you'd been there before – like it was familiar, even though it couldn't possibly be?' He was leading her in gently, focusing on those small unexplainable things which are wondered at and then disposed of as rational thought takes over.

Jessica frowned softly. 'Once.' And the memory came flooding back, an incident she hadn't thought about in years, when she and Tom were looking for a place to live in Brighton and preferably an old place with all the trimmings. They had looked at a house in Lewes Crescent, one of the beautiful Regency buildings built in the 1830s with stunning views of the sea.

It was the oddest experience; she had known where and what every room was and where another room had been before the house had been converted into apartments. Tom had laughed uncomfortably, the estate agent had looked embarrassed and they had decided not to buy. It was never mentioned again.

'Once,' he said, 'and once can be enough, except people push such things away because they don't really want to think about them. Do you believe in life after death?'

'I don't know, Zak.'

'Reincarnation?'

'I've sort of left my mind open on the subject, but I have friends who do. Why?'

'My mother's big on it.'

'I thought she was dead?'

'I lied.'

'What for?'

'Because I despise her. All I could think of was getting as far away from her as possible. She's what you might call an ageing hippy, a New-Age traveller, a flower child gone to seed, and her dubious philosophy of life has meant me spending my whole life on the road, being dragged from one place to the next – pushed on, fucked on, shat on by every Tom, Dick or Harry.' No running water, no flush toilet, no nothin'. A dead-head existence which had begun to gnaw away at him. 'She had my sister in a bloody turnip field near Glastonbury Tor, can you believe that? Refused to have her baby anywhere else, said "it was natural, it was holy", said "it was blessed".' He snorted with contempt. 'Avalonian shit. Mud, dogs, drugs and frigging folklore.'

'What has all this got to do with your father and reincarnation?'

'It doesn't matter,' he said tiredly, 'you'd think I was crazy . . .'

'Try.'

He swallowed, ran his hand down her thigh. Sometimes, he thought, sex was his saviour.

'You can accept that there are things people don't really understand, like the things I've mentioned?'

'Like *déjà vu* and reincarnation?'

'Yeah,' he said and cupped her knee with his hand, felt for the warm moist place at the back. 'My mother studied and read up on it. She believes not only in the survival of the human personality after death, but in the return of the soul. She's backed it up with centuries' old religious and philosophic writings that explain man's existence as a series of rebirths.' He hesitated. 'It's sort of convincing.' Even to me.

'So?'

'I didn't want to believe it, not any of it because she talks such shit most of the time.' He thought of Astra's face, beautiful in its fury. 'She said I was special, that I was "meant", said that if I left the tribe I'd regret it because I would lose a God-given opportunity.' His mother had meant a penance – for all that he had done. 'That I was making a really *big* mistake.'

'Why?'

'She said that *he* would come after me because I'd failed him.'

'Your father?'

He nodded. 'She said that I'd let him down, that I was no good. Bad. That the only place I was safe was with her.' But there was no safe place, no penance great enough to satisfy; she had been kidding herself about that.

'You're not bad,' Jessica protested quietly, 'and even if your father did come after you he wouldn't *hurt* you. Surely?'

'I said I didn't know what, or who, my father was.'

'I still don't understand.'

'My father's dead, Jessica.'

Her hand stopped playing with his hair and he felt her grow very still.

'But how . . .?'

'I told you it was crazy.'

'Just go on,' she said quietly, 'let me hear the rest.'

'My mother said he came from "out of Time" – another time, Jessica – like fifteen hundred years ago.'

'Doesn't do things by halves, does she?'

'Sometimes,' he said slowly, 'sometimes, especially lately I've . . .'

That fathomless feeling of being watched and followed.

'What?'

'I don't know.'

'People can't step out of one time and into another, Zak.'

'I know that lying here with you in the cold light of day, but at night . . .' he faltered, 'things seem different.'

'Especially when you've had a nightmare.'

'I know what you're saying and part of me wants to agree with you . . .' he struggled for a moment, 'but some things happen which defy rational explanation; like that "once" which happened to you.'

And Uther coming out of the night and the rain to rape his mother to spawn a son. Like something out of a Dark-Age legend. It wasn't true, of course, it was crazy crap, but Zak shuddered all the same.

'I take your point, but I think you're letting your mother's weird and wonderful theories get to you,' Jessica said and began stroking his hair again. 'Maybe she's brainwashed herself and those around her, including you to a certain degree, and it wouldn't be difficult, would it? Travellers or hippies or whatever, by definition, never stay in one place long enough to absorb what's happening in the "real world" because they don't want to. They live in their own world and develop their own beliefs. In a way – and I know you won't agree with me – I can see why that sort of life has such an appeal.'

'No, Jessica.'

'It just wasn't meant for you, Zak, that's all.'

'It's not meant for anyone *today* – there's no room for travellers and gypsies any more. This is the nineteen-nineties when most of England's green and pleasant land has been concreted over, or carved up for motorways. There's nowhere for them to go.' And he felt sad suddenly, full of regret for all that had been and would never be again.

'Perhaps they should still be allowed to try.'

'God knows, my mother thinks so.' He moved his head to look at her. 'It's the children, Jessica, don't you see? They have no choice.'

'Your mother probably thought it was a good idea.'

'My mother was too busy living on another planet to wonder whether it was a good idea.'

'And your father?'

'My father's from "out of Time", remember? Popped out of a stone circle and raped her one night.'

'For heaven's sake, Zak . . .'

'That's what she told me. Good, isn't it? Great imagination, my mother. That's what travelling does for you – it's made me what I am.' Not forgetting a few other odd little ingredients thrown in for good measure.

'I like what I see,' she said gently.

'Do you, Jessica?' His tone was heavily sarcastic. 'You know that phrase from the Bible – the one where God says about Jesus: "this is my beloved son in whom I am well pleased"?'

'Yes.'

'It keeps going round and round in my head for some reason, driving me crazy, because I have the distinct impression that *my* father would think quite the opposite about his "beloved" son and he wouldn't just leave it at that, either.'

Jessica looked down at the boy's head lying on her stomach.

'Stop it, Zak. This is nonsense, you know that.'

He took a deep breath, but said nothing.

'Your mother didn't want you to leave, that's all, she was trying to frighten you into staying.'

'Maybe.'

'Oh, Zak,' she continued patiently, 'if what you've just told me contained even a grain of truth, what could you have done that would so anger your father, dead or otherwise, or anyone else for that matter?'

Zak closed his eyes, blinked them open again and stared at the net curtains billowing delicately into the room, like so much gossamer. A wind really was coming.

'You're right,' he said too easily. 'You must think I'm nuts.'

'No, but I do think you spend too much time on your own, and you live alone, don't you?'

Lonely, save for a few faint stars . . .

He nodded. In a basement hovel, actually, Jessica. A filthy hole without running water or a place to have a decent shit.

'And you've just had a horrible nightmare. Give yourself a break, Zak and stop torturing yourself.' She was smiling now. 'Besides, whatever's in your past, I know you're a good person – call it women's intuition if you like.'

I'm afraid your intuition is not half as good as mine, lovely Jessica. You see, sometimes I *know* things, and it gets me into trouble. Sometimes a sort of darkness falls on me and I do bad things, really bad things.

Zelda had been one of those bad things; she had got herself pregnant by him and he was supposed to hang around and act the partner; the tribe had said so. A shot-gun wedding New-Age style. Christ, he hadn't loved her, in fact he hadn't even wanted her again after the first time. In the end he had saved everyone a lot of trouble by giving her an abortion and right in the centre of one of those sacred stone circles. Seemed sort of fitting to do it there, like a traditional old-world sacrifice. He hadn't told Zelda,

337

of course, because she wouldn't have let him, he had just got her a little drunk and promised her a night of love under the stars and beneath the moon.

He had loved, or fucked her – call it what you will – and because he had wanted it, the fucking had done everything: a hot jet of godless Zakky semen, as lethal as a dose of strychnine.

Because he had wanted it.

Her eyes had bulged in appalled realisation and the mouth in that upturned frantic face had ripped open into a primitive howl that had gone on and on. Above them the moon rode the darkness turning the river of blood staining the ancient stones to silver.

There was something unsettling about that memory – the moon and the stones and the blood, and in the deepest part of his heart he knew it disturbed him far more than what he had done to Zelda.

Yet he hadn't meant to harm anything or anyone; what he had done had been for the best.

After all, what sort of world would that potential child have been brought into? What sort of shabby existence would Zelda and the tribe condemn it to? It wasn't even really wanted and that was the truth. Zelda had wanted *him*, not a baby, and getting pregnant had been the means by which she had thought she could put a leash around his neck. Well, she had been wrong; all of them had been wrong.

Much later his mother had cursed him; but it wasn't his fault Zelda had bled to death, unfortunately that little technicality had somehow been out of his control. For an instant Zak looked perplexed and old. So much blood.

Sometimes, he thought, I feel I am lost, that I am losing myself.

There was no way he could tell Jessica, of course, yet he wanted to tell her, he really did, but it would only frighten her and he didn't need that, and neither did she. Enough was enough.

Zak felt better suddenly, as if he *had* told everything or maybe it was just lying with her like this and talking and being together that had made things better; all he had ever wanted, and even the gremlins of the night no longer seemed to plague him in the same way. Perhaps all he had needed was a taste of confession, but just a taste.

'You're good for me,' he said, 'I don't think you know how much.'

'Maybe you're good for me too' she said softly. He made her forget – everything.

His eyes came to rest on the smooth skin of her belly and he began to kiss and caress – her midriff, the sides of her body, raking a path up to her breasts, rolling her nipples across his tongue, suckling her like a baby.

Oh, Jessica.

His hand slid up between her legs, inside, and he left it there, not moving, whilst his lips played and toyed and tantalised her body, her face. He wanted to please her, totally and without reservation, take her to exquisite new heights and by doing so make up for all that he had done.

He would be soft and gentle and tender, he would be just a little cruel, just a little rough, and then he would wait until he was sure she was truly satisfied, that she would want, ultimately, no one else. Sacrifice his own pleasure for hers.

Sex was the only thing he had to give and he was using it to gain power over her. Yet he was beginning to discover, and almost too late, that there could be something else, that making-love sex could change and heal and deliver two people. Couldn't it?

Was it possible, he wondered, to achieve salvation through sensuality?

Even as this thought passed through his mind she was squirming beneath his touch, his very skilful ministrations.

Tom had neglected her and Jessica had neglected herself, but he would make up for all that, for everything, he told himself; that was what he was here for. To stay. They would be together now, he could feel it and he thought he had never been so happy.

He heard her whisper his name and longed to weep in gratitude; began licking her mouth with his greedy tongue, her jaw, her neck, her breasts . . . made her come with his magic fingers.

'Love you, Jessica.'

The lists were endless: guests, food, drink, fireworks. Jonathan had gone mad and Emma had never seen him quite so intent or so feverish about making something work. She had even had to query him on costs, afraid that he was going over the top where money was concerned – this was an *engagement* party, not a wedding.

But he wasn't happy, she knew that, and all the nagging doubts were creeping back, doubts she could hardly explain even to herself.

Emma pushed the ledger away and held her hand out to scrutinise the ring on the finger of her left hand. His moods had definitely worsened and he was using all this extra work for the party as an excuse to avoid her and even when they *were* alone he could hardly look her in the eyes. Let alone touch her.

'Right. Anything else?'

It was Keith. He was standing in the doorway rubbing his hands together.

'The shredder – over in the corner.'

'What the hell does he want a shredder for? This place is hardly a cover for MI5.'

Emma declined to answer, but had wondered the same thing herself.

'It's just for show,' Keith chortled, 'isn't it?'

'Never mind about that. He wants the photocopier moved into the far corner as well, I think.'

'Bloody hell,' he exclaimed with resentment, 'he can't expect me to move that on my own. It'll have to wait until he gets back; after all, this is all in aid of *his* party – sorry, correction – *yours*, not mine. I'm doing him a favour in case he hasn't realised it. Where is he, anyway?'

'Sussex University.'

'About a gig?'

'Yes.' He surveyed her with interest. 'You look down in the dumps, what's up?'

'Nothing. I'm fine.'

'Garbage. You should see yourself from where I'm standing.'

'I said, I'm fine.'

'Lover boy isn't, though, is he?'

'What do you mean?'

She was all eyes, all ears, and he could almost sense desperation seeping in.

'A bit tense, isn't he?'

'It's this party, you know what a perfectionist he is,' she offered lamely.

'Oh, I don't think it's that.'

She reddened. 'What, then?'

'Keeps things pretty close to his chest, doesn't he?'

'Why don't you get to the point?'

'I'm not making any point, Emma, he's just acting like someone whose got something really big preying on his mind.' He looked out of the window, unable to meet her eyes. 'How should I know what it is?'

'Well,' she said, 'do you have any suggestions?'

Keith shrugged. 'Why don't you ask him?' He wasn't going to break the news to her that Mr Universe and future hubby was a wooftah and, what's more, a wooftah in love with the guy downstairs. It still made his eyebrows curl just thinking about it.

'I have.'

'Maybe he's having second thoughts.' He should have.

'What a rotten thing to say.'

'Well,' Keith said, 'let's be honest, you have had to push him practically every step of the way, haven't you? I mean, he's never seemed exactly over-enthusiastic about marriage, has he?'

'How would you know?'

'Oh, come on, Emma. Stop hiding your head in the sand. You just don't want to face facts, that's all.'

'If he didn't want to go through with it, why is he putting so much energy into this party? He doesn't have to, you know; in fact I actually tried to persuade him to make it more low-key, but he insisted.'

'Don't kid yourself. This party is as much about advertising the business as your engagement.'

'You would see it that way, wouldn't you?' she exclaimed resentfully. 'Well, what about this?' It was *the ring*. 'Do you think he'd spend nearly five hundred pounds on a ring if he didn't want to marry me?'

'I don't know.'

Her flush deepened. 'It really is pointless talking to you, isn't it Keith?'

'No, it isn't. In fact, I could put you right on a lot of things if you'd spend just one night with me.'

Her mouth fell open. He wanted to laugh and he did.

'God, you're disgusting.'

'No, just realistic.'

She scoffed. 'And what do you really think I'd get from spending a night with you, except perhaps some sexually transmitted disease?'

'Ha ha. Very good, Emma.' He began to clap. 'No. What you would get from me would be some good honest pleasure, a laugh, a good time. What more do you want?'

'A lot more than that. A lot more than you.'

'Oh, I forget, I use the wrong aftershave.'

'Amongst other things.'

'Bitchy, bitchy . . . tut, tut,' he said.

'You think sex is the answer to everything.'

'It is when it's wrong.'

They looked back at each other until Emma dropped her gaze.

She knows he thought; *she knows something*.

'There's nothing wrong with us,' she lied, 'and there's nothing wrong in planning a future together – having a dream.'

'How luridly romantic,' he said, 'pass the sick-bowl, please,' but then he was tapping the side of his nose in an irritating but knowing gesture. 'Now let me guess what your little dream might be. Could be difficult,' he mocked. 'Oh, I know – a husband and a couple of kids, a house, a three-piece suite and a set of French casserole dishes from Harrods.'

'You think you're so funny, don't you?'

He shook his head and sighed heavily. 'Well, if that's what *you'd* call "a lot more" then it is a bit of a joke, isn't it? Whereas, if you bothered to take your rose-coloured blinkers off, you might discover that there's a whole big wide world of experience out there.'

'I like the world I've got, actually.'

'You mean the prospect of a husband in tow and a life spent with misery guts. Sometimes I don't even think you like him.'

'Oh, stop it.'

'Come on,' he said with contempt. 'Your only ambition is to get married.'

'Not exactly.'

'Yes it bloody is.' He raised his eyes to heaven. 'I thought girls like you were extinct – you know, the ones with tunnel vision, or no vision at all except marriage.'

'There's nothing wrong with marriage.'

'There is when it's just for the sake of it and because you can't think of anything else to do. Maybe you're suffocating him. Have you thought of that?'

'Don't be ridiculous.'

'Like I said, it's a thought.'

'Why don't you stop thinking and give your brain a rest?'

'Because, my dear . . .' he mouthed in a Texan drawl, 'you might find it surprising, but I'm worried about you.' And he was, actually, and not just about her – wonder of wonders, he was even worried about Mr Universe.

'Thank you for your concern, but I'm really quite happy.'

'But you're not, that's the point. Isn't that why we're having this conversation?'

'We were talking about Jonathan.'

'It comes down to the same thing.'

She bit her lip, fell silent. 'It's probably about money.'

He studied her pretty bovine face and sighed. 'Business has never been better.'

'How are you so damn sure?'

'Because I am,' he said, 'and so are you.'

She frowned and looked back at him warily, even fearfully. 'There's no one else, is there, Keith? You'd tell me, wouldn't you?'

Christ on a bike. He had a sudden desire to shake her until her teeth rattled and then tell her all he had seen, but instead he only shook his head. 'I don't know, Emma. Talk to him, can't you?'

He had said too much and achieved very little and now he wished he had said nothing at all. He was even beginning to discover that she bored him and that his initial attraction to her was on the wane, even all her quaint little dreams which once seemed so amusing had now become jarringly irritating. He rubbed his forehead with the palm of his hand and wondered if he was tired.

'But you would tell me,' she repeated in a small voice, 'wouldn't you?'

'Yes,' he lied, 'I suppose I would.'

He walked away from her and over to the window, suddenly feeling uncharacteristically depressed and wanting out of this place and away from their noxious problem before it blew up in their faces.

There was a spot going in local radio, maybe he'd apply for it. Perhaps it was as simple as that, that he'd just been here too long and it was time to move on. The thought cheered him a little.

Keith gazed heavenwards and realised with a trace of wonder that the sun had disappeared, that there were big fat clouds moving like galleons across the sky. Black clouds.

'I think it's going to rain.'

10

Fay had her head stuck out of the window, face upwards so that the rain would fall on her. It had begun two days ago with a fine soft drizzle and stopped abruptly, teasing – you could almost feel the general population holding its breath – and then started again with a vengeance.

She brought her head back in at the sound of thunder, but laughed gleefully, standing framed in the window, her hair hanging in two saturated curtains either side of her doll-like face. She stood there a long time watching water cascade down and over everything in sight, hugging herself as thunder rumbled some way off and sheets of lightning lit up a distant sky, but it was rolling this way, slowly but surely, and she was glad.

Fay glanced down into the garden and grudgingly admired Jonathan-the-prat for his quick thinking in putting up a marquee. The party people could grab some fresh air and view the storm without becoming drowned rats.

A storm for All Hallows' Eve. How apt.

Her face darkened as she looked through the sheets of rain and across the garden to where her sister would be. There was something close to disgust in her expression and contempt that Zak should have found Jessica's charms preferable to her own, but there was also envy and unease because it was she who was now alone and an aching twist turned and tightened in her chest.

Fay wheeled round and stalked across the room, her eyes flitting to the dress hanging on the back of the bathroom door, the one she intended wearing to the party – a little black lycra number which left nothing to the imagination: backless and almost frontless. She giggled and the giggle seemed to resound in the big vaulted room like an echo. On her arms she would wear several big spangly pewter bracelets and around her neck a Celtic cross tied with a leather thong – a talisman representing long life. Zak would like that. She would make him like it, she would make him like everything. Whatever had attracted him to Jessica in the first place must surely have palled by now. He seemed installed in that house, had slept there, even. She knew it all because she had watched and waited and grown ever more outraged.

Had they had sex? She couldn't believe it – not Jessica – because she was still in love with good old Tom, whatever she might say to the contrary at this unfortunate juncture in her rather staid life. Then why was Zak there? To finish the portrait? Fay's milk-white brow buckled into an unappetising frown as she thought of her sister's apparent burglary. Maybe he was simply keeping her company until her little crisis had passed. How cringingly gallant.

Day in, day out with boring old Jessica in that mausoleum of a house – it was so bourgeois, so bloody middle-class, couldn't he see that? What did someone like him want with the hideous trappings of such suffocating respectability?

And Jessica must be ten years older, she pondered meanly, whereas there were barely five years between herself and Zak. Quite acceptable.

Her temper wasn't, however. Last night she had got drunk (alone, of course) and had crept downstairs and into that creepy basement and proceeded to spatter Zak's few pathetic things with paint – rich, creamy, lumpy red paint. In the glow of her torch she had thought it looked like clotted blood, like gore, as if a very grisly murder had taken place down there. It had seemed terribly funny at the time, hysterical in fact.

She had awoken this morning to a splitting sick-making headache and an instant replay of what she had done. All in glorious technicolour, naturally. She threw back her head and glared at the ceiling. Zak would know it was her, of course. By the time she had pulled herself together and decided to right things if she could, people had been swarming about the place with tent poles and seats and that bloody great marquee. Too late.

If he'd been nice, even a little bit nice, it wouldn't have come to this. With her, he could be free, they were two of a kind. Why was he refusing to see that? Anger began to boil up inside at the inconsistencies of fate and she tore the sheet away from her canvas in a fit of rage and then became very still. Fay was breathing hard and looking at the work through eyes grown narrow and watchful. It was beginning to have that effect on her, the picture; an unattractive blend of suspicion and muted awe.

She spoke softly to herself. 'I don't like it,' she said, 'and I don't know why.' But her dislike went deeper, spiralling downwards into an odd feeling of panic hatred. Her gaze focused on the dark shadow of the man beyond the standing-stones, a big shit, she decided, even if he were still an unformed almost shapeless smudge. 'Tomorrow,' she said, thrusting her face close to the painting, 'I shall paint you out.'

And she felt better.

* * *

'I think the party's already started,' Jessica said, 'there are a few fireworks going off, but God knows how they're staying dry in this downpour.' A wind was getting up, too, she could hear its low moan as it wove its way uncertainly through the trees and pressed against the building, longing to be let in.

Yet the rain was glorious, heavenly to her, full of promise, as if it presaged something good after the long protracted summer which seemed to have brought with it nothing but misery. The sun, she thought, had turned everything to dust.

Zak came up behind her and slid his arms around her waist, rested his chin on her shoulder.

'I won't go if you don't want me to.' There was pleading in his voice.

'No,' she said, 'you must, you promised.'

'Yes, I did, didn't I?' and now he regretted it because when he was away from her now, even for minutes, he felt anchorless and churned up, ill at ease. He wanted to say, 'Don't make me go, let me stay here with you and be safe.'

'It's Hallowe'en, isn't it?'

He nodded. 'One of my mother's favourite feast days.'

'I should have known.'

'Don't worry. It's not one of mine.'

'I didn't think it was.' He had hardly mentioned the nightmare episode over the last two days, or the past where all his fears lurked, that strangeness; and she was more glad than she cared to admit.

He closed his eyes and when he opened them again, Jessica was looking up at the black moonless sky.

'It's going to rain for a long time.'

'Yes.'

'I love the sound of rain falling,' beating down on roofs and trees and earth, it was comforting somehow, like the sweet echoes of old and pleasant memories. 'All these months I've missed it and I hadn't realised how much.'

'I know,' he replied, 'but there'll be flooding from this amount of rain . . . the earth is baked solid and the water will simply run off and create havoc.' Filling sewers and drains and gullies and all those low-lying areas which have flooded for time immemorial.

The year before last his mother's caravan and the rest of their shabby convoy had sunk into a foot of saturated mud after heavy rain. Water had seeped into everything and Astra had wept in frustration and grief at the destruction it had wrought. There had been no dry wood or means to make a fire, no heating of any kind, and so they had shivered for days. Just as people had done long ago during those Dark-Age times his mother revered and romanticised so much. People had died young then: in pain and in squalor, flea-ridden, lice-ridden, disease-ridden, malnourished, filthy and stinking.

And witches had been burnt at the stake.

'There's always a catch, isn't there?' Jessica remarked sadly.

'Always.'

He watched a rocket hurtle skywards in a trail of gold, watched it explode and shrink to a loop of nothingness.

'I won't be late.'

She leaned her head back so her cheek touched his cheek and said with mild exasperation, 'Take your time and enjoy yourself. You've hardly been out of the house, and it will do you good.'

'It will bore me.'

'I'm surprised I don't bore you.'

'Never.'

'We're so different . . .'

'It doesn't matter.' He pressed his lips against her neck. 'You must know that by now.'

'I'm not big on vanity.'

'Well, you should be,' he said gently and turned her so that she was standing directly in front of him. 'I have never been happier than I am now and it's because I'm here, with you.'

'Why do I find that so difficult to believe?' she said with a trace of despair.

'Because you have no faith in yourself,' he said softly, 'but it will come back.'

'Will it?'

'Oh, yes.'

He opened her robe and began running his hands very slowly over her body. 'And this,' he said, 'makes me happy too and yet it's only part of it.'

She looked steadily at him, feeling weak and a little intoxicated.

'You're so good, Jessica,' he said. 'A good woman.'

'Now that does sound boring.'

'Oh, no. A good woman is the most valuable thing in the world. In the place that was once called the Orient they would have said that you were a pearl beyond price.'

She threw her head back and laughed in delight.

He smiled crookedly, inordinately pleased. 'I like to make you laugh.'

She brought both her hands up to his face and held it, watched it, thought of the finished picture hanging above the mantelshelf behind them and how little of him she had really captured on her carefully painted canvas.

'You could do anything, be anything, if you wanted.'

'I want to stay here and take care of you.'

'Being here with me would never be enough.'

'Yes, it would.'

'Oh, Zak.'

'Yes, it would. I don't want anything else.'

'You've got your whole life ahead of you.'

He said nothing for a moment, but then, 'You'll think I'm nuts . . .'

'Again?' she broke in, and laughed.

'Listen, lady,' he grinned, but she could see how serious he was, 'let me finish.'

'Okay.'

'I feel I've been leading up to this time with you all my life, don't ask me how I know, I just do,' his expression was very grave. 'And, for the record, I don't want to look any farther, I don't need to.'

'Don't be so serious. Please.'

'I want to be; I've never been more serious about anything. I've been a nothing and a nobody – a misfit wherever I went . . .' he hesitated for a moment, 'and I *have* been bad, Jessica.'

'We're all bad sometimes, aren't we?'

'Not like me.'

His face seemed terribly young then, and hurt, like a child.

'Stop it, Zak. Why do you do this to yourself?' She had a sudden confused desire to save him from himself.

'You should ask me what I've done that's so bad.' There was something in him now that wanted to tell her everything and absolve himself.

She shook her head. 'No.'

'Why not?' he said in a small voice.

'Because I'm happy,' she said firmly. 'Because I've had enough of "bad" things and I don't want to hear any more.'

Not now, not at this moment with the rain battering down on my roof and with this beautiful boy's hands on my body, his beautiful face looking at me with the sort of desire and need I have not experienced in years. Ever. I will have this time, she vowed to herself, however long it lasts – unsullied and unspoilt by the world beyond this house and all its tragedies.

It would all catch up with her anyway, soon enough, once the spell was broken and Zak had gone. Because he *would* go.

'How do you know I will go?' He looked startled, afraid.

Jessica stared at him with disbelief. 'How . . .?' She gaped at him. 'You read my thoughts?'

He blushed furiously, silently cursing himself. 'I sort of feel them,' he said awkwardly, 'it's always been there.'

'You can "feel" everything?' She was looking at him in bewilderment, unable to comprehend.

'Oh, no,' he answered quickly. 'Not everything.' Only *nearly* everything.

There was a new look in her eyes, guarded and questioning. 'That could be rather unnerving, Zak, even worrying.' She smiled with an effort as all the things he had told her, those strange unsettling things that had a way of creeping under your skin, came tumbling back.

'I know,' he said quietly, 'but there's no need to worry, it's nothing, really.' God, what a fool he was.

She was looking back at him carefully, warily, and he knew he had made a terrible mistake.

He licked pale lips. 'Apart from my mother,' he continued rapidly, 'you're the only other person I've told.' Astra had known anyway, from the first, even tried to protect him in her curious clumsy way. She had tried. It wasn't her fault, he realised at last, that she was who she was, that she was weak and gullible and sick for men. Hadn't he been sick for women, their bodies, anyway?

She was his mother and there was always a part of a man that needed his mother. Someone had told him that once, but he couldn't remember who it was, perhaps because he had despised them for saying it. Zak frowned, there was a dull half-questioning expression on his face.

'Zak,' Jessica's voice came, 'are you all right?'

'Only a headache.' He scrutinised her sharply. 'Are you all right? I haven't frightened you?' But he had, and enough to break the spell.

'No.'

He could almost believe her.

'Look at me.'

Jessica looked and found her vision swimming slightly, felt his hands move across her back and the splaying of his fingers against her skin, his hot open mouth closing over hers, down her neck, across her shoulders, felt her robe fall.

'How do you know I will go?' he asked again and in a whisper that was so seductive she almost swooned. 'How?'

Jessica made a soft, despairing sound. His hands were low, lower, cupping her belly tenderly, then beyond: holding, probing, caressing; felt his strength, his thoughts enter her flesh, her bones. 'I don't know. I don't know.'

'Oh, Jessica,' he said with regret and longing. 'Jessica, Jessica.' He pushed his face into her hair in an agony of remorse, pressed his body hard up against her as if the action and his will alone might make them truly one and therefore inseparable. Safe.

And then she was beneath him and he was inside her and when the loving was over he raised himself gently above her, arms like pillars on either side of her body, his mane of black hair falling like a cloak around them, sealing their expressions from the world.

Zak looked into Jessica's face for a long time, in the sad wistful way of a man looking at a memory.

Outside, the rain had slowed and a mist was ghosting up from the turf.

'You're late.'

'I had things to do.'

Dazzling white lights flickered and danced manically about the room, alternately illuminating Jonathan's handsome, if petulant face. Zak ignored him and glanced around what only hours before had been an office, but now was a pleasure dome, all soft drapes and cushions and swathes of voluptuous black and red satin. Great sweeping arcs of material had been hung from a central point in the ceiling, terminating at points in the lower corners of the room and tied in huge glistening tassels of silver. Above them strange ghoulish mobiles hung, Jonathan's token acknowledgement to Hallowe'en.

A few shadowy people milled about here and there, flitting from the garden and back into the house, anxious to see if anyone else had yet arrived.

'You'd better get on with it, then,' he snapped. 'I suppose you know what to do?'

'I suppose you want me to stay?'

Jonathan's mouth curled upwards into the pretence of a smile.

'I think you know the answer to that.'

Zak shrugged, not caring, not wanting to get involved, but wanting, more than anything, to get this long night over and done with.

'By the way,' Jonathan said (smugly?), 'Keith's going to be late, which means – '

' – you want me to stay until he arrives.'

'Right.'

Zak closed his eyes and deliberately turned his face away from Jonathan. He opened them again to find himself looking at the window which was black and closed off by the marquee. Closed off.

'How long?'

'Not *that* long. I'll make it worth your while.'

'I don't care about the money.' Oh, but he did, he was badly skint and the knowledge ate away at him, making him feel small and pitifully vulnerable.

Jonathan raised his eyebrows. 'Lucky old you. Renting ourselves out, are we?'

'Fuck you,' Zak spat. 'Do you want me to do this, or not?' He saw Emma coming towards them out of the corner of his eye.

Jonathan held up his hands. 'All right, all right. Sorry. I'm sorry. Okay?'

'One more word and I'm out, okay, man?'

'Okay, okay,' Jonathan gushed. 'I've said I'm sorry.' He wanted to rage at himself for behaving like a prat all over again, but it was too late for that.

Zak wheeled round and moved over to the disco equipment which looked like something out of *Startrek* – a mixture of dull silvers, blacks and steel-greys with throbbing lights pulsating the perimeter. It looked as if it were about to take off.

Yet behind the sleek exterior sat the proverbial dual turntable and stacks of CDs and albums. Zak twirled one of the turntables dully with his finger and stared uninterestedly at the lines of switches and buttons, the dead microphone.

Keith had lined up exactly what he should play and the rest was easy; there had been no pressure put on him to give any 'DJ-speak' which was just as well because he would have refused; that sort of circus was left to the clowns of this world like Keith. Except that beneath his funny-man skin, Keith was a decent guy. Stupid, sometimes, but decent nevertheless.

He would do well.

He would leave here soon.

Thoughts. Hidden knowledge. Zak blinked and took a deep breath as the odd moment passed – like wading through glue and there had been too many of those lately, too many mysteries and mistakes. He looked down at his hands resting on the turntable and wondered if it was all slipping away.

A beam of light picked out a face on the cover of the first album. The face was grinning and the grin was full of unnaturally white teeth. Zak picked it up and placed it gently on the turntable, picked up another and placed it on the second and Tina Turner blasted her way through the speakers.

From that point the evening was a blur. People clustered near him, then backed off, girls hung around waiting for a look, a smile, *anything*, but he could hardly see their faces in the glare of the lights and even if he had it wouldn't have made any difference. Some of them wore masks, hideous feline things like crusts over their eyes, moving to the mind-numbing noise, because Tina Turner and Meatloaf and Simply Red had given way to hard-core: ear-bleedingly loud, metallic noise, and the bodies freeze-framed by strobes in clouds of dry ice seemed like beings from another planet.

Into his nostrils wove tendrils of hash-smoke, in his hand

a tab of Ecstasy grew moist and crumbled to nothing; a gift from someone called Angel who reminded him of his mother.

He felt a hand coil and tighten around his ankle. Zak jumped and looked down and into Fay's unsettling almond-shaped eyes. Light and shadow fled across her face as lights soared and fell in the pleasure dome. She was smiling inanely, she was high, her pale face flushed at the cheek bones, her rose-bud mouth pulled into an unpleasant grin.

He pressed his foot down automatically as if he were treading on a loathsome and poisonous insect. She released him with an obscenity that could be read, but not heard above the scream of the rhythmic noise, and then she was gone and a part of him wondered if he had imagined her.

He saw Keith approaching the daïs and heaved a huge sigh of relief. It was late, almost eleven, and he felt light-headed, giddy from the smoke and the glasses of wine Jonathan had plied him with. Maybe he was trying to get him drunk, and that made him smile, made him sad in a curious kind of way.

'Thanks, man,' Keith yelled into his ear.

Zak nodded and then placed his hand on Keith's shoulder, left it there, feeling Keith's comforting body heat burn its way through his awful luminous black and white shirt.

'Hey,' Keith yelled again, 'are you okay?'

Zak smiled, stepped down and gave him a small wave, but Keith's face was still and puzzled, but then he was turning back and doing his thing – head-phones on, arms up to the elbows in albums, big wide mouth glued to the microphone.

Zak weaved his way through the frantic crowd and in the direction of the garden for some fresh air, but first there was the marquee to manoeuvre and he waited for a moment on the edge, listening to the rain beating down hard on the plastic canvas, watching couples languishing in each others arms, sticky limbs entwined with more sticky limbs, and in the middle one guy stomping all by himself around the ancient bird-table which poked incongruously through a hole in the marquee floor.

'Not exactly a scintillating performance ' it was Jonathan, 'but adequate.'

'Do you mean him – ' Zak pointed, 'or me?'

'Always have a clever answer, don't you?'

'I try.'

Jonathan felt foolish suddenly. 'I always seem to say the wrong thing . . . or put my bloody foot in it.'

Zak said nothing.

'You're not squatting in the basement any longer, are you?' Jonathan's voice was soft, no trace of sarcasm now.

Zak kept his gaze on the guy stomping all by himself.

'Some of your stuff's been damaged,' Jonathan continued, 'looks like someone's been throwing it around and splashing it with paint . . .' Red paint, in fact, and when he had pushed open the door and seen the mayhem he had expected to find Zak lying there with his throat cut and he had nearly thrown up.

'Shame,' Zak said drily, 'and I forgot to renew my insurance.'

Fay stirring her cauldron, of course. So busy in his absence.

'You'd better take a look.'

'Now?'

'Why not? Besides I think I might get someone in to really go over the place once and for all and then maybe I'll renovate. It's as good a time as any to breathe new life into the place.' And sweep away the memories. 'I put your things on one side, the bits and pieces that escaped the carnage.'

'You shouldn't have done that.'

'I wanted to.'

'You shouldn't have wanted to, either.'

'I couldn't help myself.'

'But I could have.'

Jonathan swallowed. 'I don't understand.'

'It doesn't matter,' Zak said and looked back at him with weary inevitability. 'Lead the way, then, and let's get it over with.'

Jonathan pushed a flap of the marquee to one side and there were the stone steps, slick with moisture and worn away in the centre by countless feet, there was the warped and ancient brown door with its peeling paint opening on to the two decaying rooms he had come to despise so much.

He didn't want to go in.

'What's up?' Jonathan asked.

'Nothing.'

Jonathan struck a match and disappeared inside, lit the remains of a candle sitting on the mantelshelf. Above them the ceiling throbbed and groaned.

'Christ,' he exclaimed, 'they'll come through any moment . . .' and he wasn't sure he was joking.

Zak hovered just inside the door, flicked a tired glance upwards and then switched his gaze to Jonathan.

'I wanted to apologise, actually,' Jonathan began. 'I've handled things rather badly.'

'You haven't handled things at all.'

'I know, I know.'

'It's not a sin to be gay.'

Jonathan flushed in the candlelight.

'Perhaps not,' he whispered, 'but it feels like it.'

'Admitting it to yourself would be something,' Zak said, 'you'd feel better.'

'No, I wouldn't, that's just it. I want to be normal, like everyone else,' he said helplessly. 'You see, I don't like to be different, or be seen as different. Not like you. I just want to fit in.' Act as though you are one of them and you will become one of them; his very own home-spun philosophy.

'No one's normal. No one's got it all, Jonathan.'

'I thought that – you and me – I thought . . .'

'No.' He still didn't understand that the sex they had shared had meant nothing to him – a little warmth in the dark, a little comfort to see him through the night. Just sex.

Jonathan sighed dreadfully.

'Look, I'm sorry. All right? But I don't have time for this.'

I want to go. I want out of here. I want Jessica.

'Sure,' Jonathan nodded, but his voice was unsteady. 'Of course. I understand. I'll get your money.'

Zak nodded. 'Yeah. Why don't you do that.'

But Jonathan made no immediate move to go, he only stood there, watching him: a tall, blond confused boy who didn't really know who he was.

'Hurry *up*, man.' Zak squeezed his eyes tight shut in frustration and Jonathan jumped.

'Sorry,' he stammered, 'really. I was miles away.'

And considering one last try, but he couldn't blame him for that. 'Just get my money.'

Zak took a deep breath as Jonathan scurried out of the basement and reached for the few belongings that might be worth keeping, which was a joke really. He picked up each one and examined it separately in the poor light, saw droplets of red paint on everything: his few books, a woollen scarf he had had for years, a leather belt with a silver buckle, a bottle of paracetamol, nail-clippers . . . Dropped them, one by one to the floor because he didn't want them any more, except William Blake's poetry, a dog-eared leather-bound little book which had been like a friend to him.

There was someone standing in the doorway and he swung round expecting to see Jonathan, but it was Fay.

He cursed under his breath.

'You hurt me,' she said, 'in there.'

'Did I?'

'You know you did.'

'Do *you* know when *you* hurt people?'

'Don't try and lecture me.'

'You're right,' he said, 'I suppose it would be a waste of time.'

'You bloody hypocrite.'

He eyed her with uneasy distaste, could feel the hate coming off her like heat from an oven.

'I've got to go.'

'To Jessica?'

'To get my money.'

'And then you'll go to Jessica.'

'That's none of your business.'

'Yes, it is.'

'Like I said, I've got to go.'

He came towards her and she pushed him back with both hands and the action was so unexpected he fell.

'For Christ's sake,' he seethed.

'You can spend some time with me, can't you? Or do you find me so repulsive that even being in the same room is too much?'

'Yes.'

'What did you say?'

'I said "yes".'

'You bastard.'

She was drunk, of course, or maybe she'd taken a tab of something and it was having a bad effect. It happened all the time, but not to the Fays of this world because they were usually smart enough to avoid it since it made them demented. Or, at least, more demented than they usually were.

He was looking back at her and she was looking back at him. He tried to get up, but she pushed him down again.

'You're making me angry.'

'I'd like to see you angry. I'd like to see you lose control – now that really would be interesting.' Her eyes darted to the opening leading to the other room. She wanted to push him in there and through the secret door; the thought was jumping up and down in her mind in livid red letters – push him into that stinking rancid pit.

In an instant he was up on his feet and she was running at him, head down, feet pistoning on the patched linoleum floor, grunting with the effort. Zak was catapulted through the doorway and came up hard against the stone sink, winded and shaken. In the sick moonless dark she came at him again, hands stretched out in front like claws, hair flailing across her face, a small smile on wet lips which hissed, then sprayed his face with spittle.

He tried to speak, but nothing would come.

Get out, Zak.

He moved to one side as she advanced, but felt her fingers catch in his hair and jerk his head back and he lost balance, buckling to the floor. She clapped her hands and shrieked with delight, and all the time his heart was pounding and he felt dizzy, strange, remote.

Get out.

Something was coming and he was afraid.

Up above he could hear Keith's voice boom through the speakers, something about Rastas, raggas and ravers and then the whole world seemed to shake and stomp and sway.

There was a loud ominous creaking.

Plaster crumbled.

Somewhere timber splintered and snapped.

And the photocopying machine lurched drunkenly through the ceiling.

From where Zak was lying it looked like something out of one of his nightmares: it was big and grey and hard as granite and it fell like a stone, plunging through the floor-boards and into the blackness beneath. Even as it struck him and the bones of his legs fractured and smashed he was wondering about the white things which came after, pouring through the ceiling like confetti, like white wiggling worms. They fell on his face, his hands, his feet and he smiled with surprise and bewilderment; it was only paper, tiny bits of shredded paper falling through the sky, just like he was.

There was no pain in the blackness only screaming and he thought it was Fay until he saw through half-closed lids that it was Jonathan – Jonathan shuddering and crying over the rim of the jagged hole, and above that hole there was another, brighter one, through which others peered, eyes like black dots in deathly-white faces staring mindlessly down into the dark, and then he passed out.

He had fallen through the floor and landed on the photocopier, lying there a moment before sliding from the machine on to his crushed legs.

When he opened his eyes again he found himself half-sitting, half-lying in something soft and wet and stinking:

waste and rat-droppings and bugs and fungus; dead birds that had fallen down from the eaves and through the decaying cavities in the brickwork; and other nameless things. He looked down at his shattered legs, they were beginning to itch and crawl with excruciating pain as if they had just woken to the surprising fact that every bone from ankle to groin had been smashed to pulp.

His heart was palpitating and his head felt strange and full of cobwebs. He thought of a girl called Saffron who had wanted him as Zelda had wanted him and how he had put paid to her wanting in his usual and unique fashion. Ironic that the injuries she sustained were much the same as his own now were; rough justice, his mother would have said. He wondered if she would have believed that his punishments had never been designed to kill, only hurt.

Zak hadn't thought about Saffron in a long time, hadn't cared, and he gave a harsh grating sigh which caused the pain in his legs to shoot up a thousand degrees and the world went grey. He clamped his mouth shut on his agony and tried to concentrate on his surroundings which were as unwholesome as he had always imagined this black hole to be. He saw that he was in some sort of room, perhaps a cellar, and the cellar had three solid brick walls and one archway entrance leading off into God knows where. Another rancid pit of a cellar like this one? It was old and damp and teeming with unappetising life; it also had the stench of an abattoir – and something else, some dark meaning stroking his spine.

Through gaps in the debris his enfeebled eyes could make out odd details emerging from the shadows: rotted wineracks, broken glass, a great barrel sitting against one wall and directly above the barrel and embedded in the ceiling were several large rusted meat-hooks and something was hanging there. His eyes grew wide and terrified as he saw the something was the shape of a man and the man was looking back at him.

Zak closed and opened his eyes, twice, prayed it was the pain distorting his senses, but let out a strange sob of disbelief because the face of the man was smiling and the face of the man was his father. No escape now and the thought brought a hopeless chill, a return of all the horror he had ever felt.

So this is how it will end.

The shape moved and the face hung in the darkness like a nasty Hallowe'en treat and Zak blacked out.

When he surfaced again Keith and Jonathan were there, gathered impotently behind the photocopying machine and rotten timber and other muck that had fallen through; they would have to remove all that shit before they could even touch him. Together they looked quickly around and up to assess the damage and where they should begin. Zak heard, rather than saw, Jonathan vomit. Heard Keith's appalled curses because the shape on the meat-hook was real and because there were three. Dead a long time. Ah, but the smell, crushingly ripe, as if they had died only the week before. This was a bad place.

His mother had told him there were such places in the world, places where badness hid and accumulated like dust; and just like the rot in the woodwork, it spread outwards like a stain, infecting everything.

At least it was not his father; only the darkness and his pain playing tricks and the relief was a little like swooning. Now they would save him and take him up and out of this hideous place and into the fresh rain-soaked air and he could go back to Jessica. He could hear the sound of police sirens, the manic bell of a fire-engine coming from far away and he thought the noise had never sounded so beautiful.

Jonathan was close now, but not close enough, staring at him white-faced, filthy, sick; and Zak knew what it had cost him to climb down into this stinking pit. He was brave, after all, and he wondered if he knew.

A roaring sound, far off, a swell that was growing, boiling and rolling.

Oh, God.

Something was coming and he was afraid.

Jonathan was joined by Keith and now they were both looking at him with round frightened eyes. Zak parted his lips, tried to speak, but his mouth was full of blood and he only combed the foul air with a shuddery sigh.

Get out, his mind shrieked. *GET OUT*.

And they did.

Don't leave me.

He watched them trying to scramble out of the rancid pit, saw how they used the barrel as a springboard to escape, legs and feet slipping and sliding upwards and finally through the jagged hole in the ceiling, their frantic movements causing the human husks on the meat-hooks to sway gently as if a vagrant breeze were blowing through this dark underworld. And then they were gone and he was alone. All except for the roaring sound which was much bigger, much closer – a babble of goblin voices, the greedy heartbeat of some stalking giant, the ground-swell and vibrations of an approaching earthquake.

The measured and relentless thud of drums beating and echoing down through eternity. With failing eyes he scanned the gloom.

Something was coming and he was afraid.

368

Zak opened his mouth as if he would speak, but there was only that sigh again – a sad, desolate sort of sigh filled with grief.

Love you, Jessica.

The rain was still falling, good and hard, even after thirty-six hours, and the weight of water on the battered earth ran off into drains and sewers and cracks and holes, filtering through to basements, coalholes and beyond to even lower levels.

The Crescent had been built atop the foundations of older dwellings, cottages erected during the time of Cromwell and beneath these foundations were storage vaults, cellars, smugglers' holes – older things; many no longer in use, forgotten and boarded up like rooms in an empty house. There was also a redundant sewer network which had been sealed-off at the end of the last century and running parallel to the Crescent, in some places only separated from a cellar or a vault by a layer of bricks. Into these places the water poured, forming vats and clots and cavities which eventually burst open under the pressure of the in-coming water. This water formed a torrent and the torrent formed a wave and the wave ran howling through these long forgotten places like a frenzied monster.

Zak saw the monster and he knew him.

Fay sat in the bath for a long time, until it was almost cold and then she shivered and puked a bit, but she still sat there, regurgitated red wine trickling from a corner of her mouth. She was trying to be quiet because she shouldn't be here; the building had been declared 'unsafe' by the Powers That Be, but she was too drunk and too tired to care. Tomorrow was soon enough to tackle that little problem. Besides she had nowhere to go. Under other, normal, circumstances she could have stayed with Jessica and been welcomed no doubt because that was the way Jessica was, but no more.

Fay lay back and stared at the ceiling, each hand clinging to a side of the bath as if she were afraid to let go.

No one could make her leave if she didn't want to.

Besides, the busy-bees downstairs had other things on their mind – all those pretty men in uniform, the police and firemen – she could hear their voices, their shouts even above the rain. They were still looking for him, they had been looking for him for hours, even called in a police frog-man once the flooding had subsided. The other bodies had been recovered with ease, the disgusting husks that had been down there for God knows how long, fished out with poles as they whirled around on the surface of the water. No wonder that old door had been boarded up and papered over: someone's grisly secret come back to haunt them.

Zak's corpse wouldn't float, of course, Zak's flesh-covered body would sink because it had substance.

Fay shivered again as a vision of that appalling wall of water formed uneasily in her mind, it had exploded outwards from the creepy blackness of some long-abandoned tunnel with incredible ferocity, bricks and filth and rubble erupting into that ghastly place as if the artery of some enormous beast had just been severed. She swallowed hard. It had all happened so *fast*, everything.

Her fault.

No.

She sat up and lashed out at the stained water in the bathtub with her fists, brought her legs up and sobbed impotently against her wet knees.

If he had just been *nice* to her – would that have been so hard, such a big sacrifice? Then she wouldn't have pushed him and pushed him and he wouldn't have fallen . . .

He knew what she was like. He should have known what would happen.

Fay put her hands over her ears as if she could still hear the splintering of rotten wood, the thunder of the water and the weeping, the weeping of Jonathan-the-prat which had gone on and on; an odd sort of crying that had made her wince – ugly whooping grunts which had made her want to shake him until it stopped.

Gradually, his girlfriend (and everyone else for that matter), had begun staring at him in muted astonishment until realisation slowly dawned in their addled brains. Emma's dim little face had crumpled and she had crept out of that damned place like a mouse looking for cover.

So much for love and marriage. So much for secrets.

'People get what they deserve,' Fay muttered over the rim of her knees, 'people bring things on themselves.' Her eyes fell on the stuffed fox standing by the loo; it was looking back at her gravely. 'It wasn't my fault . . .'

Be sure your sins will find you out. Her mother had said that – often.

Fay swore and pushed herself up and out of the bath, shivered again and felt goosebumps run up her back. She would go to bed now and sleep and forget, but tomorrow she would wake up and think about what had happened all over again. It would fall on her like a ton of bricks as soon as she opened her eyes. And the police wanted to see her; two interviews in ten days. Wasn't she the popular one?

There was a noise: a squeal and a crash. Fay awoke to darkness, pitch-black night and rain battering against the windows. There was probably a line down somewhere and the lights had fused, or maybe the electricity had been cut off by one of those conscientious dick-heads downstairs.

371

She was lying across her bed with not even a sheet for cover and she felt cold, only the white gauze curtains surrounding her bed coming between her naked body and the damp night air.

Thunder rumbled somewhere and a sudden gust of wind rattled the glass in the window frames and made her jump. Fay bit her lip and looked about the room; she didn't like the dark, never had, because everything seemed different, everything had a different shape. A different face.

Lightning lit up the room with ghostly luminosity and she gazed into the white glare. Max was sitting in the doorway and watching her.

'Stupid, bloody cat.'

She would find her torch, light some candles. She slipped out of bed, threw a sheet around her shoulders and padded soundlessly across the studio to the kitchen. The torch was on the windowsill where she had left it two days ago (after her sweet little visit to Zak's basement) and the thought made her shudder and shrink a little inside herself. She switched the torch on and searched for some candles; several unused ones lay rolling around in an empty drawer. She lit them all and clustered them together on a plate. With the torch in one hand and the plate in the other she walked back into the room.

If someone had been able to ask Fay why she had glanced at the picture standing on the easel she would not have been able to tell them, but in the moment of that glance she knew there was something wrong. Screwing up her eyes, she tried to focus, then lifted the torch up and stared into the painting.

There was a spreading coldness in her stomach. He was bigger, the smudge that was a man was bigger – and closer, she was sure.

Very carefully and without letting her eyes leave the picture, she set down the candles and the torch on the floor and then picked up a tube of paint, unscrewed its top and squeezed a worm-sized green blob on to the canvas and over 'the man'.

And he was gone, obliterated with one squeeze.

'Just your imagination,' she whispered, but wished – and how she wished – that the lights would come back on. Good old electric light would frighten all her bugaboos away.

She got back into bed and even allowed Max to join her. She propped herself up with some pillows and finally fell asleep sitting up as another storm came sweeping in from the east, a vicious soulless thing that would destroy much in its path, including a few dogs and cats and the odd human life.

When Fay awoke the second time Max was standing at the bottom of the bed, and the fur along the animal's back was standing on end and he was yowling in that slow blood-curdling way cats do when they are petrified, eyes fixed on something in the dark because the candles had burnt out and the torch had died.

A board creaked and Fay froze and shrank as terror ran up her arms and congealed in her throat.

She saw him then. He was standing in front of the picture.

Her eyes bulged and all the saliva dried up in her mouth. She wanted to speak and break the thick frightful silence, make it stop.

Breathing. Heavy, slow, hideous breathing coming from the other side of the gauze curtain.

'Zak?' she pleaded.

But it wasn't Zak. He was too big for Zak, much too big. And Zak was dead. Oh, but he was like Zak.

Fay moved her head very slowly and as she did so the curtain began to part and she could see the vast ragged shape of a man and she opened her mouth to scream, but no sound escaped her, nothing would come. Even when he took her hair in his two great fists she still didn't scream, and she didn't scream when he dragged her to the floor and she saw his filthy naked body in the glare of a lightning flash.

When he entered her, he tore her and then Fay was able to scream. No scream of pleasure this, no pain-pleasure trip in this sex – Fay's scream was pure shriek of agony, the sort of shriek that is ripped from a mother's throat during the torment of childbirth: a pain so enormous it was tearing her in half. The face of the body pumping and hurting and floating eerily above her was silent and empty and merciless and full of vengeance.

And, like Zak, she knew who it was.

Fear, like love, can weave strange magic. For a time fear closed down Fay's vocal cords, and fear made her lovely red hair fall out of her pretty head and when it grew back, fear made it white.

Jessica stood at the window looking out into a garden that was green and still and nipped by frost.

She didn't want to stay here any longer, not after all that had happened.

She trembled just perceptibly and thought of Zak. Even after a week of dredging the sewers and underground systems they had never found him, not a trace, nothing. The police had been mystified and finally concluded that the body had been swept out to sea somehow and if she thought it were possible, she would wish that for him. He had loved the sea.

But there were sluice gates, *closed* sluice gates all the way to the coast; there were twists and turns in the network of tunnels, and grills and gullies and little walls and dams; there was the photocopier which had plugged the entrance . . . but nothing. Yet they had successfully retrieved the others, three pre-war bodies rotting slowly down through the years hung on meat-hooks by some maniac.

An appropriately nightmarish ending to this hideous summer.

Perhaps Roz had been right and there was something wrong about this place – the gardens, the Crescent, that house – *something*.

Something which could leave a mark, a taint; something waiting for a catalyst to provoke a feeling, an event. Zak?

Jessica shook her head wearily; she was tired and sick at heart and these were nonsense thoughts, but a picture of Fay took shape in her mind and she shuddered. Too many things had happened – enough to make anyone want to move. Except, by going, she would leave Zak alone. Madness, of course, but that's what it felt like. She closed her eyes for a brief agonising moment as that same inexorable question came back to torment her again: why had she insisted on him going to that party? He had been reluctant anyway, but she had said a promise is a promise and so he had gone.

Even their parting could not be cherished in her memory because she had let him down and become wary of him – his wild talk, his strange power, his father . . . things she didn't want to think about any more.

So many regrets, so many memories crowding in on her.

She looked at his portrait fixed above the marble fireplace; the best thing she had ever done, but she closed her eyes on the beautiful savage face, overcome by sadness and pity for what might have been.

Jessica switched her gaze back to the window, watched a plane make a vapour trail across the sky.

Zak would understand her plans for the future and Tom, that she would not want to be alone.

She would go to Champneys with Roz and talk things through and then she would tell Tom that she would have him back. Her husband had failed her because he was weak and infidelity was a form of weakness, and she accepted that now. Despite what he had done Tom was basically a kind man and decent in his way and more importantly, she would need him.

He would assume it was his, of course – men did, didn't they? And it was just about possible. Tom could not conceive of his good and faithful wife having an affair, and she would never tell him.

Jessica laid a protective hand against her lower belly because Jessica was pregnant.